He's about to be conquered and hasn't a clue . . .

After college, Birdie Ferguson hits London like a ray of California sunshine. She's fresh, cheery, and positive she's about to be the best Executive Assistant her father has ever had. But her chipper outlook is guaranteed to clash with her stuffy coworker Oswald Attenborough, who has probably never had a belly laugh in his life . . .

Oswald knows he's not good enough for the boss's daughter. Although he's born of aristocracy and is proving himself at Lynford International, he's always had to play second or third fiddle to his Peers. But now he's ready to take his talents elsewhere. Until he's tasked with mentoring Birdie. Despite his own reluctance, he can't help but notice life's a lot less dreary with this West Coast beauty around . . .

Books by Shea McMaster

The Robinsons series
Her Foreign Affair
Her Unexpected Affair
Her Improper Affair

Rachel Dahlrumple

Writing as Morgan Q. O'Reilly
Frozen
Chinook, Wine and Sink Her

The Open Window Series
Til Death Undo Us
Courage to Love
Weathering the Storm

Published by Kensington Publishing Corporation

Her Improper Affair

The Robinsons series

Shea McMaster

LYRICAL PRESS
Kensington Publishing Corp.
www.kensingtonbooks.com

Lyrical Press books are published by
Kensington Publishing Corp. 119 West 40th Street New York, NY 10018

All Kensington titles, imprints, and distributed lines are available at special quantity discounts for bulk purchases for sales promotion, premiums, fund-raising, and educational or institutional use.

Special book excerpts or customized printings can also be created to fit specific needs. For details, write or phone the office of the Kensington Special Sales Manager:
Kensington Publishing Corp.
119 West 40th Street
New York, NY 10018
Attn. Special Sales Department. Phone: 1-800-221-2647.

Kensington and the K logo Reg. U.S. Pat. & TM Off.
Lyrical Press and the L logo are trademarks of Kensington Publishing Corp.

First Electronic Edition: November 2016
eISBN-13: 978-1-60183-821-6
eISBN-10: 1-60183-821-2

First Print Edition: November 2016
ISBN-13: 978-1-60183-823-0
ISBN-10: 1-60183-823-9

Printed in the United States of America

To my husband, the fabulous Mr. McWonderful.

At the time I wrote this book, times were tough and not looking up. Your support has kept me writing through all our trials – a priceless gift.

Acknowledgements

Author Maya Blake answered many, many questions about London locations and British customs to help with the authenticity of this book. Any cultural mistakes are my own and not intended to cause offense.

Super sprint writing partner Carmen Bydalek helped me bust down blocks and kept me at the keyboard long after I would have given up had she not been there to egg me on.

Lizbeth Selvig also provided feedback and helped me tweak a few sentences. She's been studying the Brits far, far longer than I have. Her more recent travel abroad eclipses my short few days spent in London more than thirty years ago.

Last, but never least, the alpha reader who has been with me from the start, Jennifer Weilbach. We knocked another one out!!

Chapter 1

The last notes of the organ music echoing in the vast reaches of Grace Cathedral held the congregation in thrall. Birdie sat in the front pew of the magnificent cathedral on San Francisco's Nob Hill as her brother's wedding began. Behind her, approximately four hundred thirty-five guests filled only half of the nave. If she understood correctly, the number would be a tight fit at the reception venue, a ballroom at the St. Francis Hotel on Union Square.

At the altar, Drew took Meilin's hand from her father. The two had eyes only for each other. The loudest sound heard over small rustles was Mr. Wu's footsteps as he found his seat in the pews.

Beside Birdie, her mother sniffled into a lacy handkerchief. On her mother's left, sitting on the aisle, her father had three more hankies tucked in the pockets of his suit. They held hands and shared a smile very similar to that of the bride and groom. It hadn't been so very long ago they'd said their vows.

Across the aisle, on the bride's side, the first three rows were jam-packed with what she imagined Chinese mafia might look like. The older men were stern-faced and their ladies dressed very much like the royal court of London, complete with fascinator hats. Most of that group represented the closest of Meilin Wu's family—parents, brother, sister-in-law, nephews, aunts, uncles, and cousins. Behind them the rows were filled with more distant relatives, many friends, and scores of business associates. Many of them the old guard of Chinatown.

On the groom's side, not quite as many pews were filled, but they held a surprisingly large number of friends and family from England. Several of whom were scheduled to attend the smaller ceremony back in Sussex in less than a week. The larger portion was local friends and business associates of her mother and grandfather. A few friends from Stanford. Not a bad showing paired with the Wu dynasty.

At the front, the bride and groom stood facing one another, absolutely absorbed in each other and the words of the priest at the altar. Birdie had heard the words so many times in the last year she nearly had them memorized.

Still, she had to admit her brother cleaned up very well. His bride, who never needed any cleaning, looked radiant. Birdie had no doubt Drew's tux had been custom made in China; it fit too perfectly to be rented. The embroidered red silk vest, matching tie and handkerchief were also a dead giveaway. For all their marked differences, the pair were two halves of a whole. Him tall, blond with blue eyes, her small with dark hair, pearl smooth skin, and soft green, almond-shaped eyes. The expressions on their faces were identical. The two were love-struck for sure. A small part of her melted at the observation.

As beautiful as they both were, it was easy to assume animal attraction, although anyone who knew them knew it went so much deeper.

Despite being half way around the world, Meilin and her family had pulled together a beautiful and elaborate wedding. Starting with the bride herself.

Meilin wore a flowing strapless gown of white silk accented with a band of embroidered red trim on the overskirt and a three foot train of more embroidered red silk trailing from under the skirt split down the back. For her veil, she'd combined a clever mix of a supersized, heavily ornamented gold, diamond, and ruby Chinese hairclip over her hair gathered into a low knot with a long white veil flowing from it. Long, dangly gold earrings with more rubies, and the engagement ring of a large ruby surrounded by diamonds set in yellow gold completed the look.

The simple truth was the woman was gorgeous and Birdie's brother clearly knew it. Frankly, most everyone in the church had their eyes glued to Meilin as she stared raptly at Drew. To Birdie, the droning of the priest was white noise.

Lined up on Meilin's side of the altar, six attendants, each one dressed in ankle-length, red and gold, Mandarin styled gowns, strung out behind her. Long beaded earrings in matching red, hair ornaments of tiny red flowers, and cascading bouquets of red and white roses completed the look.

One near-miss Birdie had survived. Not that she didn't like Meilin, and she really would have been honored to be asked to stand up with her, but the woman had what looked like a line-up from the Chinese Imperial

Court on her side. Birdie would have stood out with her fair coloring and extra inches of height. She most definitely was not offended to be left out. Her presence would have thrown off the beauty of the picture.

Drew's side was a little more mixed up. One of Meilin's countless cousins, Jack Ling, stood as best man, while a few school mates, from both Eton and Stanford, created the line of groomsmen; they all wore red silk vests, although not embroidered like the groom's. A line that included Oswald Attenborough.

Of course Drew would ask Ozzie. Birdie's lip curled on its own. As luck would have it, Ozzie's eyes flicked her way at just that moment. Amusement sparkled in his eyes from behind rimless glasses. Damn him. She gave him a glare in return, which only seemed to amuse him more. Time to rethink that tactic. Not ready to admit she might be squirming under his regard, she shifted slightly in her seat. Nope, not squirming. The pew seat was hard.

So many things had changed over the past twelve months. Drew had met Meilin a year ago, then spent a tumultuous summer trying to learn Mandarin and court a woman engaged to someone else. Then it was off to Beijing where he took over lead of the family's office with Meilin at his side. Who, much to his great relief, also served as his interpreter. Drew's Mandarin teacher claimed Drew hadn't been his worst student, maybe, but darn close. Drew claimed he knew enough to make a polite greeting, say thank you, order dinner, and tell Meilin he loved her, and swore that's all he needed to know.

Meilin was also Drew's right hand when it came to making acquisitions for Lynford in China. Great choice on Dad's part to hire Meilin. She could tell a dining table from a tea table, a chifforobe from a dresser, and the difference between a Chinese teapot versus Japanese. Drew could charm, wheel and deal, mind the financials, and negotiate the fine lines in the contracts, but Meilin made sure they dealt only in quality goods and didn't get screwed over doing it. Dad considered it a major coup.

They'd made a few trips back, as Meilin still owned an interior design business in San Francisco, and they'd traveled to England for Christmas for the big family gathering. Birdie had only had her brother to herself for seven months, four of those sharing an apartment while Drew finished his International Law degree. As far as she was concerned, it hadn't been long enough. She missed her brother when he was away. Until that Thanksgiving, just nineteen months prior, when her mother had been forced to admit Wyatt Ferguson hadn't been Birdie's biological father but rather the one who'd raised her for eighteen years, she'd never had a sibling. It wasn't until she had him that she ached for what she'd missed growing up.

For a moment, her gaze once more stole away from the main attraction and drifted down the line of very well dressed groomsmen. Jack Ling grinned, very proud to be chosen for the honor of best man after introducing the couple. Next to him, Oswald stood at attention, his face carefully blank. His usual expression, especially around her. Very unlike his more carefree uncle, Larry Attenborough, sitting two rows back, who loved nothing more than to dig out the deep, dark details of everyone's lives. He was fun to tease, unlike that stiff-necked nephew of his. Make that the very handsome and hot nephew. Oswald of the thick dark blond hair, light colored eyes behind frameless glasses, and a lean, muscular physique that layers of cloth couldn't entirely hide. Too bad he was such a dork and killjoy. Behind Oswald were two of Drew's friends from London, Phillip Hammond and Calvin Whetmore. It said something that they'd flown all the way here just for this event. Two more friends from California finished the lineup.

It about drove Birdie crazy the wedding was taking place in the middle of the week merely because it fell on the summer solstice. But that was Chinese superstition for you. Meilin's mother had consulted with an elder who'd declared this the most auspicious day for Meilin to marry.

Of course part of the reason Birdie was happy to be in the audience was she had been too wrapped up in the last year of her master's program. A sigh of relief left her, glad that was past. With this wedding out of the way, it was on to her future now.

This time next week, she'd be setting up her life in London and beginning her own career at Lynford. Eventually she'd be taking over for Dad's retiring executive assistant, Eleanor Cuthbert. The next six months were a carefully constructed program to move her through all the divisions, working her way into the top office. The only problem with that was Oswald, currently in line with her and Drew for the day Dad decided to fully retire, had been hovering around the office, covering for Dad who'd taken more of a traveling role. Her mother described it as an extended working honeymoon. Impatience to get to London and start staking out her territory rode Birdie hard. Perhaps she'd never be named CEO of Lynford International Importers, but she'd sure have a say in the running of the company. Both Drew and Oswald had more experience with Lynford and had the required old boys' club equipment between their legs.

Good old Oswald.

Ozzie. A little boring.

Ozinator. Intimidating.

Ozichu. Electrifying.

Ozimander. Flaming hot.

Ozmantis. Insect-like fighter. Hadn't she heard a rumor he was big in mixed martial arts in London? Drew had said something about it once, but she hadn't really been listening.

As if she'd said his name out loud, he turned his head just enough to look directly at her. She really hated it when he did that. It seemed like every time she tried to get a good long look without him noticing, he'd turn his head and catch her. Instead of looking away as she usually did, this time she held his gaze and lifted a brow. For just a flash, a twinkle of amusement zapped in, then out, of his eyes. In all probability it was the angle of the candle flames reflecting off his glasses. Or he was laughing at her. Having never heard him really laugh, she didn't believe he knew how.

The hell with that. Narrowing her eyes at him, she gave him a good glare. Laugh at her, would he?

Not for long.

School was over and done, and she was on her way to London.

They'd see who got the last laugh.

The priest pronounced Drew and Meilin husband and wife. Didn't even get out the words telling Drew to kiss his bride before he had her tipped back nearly to the floor, much to the amusement of everyone present. Bet the photographers loved it.

Drew finally hauled Meilin up from the dip, lifted her into his arms, and strode down the aisle with a huge grin on his face. Meilin laughed up at him and snuggled in while Martin, the family butler, stood in the shadows at the side of the nave, hands over his face. So much for the perfect picture of the new Mr. and Mrs. walking down the aisle. Maybe they could call it their *Officer and a Gentleman* moment.

The attendants started pairing up and following the newlyweds. As Oswald and his bridesmaid passed, he turned his head to look straight at Birdie.

Oh damn. He smiled. At her.

And didn't that just make him the best looking thing she'd ever seen? His smile completely transformed him from an uptight British stiff to a Hollywood handsome hunk, a little like a blond, young Pierce Brosnan, but with glasses. He certainly wore a suit as elegantly and easily as the actor. Enough to steal what little breath she had left when he was around. This time was no different, she had to admit, as her heart pounded in double time. Deep inside, something melted, akin to a nuclear meltdown. Damn the man.

The moment passed and Birdie dropped back into her seat, the stack of enameled silver bangles on her wrist joining in with the recessional music, causing her mother to turn and look at her with concern.

"Birdie?"

"Yeah, Mom. I'm good." She needed to take a powder room break, if only to get some strength back in her legs and wipe up some drool.

She wasn't good, but she would be. Too bad she didn't have an excuse to leave the reception early. Last thing she wanted was to find herself forced to dance with Ozzie. And knowing Drew, it would happen.

Once the participants passed down the aisle, Birdie's parents stood and allowed Meilin's immediate family to precede them toward the exit. Dad tucked Mom's hand around his arm on his right and held out his left to Birdie.

"I'll get Gran," she told him.

The old lady sniffed from the aisle seat of the second row, but stood to her full height only a few inches shorter than Birdie and accepted her assistance, and they fell into line behind her parents, her grandfather Dailey right behind them. As elegant as any woman there, Gran maintained the slender build and blonde hair Birdie had inherited from her. The woman may have been seventy, but she easily passed for sixty. The result of good living and strong genes. Didn't mean she was as sweet as pie. The opposite was true, in fact. Hard headed and extremely proud of the Robinsons' vaulted position in British society, the woman's ideals and prejudices had been a pain in Birdie's back side from the start. And yet, they'd found enough common ground to sort of like each other. Or at least tolerate each other and get along with a veneer of civility. Most of the time.

"You next," the old bat whispered at her.

"Not bloody likely," she whispered back. The curse earned her a pinch on the inside of her forearm.

"Unless I miss my guess, the next to head the company will be a pair. A married pair."

Birdie stared at her grandmother. The cranky old witch, who could never seem to find anything right about Birdie from her speech to her posture, had a positively wicked gleam in her blue eyes. It unnerved Birdie that the look was as familiar as the one in her own mirror. "You mean Drew and Meilin? Possibly."

"I didn't say that."

"You're an evil woman," she told her grandmother.

The woman's laugh rang out in the church, enough to rise above the general murmur, enough that both Mom and Dad looked back over their shoulders.

"Doesn't mean I'm wrong." This time she patted Birdie's arm. It was less comforting than the pinch.

"Well, we've got a long time to figure it all out."

"So the young always believe," her grandmother said cryptically.

"Not going to let you ruin this day, crazy woman. My brother just married a beautiful, wise, and loving woman. My parents are so happy they're nearly stupid with it, and I am done with school. The sun is shining, the sages say this is a lucky day, and I'm going to enjoy it to the max."

"Never said you shouldn't. And mind your manners. Respect your elders. We've been in your shoes. You should listen to us more than you do. And mind your language. We don't want her family to think we're baseborn."

"Anything else, Your Majesty?"

This time the old woman slapped her shoulder. "Be good or I'll sic Oswald and Larry on you."

Now there was a threat to make her shake in her Jimmy Choo's. "Yes, ma'am. Thank you, ma'am. Anything I can get you, ma'am?"

"Just hush up, get me through that receiving line, and deliver me to the party."

Sounded like a good life motto to Birdie.

Get me to the party.

"Easy peasy lemon squeezy, Gran."

Something good to focus on for the coming year or two.

Because it would be a party when she got to London. She'd make sure of it.

Chapter 2

Speaking of parties, Birdie had to give Meilin and her family props for the reception. Not far from the cathedral, limos dropped the family at the Saint Francis Hotel as the sun was beginning to lean toward the west with a few hours left to sunset. They'd been ushered into a ballroom filled with forty-three round tables set for ten each. The bridal party had a long table set on the other side of a parquet dance floor, behind them an incredible view of the city beyond filmy curtains. The room sparkled with crystal, candlelight, the guests, and particularly, the newlyweds. Not that they paid much attention to anyone other than the photographer and videographer.

Which meant Martin and the wedding planner hired by the Wu family had the job of making sure things kept moving. Receiving line, first toast, various speeches, the buffet, and the cake cutting. Jack, Drew's best man, kept the crowd in stitches with his speech. Dad nearly brought them to tears with his emotional acceptance of Meilin and her family as part of the Robinson family. Meilin's father unbent enough to allow that he considered Drew a very good son-in-law, even if he wasn't of Chinese descent. The crowd laughed, but Birdie didn't think he'd been joking.

Somewhere around her third or fourth glass of champagne, the after dinner dancing started. She'd had to swipe one of Dad's spare handkerchiefs, for there was not a dry eye in the room. Anyone watching Drew and Meilin dance felt a touch of magic as the power of their love seemed to sweep across the room like a warm breeze. Or maybe it was the influence of the wine making her overly sentimental.

A small prickle of awareness made the small hairs on the back of her neck rise. She'd piled her long blonde hair on top of her head with a small red clip Meilin had given her. Meilin had also chosen a dress for her, embroidered red Chinese silk, but styled as a simple sheath with a slit up the back, much like the dress Birdie had worn for her parents' second wedding a year before. Western in style, but Chinese in material. It was a beautiful compromise that tied her into the wedding party. Mom's dress was similar, but floor length and gold rather than red, to set off her red hair and make her stand out from the bridesmaids, while complementing the mother of the bride.

The prickle grew stronger, and Birdie raised her champagne glass as a cover to search for the source of her intuition, or whatever. Something woo-woo in nature.

Over the rim of her crystal flute, her gaze caught on the intense regard of Oswald. While the rest of the room watched the newlyweds, Ozzie's eyes were on her.

A wash of heat covered Birdie, and she tossed back the remains of her drink to hide what felt like ten shades of scarlet painting her skin. Her blush intensified when she recalled the twenty she'd slipped the DJ. The agreement was that if he saw Ozzie leading her to the dance floor, he was to put on Ozzy Osbourne's "Crazy Train." Sophomoric on her part, but it annoyed Ozzie, which was the entire point. Anything to get that stick unstuck from his uptight backside.

She was saved by Drew coming to take her mother onto the dance floor while Meilin grabbed her father. Next up they'd swap parents, Drew dancing with her mother, while Meilin danced with his father. The plan was then for the newlyweds to dance with their grandparents and siblings. Then the dance floor would be opened to the masses. Birdie had time for another glass of bubbly. Another hand beat her to the bottle.

"I think you've had enough for now," Ozzie said in her ear, then took the seat beside her as he set the bottle out of her reach. No one else at the table seemed to notice Ozzie's invasion. Indeed, he was so close to the family they all accepted him as one of them. Gran merely nodded at Ozzie, then turned her attention back to the dance floor. Drew would dance with her next. Something sedate enough she could follow with her new hip.

"Not your call to make," Birdie shot back, but let the bottle sit where he'd put it. For the time being. "What are you doing here? You're supposed to be up at the table, or standing next to your bridesmaid waiting for your turn to dance." Yep, the ushers and maids were lined up on the side of the dance floor in front of the head table.

"My bridesmaid, as you say, has a boyfriend. Said boyfriend made it clear I'm not to dance with her. So, he's relieved me of groomsman duties." Ozzie lifted her so-far-untouched water glass and took a sip.

"And the principal parties have no objection?"

They both looked toward the dance floor. Nope, they weren't seeing anyone else but each other.

"Pictures have been taken." Ozzie shrugged again and drained the rest of glass. "Warm day to be trussed up like a penguin."

"My water should have helped." Too bad it would have been rude to pour it over his head. Maybe later, if he annoyed her.

"It did, thanks." The big grin he gave her was the one rarely seen. The panty-melter.

"So, again, what are you doing here? Have you appointed yourself as my undesired babysitter?" She leaned forward and grasped the champagne bottle once more.

Ozzie stared, but this time didn't stop her from refilling her glass.

"What do you want, Ozzie?" she asked at his continued silence.

In a move that irritated her, he shrugged. "Seemed like a good place to sit and watch the proceedings."

"It is at that." She smiled at Drew when he came to escort Gran onto the dance floor. Because Meilin didn't have grandparents here, she tugged on Grandpa's hand. He was only too happy to follow her and then showed off his superior dancing by whirling Meilin around the room as if they danced on an enchanted cloud. It was even more entertaining when Gran caught sight of them and put her nose up in the air.

"So, what do you think, Ozzie? Planning on spending the evening dancing the night away?" She glanced toward the DJ until he caught her eye, then returned his nod.

"I can dance well enough, I suppose, but it's not my preferred entertainment."

"Oh? What would that be?"

He never had the chance to answer. Drew interrupted after he passed Gran to Grandpa Dailey, then came to the table for Birdie.

"Saved by the wedding traditions," Birdie joked as her brother spun her onto the dance floor.

"Saved from Oswald?" Drew grinned down at her.

"No, you saved him from my inquisition."

"Think I'll hand you off to him next. You may think I'm completely mesmerized by my bride, and you'd be right, but there's no missing the sparks between you and the young Mr. Attenborough."

Birdie scoffed. "Oh, please. Drop that line of conversation right now. You and Meilin are off to a good start." She nodded at the smiling faces whirling by. Mom and Dad, also in their own little world, not quite dirty dancing, but close enough.

"We are." Completely sure of himself, his grin was smug and proud at the same time. "It will be fun watching you and Oswald work things out."

Refusing to answer that redirect, she pinched his arm. "So, honeymoon in England? Why not somewhere more exotic?"

"Meilin thinks the country house is exotic enough. She hasn't had enough time to absorb all the history. We'll also do the tour up through Scotland and across to Ireland. She has a client wanting a design based on Scots and Irish manor homes."

"Fun times. Work and a honeymoon at the same time." Birdie shook her head.

"Meilin loves antiquing, so now I love it too."

With a sad pout, she said, "Whipped already."

Drew threw back his head and laughed. "You'll see." He glanced over his shoulder. "About time to pass you off to Oswald."

"Not unless you want the next dance to be 'Crazy Train.'"

That got Drew's attention. "What?"

"I bribed the DJ to play that if I ended up dancing with Oswald."

Drew rolled his eyes. "Fine. I'll give you to Dad."

"Or you can just drop me back at the table when the song ends."

"Not like you to sit out during dancing." Still, he guided her in the direction she wanted to go.

"I'm sure I'll dance, once the obligatory nice dances are over. Later, when everyone is a little more lubed up on champagne, is when I'll really let loose."

Without a reply other than the shaking of his golden head, Drew stopped by the family table, then bowed as the music faded out. "Enjoy yourself. I'm only dancing with my wife from here on out."

That's what he thought. Birdie smiled and gave him a little wave as the maid of honor pulled him into a dance before he made it halfway to his bride. Much like she found herself being pulled onto the dance floor by Phillip, one of Drew's friends from London, a moment later. By the time the set was nearly at the end, she was ready to slow down, or better yet, get off her feet long enough to have another glass of champagne.

She'd just smiled at her last partner, one of Meilin's many cousins, and turned to find her seat when a strong male hand took one of hers and spun her into his arms.

Surprised, she looked up to see Oswald and his usual blank expression staring at her. "Really, Ozzie, I'm ready for a break—" He already had his right hand on her waist and her right hand captured in his left. Classic dance position of her grandfather's generation, which oddly felt right, although when it came to slow dancing she was more used to linking her hands around her partner's neck with both his arms around her waist. This time his touch, palm to palm, palm to waist, captured her breath while her body went into a wild form of shock. Almost like being Tasered, but instead of pain, the shock felt…erotic. Something she'd never once felt before, but oddly enough she recognized it.

"And now," the DJ interrupted her stunning revelation, "we're going to slow things down with a special request. This one goes out to the couples from the bride and groom."

Expecting to hear Ozzy Osborne's crazy laugh, Birdie glanced over her shoulder at the DJ as opening strains of "Unchained Melody" began. The DJ shrugged and nodded toward Drew and Meilin who danced nearby. Both of them gave her wide grins. The dirty rats. They'd stolen her poke at Ozzie.

The same man who now expertly led her into the slow dance, his body guiding hers as if they'd danced this way their entire lives. It thrilled her and unsettled her all at once as their gazes locked. For the first time she noticed his eyes were more a pale blue than gray, something his glasses had hidden until now. She'd never been this close to him before. The spin he navigated her through only brought their bodies closer until they were plastered together from knee to chest. A warm flush washed her from head to toe, and she tore her gaze from his, looking over his shoulder.

"Cat got your tongue?" he asked. "Or do cats even bother with bird tongues?"

Birdie concentrated on not looking at Ozzie. "No. I'm just a little winded from dancing." She certainly was short of breath. And her mouth was dry. Both conditions she absolutely attributed to the previous vigorous fast dancing. Not the way he held her, like something delicate.

* * * *

Well, if Courtney didn't want to talk, that was fine with Oswald. Although the distraction from the song would have been nice. Damn Drew and his idea of a joke. Since Oswald was pretty sure Courtney had asked the DJ to play something from Ozzy Osborne, the switch wasn't exactly appreciated. Even something slow from the Brit rocker wouldn't have been nearly as erotic as the Righteous Brothers.

While Courtney stared over his shoulder, he studied the rosy flush that heated her entire body, most of which was pressed against him. In fact, as he spun her again, one of his legs nudged between hers, and he was fairly certain part of the blush came because she could feel his erection. His hand, on its very own, had traveled from her waist down to the very top curve of her beautiful backside. She was slender enough he could nearly wrap his arm completely around her, fitting her body to his like they were two puzzle pieces made for each other. The very thought of his piece fitting into hers, of course, only made him harder yet.

He wanted nothing more than to take her mouth and waltz her away to his room for the night. Something that could never, ever happen. As she was the daughter of his boss, and he was essentially the hired help with only a tenuous claim to a somewhat noble bloodline, he'd never be good enough to kiss her toes. So instead, he breathed in her fresh scent of lemons and sunshine, and admired the rosy hue of her cheek, the mischief dancing in her incredibly blue eyes, and the graceful lines of her smooth neck decorated only by a long gold chain with a charm of some sort hanging from it. A tiny book with castle towers? A closer look would also allow him to better study the swell of her breasts, which looked to be perfect handfuls. Pulling his thoughts upward, like the spark in her eyes, the lights danced off the highlights of her naturally blonde hair, enhancing the aura of gold that surrounded Courtland Robinson's precious princess. The slightly disheveled strands now hanging down in soft curls from the previously polished up-do lent an attractive smudge to her perfect image of an angel. An angel who would inspire the devil to lay her out on one of the tables covered in white linen and damn the audience.

An angel he had no business thinking about in the carnal way currently trying to push more ideas into the forefront of his brain.

Fortunately, or sadly, the song came to an end, and Courtney quickly separated from him.

"Thank you for the dance," she said stiffly, her many bracelets making a silvery sound as she dropped her arms.

Unable to speak, he merely gave her a half-bow, then waved her ahead of him back toward the table assigned to Drew's family. Who were somewhere on the other side of the dance floor as the music switched to something from the eighties. Neptune Satellites if he wasn't mistaken. One of their least offensive rocker tunes. Probably a nod to the those who'd come of age in the eighties.

As he stopped by the table, she kept walking in the direction of the door to the ballroom. The gentle sway of her hips was enhanced by the slit up the back of her dress. He wanted nothing more than to follow her and lower the zip until the dress slid from her slender shoulders. Did she wear red lace beneath?

"Come dance with me, Oswald." A soft hand touched his arm, and he turned his attention to one of the bridesmaids. Ping? Yuahua? Junlei? No, Junlei was the one cuddling an infant at a table toward the back. He kept getting them mixed up, in part due to their matching dresses and hairstyles, and unfamiliar names, despite their very different personalities. Especially when he only wanted to think about Courtney. No other woman could break his focus on the one woman he wanted with a need so strong he could barely breathe. Meilin's friends were bright and beautiful, but they weren't Courtney and that wasn't their fault.

"Of course, my lady." He gave her a smile and watched as her eyes widened. A gentle hand in the middle of her back was enough to guide her back to the dance floor.

"Wow. You should do that more often." The woman fanned her face, then took his hand and led him to the middle of the floor where Drew and Meilin danced in the center of their friends.

"Do what?" He took control and guided her into a jitterbug that went well with the beat.

"Smile." She gave him a coy one. "Then again, if you smile, I'll get bumped out of the way far too soon."

Oswald laughed. It was better this way. Let Meilin's pretty friends pass him around and he wouldn't have time to think of blonde hair and blue eyes.

Chapter 3

In the ladies' room Birdie blew out a frustrated breath. As she'd left the ballroom Ozzie was already headed back onto the dance floor with Yuahua, one of Meilin's closest friends. Just as well. Birdie was probably mistaken about what she thought she'd felt against her stomach as he'd pulled her close during the dance. Who knew those old music groups could be so sexy?

A damp paper towel gently patted against her throat helped cool her down. The warm day and the closeness of the guests shoehorned into the ballroom made it hard to keep from sweating. Dancing only made it worse. Someone needed to turn up the AC in there.

The outer door to the lounge opened, and she heard whispers and giggles. Not only female, but a low male voice as well.

Good God. She recognized that voice. Drew.

She stepped from behind the wall near the sinks and caught her brother kissing his new wife.

"Stop that, you two," she called out.

Meilin squeaked and Drew cursed.

Birdie shook her finger at them. "This room is not empty and is not to be used for sneaky nookie in the middle of your party. Drew, get out of here."

"What if I pay you a hundred quid to guard the door for fifteen minutes?"

Arms folded across her chest, Birdie planted herself firmly in the arch separating the anteroom from the tiled room behind her. "Not on your life. You are not bumping uglies in a nasty, dirty bathroom. Save it for your suite."

Drew groaned and buried his face in Meilin's neck. The shameless woman merely laughed and patted his head.

Birdie pointed at Drew, then the door. "You. Out."

Pouting and complaining, adorably, he went, leaving Meilin giggling her fool head off. Which was a little scary in itself. Meilin wasn't the giggly type.

"Time to get you situated, woman." Birdie took her arm and steered her toward the sinks.

By the time she helped Meilin freshen up, the bridesmaids had swarmed the ladies' room, and Birdie vowed to wear a simple wedding dress should she ever get married. It shouldn't take two women to hold the skirt up just to cop a squat.

Fluffed and primped herself, Birdie had her hand on the doorknob when Meilin caught her shoulder and spun her around into a hug. "I'm so happy to have such a cool sister," the bride gushed. Very un-Meilin-like, but Birdie figured she had a right on such an emotional day.

"I'm happy too," she assured her new in-law. "Now let's get out of here." A loud, pounding knock sounded on the door. "I think he's about used up his limited store of patience."

Ping grabbed Meilin's arm. "Let's do this like going down the aisle, but Birdie first!"

The ladies all agreed, and barely refraining from rolling her eyes, Birdie made her exit to find Drew, Jack, and Ozzie waiting in the hallway.

"Patience, dear brother, patience," she advised, patted him on the chest, then headed back to the ballroom. As she thought about it, a trip to Vegas or a Justice of the Peace was starting to sound like a great way to get married. Never mind what her mother had been planning for the past two decades.

Back at the table, she picked up her empty champagne glass and waved at a nearby waiter. The dance floor was full, but her grandparents were sitting this one out.

"Where are they?" Grandmother Robinson demanded, not one pearl or one strand of fluffy styled hair out of place.

"Took a break to freshen up a bit, Gran. They're on their way back," she assured the self-proclaimed keeper of the family dignity. In addition, she pointed toward the entrance to the ballroom in time to catch the first of the bridesmaids leading the procession back. Finally Jack appeared escorting Yuahua, followed by Ping hanging on Ozzie's arm. The attendants formed a path, and the bride and groom made their second entrance into the ballroom to the sound of applause as the DJ announced it was time for the bouquet and garter tosses.

Birdie glanced at her watch. Finally getting down to the last of the required photo ops. She'd soon be able to escape to the room her parents booked for her in the hotel. Out of town guests were all parked on the same floor. Drew and Meilin had the Windsor suite for two nights, after which the family would travel together to England. Maybe another hour and she could quietly sneak away.

The waiter returned with a full bottle of bubbly and refilled all the glasses on the table while the guests gathered around the dance floor. Since their table was on the edge of the floor, Birdie sat with her grandparents to enjoy the spectacle in comfort.

It took an hour, but once Drew and Meilin left for their elevator ride to heaven, his words, Birdie guzzled down one more glass of champagne, vowing to herself she'd chase it with water in her room, kissed her parents, then headed for the door, a tad more wobbly on her heels than she'd like to admit.

So far she'd managed to avoid Jack and any more dancing with Ozzie. Ping was the lucky winner of the bouquet toss and had kept Jack on a tight leash once he caught the garter.

There was only one flaw with her perfect escape plan. After she slipped into an empty elevator, Ozzie stuck his hand between the doors just before they closed.

At his raised brow, she gave him a twisted moue, then reached out to punch the number for her floor again, this time her fingers colliding with Ozzie's hand reaching for the same button. The resulting electrical charge was enough she snapped her hand back.

"Giving up on the night?" he asked.

"Completely worn out. You?" To emphasize her exhaustion, she braced herself on the rail and reached down to undo the buckle of the ankle strap and pulled off one shoe.

Ozzie cleared his throat. "Yeah, me too. Totally knackered. That looks difficult. Need help?" Ozzie's voice sounded a little strained.

Ignoring him, she removed the other shoe to the accompaniment of her bracelets. "There we go, easy peasy lemon squeezy. Ah, that feels good." Eyes closed, she sighed and wiggled her toes into the thick pile of the rug lining the floor. The fact she was now four additional inches shorter than Ozzie made her think it had been a mistake to remove her shoes, but losing them felt too good to worry about anything else.

"Yeah, I guess so," he all but croaked.

At the hoarse sound of his voice, she opened her eyes, then decided she had to be drunker than she'd thought. The very proper Oswald stared at her with what she could have sworn was lust in his eyes. The fact his regard made her breath catch in her throat only underlined her thought, because in that moment she couldn't lie to herself. The man was seriously hot. If he ever took those glasses off, he'd be devastatingly handsome instead of garden variety male model beautiful. His eyes glittered with a fire she'd never seen in them before.

"You drunk?" she asked. "'Cuz I might be just a little, drunk, that is." His stare certainly made her head spin as the elevator walls seemed to press inward, making the small car even smaller.

With just one step, Oswald was close enough she could smell the remains of his cologne, feel the heat of his skin. "Yes, I had a little too much. The bar had your father's favorite whisky. Come to think of it, it's my favorite as well."

Yeah, now that he mentioned it, she could detect a faint trace of the distinctive Scotch that was always in a decanter at home. Wasn't much to her liking, but the men had strange tastes, anyway.

"You need an escort to find your room?" Ozzie asked the question as the elevator dinged on their floor.

"No. No, no," she stammered. "I'm good."

Which didn't mean he didn't follow her down the hall to her assigned room. Then watched as she lifted the hem of her dress enough to pull the keycard from the top of her stocking. In the silence of the hallway, the increase of his breathing was clear.

"Let me help," he said. The hand he placed on her thigh was hot to the touch, although dexterous, as he plucked the card from where she had it half extracted.

Thank goodness for the wall at her back. Otherwise she would have fallen right over. It was fifty-fifty as to whether she would have fallen into his arms or on the floor. Good old Mr. Wall kept her from doing either.

Ozzie quickly opened her door, then wrapped his arm around her waist and eased her into the room. Surely not as fancy as the suites occupied by the parents and the newlyweds, her single was still luxurious if somewhat small. She had a great view of Union Square and the Bay Bridge.

Ozzie didn't bother checking out the view. He kicked the door shut and had her backed up against a wall before she could utter a squeak. His lips were hot on hers, and oh, so soft as he kissed her. Tentatively at first, until she slid her hands up his chest, then more insistent as her body felt as if it had burst into flames.

Always a man of few words, he didn't say a single one, not verbally, anyway. Instead he spoke with his hands, body, and lips. While she debated the need for air weighed against his kiss, his mouth took command of hers. Air lost.

She'd been pretty sure she knew what being kissed felt like, but it took only a minute, or a lifetime, to discover she'd never really been kissed before. And Ozzie didn't kiss like a proper gent. In fact, he stole her senses like a plundering pirate.

Neither had she ever been touched so well. Not that she'd had many men touch her. There'd never been anyone who intrigued her enough to divert her from her studies. Not like Oswald diverted her now.

His hands, so big and strong, slid over her hips, down her thighs, his fingers then slowly worked the skirt of her dress up her legs. That alone was enough to send her already dizzy senses on a new world tour. First his fingers found the lace tops of her stockings, followed by the bare skin above them, pushing the silk of her dress up, up, up. The cool air of her room washed her legs as more skin was exposed until his hands gripped her bottom. A mostly bare bottom thanks to her not-so-sexy thong. No, she'd worn the one that had a little stretch and helped hold her tummy in, while not revealing panty lines in the clinging dress.

She'd just begun to feel a little self-conscious when he lifted her off the ground, settling his groin between her legs, and pushed against her firmly enough to hold her on the wall, allowing his fingers to slip between and under the thin barrier of her panties. Instinctively, her legs wrapped around his waist, as tightly as her arms twined around his neck.

The man had mad skills. He never stopped devouring her mouth while stroking the tender skin, the folds that protected her very private vale between her legs.

Enough bubbly wine swam in her bloodstream that she couldn't track each nuance of his touch. Somehow he snuck one hand behind her back and eased down the zipper of her dress until it sagged around her shoulders. Much too hot, her skin too sensitive to bear even the whisper of silk, she pulled her arms from the dress, pushing her bracelets off at the same time, letting them fall in a clatter to the carpet, and wrapped her arms around his neck again. The dress folded between them and fell off completely when he set her down near the bed.

He was much better at this than she was. Rising up on her toes, she slipped her hands beneath his coat and pushed it off his shoulders until he let go enough to shrug it off. Fussy Ozzie let the jacket of his tux fall to the floor, before reaching for the back strap of her bra. Somehow that disappeared too and her breasts pressed against the starched front of his shirt and the soft silk of his vest.

Ozzie's hands came up between them and wrapped around her breasts. It felt so good she dropped her head backward and let him cradle her needy flesh.

"Beautiful," he murmured.

A tinge of embarrassment sent a small wave of heat across her skin. It disappeared when he bent to touch his lips to first one nipple and then the other.

"More," she whispered, grasping his shoulders, wanting to feel his skin without the layers of his clothing between them.

He spared one hand to tug on his tie, loosening it, then undoing his collar. Birdie raised her head and took over undoing the studs holding his shirt closed while he unbuttoned the vest.

His arms went around her, and he cursed under his breath.

"What's that?" She finished with the front of his shirt and pressed her hands against the warm skin of his chest. So defined, and hard, and warm. He had a little hair, but not much. Just enough to tickle her palms.

"Cufflinks," he responded. "Damned nuisance."

She snuggled closer, enjoying the warmth of his chest against hers, letting her hands glide over his skin, down his sides, and around to his back where she discovered more muscled contours. So different from the boys who'd tried to get her into bed, or out of her swimsuit in the pool.

This was different. This was her wanting Ozzie as much as he appeared to want her. Finally, with a final curse, he shrugged the vest and shirt from his shoulders, then wrapped his arms around her back again, his hands soothing and heating her at the same time.

"Okay there?"

"Yes. Very okay," she said with her lips against his skin. "Touch me. All over." As much as she wanted his touch, a tiny part of her had trouble believing this was happening. Never, ever, had she truly imagined Ozzie wanting her. Well, she'd certainly managed to believe he wanted to strangle her a time or two, but this? No. How had she not picked up on this? The way he made her feel now was almost too much, and yet, not enough. She wanted him like she'd never wanted anything else in her life.

"As you wish," he whispered against her ear, causing shivers of heat to race along every nerve in her body. From there his lips traveled down her neck, teasing and gently nipping. His hands stroked every inch of her back, pulling her closer, reverently touching, inflaming her as she did the same to him, her lips brushing along his collarbone.

When his hands once more palmed her rear cheeks, she wanted to feel his. Not that his clothes could hide the perfect shape of them, but she was suddenly hungry to feel his flesh, every bit of it. She followed the waistband of his slacks around to the front. One of his hands stopped her when she fumbled with the fastening.

"Easy, love. Not yet."

"Not fair," she complained. "I want to touch you too."

"No. Never said this would be fair."

Her world tilted, then stopped. He'd laid her back on the turned-down bed. It took another few seconds for him to tug the covers out from under her. He didn't give her a chance to move before he crawled between her legs, holding her down with his hips perfectly aligned with her pelvis.

"Okay?"

In answer she reached up and gently pulled his glasses from his face. "I want to see your eyes." Somehow the glasses found their way to the bedside table as she stared into the most beautiful sight she'd ever seen. Oswald's silvery blue eyes darkened with his focus one hundred percent on her. This time it was a shiver of pure heat that weakened her limbs. She reached up to lock her hands behind his neck and pull him down for a kiss. The move, while foreign to her, felt completely natural and right, their gazes never leaving one another until their lips met.

The kiss was hot enough to melt her into the linens beneath her.

Oswald kissed her until they both needed great gulps of air, but he didn't pause upon leaving her lips. He began an exploration of her face, never giving her chance to kiss him back. Instead she tunneled her fingers into his soft, thick, close-cropped hair. He could grow it a little longer, she thought, the better to touch and pet.

At her earlobe, he used his teeth to gently nip, sending a shot of fire straight to the quivering spot between her legs. The minutes passed while she lost herself in his touch as he moved down her throat, across her collarbone and shoulders, around her now aching breasts, teasing her, avoiding the nipples so peaked they almost hurt. His hands cuddled her breasts, gently squeezing, molding, shaping them to his heart's content, driving her mad.

The hard length of him pressed into her, reminding her she wanted his pants off. His shoulders blocked her way, and when he settled his lips around one nipple and sucked, she tossed her head, forgetting her goal to undress him. Involuntarily her hips rose, pressing her needy parts against the part of him she wanted inside her.

Oswald switched to the other breast and suckled the nipple, his fingers rolling the wet one, ramping her up more. If he kept that up, she might very well come from the nipple attention alone, but she'd sure hate for her first orgasm with a man to happen that way. This time she wanted everything.

She might technically still be a virgin, but she knew what went where. She knew how it was supposed to happen. All those romance novels had to get that right, didn't they? And yes, after one bad experience she'd sworn to herself to wait for the right moment. The right man. Sure, she'd been kissed, had even participated in petting, but she'd never gone all the way. The way he inflamed her, she knew Ozzie was the right man.

She tugged on his ears until he looked up at her. The sight of him with his mouth around the peak of her breast was almost as arousing as the feel of him there. And then he grinned and all her brains fled.

The man was downright gorgeous when he smiled, especially without his glasses on. No wonder women followed him both with their eyes and their feet. He certainly hadn't lacked for dancing partners at the reception, every single woman hoping he'd be with her like this tonight. Instead, he wasn't with them. He was with her.

She fought to find air. Ozzie. With her. Making her feel things she'd only dreamed about.

Their gazes locked, his grin faded as he wrapped his lips once more around her nipple and sucked it into his mouth. The intense heat emanating from his eyes started a core meltdown.

Every nerve ending in her body spiked as if she'd been hit with a live wire. She especially wanted to connect their parts. Once more, her hips rose, and she pressed her very wet panties to the front of his trousers.

"You're killing me," she moaned. "More."

He didn't speak—his mouth was too full for that—but he did move his free hand down her stomach and into the front of her panties.

His fingers passed through the trimmed patch of hair before touching the heated core, riding the slick juices his touch produced to slip between her folds.

"So sweet," he managed to say around her breast. Or rather moaned. The vibrations an incredible, new, never before imagined sensation.

She wished the man had four hands and two mouths so he could touch her and lick her everywhere at the same time.

"Please," she begged, her body aching to be possessed fully by him. Only him. She'd never wanted a man the way she wanted him now, a fact that she'd have to think about later.

In answer he pulled his hand from her panties, rolled to her side, gripped the waistband, and tugged them downward. When the stretchy fabric caught on her hips, she reached down to help, lifting her hips to speed things along. All at once they gave way, and she felt him rip them down her legs and off. Heaven only knew where they landed because his hand drifted up her stocking-clad leg, urging it to fall to the side. Mouth still working, he once more moved between her legs as he kissed his way down her body, skimming her stomach, moving lower, until he slipped one hand beneath her hips and lifted her to his mouth.

Oh! She'd never been kissed there before. It was wonderful and naughty. Her mouth watered at the thought of returning the favor to him. What would he taste like? Would she like it as he seemed to like tasting her?

Only briefly he touched her clitoris, leaving her writhing in need. How could he? She'd be sure to torture him when her turn came around. She'd never given a blow job, had never wanted to wrap her mouth around a penis, but when it came to Ozzie, oddly, she didn't want to wait a moment longer. But wait she would, because he wasn't letting her move beyond burying her fingers in his hair.

"Yes. There." *There*. The man was going to drive her to insanity if he didn't...

One finger entered her, stroking, seeking, touching every part of her. She'd touched the smooth walls of her channel, but it hadn't felt this good when she did it. No, his finger was larger, more invasive, but in the right way.

"So tight." He worked his finger gently, slowly stretching her until he could add another.

Oh yes. That was what she wanted. "More."

"Slowly, love. Don't want to hurt you. You're so tight, it's as if..." He delved deeper, then stopped.

She was watching as his startled eyes flew open and met her gaze.

Not wanting to speak, she merely nodded and burned with embarrassment. His gaze noted her hot flush, his eyes softening to something that looked a little like affection.

"I'll take proper care of you." His softly spoken words created a vibration she felt very deep inside.

She nodded again. He would. She knew that much about him. He lived up to his word.

Ozzie bent his head again, and when his lips closed about her clit, her eyes rolled up into her head, and she dropped back on the downy pillow. Nothing felt as good as this. His lips and fingers thrilled her, brought her alive in a way she'd only read about. No wonder women trailed after men like him. Not only was he gorgeous to look at, but he knew where and how to touch. The room spun as he took her higher, digging himself deeper under her skin, molding her into someone new.

The man was a god as he suckled just right, lightly biting down, filling her with wickedly wiggling fingers. Before she knew it, she was flying, light bursting behind her eyelids, sending her into the stratosphere, her body no longer her own as her head tossed back and forth on the pillow, the blood pounding in her ears the only sound she heard.

"Again," he demanded.

* * * *

Oswald watched as Courtney shattered under his touch for the third time. How he wished his conscience would let him strip off the rest of his clothes and crawl right up into her body where he knew the fit would be more perfect than anything he'd ever experienced before. The grip of her muscles around his fingers was enough to tell him she didn't have much experience. In fact, the tightness he'd encountered on his first foray into heaven, and her blushing nod, had confirmed what his gut had been telling him all along.

This woman was a virgin.

And he'd be damned if he took that from her now. Not with the level of alcohol bubbling through her system. Not with her parents downstairs in the ballroom. In fact, he'd have to find a graceful way to exit before she worked her wiles enough to tempt him into completing what he'd started when he touched her.

"Come 'ere," she whispered, eyes still shut as her body relaxed into the soft mattress. Maybe now she was exhausted enough to fall asleep so he could make his escape.

Slowly he pulled his drenched fingers from her, taking time to stuff them into his mouth and suck her taste greedily from them. Good God she was just as sweet as she looked. And the remaining trace of her signature lemon scent blended perfectly with her luscious juices. If ever there was a woman made for bedding, she was it.

"Oz," she called softly.

This time he obeyed, slowly working his way up her body, worshipping as he went. Her eyes were open just enough to watch him, something he found incredibly erotic. If only he could answer her demand to see this all the way through. If she pushed, he'd go down on her again and again until she passed out. A state she was already close to if he was any judge.

Courtney pulled him down on top of her, and he had to work to resist the temptation to dry hump her. She didn't deserve a horny bastard like him rubbing against her only to get off in his pants.

She licked his lips. "So that's what I taste like."

"Mmm, delicious." Even better when she opened her mouth and kissed him. Long and deep, their tongues lazily dueled, neither one wanting supremacy, only the intimate tango of two people enjoying the give and take, take and give, of being close, making love without intercourse. Warmth like he'd never felt before started in the vicinity of his heart and spread throughout his body, making it even harder to think about walking away from her. No one had ever taken the time to play with him like this, and Oswald discovered a new joy. Kissing had never been about intimacy before. Never about merely kissing just to be close.

He never wanted to stop.

That thought brought him back to his senses. Mostly. Head swimming with new emotions, he rolled to his side, cuddling her close.

"Don't let me fall asleep. I just want to rest a moment...."

"Take your time, love." He'd hold her until she was deeply asleep, and then he'd exit stage right. Too bad he wasn't the one taking off for a couple years in a foreign office like Drew. No, he had long months of torture to look forward to. Just this afternoon Court had asked him to mentor Courtney when she joined the London office. Court and Randi wanted to travel more and visit each of the satellite offices, leaving him in charge of the home office. With their daughter in Oswald's direct care.

Like he could be trusted with her care. He was the one she needed protection from. Hell, he needed protection from these feelings erupting from his heart.

And if being assigned as her mentor didn't suck, he didn't know what did. Now that he'd crossed the line and touched her, how would he keep his hands off her at work?

Chapter 4

Birdie woke to sunlight peeking around the edges of the curtains of her room. And a bed empty of Ozzie. In fact, all signs of him were gone, from his cufflinks to his tie. She pushed her hair from her face and realized she'd fallen into a deep sleep right after he'd snuggled her into his arms. When had he left?

Why had he left?

A sunbeam worked its way between the curtains and stabbed her in the eye, bringing with it a pounding in her head. Damn. A hangover. She'd never gotten around to taking a couple aspirin along with a quart or two of water. Neither had she removed her stockings, washed her face, or brushed out her now impossibly snarled hair.

With a groan, she dropped back on the pillow and tried to block out the morning. But she was naked between the sheets, and her body gloriously relaxed. Down there her parts pulsed with a satisfaction she'd never felt before. She smiled at the memory until she remembered she hadn't taken her turn to satisfy him. Which meant, dammit, she was still a virgin. Mostly. Did it count that he'd had his fingers inside her?

From the desk across the room the phone rang, driving another spike of pain into her head. Brunch with the family. She rolled her head enough to glance at the clock and noticed she was supposed to be downstairs right now.

Instead of running for the hotel phone, she grabbed her cell phone from the bedside table where she'd left it before the wedding and reception. Saw three texts from her mother.

She punched out a fast reply: *Just woke up. Give me 30.*

The return ping was fast. *You okay? Need me to come up?*

As if. *No. I'm good. Just a little hung over. 30 mins.*

Another fast reply: *Okay. See you then.*

Well that bought her a little time, but not much. She could only imagine the conversation between her parents downstairs. Surely she'd get concerned looks and maybe some inquiry. However, she was a grown up. As Ozzie now knew.

As tempted as she was to stay in the shower for a solid hour—it felt that good—she rushed through it only taking time for an extra dose of conditioner to comb out her tangles. Thoughts of seeing Ozzie again helped speed her through getting ready. Wet hair twisted into a simple up-do, she casually tossed on her favorite yellow sundress and a pair of sandals, completely skipping makeup except for the lip gloss she applied in the elevator down. With a minute to spare she sauntered into the private dining room set aside for the wedding party brunch that included out of town guests staying at the hotel.

Which meant Ozzie would be there.

Or should have been there.

A quick glance didn't show the sneaky Englishman anywhere. Frowning, she searched the room again. Skip out of her room while she slept and then hide out in his? Was he so cowardly? Or aghast at what he'd done? Her mood deflating a little, she bit her bottom lip in confusion at the thought, then caught her mother's concerned look with a questioning brow raised. Oops. Time to look happy for the newlyweds.

Pasting a smile on her face, she stopped by the drinks table just long enough to pick up a glass of orange juice. Mom was already pouring her a cup of coffee at the table. A spot was open for her between Mom and Grandpa. Mom's dad still looked handsome and vigorous with a full head of steel colored hair at seventy-one. Birdie only had the two grandparents now, Grandpa Dailey and Grandmother Robinson. The first adored her, the second wanted to improve everything about her. But she knew the old woman loved her in some warped and twisted way.

Birdie slid into her seat and gratefully accepted the cream pitcher her grandfather passed her.

"Feeling a little under the weather this morning, eh?" He nudged her with his shoulder.

"Nothing some coffee and juice won't fix. Maybe half a pound of bacon."

Grandpa snickered. "If you want a Bloody Mary, they make a pretty good one here."

"No thank you. Vodka on top of last night's champagne? Sounds like a nightmare in the making. Especially if we have to sit through the happy couple opening five hundred gifts."

"Only two hundred," her mother answered. "The rest are at the Wu's house."

"Oh thank God. I hope most of them are gift cards."

"I expect so. Most of what's on the table are envelopes."

Birdie had kept her gift very small. Personalized His and Her leather travel tech organizers. Perfect for holding passports, phones, charging cords, earbuds, and a little cash. She'd even thrown in matching luggage tags, also personalized. Useful for all the traveling in their future. For the bridal shower she'd given Meilin a pair of panties with "Groom Landing" printed on the front. Not every gift had to be practical.

"Am I the last to arrive?" She looked around the room, making note of all the groomsmen minus the traitorous Ozzie, who was still a no-show. The rat.

His uncle, the ever nosy Larry Attenborough, looked up from his plate and gave her a wide smile across the table. "Looking lovely as usual today, Miss Birdie."

"Courtney," she corrected absently. Too many people were looking at her with speculation in their eyes. Was her almost un-virginized state that obvious? Or was she too obvious about looking for Ozzie?

Dad leaned around Mom. "Everyone is here, except Oswald who caught a ride to the airport about an hour ago. His flight is in a few hours. He needed to get back to be ready for a meeting on Friday morning. This way he'll be able to grab a few hours sleep once he gets in."

"Ah." She busied herself sipping her juice, then stirring her coffee.

"Want me to get you something from the buffet?" Dad asked. "Eggs? Sausage? Rolls?"

"Um, sure. A little of everything, I guess." Not that she was especially hungry, but food would help the last of her hangover.

Dad pushed back from the table and came around to kiss the top of her head. "I know what you like, puddin'." The silly nickname made her smile up at him. For all the years they'd missed, they were making up time. If a childish nickname made him happy, then it made her happy. They'd had a rough start, but things were cool now. Last night while dancing with him she'd even called him Daddy and nearly brought both of them to tears.

"So other than opening gifts, what's on for today?" she asked her mother.

"Not much else. Some folks want to see Alcatraz. Your aunt wants to go shopping. Thank God we're already on Union Square and won't have to travel far. Your grandfather is taking your grandmother to the Legion of Honor Museum. I think Albert is taking the kids down to Great America. We'll all meet back here for dinner at seven."

It was a given that Dad's sister, Liza, wanted to see the best of what San Francisco had to offer in the way of shopping. Heck, they could even do a quick cruise of Chinatown, which was also close by.

"I'll go with Liza. Not that I need much." Other than some sexy new underwear. Oh yes, she wanted something better than the plain Lycra she'd been wearing last night with the idea of holding her up and in. If she was starting a friendship with benefits, it was time to up her game in the lingerie department.

Birdie looked to Drew's two friends from London. "You two on the Alcatraz trip?"

"Yer," Phillip Hammond answered. "Don't need to follow the women around and carry shopping bags when I can do that anytime at home." His smirk said he wouldn't do it there, either. "What are your plans on arrival in London?"

"I'm not sure what Mom has planned. Other than the next event on Sunday, and then on Monday I report for work."

"Once you're settled in, I'll be happy to squire you about town, help you get a feel for things," Drew's other friend from London, Calvin Whetmore, offered. The smile on his face was just a tad too smarmy for Birdie's taste, although she thanked him.

"I'm sure I have plenty of guides, not to mention my own brain, to get around. Plus, it's not like I haven't been there before." Granted it had never been longer than two weeks at a time, but she had been on the tour of London and knew the Vauxhall area around the condo and offices fairly well.

"We'll look you up in a couple weeks," Phillip said. "Get you introduced around so you have some friends to hang with."

If nothing else, they might know a few of the more fun night clubs. "That'd be great. Thanks."

Dad returned with a pair of plates, each one loaded with more than she could eat, but he had a fair sampling of the buffet tables. Had Drew been sitting beside her, he'd happily help, but the newlyweds were occupied on the far side of the room.

However, before she took off for the day, there was one person she very much needed to talk to. Jack.

Shortly before graduation, he'd done his best to talk her out of moving to London. He'd used the argument that her grandfather needed her here in California. If she wanted to run a company, there was one readymade for her, especially with her mother moving halfway around the world.

It was a good argument, and one she'd discussed in depth with her grandfather. While he'd miss her, he said, there were plenty of people who would love to buy his business, so she wasn't to worry about it for even a second. She glanced his way, and Grandpa winked back at her. They were good. Always had been. More often than not, they teamed up as co-conspirators in teasing her mother. Mom claimed she was the sandwich generation, or more specifically, the turkey in the middle getting squeezed between the elder and younger generations.

So she just needed to clear the air with Jack. It took a little maneuvering, but once she'd finished eating, she got up from the table, picked up a fresh glass of juice, then wormed her way into the group surrounding the newlyweds. It didn't take long to cut Jack from the group and get him off to the side.

"Jack," she started.

"Courtney, we really don't have anything else to say to one another." Although he smiled for their audience, she couldn't miss the hurt in his voice.

"I don't want to leave with you mad at me. You're a good friend. I've very much enjoyed, and appreciated, having you around. Once Drew left, you became my best buddy."

Jack winced at the buddy designation, but he also sighed and looked at the ground for a second before raising dark eyes that held a lot of sadness and hurt, but also resignation.

"I'd say you were more than a buddy, Courtney."

She rested a hand on his arm. "I know. But I never tried to lead you on. I made it clear from the beginning my aim was London, and now it's happening. My next goal is to become indispensable to Lynford."

"And rule the world as the first female CEO of the family business. I get that." He sighed and looked toward the newlyweds and their court of admirers. "I'd just hoped you'd change your mind."

"I'm sorry I hurt you. I never wanted to, you know."

"I know."

"And we did have fun."

Jack nodded, his eyes full of so much emotion she wanted to cry.

"Please don't be mad at me." She couldn't keep the pleading tone from her voice. It really hurt to turn Jack down this way, despite the forewarning she'd given him.

"I'm not." Jack sighed and his shoulders slumped. "As much I want to be angry with you, I'm more upset with myself. You were clear, but I ignored it. I wanted to sweep you off your feet the way Drew did Meilin. I was jealous of their romance and wanted it for myself." The crooked smile he gave her was self-deprecating.

Birdie rested a hand on his arm. "You will have it. But I'm not the woman for you. I happen to know Ping's little sister is wild about you."

"Wen?" Jack frowned. "Why she's no older than…you." A light of intrigue entered his eyes. "Really? It's hard to think of her as all grown up now. I remember her as a baby, always toddling off somewhere she had no business going. And as a teenager she was a complete disaster, always getting into trouble with her parents. I remember when she got her first piercing, an eyebrow if I recall." Jack smiled at the memory. "Maybe I'll have to look in on her, see how she's doing these days."

Whew. Great deflection if she did say so herself. "You should do that. I'm sure Ping would love to help find a way to make it look casual." Birdie gave his arm a light squeeze, then let go.

Jack chuckled, so much more like his happy-go-lucky self. "I know she would. I cringe at the thought of being at her mercy when it comes to matchmaking."

"If I say a quiet word to her? Suggest you need a distraction from missing me?" The coy look and batted eyelashes earned her another laugh. "Would that help?"

"I'm not ready for the altar, well, unless you are, but I suppose I could look around a little."

Better to ignore that altar comment. "I'll put in a word for you. Make you seem very reluctant. Can't have you looking eager."

"There is that. Jack the playboy needs to keep his reputation intact." He rolled his eyes while grimacing.

"I'm sorry you're not coming to London with us. Sure you can't get away?"

Jack shook his head regretfully. "My uncle's health is much improved, so my aunt doesn't need my help with him, and I have a large caseload this week. One even going to court."

"Court? Wow, that's exciting. And what you've been waiting for, right?" One year out of law school, he'd been itching to go head-to-head in a courtroom. "Well good for you." She gave him a huge smile. "I'm very pleased for you."

"Thank you. I'm quite pleased myself."

They stood and shared a long gaze for several seconds, until Birdie broke the silence. "So, we're good now? You won't mope when I'm around or ignore me to the point of ridiculousness?"

Jack picked up her hand and held it for a long moment, then raised it to kiss her knuckles. "No, I won't be rude. Yes, we're good. And if you change your mind about London, I'll still be here. But wait too long and I may be taken."

Laughing at his roguish wink, Birdie leaned forward and kissed his cheek. "I'm glad we're good. You're going to be snapped up very quickly, and then it will be my loss for sure."

Still holding her hand, he asked, "You going to Alcatraz?"

Birdie shook her head. "Nope. I'm for shopping with Aunt Liza. She likes to buy lots of gifts. Someone will have to remind her she has only so much space in her suitcases."

Now if only she could find out why Ozzie had run from her.

Chapter 5

It was late morning the next day, after skipping the wedding brunch, when Oswald gathered his laptop case and exited the plane. At least Court insisted on first class seats. It had made the long flight bearable. He'd even managed some sleep, although his dreams had been filled with pictures of Courtney.

Once more he damned himself for what he'd done. Now he couldn't rid his brain of images of her laid out on the bed, her lightly tanned skin perfectly covering the contours of her perfect body. The hills of her breasts, the flat planes of her stomach, the enticing valley of her cunny. A landscape he could spend his life exploring.

He'd be better off learning to draw or paint so he could capture his vision forever, because he certainly wasn't going to get another chance to see her like that again.

Standing in line at Customs and Immigration, he wiped a hand over his face trying to clear the images from his mind. The taste and scent of her from his memory. Coffee and whisky on the plane hadn't succeeded. How did he expect anything else to work?

Thank God for his job. He had that to look forward to. He had a day-long meeting tomorrow and then planned to spend Saturday in the office catching up from the week away. Sunday he'd have to see Courtney again, couldn't help that, but he could keep a distance between them. Maybe twice the length of his reach would work. As his turn came, he handed over his passport and the required documents filled out on the plane, endured a search of his suitcase, then made his way out to the cab stand. No point in bucking the system.

Oh, and he knew the system. From the time he'd lost his parents and moved in with his Uncle Larry, he'd learned. Not that Larry was such a stickler, but his Uncle Wilton and his wife had made things clear. How the hierarchy worked. The servants also made sure he knew his place. He may have been an Attenborough, but he was clearly the poor relation. A label that had followed him all his life. Even at Eton he'd been clear about his place. The heirs to their family titles had let him know he'd never reach their level.

Their methods hadn't been so simple as shunning. No, there'd been more brutal lessons. Eventually he'd learned to fight back, and had grown big enough, strong enough, to defend himself and others like him. Eventually they'd left him alone, although to this day the occasional taunt was tossed out when he happened upon one of those old school chums. They liked to remind him he had three cousins and an uncle before him in line to the title. And now his cousins had children, pushing him even further from inheriting the Barony, a small enough title as it was.

As such he'd had to make his own way. To his thinking it made him stronger. He'd built his own impeccable reputation, had his own investments that tallied up to a respectable fortune few beyond his financial advisor knew about. His was also a highly regarded name in the world of mixed martial arts. He had enough clout in that area he could open his own gym and challenge the top ranking ones in the country.

Not that it would have made much difference to the higher social circles. Oh, he was proper enough to even out a dinner party, handsome enough to escort a minor starlet or rising model, but not good enough to hang with them as their cachet rose. There was always someone with better connections, better looking, or more money to take over when the women who'd hung on his arm gained more and more attention.

Hostesses liked him because he was unfailingly polite. He knew the rules of etiquette and never overstepped his bounds or made an ugly scene. Like a well-trained background actor, he never tried to outshine those at the center of attention. Rather he made them look better. Same as properly behaved younger sons had been doing for generations.

Only he was one step beyond that. The only son of a disgraced younger son who'd had the misfortune to marry the daughter of a poor preacher because he'd gotten her pregnant. A girl who thought by catching James Attenborough, youngest brother of Wilton, it would up her station in life. In fact, it had done the opposite. James had been forced to leave university to work to support the new wife with a baby on the way. He hadn't been good for much and jobs had come and gone, each one lesser than the one before until he'd been working as a laborer on the docks.

Oswald had only been three when his father was killed by a crate that fell as it was being lifted from a cargo ship. Only two years later his mother died in their tiny, dirty apartment at the hands of a lover who'd gotten her into drugs.

Larry had been the only family willing to take him in. Thank God for Larry, the bachelor uncle. Larry had coached him on how to act around his cousins and much older Uncle Wilton who'd barely acknowledged him unless Oswald had done something stupendously stunning at school or on the pitch, whether it be cricket or football. Fortunately Oswald had brains and he'd quickly learned to use them. It didn't hurt that he had a fair athletic ability, but his brains far exceeded his physical prowess.

Larry's close friendship with Courtland Robinson had given Oswald a further boost in the world. Court didn't have a family title, but he had a family business and estate, both going back several centuries. Not nobility, but certainly a force in the business community, and status with the peerage, his clients. Because Court always treated him fairly and with respect, when Drew had shown up at Eton, a little on the small side and a target for bullies, Oswald, four years his senior, had stepped in and quietly provided not only protection, but he'd taught Drew how to defend himself.

The fact Drew had brains even more powerful than Oswald, and an open, friendly personality, had rocketed him up the academic and social scales at school. So when Drew entered university at the start of Oswald's second year, it made sense for them to share a flat, something both Larry and Court had encouraged.

So, it was only logical that Court had hired Oswald to work summers and breaks at the offices of Lynford. First he'd spent a summer in the warehouses out Tilbury way learning the flow of inventory, the shipping routes, and how to track it all. Then he'd moved to the offices, starting in the mailroom. Just as Courtney would next week. That made him smile to himself. Old Dennis had ruled the mailroom for going on twenty-five years now and wasn't likely to retire until he lost the use of his hands to arthritis.

When it became clear Oswald had a head for finance, Court had directed his internship through the accounts department. Larry had even found a few thousand pounds to give him for his sixteenth birthday and shown him how to get started investing. He lost enough on his first try that it scared him into approaching one of the upper level boys at school. One who came from a very rich family that also lacked a title. Fortunately,

Abraham had a good grasp of money and the markets, and was willing to share what he knew. Abraham still managed most of Oswald's investments because he lacked the time to do so himself. For now. Soon he'd have the capital to form a partnership with Abraham.

Oswald only had to give Lynford another year, and gladly, but he knew with Drew now stepping into the company full time, and Courtney doing the same, chances of him ever taking control of Lynford were slim. He liked Lynford, and the Robinson family in particular, but he wanted more. He wanted to be the head of his own company. In his mind it was better than holding a hereditary title from the crown. It meant he'd made it on his own, and not on the shoulders of his ancestors. Sticking with Lynford awhile longer hadn't been a problem. Not until Court had taken him aside the day before the wedding.

"I have a big favor to ask of you," Court had opened the conversation just before going into the wedding rehearsal.

"Anything." Because he owed this man his loyalty, respected him far more than a father figure, and loved him as much as Larry. The two men, close friends themselves, had mentored Oswald into the man he was today.

"I know you have plans for your future that involve leaving Lynford." Court held up a hand. "I'm not asking, but it's inevitable. You've a brilliant future in anything you choose to do. You think you've hit the top at Lynford, and maybe you have, maybe you haven't, but I'm not here to discuss that. I don't know your timeline, but I'm asking you, as a favor to me, to stay at least another year."

Not ready to confess his plans, he merely nodded. "I can hold a year." Besides, that fit into his timeline, more or less.

"I'm far from dead, but I'm old enough now I need to plan seriously for the unimaginable. Heart attack, stroke like Smithfield had last year, accident, or some other catastrophe. Drew isn't ready. Even less so is Birdie."

At the mention of Courtney by her nickname, caution stole over Oswald.

"Should anything happen to me, yes," Court continued, "the board feels Randi could step in, but she doesn't like to hear about it. On the other hand, we have Birdie who is ready to take on the London office. At least in her own mind."

Oswald nodded. Each time Courtney had a break long enough to travel to London, she'd been in the office ghosting Court's assistant, a sturdy older woman who didn't put up with any nonsense, but still blushed like a school girl when either Court or he dropped a posy or treat off at her desk. She was also old enough to retire in a few years and was amused by Courtney's not so subtle ambition to replace her.

"These next twelve months, Randi and I are planning an around-the-world trip. Mostly an extended honeymoon, but we'll stop in the satellite offices for two to four weeks at a time to get a real feel for things and see if we need to update our processes, find new sources, target new markets."

Oswald nodded again, but began to have a sinking feeling. Court had mentioned these plans a year ago, but in a more abstract way. It sounded like they weren't so abstract anymore, but rather on the eve of taking place.

"After the wedding, we're headed back to England for about a month. During that time I want to shift the balance of power to you. This shouldn't be a surprise; we've discussed it." Court took a long look around as people were herded into place, and chuckled. "According to my mum, I'm at the rehearsal for show. How did she put it? 'The only person more useless at a wedding than the groom is the groom's father.'"

Oswald smiled at the last comment, but answered the first. "Yes, sir. I'm aware of your plans."

"There's more. Since Randi and I plan to be out of the country, someone needs to guide and mentor Birdie as she goes through the training period."

Oswald's stomach dropped. His eyes sought out Birdie across the vestibule where she stood with her mother ready to help assemble the bodies of the wedding party. She was smiling and chatting with the women around her, completely unaware she was being discussed.

"I see," he said, merely to fill the silence as Court also gazed at his daughter.

"You know her by now. She's eager. Perhaps a little too much so. I'm not sure she's really ready to take on the London office, but she's determined."

Yes, Courtney was determined. And possibly a little naïve. She'd discover that when she came up against Dennis and his kingdom in the basement.

"I'm asking you to be her mentor. To keep an eye on her. Possibly head off any animosity that may come her way. I'm fully aware the employees are leery of her. They don't fully understand her position in my life. As you know, I try to keep the personal side separate. Drew grew up coming to the office so they were used to him when he began working there. But with Courtney, well, from the rumbles I've heard, they're not quite open to accepting her. Many feel she's a gold digger, taking advantage of me. Nepotism in favor of the daughter isn't as acceptable as it was for Drew. I'm afraid she might get hurt when she runs into the wall they have in place."

"She's a friendly girl, she'll win them over."

"Eventually, yes. But it's the near future that has me concerned. That's why Randi and I are putting off our travels for a month. I hope to ease her into the office culture, but as her father, it will be awkward. However, you, as my chosen replacement and as her friend, can help. You know the players on a level I don't. Most of the ones I worked with on my way up the corporate ladder are retired now. The newer ones won't like her making a fast climb. They'll see it as her milking me, using our new-found relationship to make her rise faster."

"True." Even he, and particularly Drew, had to suffer their own levels of subtle hazing, but as males, they'd been accepted faster. The men respected them and the women had flirted with them. For Courtney, the men would be patronizing and the women catty or dismissive. As many a female executive had suffered, any rise in a male dominated corporate world was often interpreted as sleeping their way to the top. Hard work was discounted by a pretty face in front of sharp brains. Courtney not only had the pretty face and figure, but the shining new family connection. Had she been raised in the company, starting at a far younger age, her road might have been smoother, but there was no use lamenting it.

The girl was in for a shock. Truly, she would be better off staying in California and working with her grandfather in his business supplying items to the world of the west coast vineyards. The culture was far more accepting of a woman in a leadership role.

Oswald sighed and accepted his fate. "Yes. I'll stay at least a year. Until you're back in the office and Courtney is settled."

Court landed a hand on his shoulder. His grin was as wide as any his children might flash. "Thank you. I knew I could count on you. And when you're ready to make your break, I hope you'll let me invest in your new venture, whatever it may be."

Oswald gave him a half smile. "Don't worry. I'll be presenting my business plan when the time comes."

And now that he'd touched Courtney, Court's request was going to be that much harder to honor, because Oswald had already taken advantage of Courtney's innocence. Or one her father believed she still held. One Oswald desperately wanted to take wholly for himself. But knew better. Courtney was off limits. And for the next year she'd stay there.

Chapter 6

Birdie dropped her tablet on her first class window seat, then swung her carry-on into the bin overhead.

"Darling," her father said at her shoulder. "You were supposed to wait for me to do that."

"Dad, I'm not some fainting flower. Go play white knight to Mom. She needs it more." She closed the bin and turned to him.

"Whether you're capable is not the point at all," he grumbled. "Appalling how your mother raised you. Her and that husband of hers." The twinkle in his eye told her he was joking.

"Well, you're her husband now, so go fawn all over her. She eats it up." The two of them shared a smile, then a laugh.

"Right, you little baggage. Settle in. We'll come invade your space later. Or the newlyweds will." They both looked over his shoulder to see Drew and Meilin gazing at each other across the cabin in the back of the section, millions of miles away from anyone else in their minds. "Well, maybe not them. Although I'm sure the grandparents will look in on you, unless you look in on them first."

Birdie rose up on her toes and kissed his cheek. "Go on with you. I can certainly get myself into my seat."

Dad took his seat in the next row up, on the aisle. Mom had the window.

Adjusting her belt, Birdie buckled in and picked up her tablet. For once she was going to read something fluffy and frivolous. Other than accepting a diet soda from the flight attendant, she didn't look up from her book until a man appeared at her row. Darn. They'd sold Oswald's seat. Or upgraded someone. She'd been looking forward to having the row to herself.

"Excuse me, uh, miss?" The man's voice was rough, as if he'd smoked three packs a day for the last three decades.

With an internal sigh, she glanced up at him. "Hello. You my seatmate?"

"Um, yes. I'd like to ask a favor if I could." Birdie noted the gravely mix of upper crust Brit with a few nuances of something not so posh. "Mind swapping seats with me? All I want to do is sleep. I don't want people bumping into me, and I don't want to have to move when you get up to…wander the cabin."

She took a closer look at him. He wore pressed jeans, designer label probably, what looked like a silk T-shirt under a worn black leather jacket. On his face he had at least a three-day growth of dark beard liberally sprinkled with gray. His eyes were hidden under Harry Potter style dark glasses. Or maybe he was trying to look more like John Lennon, or the Prince of Darkness himself, Ozzy, but with a Forty-Niners ball cap on his head, further shading his eyes. Black, long hair curled from under the cap to the tops of his shoulders lightly streaked with more strands of gray.

In one hand he held what looked like a very expensive attaché. If she'd met him on the street she'd think he was some sort of aging Hell's Angel, but lean and lanky rather than sporting a pot belly. Then again, maybe he was one of those aging rocker types. Like from those strange eighties groups her parents still listened to. Neptune Satellites, Tears for Fears, Prince, and Queen came to mind. With his face hidden, it was a little hard to be more specific. For all she knew, he could be Keith Richards. But wouldn't he fly charter? Maybe. She'd have to ask Mom as she was more the rock groupie type than Birdie would ever be.

"Okay." She unbuckled and slid from her seat, tablet in hand. No big deal, she was portable.

He stepped back enough she could get into the aisle. Then it was her turn to step back and let him get to the window seat. Not that they could bother each other much with the near-wrap around backs. Each seat was like a tiny living room. The seat even flattened out for sleeping, and they each had their own TV-like monitor and gooseneck adjustable reading light.

Before she sat again, Dad was there. "Everything okay, puddin'?"

"Sure. My seatmate wanted the window seat. I don't mind the aisle, so we swapped." She waved a hand at the man shoving his case under the seat in front of him.

The man barely spared her dad a glance, but Dad seemed to do a double take as he scrutinized the newcomer. Then he shook his head with a little smile. "Remind me later to tell you about my cousin Paul."

Before she gave him the you're-weird-Dad look, the man in the seat stiffened, but didn't look up. Dad just grinned and returned to his seat. Shrugging off his comment, Birdie reseated herself and settled down to return to her book. Thankfully it was an ebook. When stealing a little frivolous reading time, she preferred for no one to see the cover. Most of the ones she chose had covers with half naked people. It was no one's business what she read.

Since the flight left around four-thirty, it wasn't so long after take-off when afternoon tea service began.

The man next to her refused anything other than a double Glenlivet. When the flight attendant tried to offer him something else from the tea menu, he nearly growled.

"Listen, I really don't want to be rude, Regina, love." Birdie glanced at the attendant's name tag. Yup. Regina. "However, I'm going to say this only once. Unless I press the little button calling for you, I want to be left alone. No dinner, no tea. Just this one drink, and I plan to curl up like a hedgehog and go to sleep for the rest of this ten plus hour flight. That's all I want. To sleep. Are we clear?"

Birdie was slightly taken aback by the barely restrained impatience she felt coming off him in waves. Grouchy bear there. But even she could appreciate the sexy Brit accent with the gravelly voice. If Mom could hear him, she probably would have been on her knees looking over her seat back. Still, the man was older than her father. Maybe as old as the man who'd raised her as his own had been. Dear, dear, Daddy Wyatt.

However, the attendant took it in stride without a blink. "Of course, sir. I'll see you're not disturbed unless the plane is going down."

"Appreciate it." He nodded sharply, then leaned back in his seat, his head once more hidden by the wings of the seats.

"And you, miss?" Birdie now had the attendant's undivided attention.

Her row mate might not be hungry, but she was. Surprising, really, after the last week. She looked over the menu card. "I'll have the cucumber sandwiches, a buttermilk scone, and the English Breakfast tea."

"I'll have it out soon," the woman promised and moved to the seats behind.

Tablet in hand, Birdie fell deep into the story. She barely heard the attendant tell her parents dinner service would be in a few hours, and if they wanted to rest, she'd help them arrange the seats into beds.

Birdie smiled at the woman clearing dishes, even helped by reaching for the empty whisky glass of her seatmate. He didn't stir an inch at the silent movement. Apparently he hadn't been kidding when he said he wanted sleep.

When the attendants vacated the cabin, the man beside her shifted position, then gruffly said, "Thank you," in barely more than a whisper.

Birdie leaned forward enough to see his chin. "You're welcome. Go back to sleep," she whispered.

The only response was a grunt as he pulled his coat closer about his body, then settled once more into soft, even, breathing.

Wanting to stretch her legs a bit, Birdie rose and made a circuit of the first class cabin. Drew and Meilin were dismayed at the lack of intimacy between their seats, since each one was designed to cocoon individual travelers in their own private space. Other than that, they too were settling down for a nap. Grandmother Robinson and Grandpa Dailey were already tucked in and snoozing in their separate, but side by side nests. Same with Meilin's parents. Birdie only spared a brief thought for a few other members of the wedding party tucked back in business class. Dad was generous to a fault, but a line had to be drawn somewhere. As it was, her family pretty much commandeered half the exclusive cabin. The only person missing was Oswald.

Once more she wondered what had sent him scurrying for London a day early. Was she really so frightening a creature? Had she done something in her sleep that was inexcusable? Had she said she loved him while dreaming? Farted? What? And why hadn't he taken her virginity? That's probably what pissed her off the most. Like she wasn't good enough for him. Or too young. Too innocent—she snorted out loud at that thought as she was returning to her seat.

Dad grabbed her wrist. "What's up? Everything okay back there?" He nodded toward her seat mate.

"Yeah, everything's good." A thought occurred to her, and she narrowed her eyes on her father. "You know that guy?"

"That bloke? The one who looks like a washed up rocker? Probably a one hit wonder from the eighties and is still trying for a comeback." With a twinkle in his eye, he spoke loud enough for the man to hear him. By the way he spoke over his shoulder, she guessed it was intentional. Mom looked up from her book with curiosity painted across her face.

And the arrow hit the target. The man shifted, his foot "accidentally" kicking Dad's seat. Instead of getting annoyed, her father laughed. "Looks like I'm right." He looked downright smug. "Time for a nap?"

At the word nap, Birdie raised a hand to cover her huge yawn. "Looks like it. See you later."

When she woke a few hours later to the scent of hot food, she discovered someone had tucked a blanket around her. Her seatmate had one too. Sitting up straight, she rolled her neck and pushed the blanket aside. A rough grunt came from her left, and she turned to look at her now even scruffier looking companion.

"Aren't you a little old to have Mummy tucking you in?" he muttered. Like he was one to talk with a blanket draped over him as well.

"You try telling her that," Birdie challenged him.

He merely grunted and rolled the other way.

Ignoring him, she enjoyed her dinner, complete with wine and a decadent dessert. Her book was excellent company while she ate. Once the dishes were cleared away, she decided to stroll again, now that everyone was awake. She was sitting on the arm of her grandfather's seat on the far side of the cabin when she noticed her seatmate get up and head for the lavatories. What she could see of him, what wasn't covered by the hat and sunglasses he still wore, was tall and lean. He moved like a panther, all loose and relaxed looking, but one couldn't miss the aura of power around him. More her mom's type. Well, when Mom wasn't drooling over her husband, Birdie snickered inside her head. Honestly, they were cute together.

She turned her attention back to her grandparents, but kept half an eye on her seat, waiting to see if her new friend stopped to talk to anyone. Well, he didn't stop because he wanted to, but rather because her father stepped into his path.

"Excuse me," she said to her grandparents and headed around the center row of seats to come up behind the stranger.

"So is this what old rocker gits wear these days? Where are the chains? Found a new seamstress who doesn't cut up your clothes?" her dad asked.

"I see you haven't changed much. Looking a little thick around the waist there, old man. Middle age settling in? Won't catch yourself a rich widow that way."

"No need to catch a rich widow. I married the beautiful mother of my daughter about eighteen months ago now. Not that you ever bothered to respond to the invite." Dad crossed his arms and leaned against the back of his seat, giving every intention of staying as long as it took. Whatever it was he was looking for.

The stranger crossed his arms over his chest and shrugged. "Didn't get it."

"Suppose you didn't get the one to Drew's wedding last week, either, you washed-up has-been. Interesting you're in San Francisco to catch this flight, but couldn't break out of the studio for an evening to make merry and wish your cousin well."

"The boy got married?" He did a good job of sounding surprised. Or least Birdie believed him, although the look on her father's face said he didn't. "Must have missed that invite too. I was in LA until yesterday"— he paused to glance at his watch—"Uh, Thursday morning. Had to stop in SF to meet with Lucas on a project."

A bony finger poked Birdie in the shoulder, as her grandmother said, "Out of my way, girl."

Birdie turned sideways so the old woman could poke her finger in the stranger's shoulder next.

"Rupert Paul Robinson, you very well did receive those invitations," Gran said. "I had Martin send not only the engraved one weeks early, but I had him e-mailing you once a month six months prior. And take off that ridiculous disguise. It doesn't work, anyway."

"It got me on the plane undetected," he muttered, as he turned around with a cheery smile on his face. "Aunt Helen!" He took off the hat, leaving the sunglasses on as he enfolded her in a hug, then set her back and kissed her cheek. "Looking lovely and hale as always." Only then did he remove the glasses and tuck them into an inner pocket of his leather jacket.

Oh that face. It did look extremely familiar, but from where? He'd called Gran Aunt Helen, so was there a family connection she didn't know about? She glanced at Mom whose green eyes were as round as Birdie had ever seen them.

"Stop right there, you cheeky boy." The older woman poked him in the chest hard enough he rubbed the spot. "I even spoke, personally, with your personal assistant just last week to make sure you'd be there for Drew's wedding. LA is not that far from San Francisco."

"Auntie, dear, San Francisco is a twelve hour drive from LA. On a good day."

"And a matter of an hour or two by plane. You could have been there for the wedding and back in LA later that night."

"And I sacked my PA last week, so she probably withheld that little tidbit out of spite." He glanced over his shoulder at Birdie's dad. "I swear I'm never hiring another woman PA again. Sticking to men from here out. Hetero men."

"Hey," Birdie found herself protesting.

"I have nothing against gays, or women for that matter, love,"—he turned very familiar blue eyes on her—"but I can no longer afford to risk my assistant being attracted to me. I've sacked three for that very reason in the last three years." He gave a shrug. "So, am I to understand you're a new part of this crazy family?"

Birdie accepted his handshake. "I'm Court's long lost daughter, Drew's half sister. And this old bat's uncouth granddaughter." Birdie grinned as her Gran sniffed and pointed her nose in the air.

Of course Gran knew her line. "The manners of these Americans, I swear...."

"I agree," the new cousin said, with a wicked twinkle in his eye that fooled no one. "They're just hopeless, but hey, at least the Californians make good wine." He looked around the cabin. "So, are the newlyweds here too? I should give them my regards."

Birdie pointed toward the last row of seats on the far side of the cabin. Drew was just rising from his seat, trying to figure out what the commotion was.

"Oi! Drew, my man."

"Cousin Paul! What're you doing here?" Drew started across the cabin but had to stop in favor of the attendant already headed toward the knot.

"Ladies, gentlemen," the attendant said. "I must insist you return to your seats. We can't have you all standing around blocking the aisles. Maybe a couple of you can swap seats to catch up?"

"Of course, love," Paul said. "How rude of us. Oh, and when breakfast comes around, if you don't mind adding a full English for me as well? I know I said I didn't want food, but now I've slept a few hours I'm a little peckish."

"Of course, Mr. Robinson." She glanced at Birdie's dad. "I take it most of you are related in some way?"

"Forgive me, Regina, love," Paul said. "Totally unexpected family reunion here." The smile he gave her was nearly identical to Birdie's father and brother's. In addition to the bright blue eyes, his features bore a strong resemblance. Only the hair color was different.

"How lovely for you all. I hope you have time to catch up over a cuppa in London. For now, if you please..." She indicated their seats.

"Of course. Now, Court, let me by."

"Certainly." Dad looked at Birdie first, then turned to Mom. "Randi, love, mind if I switch seats with Birdie? I need to catch up with Paul."

Mom's smile was a little strained. "No, of course not. Birdie and I can have some girl talk."

Muttering, Gran turned back the way she'd come. Drew met her and took her to her seat.

Meanwhile, Birdie settled down beside her mother and caught a sideways glance. "What's that?"

Mom sniffed. "You may be an orphan by morning. I'll make sure I transfer enough money for bail into your account. Then again, any judge in the world would let me off, I'm sure."

Birdie laughed. "I have no idea what you're talking about."

"Your father never told me he was related to Khan."

"You mean, that's Khan?" Both of Birdie's brows headed for her hairline. "Really?"

Mom nodded emphatically. "Khan, lead singer of Neptune Satellites. I think that's a punishable offense, don't you?"

Birdie laughed. "Maybe, but surely not by death. I've sorta gotten used to him, and I'm pretty sure you love him. So yes, something evil, but not permanent. At least death permanent. You can scar him."

"Scarring is good." Mom nodded. "I can do that."

Chapter 7

Fresh from the airport, door closed and locked behind him, Oswald dropped his luggage in the foyer and headed for the kitchen. His jacket landed on the back of a chair at the island separating the kitchen from the small dining area. Normally he'd take the time to hang it properly in the closet, but after more than fourteen total hours of travel he had a powerful need for water. First the California heat, and then the dry air of the plane had left him as parched as a desert.

Thankfully the housekeeper had been in that morning and the fridge was full of bottled water and a casserole with that night's dinner ready to go in the oven. She'd also left fresh bread and fruit, along with the quick and easy foods he liked. Without opening the freezer he knew it would be stocked with a full week's worth of oven ready meals. He may have liked quick, but he didn't care for overly processed food. Thank God she agreed because whatever she cooked was ten times better than a frozen boxed meal. Almost as good as eating out, although she couldn't quite match the pub for fresh fried fish and chips, a treat he only allowed himself once a month.

He pulled two bottles of water from the fridge and cracked open the first one. It lasted thirty seconds as he gulped it down. The bottle went in the recycling bin as he reached for a tall glass to pour the next bottle into. No point in gorging himself, but the first bottle had needed to be fast. The second wouldn't last fifteen minutes, but he'd make himself slow down.

As he was calculating the time until putting the casserole into the oven and how long before he could crawl into bed for a well deserved ten hours of sleep, the bell rang. Nobody but the housekeeper should know he was home. His original schedule had him flying with the Robinsons, but he'd ducked out a day early without telling anyone in London other than his housekeeper and Court's assistant.

Carrying the filled glass with him, he answered the door.

"Darling, I'm disappointed in you." The pouty voice belonged to Deirdre Portman-Wright in the flesh, dressed in her usual slumming outfit. Designer jeans, glittery T-shirt, dark brown leather jacket that matched the boots with four inch heels.

"How did I do that?" The last person on this earth he wanted to talk to right now. Should have never answered.

"You missed my dinner party last night. I left the invitation on your voice mail three days ago." Deirdre reached out a perfectly manicured red-tipped claw and touched his chest. The touch did absolutely nothing for him.

"Sorry, but I was in California for Drew's wedding. I'm sure I mentioned it." He knew he had. In fact, the announcement had been in all the social columns.

The woman actually fluttered her overly made up eyelashes. "I thought that was last week."

Harsh restraint prevented him from rolling his eyes. Deirdre only followed her own calendar and never paid attention to anyone else's. "No, it was this week. Tuesday."

Her finger continued to make lazy circles over his chest. "Well you can make it up to me now. I'm dying for some fish and chips at your favorite pub."

"Sorry, love. Just got in, literally five minutes ago, and I'm knackered. I'm heading for a shower, afterward I'll warm something for dinner, and then it's off to bed for me." Then again, he hadn't had a serious workout in a while. While dinner cooked he could go a few rounds with the punching bag in the gym he'd set up in the basement and shower on his way to bed.

"Sounds wonderful. I'll join you."

Oswald sighed and took a long drink from his glass. It gave him a moment to consider his words. Wiping his mouth with the back of his hand, he let himself meet her gaze. "Really, I'm not up for entertaining." Especially the kind she wanted. After last night, or rather the night before, with Courtney, he wasn't open to taking Deirdre to bed. In fact, he wasn't open to taking anyone to bed. Unless Courtney showed on his doorstep, and then maybe he'd change his mind. Since she was getting ready to climb on a plane, that was highly unlikely. Impossible, in fact. Oswald rolled his shoulders. Yeah, a workout was a great idea.

"Darling, don't disappoint me two nights in a row. Nobody likes to eat dinner alone." The sexy pout did nothing for Oswald this time. In the past he'd indulged her need to slum from time to time, but not tonight.

"I didn't disappoint you on purpose last night, but I'm afraid I'll have to do so, consciously and with great guilt, tonight. I've been gone over a week and I need to be up and into the office before the birds tomorrow. I'm afraid my schedule is booked for the foreseeable future." And if it wasn't, he wouldn't admit it to her.

She tried the eyelash fluttering again. Still didn't work on him. "All work and no play makes Oswald a dull boy."

"I just spent a week doing no work other than playing groomsman to an old friend. I have a boss to impress and a new hire to situate next week. There's also the England portion of the nuptials to attend before the newlyweds head off to their new life. It's going to be a busy week, and tonight is my one night to get some real sleep. And I do mean sleep. Something that usually doesn't happen when you stay over, love."

Deirdre's laugh was throaty, and her hand slipped down to hold him by the waistband of his jeans. Obviously she thought she still had a hold over him. Something he'd let her believe for the last eighteen months. A hold that had been slipping from the moment he'd met Courtney. A fact that would have repercussions the moment Deirdre figured out his attraction had shifted. Not that he'd ever had the illusion of a long-term relationship with Deirdre. He was a diversion for her when everyone else was tied up, and he'd known it from day one. Since she wasn't the type who'd ever marry him, he'd been happy to accommodate her when she got the itch to see him. But he wasn't going down that road again. He just had to be careful how he broke it to her.

"All right." The smile was conciliatory, if a little brittle. "I'll forgive you this once if you include me as your plus-one for the celebrations. I haven't seen Drew in ages, and I'd like to meet his bride. I've heard she's a beauty."

"That she is." Oswald gently removed Deirdre's hand from his jeans. "She's also gentle and kind on the surface, with a steel backbone beneath. Anyhow, you'll love her. She's wonderful and good for Drew."

"I look forward to it. Call me!"

With that she leaned forward and placed a brief kiss on his chin before turning and sauntering toward the sidewalk with an over exaggerated sway of her hips. Oswald heaved a sigh of relief, and gently closed the door, double checking the locks. Now he had to figure out how to not invite Deirdre to the reception on Sunday celebrating the newlyweds.

Courtney would be there and Deirdre would have no issue with letting Courtney know about their relationship. As it had been. The one that no longer existed. The one he had to tell Deirdre was over.

* * * *

Oswald managed to stick to his plan of digging into work until late Saturday afternoon. His vow to stop thinking of Courtney, not so much. He was just considering a short break for dinner when his cell phone rang. Since Court's number showed, he answered.

"There you are," Court said. "Tried your flat and couldn't get through the office switchboard, have to fix that on the weekends. Hate calling your cell because of what I might be interrupting."

"You aren't interrupting a thing. I'm at the office and just considering a break for dinner."

"Perfect. We're at the flat, got in yesterday, and spent today getting people sorted. Randi's rustled up something involving pasta, seafood, and some of that San Francisco sourdough she smuggled over. It's just family, which includes Larry, so haul yourself over here. By the size of the salad and the pasta pot, I do believe Randi means to feed half of London."

"Who can resist an offer like that? Shall I pick up some wine on the way? A cake for dessert?"

"We're set. Just bring yourself and your appetite."

And maybe somewhere along the way he'd find his courage. How would Courtney greet him? As for him, he planned to act as he always did. Reserved. Removed. One step back from the inner circle. Larry being there would help. He loved to tease Courtney, and Oswald could watch from the sidelines.

With the flat not far from the offices, Oswald managed to make it there in fifteen minutes, and that was dragging his feet. Easy commute for Court. Probably where Courtney would stay while her parents traveled. Not that they needed a house sitter, but Court would probably insist because of the building security and the vicinity. At least there were few gangbangers in this section of well-lit and patrolled streets. Although the temptation of her living so close to the office could be harder to ignore. A brisk walk for a midday break, if one could wait long enough to avoid scandal at the office.

The doorman let him in, and the security man at the desk gave him a nod. They knew him well, and Court had probably called down to expect him. The elevator ride to the top floor was fast, and he found the flat door open when he approached. The level of trust and acceptance extended by the Robinsons never failed to impress him. It humbled him. Gave him ideas of grandeur above his accepted station in life. The only Robinsons to ever look down their noses at him had been Drew's mother, Beatrice, and his grandmother, old Mrs. Robinson. But then again, both women looked down on everyone. Mrs. Robinson had been kinder about it, more along the line of not wanting to be bothered with little boys, rather than seeing him as low class trash. That had come from Beatrice. As far as he could tell, no one missed that woman.

"Oswald!" Larry greeted him at the door with a glass of aged liquor. "Good to see you, m'boy."

Before he could get a word out, the distinctive opening of Osborne's "Crazy Train" screeched out from the speakers, then the volume dropped. Courtney looked up from the stereo set and gave him a snarky smile. One he couldn't resist returning despite his resolve to distance himself from her. Something that was going to be harder to accomplish than he'd originally thought. Especially if they continued to invite him to intimate family events like this one.

"Oswald's here," Randi sang out from the kitchen where delicious smells emanated.

"Evening, everyone." He shrugged off his jacket and hung it on the coat tree near the door. Larry handed him the drink, and they made their way deeper into the flat. The music volume was now at background level, and it was easy to let the heavy metal tune roll off his shoulders. Maybe one day he'd confess to Courtney he liked heavy metal as much as baroque, whatever the setting called for. Then again, it was a bit of fun to watch her try to rile him with her musical introductions. It was even more fun to watch her dance to the tunes rocking the sound system. The tight stretchy leggings she wore called to mind the dancers from videos made in the eighties. All she needed was big hair instead of her sleek ponytail. Still, a bloke had to admire the curve of her bottom and the long legs on display. The T-shirt she wore wasn't so loose he couldn't make out other curves. He'd probably shock her into a faint if he danced over to her playing air guitar. The very fantasy was almost too rich to ignore before he reminded himself of his plan to back away.

* * * *

Birdie wasn't quite sure how she felt seeing Ozzie again. Well, she wanted to rush to his arms and kiss him silly. Her mouth actually watered at the thought of kissing him. His taste, the feel of him was like a ghost feeling in her mouth. Oh, God, what if he could see that on her face? Cheeks flaming, she turned toward the stereo and fiddled with the play list while waiting for her face to cool.

He looked good. He also looked tired, and she guessed that was to be expected. She was pretty wiped out herself. The wedding, the travel, the dreams. Oh Lord had she had dreams. Every night since the wedding she'd dreamed of Ozzie in full color. And much to her embarrassment, she'd even dreamed of him while curled up in her seat on the plane. She still wasn't sure if it was a good thing she'd been sitting next to a stranger, who was no longer a stranger, but he hadn't said anything, not that once they'd been formally introduced she'd had a chance to talk with him. Dad had spent most of the last two hours of the flight sitting with Mom's favorite rock star, catching up on family business. Mostly she was thankful Ozzie hadn't been her seatmate as originally planned.

"Dinner's on the table," her mom called out. What was supposed to have been a small dinner party had become a dozen people. Her parents. Drew and Meilin, of course. Meilin's parents. Paul and Larry. Both her grandfather and grandmother. Ozzie. And her. Chairs shuffled as people found their seats. Corks popped as her father and Drew opened half a dozen bottles of white wine and passed them down the table. Two large bowls on each end of the table held a mountain of tossed green salad and steaming vats of seafood Alfredo. Four bread baskets held the also steaming slices of sourdough bread. Everyone had carried at least one loaf in their carry-on luggage. Birdie herself had carried two.

As she approached the table with two pitchers of water, she found the only chair left was between Ozzie and Paul. Ozzie stood holding the chair for her. After taking the pitchers from her and setting them on the table, he pushed her chair in for her, then took his seat.

"Courtney."

Well, at least he remembered her name. "Ozzie," she replied, impressed she'd managed to keep her voice as impersonal as his.

Like the gentleman he was, he poured her glass and then filled her grandmother's glass before filling his own with the crisp Chardonnay her father had imported from Napa Valley the year before.

Her father raised his glass. "To the most beautiful cook in England."

Which raised a blush on her mother's cheek. "Thank you."

The next glass up was Paul's. "To the bride and groom for bringing us all together."

"Hear, hear."

Not to be outdone, Drew raised his glass. "To our families for their unwavering support. Mum, Dad"—he saluted first his parents, then turned to Meilin's—"Mom and Dad. We're blessed to have both sets of you."

"Enough with the toasting." Birdie's mother laughed. "Eat before it gets cold. And just so you know," she raised her voice to speak over the sudden clatter of dishes and serving spoons, "the pasta is a lightened up version. Still not completely healthy, but less heavy on the fats. However, there are enough carbs to send everyone into a nice coma for the night to help regulate the internal clocks."

Everyone laughed and Birdie helped herself to a large serving of the tossed salad. Paul held the bowl for her; then she turned and held it for Ozzie. Next came the pasta bowl and finally a bread basket. If she ate everything on her plate, indeed, she'd sleep like the dead tonight. Much as she had after Ozzie had finished with her. A shock of electricity sizzled up her finger from where he touched her briefly. The sizzle zipped right up her arm, igniting newly awakened nerve endings. Nerve endings she'd never known could be awakened until Ozzie had touched her.

The same man who caught the bread basket before it completely left her hand. The same man who wouldn't look at her now.

Bastard.

Diddle with her, then leave her without a word? Well, they'd see about that.

Chapter 8

Dinner was an experience for sure. Paul sat to her left doing his best to avoid Mom's super-fan hero-worship, although Birdie thought she was admirably restrained, while Ozzie on her right barely said a word to anyone. Just sat there slowly eating, answering when asked a question, but not initiating any sort of conversation.

Across the table Larry looked on with sympathy in his eyes, but really in no position to rescue her. Fortunately most of the conversations were loud, and Birdie was able to listen to the small talk taking place around her. Mostly it was a recap of the upcoming schedule with a few questions directed to Paul, who rolled his eyes every time someone tried to call him Khan. Something she could identify with all too well.

Tomorrow morning they'd all pile into various vehicles and make the drive down to the house in Sussex. Fine. Mid-afternoon, for a selected number of friends and the older extensions of the family, Drew and Meilin would say their vows again, and the house would open up to whatever guests felt like dropping in to congratulate the newlyweds. Far less formal than the big wedding not quite a week ago. Martin had the entire event well in hand. Cook had been preparing for a solid week. All Birdie had to do was throw on her pretty dress, smile, and make polite conversation. Easy peasy lemon squeezy.

Tomorrow afternoon Ozzie would stand up with Drew for the smaller ceremony at the local church while Birdie would stand with Meilin in a pink bridesmaid's dress. Again, easy enough. But this time she'd be standing across the aisle from Ozzie. Would he look at her then?

Who knew what had crawled up his butt. Was he angry she'd fallen asleep and left him hanging? Or rather in a state of pain? She'd told him not to let her fall asleep for long, but when she'd woken several hours later he was not only gone from her room, but gone from California. The entire country! What the hell did that mean?

So all through dinner she ignored Ozzie as much as he ignored her. Other than to keep her wineglass full and make sure she had bread and butter, or more salad. Then he'd eaten what she couldn't finish of the cheesecake Cook had sent up from Sussex for dessert.

And when her head dropped forward, she admitted defeat. Mom's plan to carb-load everyone had worked on her first.

Strong male hands gently landed on her shoulder. Her father whispered in her ear, "Time for bed, Bird. You've had a long week."

She let her head drop back against his shoulder and blinked up at him. "Okay, Daddy."

At least he still loved her. His eyes softened and his lips touched her temple as she heard Ozzie say, "I've got her, sir."

One strong arm slid under her knees, another behind her back. Instinctively she raised an arm to drape it round the neck of the warm, spicy smelling man lifting her against a hard chest. "Ozimander," she whispered. Even now she recognized his scent, despite the garlic they'd all had. "I can walk myself."

"Easy, princess. Your mum is leading us to your room so she can get you tucked in."

"Mmmm." She also heard Meilin tiptoeing down the hall.

"Don't drop her, Oswald."

He didn't deign to answer more than a grunt. Lord, she hoped it wasn't because she was too heavy. That almost woke her up, but then his lips brushed the top of her head.

"Sleep." His order was soft, but gruffly spoken.

"Aye, aye," she murmured. "But I really can put myself to bed."

"Let us play," Meilin said. "Practice for your niece or nephew. Future niece or nephew."

That sounded interesting enough to almost wake up for.

"Really?" her mother asked. "Thank you, Oswald. We'll be out in a few moments. Maybe you could encourage the men to start clean up?"

"Happily." The bedroom door closed softly behind him.

"I can undress myself," Birdie muttered as her mother tried to tug off the T-shirt she wore over comfortable yoga pants.

"I know you can. But you're exhausted, kiddo. Besides, I want to hear more about this subject of babies from Meilin."

Birdie accepted her mother's help in pulling the shirt off, holding back further complaint because she, too, wanted to hear what Meilin had to say.

"No news there yet," Meilin said, sitting on the side of the bed as Birdie struggled out of the clinging yoga pants, leaving her undies in place. "We're not actively trying, but neither are we doing anything to prevent it."

Birdie's mother pulled a large sleep shirt over her head. "I think you can take it from here, Bird. I'm not removing your bra."

"Gee, thanks, Mom. Meilin, make me an auntie."

"Night, sweetheart." Mom leaned over and kissed her forehead. "Sweet dreams."

Birdie grunted as Meilin wished her good night. Just before the door shut she heard Mom say, "Haven't had a chance to do that in years. Probably never will again."

Birdie didn't hear Meilin's response because the door shut, blocking the light from the hallway and plunging her room into darkness. She finished removing her underwear, then pushed her arms through the sleeves of her nightshirt and snuggled under the covers.

* * * *

Oswald looked down the hall, one of the large serving bowls in his hand, as Randi and Meilin returned to the dining room. As soon as they'd disappeared, Meilin's mother had organized the men into clearing the table and general kitchen cleaning duty. Since he'd been raised as a gentleman and knew how to clean up after a meal, he fell in with the others, hoping it would erase the feel of Courtney in his arms, her lemon fresh scent from his nose. He'd had to stop in the loo for a moment to get himself under control enough to face everyone else. The attraction he felt for Courtney was growing each time he was near her. On the one hand he'd been dismayed at the presence of Randi and Meilin in the bedroom, but on the other, he'd been thankful for them as well. Their very presence was the reason he could do his part now.

He still couldn't figure out the name she'd murmured. Ozimander? Was that some strange Pokémon reference? He'd have to ask about it later.

Court was in charge of putting the few leftovers away, since he knew where the dishes were kept. Paul was up to his elbows in suds while Drew dried dishes. Mr. Wu and Larry were setting out fresh coffee and cream on the table.

"Impressive," Randi said as she passed him.

"We're well-trained, ma'am."

Randi laughed. "So you say. Although I can see room for improvement, I'm not complaining." She patted his shoulder. "Don't let me get in your way."

Since Birdie had crashed, the party wound down quickly. Oswald downed one cup of coffee, then made his excuses.

Court escorted him to the elevator. "Your car can carry three more, right?"

"Yes." Right now he was wishing he drove a two-seater with little cargo space.

"Stop by around ten, if you please. I'm sure we can put at least two with you and make things a little more comfortable driving down."

"Will do."

"And thanks for helping me save face tonight. Not sure I could have carried Birdie. You probably spared me from a heart attack or a hernia in front of an audience."

"My pleasure, sir." Oswald barely kept himself from grimacing over that statement. Sure, tell his boss he'd enjoyed carrying the man's daughter to her bed. His only regret was he wasn't wrapped around said daughter this very moment.

"See you tomorrow." Court slapped him on the shoulder and turned away as the elevator doors slid open.

The next morning his suspicions from the night before were confirmed. Birdie and her luggage were deposited into his car. Drew and Meilin were also assigned to him. So while he loaded the rest of the luggage in the boot, Drew handed the ladies into the vehicle. Birdie in the front passenger, Meilin directly behind her. As he climbed into the driver seat, Oswald wondered how long before Drew complained of the shortened leg space. Not long as it turned out. He didn't even bother trying to climb into the seat behind Oswald.

"Bird," Drew demanded. "Swap with me."

Beside Oswald, Birdie sighed and rolled her eyes. "That didn't take long."

Meilin laughed. "I'd rather get a little sister time back here, anyway. Let the boys chat up front."

Birdie smiled up at her brother as he swung open her door and reached in to pull her out. In an exaggerated, deep, grunting voice she said, "Yes, caveman, little womans gather in the back seat."

Drew gave her a huge grin. "Funny."

Oswald climbed from his seat as Birdie made the circuit around the back of the car. He held the door for her, then shut it once she'd pulled her long legs in. Settling once more in his seat, he asked, "Enough room back there?"

"I'm good," Birdie responded and Meilin piped in with the affirmative as well.

"All right, then. Strap in and we're off."

"This is good," Meilin said. "We can have girl talk while they discuss soccer or something."

"Over here it's football, or if you want to keep them straight, we can call it footie." Drew glanced over his shoulder. "Or there's always cricket and rugby."

Oswald figured he could deal with that. Even with the four bodies, each with their own shower fresh scent, he could make out Courtney's unique lemon fragrance. It was a very pleasant switch from the expensive perfumes he was used to from Deirdre and her ilk. None of them would choose such an innocent scent as lemon. It was perfect on Courtney.

"I still can't get used to this driving on the wrong side of the road business," Meilin said.

Oswald glanced aside at Drew and caught his smirk.

"It takes time," Courtney assured her sister-in-law. "I haven't tried driving in the city yet, but Dad lets me toodle around the village. Feels like driver ed all over again with him trying to appear calm and pretend he's not stomping on the invisible brake all the time. He did the same with Mom until she refused to drive with him in the car."

Drew laughed out loud at that. "You both were raised on California traffic. You just have to forget your hang-ups about swapping sides and you'll figure it out just fine."

"I can get around London perfectly well without a car," Courtney said. "Besides, most of what I want is within walking distance, anyway, or I can get to it from the Tube. Easy peasy lemon squeezy." Oswald had heard her use the strange phrase before, but considering her lemon scent, maybe there was a deeper meaning. If so, she wasn't giving it away now, rather she continued rambling on. "On rare occasions, a cab works. It would be a waste of time to get the car out only to have to try and find parking."

"And then try to parallel park from the wrong side of the car." Meilin's nod could be seen in the mirror.

Oswald allowed himself a smile.

Fortunately traffic was reasonable for a slightly overcast Sunday morning. Oswald maneuvered his vehicle through the cars darting here and there, many headed out of town for the afternoon.

"Why didn't we just drive down yesterday?" Courtney wondered behind him.

If he adjusted the mirror he'd be able to see more than part of her cheek, but he resisted the temptation and let the conversation flow between his three passengers. The bantering and teasing was very much what he'd come to expect with Drew anywhere nearby. Not something he engaged in well, but that didn't mean he didn't enjoy listening in. For him it was enough to listen to Courtney's voice as she joked with the other two.

Two hours later, as they neared Chichester and the Robinson estate, the sun broke through and brightened the landscaping.

"It's so green and beautiful," Meilin said. Oswald guessed there was a dreamy quality to her tone. "Not that San Francisco isn't green, or Beijing, but there's something special about the English countryside. Also, you can't beat the air quality here."

"It's all the historic homes," Drew answered. "It imparts a sense of history neither of the other cities embody. Although San Francisco has its own historic charm."

"Don't get me wrong." Meilin poked his shoulder from between the front seats. "I love nearly every part of San Francisco. But it's just different. This has a romantic air to it. I can almost see the coach and fours trotting along."

"Being chased by a masked highway man intent on getting the girl and the jewels."

Leave it to Drew to think of such a thing. Oswald had no such romantic fantasies. He hadn't been raised with a nanny who read him adventurous bedtime stories. Larry had had a housekeeper who cooked dinner and waited around until he got home from work. Otherwise, Oswald had sort of raised himself. He'd had a bachelor uncle who taught him the ways to wine, dine, and generally woo whatever he needed from someone. A handy talent he could employ when motivated enough, but not one he put a whole lot of effort into. Rather he preferred to watch and listen to find his way around getting the things he needed. Usually without anyone being wise to his maneuvers.

Before long they pulled up in front of the house. A Tudor era mansion was more like it, but he'd been there often enough to him it was a warm and welcoming house. They weren't the first to arrive, but neither were they the last. Martin was already pulling luggage from Court's SUV. Phillip Hammond pulled up behind Oswald and sauntered around the bonnet of his car to help the elder Mrs. Robinson from the front seat.

Behind him, Courtney was already swinging her door open. He was there in time to hand her out of the car while Drew attended to his wife.

A jolt of electricity shot up his arm when Courtney's fingers made contact with his hand. Her startled blue gaze jumped to meet his, and she lost no time letting go the moment she stood on the gravel drive.

"Thank you, Ozinator."

"My pleasure." The faint blush that washed her cheeks was certainly his pleasure to watch. And a danger he didn't need to flirt with.

She turned from him to check for left behind belongings in the back seat, and he firmly directed himself to the boot rather than ogling her posterior. Martin had too many people arriving at once to handle all the luggage, so Oswald made himself useful and did the unloading himself. Fortunately, half the cases were small and most had shoulder straps. He loaded up and headed for the front door, leaving Drew to get his wife's larger suitcase.

Courtney caught up to him at the wide low stone steps to the large double, arched doors at the front of the house. "Give me mine. There's no reason for you to lug all that."

"I've got it. To sort yours out now would only slow us down. Do you know which room you're in?"

Courtney huffed with what he assumed was exasperation. "The front corner room on the south end."

Damn. Next door to the room he usually took. They'd be sharing a bathroom. That was all he needed.

"No worries then. You go find the refreshments I'm sure Martin has set out. I'll be down in a minute." They'd already crossed the great hall where the reception would be held later. The weight of the old building seemed to press down on him as he headed for the stairs.

"Fine," Courtney bit out. "Be the hero." She paused and he looked over his shoulder, one brow raised. "Thank you."

She'd tried to say it with grace, but a slight edge of irritation had snuck through.

Instead of answering, he nodded, then left her in the hallway lined with hand-carved paneling that had darkened over the centuries and had the luster of years of careful dusting and oiling. Come to think of it, the house smelled of lemon oil. Maybe that's why Courtney seemed so suited to this house. He could easily see her as mistress of the mansion, hosting a masked ball with Tudor era costumes. Pretty enough to catch the eye of old Henry himself.

At the top of the steps he looked down to see her staring up at him. Yes, she'd look beautiful in costume, far more alive than the ancestors painted in stiff poses lining the walls. Maybe he could commission a portrait of her in just that way....

Abruptly he turned away from Courtney as much as he turned away from that flight of fancy. He was merely footman to her lady of the manor, and he'd best not ever forget.

Chapter 9

No. No, no, no! She was not going to fall for stuffy Ozzie again. She'd already done that Tuesday night, and since he was showing no signs of acknowledging their brief interlude, she wasn't going to bring it up. Other than carrying her to bed, under her mother's watch no less, and the gentlemanly behavior with the help from the car a few minutes ago, he'd basically ignored her. Hadn't jumped into the conversation in the car at all other than to grunt in agreement with something Drew had said.

More bodies poured into the entrance hall, and she turned to lend assistance to her grandmother, or whoever might need help.

Only half an hour later, Birdie's mother and Martin were ushering people to their rooms to get dressed for the much smaller ceremony at the village church. Thankfully the temperature was a good fifteen degrees cooler than San Francisco had been a week ago. And everyone's clothes were less formal than they'd been for the grand cathedral ceremony. No need to help Meilin with her very fluffy wedding dress. This time they both wore traditional Mandarin sheaths of thick silk with a wealth of embroidery from neck to ankles. Meilin in cream with red and gold embroidery, Birdie in a dress of pink with cream and blue designs. Mostly birds and flowers with touches of red while Meilin had a golden dragon and phoenix on her gown. All for good luck.

Despite the simple, scaled down wardrobe, it still took the women two hours to dress, with Meilin's hair and makeup taking up most of that time. A task Mrs. Wu absolutely ruled.

Birdie leaned over and whispered in her mother's ear, "I won't be so fussy, I promise."

Mom had whispered back, "You can be as fussy as you want. I'll love every minute of it." Then she'd pressed a tissue under her suspiciously bright eyes. "Your father wants to give you the world, and when it comes to your wedding, I won't be able to hold him back; not that I'd want to, anyway."

The unexpected lump in her own throat made it hard to do more than blink and nod. As much as she'd come to love Court, her biological father, she'd also loved the daddy who'd raised her, Wyatt Ferguson. At moments like this, a bittersweet shard pierced her heart. Whenever she'd dreamed of a wedding as a little girl, he'd been the daddy to walk her down the aisle. And since she spent very little, if any time contemplating her own wedding these days, it was hard to insert Court into the picture. It would be easier as time went on, but three years down the road, she still missed the man who'd loved and held her from the moment of her birth.

Mom's arms suddenly wrapped around her. "I still miss him, too. I love Court, adore him, but there's still a piece of my heart where Wyatt lives. There's no need to push him out of your heart. He's still watching over you, and to some extent, possibly me. He loved us well. We don't have to forget that."

Birdie squeezed her mom, then stepped back and gently wiped at her eyes. "Stop that or we'll have to do our makeup over again."

Mom sniffed and laughed, reaching for another tissue to blot under her eyes. "Yes, dear."

"Everything okay over there?" Meilin's gaze reflected back at them from the mirror she sat before while her mother twisted, pinned, and sprayed her hair into a formidable do to go with the gold and ruby headdress.

"We're fine. Just having a moment of memory for a loved one lost," Mom answered. "What can we do to help other than stand around and look beautiful?"

Mrs. Wu answered, "Almost done. Powder your noses one more time and then it will be time to go."

Birdie shared a smile with her mom. Mrs. Wu was used to commanding a large extended family. Apparently the two of them were accepted if she directed her orders to them.

* * * *

At the church most everything went according to plan. The only fly in the ointment was a woman sitting next to Paul who spent the ceremony sending death rays directly at Ozzie, who appeared far less comfortable today than he had last week. Ozzie spent the ceremony looking over Birdie's head. Not what she'd envisioned at all.

Drew and Meilin made a more dignified exit from the church this time. A glance at Martin showed him smiling proudly this time, instead of hiding his face. And although she was smiling at the antics, it was a stone-faced Ozzie who held out his arm to escort her from the church. She wished he'd smile for the pictures because this time his vest matched her dress. But no, whoever that woman was, she'd managed to ruin what little good mood Ozzie had had the night before.

They went through the motions of the pictures with the photographer cajoling a stiff smile or two out of Ozzie. Fortunately Meilin and Drew had plenty of smiles to make up for him, and they were the stars of most of the photos. Although, Birdie was pretty sure her photo with Ozzie looked something like Ma and Pa whoever, the ones with the pitchfork.

"Well thanks for tolerating that, Ozibutt," she snapped at him when they'd been excused.

"Pardon me?" Behind his glasses he blinked in confusion.

"Would it kill you to smile every once in a while? Especially at Drew's wedding? I'm sure this set of pictures will be quite *lovely*." She didn't spare the sarcasm on the last word.

He responded by frowning at her. On the verge of saying something, he was interrupted by the brunette who slapped him on the arm. Although she smiled, it was sharp, her eyes glittering. "Oswald, darling. I must have missed your call. You remember, the one telling me where to be and when as your plus one."

Ice formed, skittering down Birdie's spine, entering her bloodstream, and turned her stomach into a cement mass that fell to her feet. Some instinct told her this woman was only smiles on the surface. Below, she carried more venom than a yellow bellied sea snake.

"Forgive me, Deirdre." Ozzie's gaze skittered right over Birdie's head as he turned to the woman perfectly dressed for a summer garden party in a white dress decorated with large blue flowers, complete with lacy, wide-brimmed hat to shade her face. "The situation got out of hand, and I didn't have a chance."

"Bollocks, darling. That's two now you owe me." The woman gave Birdie a cool up and down glance. "Unless this is your idea of out of hand?"

Lips pinched, Ozzie lapsed into an extremely posh accent, cool and formal, his entire body stiff. "Courtney, may I present Deirdre Portman-Wright, a friend. Deirdre, this is Courtney Ferguson-Robinson, Drew's sister, and"—he indicated Paul who sauntered up holding a pair of filled champagne flutes—"Paul's cousin."

"Courtney," Deirdre drawled. "Of course I've heard of you. Can't believe it's taken this long for us to meet." She took one of the flutes from Paul.

Birdie refused the flute he offered her with a shake of her head. The way her stomach was roiling, she'd only burp it right back up again.

"Pleased to meet you." Well, she was anything but, however, this was her brother's reception and not a honky-tonk. Not that she'd ever been in one, but she was tempted to give this woman a wallop.

Paul bent toward Birdie, and she turned to accept his kiss on her cheek. "You look lovelier than ever, dear cousin. You and our boy Oswald looked like a perfect matched set of bookends up there today. Pity the boy won't smile."

"I was just saying something about that to him," she muttered.

"I've been sent to gather you, cousin dear." The phrasing sounded mocking coming from Paul. Probably more from the formality demanded by the situation than anything else. "They want more family pictures, and you and I are all who are missing." He spared a glance for his date. "Don't tear Oswald apart while we're gone. I'm sure he has more wedding duties. Save it for later."

Deirdre wrapped a perfect, lethally manicured hand around Ozzie's arm. "I wouldn't dream of causing a scene here." Sunlight danced off the facets of the diamonds on her fingers and wrapped around both wrists.

Birdie felt practically naked beside her. Her only jewelry were the diamond earrings her mother had given her for Christmas a couple years back, a simple sapphire and diamond bracelet, a Christmas gift from her father, and the storybook locket from her grandmother. Nothing to compete with what the brunette wore.

Paul grinned at her. "Good to know. Guard your bollocks, Attenborough."

A few steps, and what she hoped was far enough not to be heard by the pair left behind, Birdie glanced up at Paul, who was looking very handsome in an oatmeal colored linen suit. "Are those two an item? Or were they?"

Paul rubbed his chin. "Not sure I know the true extent of their relationship, but I know he's escorted her to many society events. Rumor has it she thinks he's her toy, but if it's any more serious than that, I have no idea. She clearly expected him to invite her to this event, but when she saw the announcement in today's paper, she called me and insisted I bring her. Not that I know her all that well, but I've escorted her once or twice." He gave her a long look. "Thinking of claiming him for yourself?"

Heat flashed over her skin, and Birdie looked away, tightly gripping the stems of her bouquet. "Of course not. He's far too stiff for me."

"Right. That would explain why I heard you murmur something that sounded like Ozzie in your sleep on the plane the other night."

Birdie snapped her head around to stare at him. "I did not."

Taking her elbow, Paul laughed. "My mistake."

* * * *

"Oswald."

He wanted nothing to do with Deirdre today. So far she'd ruined the church part of the day for him. Staring over her head, he watched Courtney walk away with Paul.

What was it she'd called him this time? Ozibutt? He almost smiled over that one. She had quite a growing list of nicknames for him.

It struck him then just how attached he was growing to her. Blonde, sunny, sweet, beautiful Courtney who often imitated her nickname. Happy as a chickadee on a sunny morning. A canary who sang for the pure joy of it.

And a walk that drew attention to her ass, lovingly caressed by the narrow silk dress hugging her body.

"Oswald," Deirdre cajoled.

Right, honey instead of vinegar.

"Yes, Dee. I wanted to invite you, but the parties were formed up last night, and I had a full car this morning. Not to mention, my attention needed, needs, to be focused on the event."

"Darling, your attention is wandering. Was Courtney the second party in your car?"

"No, she was the fourth. I also had Drew and Meilin." He finally looked down to see Dee peering up at him from beneath the ridiculous brim of her hat. "You know, Drew's sister, Meilin's sister-in-law."

"Aw, you got stuck with her, and now again as best man to her maid of honor."

"Something like that." Well, nothing like that, but better not to mention that to Dee. "So, you snagged Paul into driving you down. Didn't realize you knew him that well."

"No, not really, but he's been useful a time or two. And since I know he's related, it only made sense to call him. Had I been ten minutes later I would have missed him. He was just on his way out."

"What a shame that would have been."

"Don't you dare be angry with me, Oswald. You promised to bring me. Add to that ignoring my dinner invitation, then turning me away at your door, I'd say you now owe me three. And I have the perfect way for you to make it up to me."

"No."

"What?" Deirdre blinked up at him. "Did you just tell me no?" Sharp nails dug into his arm. Figuring it was a better way to pay than shaking her off, he didn't flinch at the bite.

"Yes, Dee. I said no. In the next twelve months I have to play mentor on top of other increased duties at the office. I won't have time for running off to long weekends in the country, or intimate dinners for two." He stared into her startled brown eyes. "I'm terribly sorry, but I can't be your plaything anymore. Certainly there are plenty of others ready to step into the role."

Her grip softened and she used the fingers of her other hand to walk up his arm. The move was pure coquette and ridiculous. "You're not my plaything, Oswald. You're a good friend who just happens to share some pretty awesome benefits with me. I've always seen us as a team. The two of us against society."

Of course she did. Oswald shook his head. "Dee, I don't have any idea what you're talking about. I do know you set me aside to go play with your other friends with benefits often enough we've never had any exclusive understanding between us. It's merely time to acknowledge that. I'm stepping aside to let someone else step in. I know you have legions of men who would love to team up with you. I'm sure you can pick one smarter, richer, and better connected than I am. I'm pretty sure there's at least one Viscount with his eye on you."

By this time her eyes were narrowed on him. If he were the type to squirm, he'd be doing it like a bug on a pin. Other than a mild disgust, he didn't feel a thing for Deirdre and wondered if he ever really had. When she was in a good mood she could be witty and good company. Of course she was also quite experienced at shagging. Again, he wondered how he'd ever been amenable to sleeping with her. Today he found the scent of her regular perfume cloying and overly sweet. It didn't mix well with the flowers around them in the garden. Unlike a certain scent of fresh lemons.

"This is not the end of it, Oswald. I'll let you alone to do your duties today, but back in town we're having dinner Tuesday night and talking this thing out. Pick me up at seven." Eyes on him, she spun away, then snapped her attention to the party still posing for photos. "And sunny little miss won't be a part of it."

Gut churning, Oswald watched her saunter away, skirt flaring, then swinging side to side with her sensual stride. And not because she'd chastised him, but because she'd taken a swipe at Courtney. Logically he'd known sooner or later Deirdre would tear into him with those claws he knew she had. He always figured his hide was tough enough to bear it. But if she brought Courtney any deeper into this… Well, never having to defend a woman before, he had no idea what he'd do. But he wouldn't let Deirdre rip Courtney apart before she ever had a chance to become known in society.

Chapter 10

By the time the guests started filing out, a migration begun when the elder aunts and uncles had been picked up by the bus from the senior home, Birdie was ready to collapse. Inside, at one of the tables set up in the great hall, she flopped herself in a chair and kicked off her heels. If she took the time to think over the past several hours, she'd guess she'd spoken with every single person who'd been there. Sitting and chatting with Paul had been especially fun. His irreverence for the society around him translated into stories of infidelity, underhanded business dealings, and other shocking scandals.

Sadly he'd taken off back to London. On the other hand, he'd taken Deirdre with him, so the good more than balanced out the lack of his company. A shudder snaked down Birdie's spine at the thought of the beautiful but viperous woman. How could Oswald associate with her?

One of the servers brought an ice bucket with a barely opened bottle of wine and a handful of clean glasses.

"Thank you," Birdie said. "You're an angel."

The young woman smiled and returned to clearing the tables in the Great Hall.

Drew and Meilin had already departed for their suite upstairs. Chased up an hour ago so guests could start making their own ways home.

Cook had outdone herself, and there weren't many leftovers. The crowd had done justice to the groaning sideboards loaded with every treat imaginable. Beef, ham, and even a turkey or two had been reduced to bits. Dim sum demolished. Cake and pastries reduced to mere crumbs. Personally, Birdie didn't think she'd eat for two days.

With a sigh, her father dropped into the chair next to her. "I think I was overly ambitious in thinking we'd jump up tomorrow and head into the office. I'm declaring a one day holiday. We'll laze about tomorrow before heading back into town late afternoon."

Birdie raised a brow she now recognized as a Robinson inherited trait. "Are you sure? Because I stayed mostly sober in order to be ready for jumping into work tomorrow."

Her father reached for the bottle of champagne and filled her glass. "I'm positive. I'll even give Oswald the day off. Lord knows we could all do with an easy day. I want to bask in the glory of the summer garden before burying myself in the office for the next month. Lots to do before your mum and I head across the Channel."

He grabbed a glass, then half filled it for himself. Before sipping, he stopped and gazed at her, his bright blue eyes soft with love and affection, and raised the glass.

She raised hers.

"Here's to the most beautiful daughter a man could ask for. Brilliant, strong, capable, loving, and cheerful under adversity." The toast made her throat tighten. "My wish for you is to find happiness above all in this life. I hope part of that happiness includes a life partner who will appreciate all those qualities and do his best to protect and shelter you from life's storms. One who sees not only the outer beauty, but the far more compelling inner beauty as well. All of which will add up to a full and joyous life."

Unable to speak, she cleared her throat and gave him her most brilliant smile. They clinked glasses, the sound of crystal ringing between them, then drank.

She heard footsteps on the ancient, creaking, polished wooden planks on the floor and glanced over her shoulder to see Ozzie approaching, his eyes carefully averted from her.

"What time do you wish to leave in the morning, sir?"

Just the sound of his voice touched something deep in Birdie. Something that ached to be filled. A hunger she'd only ever felt with him. And although he'd been the one to kiss her, to touch her, to awaken this need, he pretended it had never happened. That he'd never seduced her into baring her body, and a bit of her soul, to him.

"About three tomorrow afternoon, Oswald. I've just told Birdie I've declared a holiday. It's a lovely time to be in the country and I want to enjoy brunch on the terrace and a stroll through the woods before heading back to the hectic pace of London."

Oswald stopped in his tracks, only inches from the back of her chair. She could feel him there, sense his shock. Could even detect his spicy scent. Squeezing her thighs together didn't help alleviate the need down there.

"Are you sure? I'm happy to drive. I figure if we leave about half past five, we'll miss the worst of morning traffic."

"I'm sure, Oswald." Dad's voice was firm. "The holiday includes you too. If you wish to have a lie-in to make up for all the travel fatigue, I wouldn't blame you a bit, since I want the same and Birdie has a few shadows to chase from under her eyes. I know you youngsters have greater stamina, but even you two are showing a little wear around the edges. There's nothing at the office that won't keep for one more day."

"Right. Anyone you need me to run to the airport?"

"Sit down, Oswald. It's hurting my neck to look up at you." From the smile on her dad's face, she guessed not, but it seemed they all conspired to get Ozzie to unbend just a little.

The chair he pulled from the table scraped on the wood floor as he dragged around so he'd face Birdie and her dad.

"Thank you," Dad said. "No, no one's headed for the airport tomorrow. Meilin's parents are staying until the end of the week. The grandparents will take them on a tour of the local surroundings and then they fly out on Saturday. It's all arranged."

Oswald nodded, his face solemn as always. "Not sure I know what to do with myself. Can't remember the last time I lazed about the country."

"I'm sure you'll figure it out." Dad patted him on the shoulder. "More champagne? We have more in the bottle and clean glasses here."

"No, no thank you. I've had plenty enough to insure a basic headache in the morning."

Dad laughed. "I haven't seen you with a hangover in nearly, what, is it fifteen years now?"

"Close to it, sir. That once was enough."

Birdie inspected the slight flush crawling up Ozzie's neck. "Sounds like a story."

Ozzie scoffed. "Not a very interesting one. A lesson learned, is all."

The closed look on his face was a sure sign he wouldn't budge if pressed. Besides, she was too tired to dig.

"Well, since it's a sleep-in day, I'll take myself off to a bath and bed." She bent to retrieve her shoes and straightened to find her father's hand extended to help her stand. The manners were taking some time to get used to, but all in all, she liked them. Good, old-fashioned men were something new and quite attractive in her world. Standing, she went up on tiptoe to kiss her father's cheek. "Night, Daddy."

"Good night, princess."

"Ozzie." She gave him a nod, then did her best to walk gracefully toward the stairs.

"Courtney." His reply was soft, but she heard it and smiled, assured he couldn't see her. At least one person accepted her wish to be called by her birth name. Not that she cared much anymore, but just Ozzie's acceptance of her wish was enough. At the office she'd insist on it as well. Just one way to keep a professional barrier between her and the stone-faced man who she hated to admit confused her.

* * * *

Oswald watched Courtney walk away, her stroll no less enticing without her heels on. He could see her barefoot in the garden, stopping to touch the flowers, or inhale their scent. He could see himself taking her down onto the grass and making love to her in the fresh air.

No. No, he was not going to indulge in that fantasy anymore.

The sun on her golden head had been like a special spotlight all afternoon. Although he'd purposely put as much distance between the two of them as possible, he'd still known exactly where she was and to whom she spoke. She'd laughed the most when sitting with Paul when Deirdre was off elsewhere. Hammond and Whetmore had cornered her more than once, although she hadn't been as relaxed with them. Smart girl. Phillip Hammond was all right, but Calvin Whetmore wasn't. More than once she'd looked Oswald's way, meeting his gaze boldly. He'd wanted nothing more than to cross to her and whirl her away into a private corner, or even into the woods, and forget the rest of the world existed.

Now he was faced with the possibility of too much privacy. The only thing separating their rooms was a shared bath. The very fact she was heading for a long soak in the oversized tub made him feel very dirty and in need of a bath. With her. A fact her father—his employer—probably wouldn't like very much.

"Will it be a problem working with her?"

Court's voice brought Oswald back into the great hall. "I'm sorry, sir?"

"Working with Birdie this next year. Will it be a problem for you?"

"I don't expect it to be. No more than working with any other intern or new hire." He'd mentored a few before, as had all the department heads. Although he'd never once dreamed of covering them with bubbles. Would his quarters smell of her lemon scent? Or would she choose lavender to bathe in?

"Ah, but you're not usually attracted to the interns or new hires. Randi and I have both noticed you can't always keep your gaze off her."

Oswald's eyes widened as the older man he admired so much smiled at him. Bloody hell. Court wasn't trying to play matchmaker, was he?

"She's a pretty girl. Most of the time I'm trying to figure out what she's saying. The American accent throws me."

It was no surprise when Court met that idiotic statement with a skeptical look.

The sound of a woman's heels click-clacking on the tiles of the kitchen reached them as the door to the kitchen swung open.

"Brilliant job today!" Randi sang out as she left the kitchen and headed across the great room. "There you are, honey," she said to Court. "I've been looking for you. We need to get some sleep if we're taking off early."

"Come sit down, my love. Have another glass of champagne, since Oswald won't drink with me. Birdie's just gone up."

"Well one of our group appears to be smart." She laughed when Court pulled her down onto his lap.

"I'm the smart one," he told her. "I've declared tomorrow a holiday. We won't head back to town until around three."

"I won't argue. We could all do with a day to sleep in. Frankly, I'm exhausted." She wrapped her arms around her husband's neck, and Oswald had a snapshot of what he wanted in his life.

A relationship like Court and Randi's. A woman who was loving and not afraid to show affection. It was a miracle these two had found each other after twenty-two years apart. Maybe there was one more miracle up God's sleeve, one that ensured Oswald found such a woman for himself.

The fact that such a woman already existed twisted his guts. The very daughter of these two people had been raised in a home filled with love, despite the separation. It showed in her very nature. One that could easily be taken advantage of. How he'd love to be the one to protect her from the harsh realities of the world.

A wonderful dream. One that could never come to fruition.

"Hey, Oswald, I've been meaning to ask you." Randi turned her attention on him. "Who was that woman Paul brought today? I met her, Deirdre somebody, but I have no idea who she is."

"Good question," Court said. "I mean, I know who she is, but why was she here today? And why was she with Paul?"

Randi looked at Court. "You know her?"

"Sure, she's one of the socialites. Has a regular posse of men she calls on to escort her various places. Oswald has been seen in her company a fair bit."

"Okay... But that doesn't really answer my question. Why was she here today?"

Oswald cleared his throat. "I'm afraid that was my fault. She was under the impression I promised to bring her as my date, but between last night and leaving this morning, I forgot to call it off." He shrugged. "She's a bit furious with me over that. I guess she saw the wedding announcement in the morning paper, figured I'd stood her up, decided she wasn't going to settle for that, called Paul just before he left, and so here she was. I apologize. I didn't really want her here, but I never should have ignored her that way. I know what she's capable of when she's displeased with an individual."

Court's brow rose. "I didn't realize you two were so close."

Oswald shook his head. "It's not a matter of being close. It's a matter of me not kowtowing to her demands. I'll pay for it."

"I just hope Birdie doesn't get in the middle of your payback. I saw that woman glaring at her more than once this afternoon." Randi's frown wasn't something Oswald saw often. In fact, other than teasing, he didn't think he'd ever seen her scowl in such a manner.

"I'll do my best to keep Courtney far away from her. However, between now and the holidays we'll attend many of the same charity events. As Courtney is coming up in the company, it will only make sense for her to attend, and I'll be the one best suited to escort her, for several reasons. At least initially. One, to introduce her in the right circles, and two, because of my connections and temporary position with the company while you two are traveling about. Three, I know the players from many years interaction and observation. I can steer her toward the people who will do the company the most good. From there she may meet someone else who would make an appropriate escort." Or not. In fact, he could not think of one man who would do a good job. Possibly Hammond. He was harmless enough by all accounts.

"All true, I suppose," Randi murmured. "But also because we trust you to look out for her." The smile she sent him was about as brilliant as any he'd ever seen.

"Yes, you can trust me to keep her safe. I won't court her, merely provide escort. I know that role well enough."

"Won't bother me if you do court her…as long as your intentions are honorable," Court said. "Don't toy with her heart if you don't mean to capture it."

Oswald blinked. "I'd never…"

"Oh you're a right proper gentlemen," Court cut him off. "You'll do everything by the book of etiquette. However, if you fall for her, and I doubt there's much you can do if she falls for you, do it for real. Otherwise, I know you'll keep your hands to yourself."

Not a topic of conversation he wanted to have. Not now, not ever. "I assure you, your daughter is safe with me. I won't touch her, nor will I allow her to get hooked up with someone who only wants to play. She deserves so much more than that. She certainly deserves a man far better than me."

"I seriously doubt there are many men better than you, Oswald." Randi narrowed her gaze on him. "In fact, I bet your intentions, whether you want to marry her or not, are far and away purer than any other man in London. Your reputation as a gentleman is impeccable." She nodded at his look of disbelief. "You're a very good man, Oswald. We'd be proud to have you officially in the family. You're halfway there already." She unwound her arms from around her husband's neck and stood. "Well, now you know how we feel. We won't meddle…very much." Her green eyes twinkled, a look that sent a spear of true fear through Oswald's gut. "We expect you for dinner whenever you can make it, just like this last year, but we won't push."

Unable to think of a reply, he merely stared at the tiny woman standing over him. Smiling, she shook her head, bent to kiss his cheek, then turned to her husband.

"Time for bed, honey bunches." She held out a hand to Court, and he accepted her invitation.

Oswald finally found his voice. "I have no intention of marrying. Ever."

At the foot of the stairs, Randi looked back at him. "That's a real shame. You owe it to the world to pass on your superior genes, don't you think?"

Court's hand landed on her bottom. "Impertinent chook. Leave the boy alone. If he doesn't figure it out soon for himself, I'm sure Birdie will, and then he'll be toast."

Toast.

Oswald shook his head and reached for the champagne bottle. Not a one of them seemed to understand. They were all mad as hatters.

Chapter 11

Tuesday morning Birdie straightened her skirt as she rode the elevator up to her father's office suite with him beside her. His company owned the twenty story building, but only occupied five floors. The top five floors, and the penthouse was their destination. On the far side of the floor from the executive suites, the Human Resources department could be found. No problem. She'd been there before and had met with Danielle Richards, the VP of the section. But her father insisted on escorting her there.

As befitted a new hire in an office environment, Birdie had dressed with care. A skirt neither too tight nor too short in gray gabardine was topped by a silk shell and crocheted cotton sweater, both in a soft sunny yellow. As her legs were still tanned, she'd skipped the pantyhose and wore sensible flats. She was tall enough she didn't need to emphasize her height when she already knew some of the older men and women she'd be working with were her height or shorter. Nothing here to scream out her status as the boss's daughter. It was a good outfit for her first day, although knowing she'd be in the mailroom, she had a selection of gabardine slacks and cotton shirts hanging in her wardrobe. Drew had already warned her she'd see some action that might get her fancy clothes mussed by the end of most days.

"You don't have to walk me to Ms. Richards' office, Dad."

"It's not like I got to see you off on your first day of school. I guess this is my one and only chance to make up for that bit of absenteeism."

She had no answer for that. The twinge of guilt she felt wasn't really hers to feel. The little smile she gave him was answered with one very like her own.

"Nervous?"

"No."

He met her denial with one of those raised brow looks.

"Not really. Maybe a little." With a touch of chagrin she admitted a bit of what she felt. Sure wasn't going to admit to the Air Forced sized butterflies acting like a bombing raid in her stomach.

"I mean, I've had jobs before, so that part is no big deal. This is a career. The next step up."

Dad nodded. "Makes sense to me."

"All you have to do is ignore me. I'm not riding on your coattails, right?" She hitched the strap of her bag higher on her shoulder and narrowed her eyes on her father.

"I won't show you undue preference." He lifted his hand with three fingers up. "Scout's honor."

"Were you ever a Boy Scout?"

He laughed. "No."

"I didn't think so."

"I do have to tell you, there might be a mild amount of fun at your expense. Most employees experience it, particularly in the mailroom or amongst the junior clerks. If it veers into hazing, I expect you to report it. If not to me, then to Danielle directly."

The seriousness on his face made her stomach clench just a little. "I can handle teasing."

"I know you can. It's just…" The elevator dinged open on their floor.

"It's just, what?" she asked as he guided her with a gentle hand on her lower back. At her own glance with raised brow he dropped his hand.

"Drew dealt with some," he said quietly, walking close enough those in the cubicles wouldn't hear, "but since he'd been in and out of the office from a young age, it wasn't as bad as it could have been. Maybe slightly more pointed than for others, but he handled it well. The difference is you're female, and a very new face, or rather concept around here. I've made no secret of my daughter, but I have no idea how the employees will react. Most will be respectful, if a little distant. Some might use you to express some latent discontent at their lot. I have no way of predicting or heading off such reactions."

They stopped in front of Danielle's door. "Just be careful, smile a lot, and don't try to change the world your first day here."

Birdie gave him her most confident smile. "I'll be good. I'll listen more than I speak and ask intelligent questions. Hey, I even brought cookies for the mailroom staff." A pat on the side of her overlarge shoulder bag produced a slight drum sound.

Dad laughed. "Good start. Old Dennis likes his sweets." He rapped two knuckles on Danielle's door and opened it when she called for them to enter.

A woman not much older than her father rose from behind a desk with a view of London behind her. "Good morning, Court. Ms. Ferguson." Hair that had once been penny bright was a soft shade of auburn now. Mom had told her about meeting Danielle years ago. She maintained a slender figure and wore an outfit not that much different than Birdie's, only her navy skirt and pale blue blouse were both silk, and her tastefully moderate navy pumps had a three inch heel that made her legs look great even if her ankles were a little thick. Middle-aged, but making it look good with pale skin and few lines.

"So happy you've joined us."

"Ready to take on the next Robinson?" Dad asked.

Danielle managed to look down her nose at him despite his six inches of height on her. "I've taken on a couple of Robinsons when they were barely out of short pants. One barely out of nappies. Since women are generally smarter and easier to work with, a grown up one should be a breeze."

It was easy to smile at the wink Danielle gave her. Dad laughed. "I guess I've been put in my place once again. Well, since I had to swear on my father's grave that I wouldn't follow her around snapping pics of her first day of school, as it were, I'd better take myself off to my cushy office chair and leave it to you ladies to plot how to run the company."

"Ah, I always said you were one of the smarter ones." Danielle patted his arm. "Off with you now. She's a big girl, and I'm sure is more than capable of getting along."

Feeling saucy, Birdie gave a slight curtsy of the variety her grandmother had taught her. "Thank you for the escort, Mr. Robinson. I'll see you at home at the end of the day."

Dad rolled his eyes. "Memo to self, tell the wife to cut back on viewing period dramas. Come hunt me up at the end of the day, and we'll walk back together."

"I'm a big—"

He leaned down and kissed her cheek. "Humor me."

"All right. If I must." While she rolled her eyes, he chucked her under the chin, then strolled out of the office.

"Nice little family scene there." A wide smile negated the rebuke. "He's a good man, but he's also a father and fully entitled to worry. We'll make sure there's nothing for him to worry about."

Couldn't help but agree with that, so Birdie nodded. "What's first?"

"Paperwork, what else?"

Paperwork, then viewing the new hire video on company policies filled the hours until noon. Danielle invited Birdie to join her and her assistant, Anita, for lunch. The café at street level did a lively business at the noon hour, but they also made an excellent chicken sandwich and latte. The latter was definitely needed to give her some pep for the afternoon. Jet lag and party lag still tugged at Birdie's energy, not that anyone other than her family would notice, but she felt it.

Anita, a blonde woman in her thirties, happily married and a little pudgy from her last pregnancy, she said as she patted her stomach, was friendly enough Birdie felt she had passed the first round of meeting new people.

A short time later, she had to reevaluate that thought when Danielle showed her the way to first the locker room where she could lock up her purse or anything else in the line of personal belongings. Next stop was the actual mailroom at the back of the ground floor.

"We process the mail for the entire building here. Each company sends down their own mail clerk to help with the sorting, then they take the mail for their company and distribute it. We found it far more efficient than letting the postal service do the distribution. But we're in charge of it." She pushed open a door into an anteroom where she had Birdie swipe her brand new employee badge for the set of double doors.

Inside, what first looked like pure chaos, resolved itself into controlled chaos upon a few moments of observation.

"Dennis is stationed at the back wall where the mail is delivered by a truck each morning, and again at noon the bigger packages arrive. I'm sure he'll be more than happy to explain it all to you." It took five minutes to cross the room, dodging the dozen or more people loading trays of letters onto carts with different company names on them. It also helped the carts were a different color, coded by company or floor, Birdie guessed when she saw floor numbers also noted.

"Remember, over here the first floor is your second floor," Danielle said.

"And ground floor is my first floor. Got it."

"Exactly. You'll have even more fun converting from American to British in addition to learning the routes."

"No problem. I've had some practice."

The nod of approval from the older woman was welcome. And with that they stood before a dais of about twelve inches with a large desk on it. Behind the desk sat a man who looked as gnarled as a hundred-year-old oak tree. He was lean with a hooked nose on his heavily wrinkled face.

"Who you got there, young lady? This the worker who was supposed to show up yesterday?" Faded disapproving brown eyes peered over half-moon reading glasses, and Birdie sensed he found her wanting.

"Family situation, Dennis. This is Courtney Ferguson-Robinson. Courtney, Mr. Redford, until he gives you leave to call him Dennis."

"Hello, sir." She gave him a friendly smile and held up the box of chocolate chip cookies she'd dug up from her bag in the locker room. "Had occasion to bake last night and thought you might like a sweet to go with your afternoon tea."

He took the box, all while peering at her suspiciously. "American? And escorted down by the head of hiring. Now there's switch. Going to be twice as hard to train you." He rattled the cookie box. "These any good?"

Holding her smile in place, Birdie restrained herself from wincing at the treatment of the cookies. "Chocolate chip. I've always called them cookies, but you could call them biscuits. Although I might have to bring in some hot buttery biscuits someday."

Dennis narrowed his eyes at her. "You being cheeky, missy?"

"Not unless you like cheeky misses, sir."

Dennis rolled his eyes. "Not only does she look like 'em, she acts like 'em. Fine. Ms. Richards, ye've done yer duty. I'll take it from 'ere."

Danielle nodded first at Dennis, then Birdie. "Enjoy the rest of your day."

"Thank you."

The first thing Dennis did was yell to a young man about ten feet to his left. He was tall, lanky, and had thick dark hair that fell over his face, probably to partially hide the red spots on his face and neck. He looked about eighteen. "Oi! Freddie, boy, 'ere's your shadow for the rest o' the week." Dennis looked at his watch. "Aren't you done sorting yet?"

"Yes, sir, Mr. Redford." He gestured for Birdie to join him.

With a nod to her current boss, Birdie strode over to Freddie and held out her hand. "Name's Courtney. Pleased to meet you."

Freddie gave her a quick shake, then turned his lanky body to the pair of carts parked side by side. "With you shadowing, you might as well push one yerself. We might even complete our circuit in time for a tea break."

"Fair enough." Following his example, she gripped the handle and pushed the cart with two bins, each about twenty-four by thirty-six inches. Each one loaded to bursting with all manner of envelopes rubber banded together. There were even a few small packages precariously balanced on top. It was surprisingly difficult to push as she followed him toward what looked like a freight elevator where half a dozen others with identical carts waited.

"We're running a bit behind." The glance Freddie gave her made it clear he'd been waiting for her to show up.

"I'm sure we can catch up." It was just beginning to occur to her she'd made a wise choice in wearing flats.

"If only these buggers would let us go ahead." Grumbles rose from those clustered around the elevator door awaiting their turn.

"You wait your turn, Freddie. Just like the rest of us."

"I got an express for the exec suites. Come on, let us through. Got the big boss's bird with me, ya know." He tipped his head in Birdie's direction. "First day and all."

That stopped the grumbles. Only it earned her a lot of stares as the clerks pulled aside making way for her and Freddie to push their carts onto the lift. Most of the stares were curious, a few resentful, some downright unfriendly. Those she could deal with, but one stare had been far too avid from a man about her age who apparently thought he was God's gift to something. Only he wasn't that good looking and his jeans and button down shirt looked like they'd been washed a hundred times too many.

"Welcome aboard, sweets," he said, casually leaning on an arm braced against the opening framing the elevator doors. "Name's Nigel. If there's anything you need, anything at all, ignore the rest of these buggers and ask me."

Birdie didn't answer, but once in the car and looking back, she gave their audience her patented friendly smile. "Looking forward to meeting you all." It was all she had time to say before the doors slid shut on shocked faces. She heard someone mutter the word Yank.

After pushing the penthouse button, Freddie said, "Don't encourage that one. Nigel's what they would have called a rake, back in the day. Fancies himself a real lady's man. Truth is every single one of those birds have had some sort of action with him, and they all hate him. Don't follow in their footsteps."

"Thanks. Appreciate the head's up."

"So, you're a Yank, are you?" Freddie's glance was anything but casual.

"Actually, dual citizenship. Half Brit, half Californian."

"Ah, that's why you look like you've been on holiday instead of fish-belly white like the rest of us."

"Guilty as charged. Undoubtedly I'll be as pale as everyone else by Christmas. No plans to spend time in a tanning bed."

Freddie grunted, his eyes locked on the numbers flashing by as they rose.

"How long you been here?" she asked.

"Going on two years now. Been hoping to get promoted up the ladder, but it seems I've made myself indispensable down in the mailroom. Heard a rumor Dennis is planning to retire, and he's picked me as his successor." The bitter edge to his tone made it clear that wasn't the career path he'd had in mind when starting out.

"Where did you want to go from the mailroom?"

"I started at the warehouses out in Tilbury. Always fancied I'd put my basic accounting certificate to use, but there've been no openings in that department." Another sideways glance came her way. "You're doin' one o' them internships, aren't you? A couple o' months in each department, then get settled in Accounts or Marketing, eh? Or higher up with the old man?"

"Something like that." The elevator stopped, the door slid open, and she followed Freddie out. The cart gave her enough trouble the doors nearly slid shut on her skirt before someone stopped them.

"Thank you…" She looked at her savior and found herself staring into Ozzie's blank face.

"Trolley giving you some difficulty? I thought that one got tossed a decade ago." Ozzie looked at Freddie who'd stopped to watch the spectacle. "Or is Dennis still holding on to it for unsuspecting new girls?"

Freddie shrugged. "Don't know nothing about that, Mr. Attenborough. Had enough for two trolleys today, found the spare since I knew I'd have some assistance."

"Well, be a gentleman and swap trolleys with the lady."

Birdie watched Freddie stiffen under Ozzie's icy gaze.

"Hey, it's all right." Birdie gave her cart a tiny shove. The thing felt as if someone had wrapped tape around the bearings, or rubber cement at least. "If this is my initiation, then I can think of plenty of worse things they could have chosen." She smiled up at Ozzie to convey her thanks for his defense, but also to let him know she didn't need it. "Besides, after the last week of weddings and parties, I need the workout. So you go on about your day, Mr. Attenborough, and let us be on about ours. I understand we're behind."

Ozzie narrowed his gaze on her, but spoke to Freddie. "Switch trolleys, then make sure this one gets a new coat of grease or gets tossed in the rubbish. I'll put in an order for a set of new ones. They're all looking a little too beat up these days."

Freddie nodded. "Thank you, sir. That would be right nice."

Ozzie pushed the call button. "Carry on."

The elevator opened but he hesitated, watching, his hand stuck in the opening to keep the doors open, while Freddie made a production of taking over her recalcitrant cart and nodding toward his easier moving model.

"Follow me, miss."

As they left the elevator lobby, she glanced over her shoulder, shaking her head at Ozzie. He merely responded by pretending to tip a nonexistent hat before ducking into the car and letting the doors close.

* * * *

The entire circuit of the top two floors took an hour and a half. According to Freddie's grumbles, about twice as long as usual. In part due to an extra heavy mail day, both dropping off and picking up what needed to go out, but mostly due to the cart she'd taken back after Ozzie disappeared. They'd traded off every so often, so they both bore the brunt of the torture. She was sweating by the time they returned to the mailroom to sort and prepare the outgoing mail they'd retrieved.

Dennis had peered at them over his reading glasses, then made a production of studying the clock. He also noticed who pushed which cart. Going back, it happened to be Freddie, but they were both slightly on the filthy side. Who knew mail handling could make one dirty? Not her. Also, she'd be rubbing in an extra double helping of lotion tonight and keeping a full tube in her purse. She wasn't about to let a month in the mailroom ruin her hands.

"Accounting has called down asking for the afternoon mail," Dennis said.

"Would have been faster but for this bloody useless trolley." Freddie shoved it toward a stack of similarly disabled looking carts. "Ran into Attenborough. Said he'd put in an order for new ones."

Dennis looked thoughtful, then nodded. "Glad to see someone upstairs being observant."

That seemed to be the end of the discussion, and she trailed after Freddie when he grabbed another already loaded cart, one that rolled easily, and headed back to the elevator.

"Oi!" Dennis called out. "New girl. Over here. You can process the outgoing while Freddie delivers that last load."

She glanced at Freddie who nodded, then turned back to face Dennis. "Tell me what to do, and I'll get it done."

Chapter 12

Oswald was in Court's office when Courtney appeared at the end of the day. Well, the usual end of the day for the non-salaried employees. There were plenty who worked an hour or two beyond five o'clock. Partly because of world-wide time zones, partly because there was always more than enough work to be done.

"Birdie!" Court stood from behind his desk, effectively ending the discussion they'd been in the middle of. Oswald gathered his tablet and a few papers. Court certainly knew technology, worked well with it, but there were some things he felt benefited from being put on actual paper. They were slowly bringing him and his current assistant into the twenty-first century, but at times it was a ponderous process.

"How'd it go this afternoon?" Court crossed the room to her and held her by the shoulders, looking her over and noting, as Oswald did, the tired eyes and smudges on her outfit. A few hairs had escaped the twist she'd worn all day and a smear of dust graced her nose.

Frankly, Oswald thought she looked like she was ready for a large glass of wine, an hour in a whirlpool, and twelve hours of sleep. A cup of tea before heading home probably wouldn't hurt.

"It was okay. The morning was paperwork. That was tedious, but easy. This afternoon… Well, let's just say it's a good thing I like walking and I wore flats. Not sure the skirt was brilliant, but it seems Dennis likes my cookies. However he feels the chocolate chips would be better in shortbread. All in all, I survived."

Court laughed and Oswald allowed himself a small smile. Somehow after her afternoon from hell, she still managed to smile. Those were the Robinson genes showing through. "How about a cup of tea?" Oswald asked, telling himself it was mere common courtesy to offer, not an attempt to show his chivalry. "Can have one up in a few minutes."

Birdie followed her father to a seating arrangement off to the side—a sofa, coffee table with a few chairs gathered around.

"Thanks, but really, I'm just ready to go home and put my feet up. Literally."

Court threw his arm around her shoulder and pulled her close. She was visibly tired enough she let her head drop to his shoulder.

"I thought the modern age reduced paperwork. E-mail replaced snail mail. Scanning and texting replaced express delivery." A yawn stole over her, and she barely managed to cover it with her hand.

She looked absolutely beautiful and adorable at the same time, Oswald thought as he carefully watched each gesture.

"Think about what correspondence was like before the advent of fax machines, computers, and the internet. In my day the mail load was at least five times what it is today. We've actually cut four staff positions down there in the last ten years." Court's hand came up to hold Birdie's head on his shoulder, and Oswald surprised himself when he wanted to knock it off and place his hand there.

"Well, start by ordering those new carts, Ozzie. Because that one relic was awful. And the fact you made Freddie take over pushing it only succeeded in ruining his bit of fun. I only saved myself from ridicule by grabbing it the first time he let go of the handle. God only knows what he'll plan for tomorrow."

"Oswald did what?" Court asked, his gaze swinging right toward Oswald.

"I met them at the elevator. Freddie had her pushing a trolley that must have had the bearings glued. I suggested he be a gentleman and switch out. Also promised to order new ones. What the mailroom has are looking more decrepit every week."

Courtney turned her narrowed eyes on him next. "Don't step in next time. I'm here to find my own way into the company, and you jumping in and reminding Freddie of his manners didn't help. Good thing he and I traded off handling that beast of a cart, so at least I've recovered some brownie points. But what you did smacks of preferential treatment, and that will not go over well if you keep it up."

"I would have done the same for any other intern," Oswald said mildly. "I'd hope our employees would exhibit plain old-fashioned good manners at all times. But your point is made. Duke it out yourself as you please."

"Thank you," she snapped, then turned and grinned at her father. "There. One battle down." Her bravado immediately faded and she visibly drooped. She opened her eyes long enough for her gaze to hit him like a Taser. Absently he rubbed his chest, unable to look away.

"Well, if you don't want a cup of tea, your mum's making something special for dinner tonight." Court pushed himself up, then took Courtney's hand and pulled her up. "Oswald, Randi's making enough for you to join us if you don't have other plans."

"Thanks, but I have some things to handle tonight. Appreciate the invite, but I'll take a rain check." He hated saying it when he'd love one of Randi's home-cooked meals, but he had a perfectly fine dinner waiting in his fridge and Deirdre coming over to placate.

"Sure we can't twist your arm?" Court grabbed his suit jacket from a hanger in his closet.

"Extremely tempting, but sorry. Not tonight."

"Your loss."

"Undoubtedly."

Court made to put his arm around Courtney's waist but she stepped aside. "No preferential treatment in the office," she reminded them both. "Save the cuddling for Mom."

Court chuckled. "Should I ring down for a cab?"

"What? And miss my five block walk home? Make you miss your daily exercise?" Mock shock took over her tired expression.

"I guess we're walking."

Courtney nodded. "I need to build my stamina. A few weeks out of school and I'm already getting flabby and pokey slow."

Oswald nearly swallowed his tongue. Flabby? Not from his view. If anything, Courtney's trim body looked tighter than it had during her graduation party. She'd toned up since completing her degree after two years of long hours in the library and eating takeout food her final quarter. Despite the walking and bicycling across the huge Stanford campus, she'd been chair-bound more than she'd liked, he'd overheard her telling her mother.

No, her perfectly respectable skirt hugged perfectly rounded hips and showcased a slender hour-glass figure that drew the eye of many a man with a skinnier woman on his arm.

He had trouble looking away.

Something Court noticed as he ushered his daughter out the door. "Oswald, walk us out. I have a couple more comments on our discussion."

"Of course."

He followed in their wake as they said their good-byes to Mrs. Cuthbert and her junior clerks who were clearing their desktops and digging out handbags. Near the elevators they came face to face with Danielle Richards and a handful of upper level managers. Not many lower managers, who'd surely been handed lists to be accomplished by morning only moments before. He'd been handed a few tasks himself, usually because Court passed them on to him at the end of the day. In fact, Oswald was still waiting for the rest of his list when they climbed on the elevator.

While Courtney chatted with Danielle, Court leaned toward him and spoke softly. "Dennis was party to the little set up?"

He shrugged. "Probably."

"Thanks for stepping in."

"Not sure what else happened today, but at least I caught that one."

"Good job covering by ordering new trolleys. I'm sure they needed replacing a year or two ago. Just never made it to the top of the list of updates."

"It is now."

"Nose around and see what else needs updating down there?"

"I'll look into it. Or ask Courtney after a few days. Maybe she'll have some better observations."

"Excellent idea." Court smiled without looking at Oswald. "Sure I can't talk you into joining us?"

"Positive. Another night, perhaps."

"Count on it. I think Randi wants to adopt you too. She's making a hard run at pulling Paul into line, so watch out for yourself unless you actually like the idea of being mothered to death."

Something warm inexplicitly flooded his veins. As he'd barely known a mother's love, the concept was entirely foreign to him now. At his age? Then again, look at how Drew had taken to his stepmother. Surely a man of twenty-four was as much past a need for a mother figure as one who was twenty-eight?

Stopping that line of thought, he followed the others out when the lift reached the ground floor.

"Anything else you need to tell me before you leave?" he asked Court.

"I had a thought, but it's flown right out of my head. We'll take it up again in the morning. Unless it hits me three steps out the door, and then I'll send a text. Don't stay too late."

Oswald nearly smiled at that. As his boss and mentor well knew, staying late was often the most productive time. It was easier to talk to Los Angeles and early risers in Tokyo. India and China were already in bed for the night, so an early morning was best for those issues.

"No worries. Enjoy your evening." With a nod to Courtney, he turned back to the elevator to return to his office until he absolutely had to leave to meet Deirdre at his flat.

Chapter 13

Birdie slept hard that night after giving her parents a blow-by-blow accounting of her first day. She skipped a few things, such as Dennis's less than patient instructions on how to process the outgoing mail. Thankfully she'd helped in her grandfather's office a time or two and had done similar work. The systems weren't so different, although Dennis tried to make it seem as if her unfamiliarity made her stupid.

By the end of the week she was gaining a handle on the rather simple, straightforward routines of the mailroom. Her decision to wear sturdier fabrics, and slacks, had proven wise. She'd toned down her already natural looking makeup and basically treated everyone as pleasantly as possible, ignoring any comments she'd been meant to overhear that were cutting. Of course the girls who'd been whispering about her had interpreted her silence as ignorance. Let them think she was stupid.

At the start of her second week she'd arrived Monday morning with a large box of iced cinnamon buns she'd made the night before and witnessed the arrival of two dozen new carts. Shiny chrome, the top basket held hanging file folders, the easier to sort mail by department or person. The wheels didn't stick or squeak, in fact they were pretty close to silent as they were pushed. Only Dennis and Freddie had looked at her with speculation, although she never confirmed Ozzie's hand in the shiny new toys.

During the morning delivery she had priority envelopes for Dad and Ozzie.

"Take 'em straight up," Dennis told her after looking over the hand addressed, heavy stationary. The cards, or paper, inside were probably just as expensive. Possibly handmade, designer paper.

As she took the elevator up, she examined the envelope addressed to Ozzie. Deirdre Portman-Wright. Huh. Could have guessed that one, but there was one for her parents as well. The handwriting was elegant script, written with a calligraphy pen. Interestingly enough, although the return address was the same, the handwriting was different. Probably two different assistants who'd been given the job of addressing a few hundred envelopes. Wonder what the woman wanted with both men.

Not that she'd seen Ozzie much since she'd started a week ago. In fact, the last three days of the week she hadn't seen him at all. At least she hadn't been consciously looking for him. She'd been too busy learning the layout of the offices, meeting the secretaries who ruled their sections, making small talk with some of the lower managers. Always a fast study, she had all the floors memorized and knew who sat where. Dad had been right about one thing, her name had preceded her, and she'd been met with various reactions from wariness to over-friendliness. Nigel was one who kept pressing her daily, much to Freddie's disgust. And she didn't encourage him. Not one bit.

At the top floor, she stepped off the elevator and headed for the executive suite. Ten o'clock. Both her dad and Ozzie were probably in some meeting. One she'd love to sit in on. Although she could see the value of working her way up through each department of the company, she really wanted to be in on the big decisions. Be there when the decision was made, then follow it as the decision filtered through the company.

Time. She had to put in her time, as Dad reminded her every so often. New kid on the block and all.

Thinking of what it would be like to sit at Mrs. Cuthbert's desk, she pushed through the glass door into the outer office where the steel-curled older woman ruled. Behind her stood the double doors to Dad's office. Ranged around to her left and right were the doors to the offices of the various VPs and Directors. Each one had an assistant at a desk guarding their doors. Ozzie's office was to the left of her father's. He alone shared the services of Mrs. Cuthbert and her junior assistant with Dad. Which made sense with Dad getting ready to turn the reins of the day to day management of the company over to Ozzie.

Of course, before Birdie took over Mrs. Cuthbert's job upon her retirement, she had several months of sitting in this outer office ahead of her. Hours where she'd learn the power behind the power. Because everyone knew it was the executive assistant who really ran the show.

Mrs. Cuthbert looked up and smiled. "This is a nice surprise. What have you got there?"

Birdie held up the envelopes. "One for the old man and one for the stuffy one." She nodded at Oswald's closed door.

"Oh he's not stuffy," Mrs. Cuthbert, a woman who could send executives running with one sharp look, practically gushed. "He's a gentleman of the old school."

Birdie bit her lip to keep from smiling too much. "Are they in? These say hand delivery on them." As if all letters weren't hand delivered in some way.

"They're in your father's office. Let me see how deep they are." Mrs. Cuthbert picked up her phone. "Sir, there's a beautiful young lady here to see you both. Shall I send her in?" The older woman smiled at Birdie and nodded. "Yes, sir."

Birdie thanked her, then turned the knob on her father's door and entered his spacious office. Very modern, it had lots of glass and chrome. Leather chairs and a sofa. His desk was something of an antique, large, heavily carved walnut, but it worked within the modern décor somehow. Even Meilin had commented on it once.

Both her father and Ozzie stood. Dad came out from behind his desk and greeted her with a hug. "This is a lovely surprise. Can you stay a bit and join me for lunch?"

"Sorry, but I was tasked with making this delivery and then I have to go back." Although lunch with Dad sounded wonderful. She held out the envelopes, handing Ozzie his and the other to her father. Her gaze snagged on Ozzie's, and she had to fight the urge to lean into him for a kiss. One her mouth hungered for to the point she had to swallow back, hard, on the desire to touch him.

Dad barely glanced at his note. "Some charitable gig, no doubt. Can you stick this in your bag and take it home to Mum with you tonight?"

Birdie dragged her attention off Ozzie's mouth and somehow managed to shrug casually. "Does that mean I can open it?"

Dad laughed. "Sure, but if it's an invite to a charity thing, then you're stuck going with us. If Mum says it fits into her calendar."

Shaking her head, she kissed him on the cheek and headed out. It was no secret he'd happily turned the social events calendar over to her mom the minute they married. Mrs. Cuthbert was a little relieved too. One less thing to track other than to note it on her calendar simply to remind him. She also had everyone's birthdays noted, as well as anniversaries and every other family event to be followed religiously.

* * * *

Oswald tapped the envelope he held in one hand against the palm of the other. An odd chill ran down his spine. After last week's dinner with Deirdre, when he'd told her—again—they were basically through, she'd promised to behave. Then to turn around and send out an invite so soon. He smelled something fishy and it wasn't the Thames.

"What's the invite for, since I sent mine off with Birdie."

Oswald tore open the envelope and extracted the card. "Charity event to raise funds for refugees," he told Court. "Saturday night, so RSVPs are due immediately." The handwritten note at the bottom of the card made it plain Dee expected him to be her escort. As hostess, she was practically required to have one, and she'd chosen him. Lucky him. Not.

"Excellent. Not that I like these things." Court moved back behind his desk and settled in his chair. "Randi and I have been looking for a way to start easing Birdie into society. Since we won't be around much the next year, this is as good as any."

Oswald nodded and settled in his chair once more.

"You're frowning," Court said.

Oswald sighed. "Dee has pretty much demanded my services as escort for the evening."

"Damn. I was going to ask you to escort Birdie. It would make a grand entrance for her, rather than being third wheel with her parents." The look he gave Oswald was bright with hope.

This required some thinking. What was Dee's angle? Was she trying to prove to him she still had him in her grip? If he showed up with Courtney on his arm, what would be the long range impact? Would there be one? Would Dee finally give up her campaign to cut off his balls? Not that she'd ever be anywhere near them again. "Since I'm trying to disassociate myself from Deirdre, if Courtney would agree to be my date, it would help Dee see I'm serious. I explained it to her last week, but you know how she gets an idea in her head…"

Court laughed. "Yes, I do. Remember the time she tried to latch on to Drew? Thank God we had the excuse of sending him overseas. Not sure he would have survived otherwise."

Oh yes, he remembered. Drew had nearly been in a panic, or as much a one he could ever be in. Deirdre had a reputation as a man-eater for good reason, and Oswald had warned Drew. Maybe a little too forcefully.

Time to spill his true worry. "I'm a little concerned she'd find a way to take out her frustration on Courtney, to tell you the truth. She'd have a hard time discrediting me, socially, but Courtney is a new face."

"Despite her being my daughter, and me being one of Deirdre's larger contributors?" Court's raised brow indicated he thought Dee wouldn't sink so low. "Would she really cut off her nose to spite her face? I mean, if she attempts to ostracize my daughter, my family, in any way, surely she realizes what it could cost her? Portman-Wrights are fairly new to the society, relatively speaking, and their wealth doesn't compare. She wouldn't risk pissing me off, would she?"

Then again, Court didn't know Dee like Oswald knew her. She might very well find a way to publically humiliate Courtney. But if he were at Courtney's side the entire night, he could protect her, not only from Dee, but from any of the stags in attendance who would love to turn Courtney's head.

"Let me think this through." Oswald tossed the invitation down on Court's desk. "I'll need to speak with her personally no later than this evening. She'll need time to find another escort, since as hostess she must have one. Then again, even if she wasn't the hostess, she'd feel off-balance without some man dancing attendance on her."

Court laughed. "True. Well, let me know what you decide. In the meantime, we have real business to get back to."

An hour later, meeting over, Oswald gathered his papers and tablet. The invitation rested on top.

"Let me know what you decide on that," Court said. "If you choose to invite Birdie, we'll have you over for dinner tomorrow night."

Oswald looked up in alarm. Invite Courtney on a date in front of her parents?

Court held up a hand. "Don't worry, we'll disappear right after dinner, and you can have some privacy to do the asking. I wouldn't put you on the spot that way."

Not much better, but he could work with it. "All right. I'll let you know after I talk to Deirdre. If I still have an arse left after she chews me out."

He left Court's office, nodded to Mrs. Cuthbert, then entered his own office and shut the door. He needed to think about this very carefully. What game was Deirdre playing?

After settling behind his desk, he spun his chair around to look out the window at his view of the Thames and the city on the other side. It was a view he greatly appreciated, but it didn't encroach on his thoughts at the moment.

A week ago, per Deirdre's demand, he'd had her over for dinner. The housekeeper had left a green salad, a frittata ready for the oven, and a small cake for dessert. Dee had arrived at seven, dressed for seduction in a red halter dress that clung like a second skin.

Dodging her hints and outright suggestions for how to finish the night, he'd used the table as a barricade of sorts. Although it hadn't stopped her from running a foot up and down his leg, or touching his hand and running her dangerous nails up and down his arm, it had kept her from crawling into his lap. That was something.

He'd let her have her say, then he'd slowly, systematically, told her in great detail why he'd no longer be at her beck and call. She'd left after coffee, greatly annoyed with him and very frustrated. Interestingly enough, he hadn't risen to her sexual challenges. Not one stirring after she laid out her best seduction with soft words, teasing touches, and malfunctioning wardrobe. He'd had an eyeful of her generous charms, all seductively presented because Deirdre didn't get dirty until the clothes actually came off. Very lady like, until the actual act took place, which it hadn't last week. No, she'd been extremely displeased with him and muttered a few words about how he'd come back to her.

So here was her first volley. An invite cleverly worded to make it clear he was her chosen escort for the evening. Not much chance of him misinterpreting her meaning. And in the past it had been enough. He'd accepted his role with no complaint.

Not this time.

The only question was, how would she make him pay? Would she cut him directly, or be more subtle by taking it out on Courtney? He spent a good hour pondering the methods she might employ, then decided that with him stuck firmly at Courtney's side, there wasn't much she could do at the event without making herself look bad in front of their audience.

Well, he wanted to make a break. Here was his chance, presented on a silver platter, or rather, on the cream stationary, hand delivered by Courtney herself.

It was a risk. Deirdre was extremely clever and more than a little spiteful when denied her way. However, he didn't think Dee would make a public move in front of Court. After all, he usually donated generously to charity, whether invited to the event or not. Deirdre was certainly counting on that. So maybe the risk was minimal.

Decision made, he picked up his phone and dialed her direct line. Best get it done and over with.

Chapter 14

Saturday evening, Birdie felt a little like she was in a fairy tale. Oh sure, she'd dressed up for social events before, but never something along these lines. Deirdre Portman-Wright, serving as her father's hostess, had opened his Knightsbridge house to a select number of exclusive guests, hoping to get into their checkbooks to support the refugees arriving daily.

It was a huge house. Bigger than the Sussex manor, and certainly a few centuries newer.

That didn't bother her so much as the fact she was going as Oswald's date. In his car. Alone. With him. Her parents were also attending the event, but they were going by limo. They'd offered to share, but Ozzie had declined.

He'd come for dinner on Wednesday, and shortly after clearing dessert dishes, her parents had simply disappeared into their rooms. Not a word of explanation, just left her alone with Ozzie, sipping coffee at the dinner table. She'd been lulled into drowsiness with wine and a dram of liquor in her coffee.

He'd cleared his throat, and she looked up to meet his serious gaze. "I have something I want to ask you, Courtney."

"Okay." Simple enough. No idea where he was heading with this, but whatever.

"The event on Saturday. The refugee fundraiser."

She nodded and took a sip of her coffee, letting it rest on her tongue for a minute.

"I'd be honored if you'd attend with me. As my date."

Surprised, to say the least, she spewed coffee halfway across the table. As she was groping for a napkin and trying to catch her breath, she'd caught the look on his face. Half bemused, half wary.

"Sorry about that. Didn't mean to catch you off guard." He thrust another cloth napkin at her. A tiny bit of the corner of his mouth ticked up. Great. Someone was amused.

Coughing and trying to wipe everything from her face to the table, Birdie bought herself a few red-faced minutes. Finally she could talk. "Sorry. Wasn't expecting that." She coughed again and accepted a refill of her water glass from Ozzie. "You want me to be your date for this charity thing? On Saturday night?"

Ozzie nodded. "If you want to go. I'd like very much to escort you there. Better than going as your father's second date, and I can introduce you to the people you need to know. Your parents will be glad-handing the same, but it might be less awkward for you to do it with me."

"Um, well, that makes sense. Sure. I'd be happy to go with you." She said the words slowly, but the only panicked thoughts that hit her brain had more to do with what to wear rather than going with Ozzie.

A genuine smile touched his face for a blink. "Great. It starts at eight. I'll join you and your parents for dinner, and from there we'll go on to the gala."

"All right. I'm guessing my mother knows what attire is appropriate." Birdie frowned. "What will you be wearing?"

"A tuxedo. The event is black tie. Let me know if you'll be wearing red or pink, and I can resurrect one of my vests from the wedding events."

"Too much like a prom date. I don't know these events well, but I'm fairly certain we don't have to match and you aren't required to buy me a corsage."

He'd agreed, they'd said good night, and then she'd gone to pound on her parents' bedroom door and found them oh-so-innocently curled up on a loveseat reading.

The next day she left work early and met her mother at Harrod's for shopping.

And now here she was, in the low slung seat, riding next to Ozzie, on her way to a fancy event wearing the sexiest dress she'd ever owned. An Alice + Olivia gown, with all-over beading in silver and black with faux jewels in blue on a background of black made for an opulent effect unlike anything she'd ever seen before. It was an Art Deco masterpiece. The deep V-neck and back didn't allow for a bra—thank God she had something to fill the top with—but the slim silhouette with a subtle flare toward the bottom of the floor-sweeping hem was more luxurious than anything she'd ever worn or even dreamed of wearing. She had a black velvet shawl for a cover up. And essential double-stick tape to prevent wardrobe malfunctions.

The whole outfit—dress, shawl, shoes and purse—had cost a bloody fortune. A fact she'd tried to point out to her mother several times. But considering what her mother had bought to wear, a silk dress of bright blue overlaid with beaded black lace, she didn't have much room to whine. Mom's dress had three-quarter sleeves, unlike her dress, which practically bared her entire torso.

Still, she knew for sure it was sexy because when Ozzie arrived to meet them for dinner tonight, he'd stopped dead in his tracks while a glazed look had slid down over his eyes. A lapse of only a heartbeat passed before he'd greeted her with a compliment, as smooth as silk.

"Anything special I need to know about tonight?" she asked. While he concentrated on driving, she admired the way the beading reflected the street lights, making her dress look like it was in motion. She was also sure his eyes kept returning to the polished gold locket she wore on an intricate gold chain, one her grandmother Dailey had given her years ago. Shaped like a fairy tale book with five castle turrets on it, the locket held a picture of her grandmother and a tiny note she'd tucked inside to remind Birdie to follow her dreams. The chain was long enough the locket nestled perfectly in the cleavage on display in the deep V-neck of the gown. The very simplicity of it served to highlight the gown rather than compete with its extravagant design.

"Follow my lead. I won't leave your side. Smile, be charming, don't challenge anyone, especially not the women. They'll be scouting you out. Be enigmatic."

"Standard party behavior. And I promise not to drink too much or plow through the buffet table."

Ozzie shot her a smile. "You'll be fine."

The smile got to her, as it always did. Mostly because it was so rare, but also because it made his face so much more beautiful. A vision of him without his glasses, or shirt, just as he'd been in her bed in San Francisco, flashed before her eyes and stole her breath. It was so not fair how beautiful he was. Her hands remembered touching his hot skin over hard muscles, and her mouth watered remembering his kiss. Not something she wanted to remember right now when he was so close and looking so good in his formal evening wear.

Swallowing the desire to slide into his lap and kiss them both senseless, she nodded and stared straight ahead through the windshield. If she didn't look at him too often, she could do this. Hopefully there wouldn't be dancing, because if he took her in his arms, she'd melt against him and cling like a vine.

There were two lanes in the drive that circled before the big house. One for limos and one for those who drove themselves. A valet opened her door and handed her out while Ozzie took a ticket from another valet. He came around the car, offered his arm to her, and together they dodged the limos and walked up to the open double doors.

Inside, whatever light touched, it glittered. From the gowns to the chandeliers and the decorations, Birdie could have sworn someone had dumped a truck load of fairy dust on it all. Greenery stood in corners and graced table tops, all threaded with fairy lights. Women dripped diamonds and every other jewel to be found on earth. Men provided a debonair background against which the women were displayed. The couples spanned the age groups from young to old.

Deirdre stood at the beginning of the receiving line looking like a queen, barely dressed in a black slip with spangled netting draped over it in the illusion of a full gown. It emphasized generous breasts, a tiny waist that gently flared into sculpted hips. Barely there spike heeled sandals gave shape to well toned legs. Many a man noticed each detail while Birdie and Oswald inched their way forward in the line.

"You met Deirdre. That's her father beside her, and then her stepmother. They don't get along, but Dee's the apple of her father's eye. Mummy dearest isn't happy about it," Ozzie murmured in her ear. The woman he said was the stepmother appeared to be no more than a year, maybe two, older than Deirdre. No wonder there was competition for the old man's attention. He looked about sixty, slightly past his prime. Not fat, but headed that way. He certainly hadn't contributed much in the way of genetic imprinting on Deirdre. Hovering nearby was a young man Birdie didn't recognize, although she'd bet Ozzie did by the nod he exchanged with the man who might have been his age. Possibly a little younger. That might have been Ozzie tonight.

"Deirdre," Ozzie said, calling Birdie's attention to the fact they'd reached the front of the line. "You remember Miss Ferguson-Robinson. Courtney, Deirdre Portman-Wright."

"Of course," Deirdre cooed and took Birdie's hand in both of hers. "So delighted you could come this evening. Make sure Oswald takes you by the bidding tables. Don't let him get off without bidding on something for you. We've had some fabulous last minute donations."

"Thank you. We'd be pleased to check them out."

The smile on Deirdre's face didn't reach her eyes, but she turned toward her father. And introduced Birdie.

"Courtland Robinson's daughter, you know."

"Ah yes," Mr. Wright said. "The one raised in the wilds of America. Very pleased to meet you, young lady."

If Birdie got that right, he was a little too pleased to meet her. Apparently Ozzie figured that as well because his arm tightened around her waist. His arm around her, his hand on her waist was the most possessive move a man had ever made on her. She was very aware of his body against her right side as Oswald shook hands with the older man, then introduced her to his much younger wife. Although she gave the appearance of being a pampered society wife, there was something slightly off about her appearance. Like maybe she'd been a stripper in a previous life and was trying to fit in. Birdie couldn't help but feel a little sorry for her, so she smiled warmly, shook her hand, and let Ozzie move her deeper into the house.

For the first hour it was all meet and greet. She sipped champagne from crystal flutes circulated by impeccably dressed waiters, murmured small talk, listened to Ozzie as he did and said all the right things. They mingled; she met the right people, made a point to admire the beautiful gowns, demurely accepted compliments on hers, and generally felt like Cinderella on Prince Charming's arm. Ozzie was absolutely perfect. At one point he'd even saved her from a bath in red wine when one of the younger crowd, as in her own age group, had turned suddenly, sending out a small wave of deep red liquid. Only Ozzie's fast reflexes had saved her from wearing it.

"Thank you," she murmured for only him to hear.

"Of course. Can't have your beautiful gown ruined, or your evening." As he said the words, he stared down at her, a tiny smile teasing his lips, a flame of heat in his eyes.

Although she'd promised herself she wouldn't be mesmerized by him, she failed to stick to her plan. His smile, directed solely at her, was more entrancing than a full moon shining down on a misty night.

"What do you say we go check out the auction tables," he said.

"Sounds like fun."

Because she was closer to the room where the items were set up, Ozzie turned her by her shoulders and pointed them both that direction. Out of nowhere, a woman about her age stumbled, and this time the entire glass of deep red wine splashed the front of Birdie, from her face to her chest, with much of it going straight down her neckline and into her panties.

Birdie gasped and backed into Oswald, who immediately grabbed her by the hips, stabilizing her on her feet.

"Oh! Love, I'm so clumsy!" the redheaded woman exclaimed. "Pardon me, I guess I've had enough tonight." The giggle sounded possibly tipsy, but not enough to believe the woman was actually drunk. In fact, the giggle had a note of glee to it.

Humiliation filled Birdie, deepening with each gasp from the people around them.

Ozzie was instantly in front of her with his crisp white linen handkerchief. "Here, mop up what you can." Then he reached out and grabbed the arm of the woman starting to push through the gawking crowd.

Birdie looked down at her chest and panicked. "My locket!" For the moment, ignoring the wine dripping from her hair and down her face, she wrapped the handkerchief around the precious charm and debated whether it was safe to open to check for damage to the contents. Squeezing the cloth, she prayed it soaked up all the red liquid before it could seep inside.

Tears at what might be lost to carelessness sprang to her eyes, and she looked up as someone else held out a square of white linen. The discovery they had a circle of observers, including Drew's friend Phillip, was not a welcome one.

She took the handkerchief from his hand, and while still gripping her locket with one hand, used the other to pat her face with the cloth that came back badly stained, not only with the wine, but her makeup as well. Deep inside she understood, this was no accident. Fury and embarrassment made her cheeks burn. Tears still stung her eyes and clogged her throat, as she told herself to buck up. Ozzie would get her out of there in a minute.

"Not so fast, Catherine. You owe Courtney a better apology than that, and more."

Birdie looked up from cleaning the wine from her skin to see Oswald holding the other woman by the arm.

Phillip produced another hanky and pressed it to her hair. "Aw, Birdie, love, now that's a shame. Catherine doesn't have the best balance when she's sober," he said as he stood in front of her, doing his best to shield her from the audience, or to look down her dress. It was a toss-up.

"I'm washable, but I'm afraid the locket and dress aren't." Damn, she'd loved this dress. True, the wine barely showed on the black fabric, but it stained the lighter colored beads and had soaked clear through to her skin, down the neckline, and dripped from her hair. Still, the dress was nowhere near as precious as the locket still held tight in her grasp. The dress had made her feel beautiful. Now it was a soggy, cold rag, the beading on the bodice making it cling even tighter. She really identified with the Cinderella allusion she'd made earlier. But most of all, she wanted to cry and refused to let them see her reduced to tears.

Ozzie pushed Phillip aside. With one hand still holding the woman, he shrugged off his jacket one shoulder at a time.

"Here, Courtney, put this on, love."

"Thanks, Oz—Oswald." Her cheeks flamed and she peeked at him from beneath her eyelashes.

"Here, hold Catherine," Ozzie ordered and pushed the other woman at Phillip. Ozzie whipped his jacket around her, then helped her into it, wrapping it snuggly about her. "You all right there?"

Birdie sniffed but nodded. "Not maimed, merely stained. I'm hoping the contents of my locket aren't ruined. It came from my grandmother just before she died." Despite her resolve, one tear leaked and slowly slid down her cheek.

Ozzie's hands held her by the shoulders, his gaze intense. "You're a real lady, Courtney. As soon as Catherine makes good, we're out of here. We'll check for damages as soon as I get you home, right?" He lifted one hand to cup her cheek. With his thumb, he very gently wiped the renegade tear away.

Unable to speak, she nodded, then raised her chin. That earned her a full out, panty-melting, heart-twisting smile from Ozzie. "Good girl."

To see that smile again, she'd maintain her calm demeanor and get out of here with what was left of her dignity.

Ozzie turned to the other woman as Deirdre pushed through the crowd. "What's going on here, and why is Phillip holding Catherine?"

"Catherine doused Miss Robinson with her wine and was about to make a proper apology," Ozzie said in the sternest voice Birdie had ever heard from him. He scowled deeply at the woman now trying to pull away from Phillip's grip.

"I-I'm very sorry. Miss Robinson, did you say?" Green eyes widened.

"Yes, Courtland Robinson's daughter," Ozzie said. "That was more than clumsiness on your part. I'm shocked, Catherine."

"It was an accident. I got bumped and my wine went flying, I swear."

"Oh, Oswald," Deirdre said. "It was an accident. Why are you getting your knickers in a twist? Of course I'll take care of the dress. Such a silly thing to get upset about." Her cold brown gaze swept Birdie, and she found herself wanting to dump a vat of red over both women; neither of them were in the least sincere.

"It's possible a piece of heirloom jewelry has been ruined." Oswald's frown deepened. "I'm not sure it can be fixed."

Catherine jumped in. "I'll replace the gown and get the jewelry cleaned. I'm so sorry. Tomorrow I'll go down to Marks and Spencer and get a replacement gown sent over to you."

Ozzie's lips twisted at the name of the department store. "I believe the dress came from Harrod's, am I correct, Courtney?"

"Yes, you are, but the dress doesn't matter. And I'm positive this was no accident." She glared at the woman trying to hold an apologetic expression on her face, although she flinched a little at Birdie's accusation. "However, I don't want to stand here dripping and debating it. The dress doesn't mean anything. I'm more worried about the locket." She turned her shoulder to the now protesting Catherine and Deirdre to face Ozzie. "Really, Oswald, I just want to leave now." Even if Catherine replaced the expensive gown, she'd never wear it. The reminder would be too humiliating. And if the contents of the locket were ruined? Irreplaceable. Especially the note in her grandmother's hand. The thought made her heart skip a beat.

"And so we shall. Catherine. Deirdre." Disdain clear in his most plummy tone, he insincerely wished them a good evening. Barely sparing them his deepest scowl, Ozzie wrapped his arm around Birdie and escorted her to the nearest exit, a set of French doors that opened onto a terrace. At least it was fairly dark outside. She was grateful he didn't parade her through the large room. Enough people had seen her looking like a rat pulled from a vat of wine.

By the time they reached the front, and Oswald had the valet running for his car, she was trembling in reaction. Angry and humiliated, she sniffed back the threatening tears.

Careless of his shirt, he pulled her close, allowing her to hide her face against his chest. "It's all right, love. You were far better behaved than those two bitches. I'll take care of you and get the locket cleaned."

Tears were still too close to the surface, so she merely shrugged.

"I'll get you home in a trice. While you shower I'll check it over, and make a pot of tea, possibly with a shot of brandy in it; then we'll watch some telly or light a fire. I won't leave you."

His kind words nearly broke her resolve not to cry. That she'd do in the shower. Alone. What confused her the most was why. She'd never faced such bullying in her entire life. No one had ever been so mean. Not for one moment did she imagine it was unplanned. The earlier miss had only made the perpetrators more determined. And she did recognize Catherine as the woman who'd nearly missed her earlier. Apparently Ozzie had as well, and he certainly knew the players better.

"Here's the car now." Still holding her close, Ozzie all but picked her up and set her in the passenger seat of his car. "Don't worry about the interior. Leather wipes clean."

Especially black leather. She choked out a little laugh, thankful he wasn't fussing about his very expensive formal clothing or the interior of his car. He buckled her in, then gently shut her door where she was mostly hidden by tinted glass.

A second or two later he tipped the valet and slid behind the wheel. "We're out of here."

They drove a few miles, Ozzie expertly navigating the traffic, before Birdie found her voice.

"Thank you." The first time she said it her voice wobbled. It was better the second time.

"Hmm?" He glanced sideways at her.

"Thank you for getting me out of there so fast. So discreetly."

"I didn't see the second one coming."

"I didn't, either. I don't think either of us would have had time to react if we had." Using the cleanest of the two handkerchiefs, she once more attempted to pat wine from her hair, her face, her cleavage. All one-handed because she refused to uncover the locket just yet. The wine even felt like it was in her ears. She stank like a wino.

"While it's not a perfume I'd normally choose, at least the red smells pretty good."

Birdie laughed. How had he read her mind? Her cell phone buzzed from her purse, and she pulled it out. "It's my mom."

"Assure her you're all right and I've got you."

"Mom, hi." Birdie nodded at Ozzie as she connected.

"Honey, are you all right? I heard you got spilled on."

"That's a mild way of saying it. I'm sorry, Mom, but the dress you bought me is probably ruined."

"I heard that too." Mom sighed. "But you're okay?"

"I'm fine. I mean my body is, but I'm terribly worried about Nana's locket. Ozzie is taking me home. He got me out of there after making the culprit apologize. She also offered to buy me a new dress."

"I don't care about the dress, as beautiful as it is. Was. We can replace it. Tell me more about Nana's locket."

"No, no. Please don't replace the dress. Even if we could clean it, I just can't, won't, wear it again. I just want my picture of Nana undamaged."

"I understand, sweetie. We'll clean the locket, and there will be lots of other dresses. Your dad is all set to take us both shopping, and believe me, that's huge for him."

Birdie smiled at the amusement in her mother's voice. "Yes, I know. I'm not worried. Not really sure I want to attend more events like this if I can look forward to more things being spilled on me. Although I'm pissed about the locket, it could have been much worse, like getting my face pushed into a cake or something."

Mom laughed. "That's my girl. So, Oswald is taking you home?"

Talking with Mom had done a whole lot to calm her down. She sighed and let the stress roll of her shoulders. "We're nearly there. I just want a long shower, and he's promised me a cup of tea and time to decompress in front of the TV. Think I'll find my coziest pajamas and take him up on that. Might have to steal one of Dad's shirts for him. His shirt, probably his whole suit, is ruined too. Wonder if that's why they used red wine?"

Mom gasped. "You think it was done on purpose?"

"No doubt." Anger once more sizzled to life. "Ozzie pulled me away from harm the first time. We weren't watching closely enough for the second round, and she got me good. From the hair down."

"This was done deliberately?" Mom's voice rose, and in the background Birdie could hear her father asking what she'd said. Mom repeated Birdie's words, and then there were two men talking angrily. Dad's voice she could make out, but with the other she couldn't tell who was speaking.

"Darling, Dad's talking with Mr. Wright. We'll be home soon."

"No, Mom, really, don't leave on my account." She glanced over at Ozzie who was obviously listening, but also intently focused on the road. "I wasn't hurt. I'm just angry and a little stained is all."

"No, sweetie, we don't want to stay at a party where guests are abused in such a manner." The last was said loud enough to be overheard. "The behavior is outrageous and beneath people who are supposed to be the crème of society. I'm glad you're headed home. Tell Oswald we want him to stay with you until we get there."

Birdie closed her eyes. "Mom, I'm not a kid. Of course I can stay home alone. But it doesn't matter anyway because he's told me he's staying." A glance his direction proved her right as he nodded. A muscle jumped in his cheek, and she realized he was gritting his teeth.

"Well, we won't be too long. Unless your father wants to go out for coffee. We might stop for dessert. Anything you want us to bring home?"

"No, I'll be fine. I think I saw a little carton of ice cream hidden in the back of the freezer."

Mom laughed again. "Nosy one. Fine, eat my ice cream. I think there's enough to split with Oswald. All right, I'm glad you're out of here. We won't be terribly late." Mom's voice dropped in volume. "Unless you want us to be late?"

"Mom!" A hot blush stole up Birdie's cheeks. "No. You two do what you want, when you want. Go out for dessert or find another party. You're dressed for a night out, might as well enjoy it." When did parents stop embarrassing their children on purpose? Lord, she hoped it was soon.

"Okay, Birdie. We're through here. And we're not leaving a donation. That's a new one. Dad sends his love." Mom made a smooching noise, and Birdie disconnected with a groan.

"Parents," she said quietly, but couldn't hide her weak chuckle.

"You have some great ones," Ozzie said as he slowed the car to turn into the underground car park.

"Yes, they are great. But still, do they have to treat me as if I were eight?"

Oswald didn't answer and she remembered, too late, he hadn't had parents for years.

"I'm sorry," she said quietly.

"For what?"

"I shouldn't be complaining about my parents. I'm beyond lucky to have them. A second chance at a father to love me."

"You are lucky. And I'm lucky to have my uncle. Larry was a far better parent than the two who made me. It's not always about who made you, but more about who loves you." Oswald circled the parking area until he found a spot in guest parking. It was about as far from the elevator as one could get, but she wasn't going to complain. She just hoped the lobby and the lifts were mostly empty. The one from the garage only went to the lobby, so from there they caught another car to the penthouse level shared with one other co-op owner. At least in this tower.

Birdie gathered her purse, wrapped his jacket around her tighter, and was ready to climb out when Ozzie opened her door and took her hand.

He didn't let go while he shut the door. In fact, he backed her into the side of the car and lifted his free hand to sweep back a sodden hank of hair that had fallen down. "In spite of the wine bath, you're still the most beautiful woman there tonight."

Birdie blinked up at him, the heat of a blush infusing her from head to toe. "Thank you, but I beg to differ. I'm pretty sure I look like something dragged from the river."

A smile lightened the severe expression on his face. "You smell a hell of a lot better than something dragged from the river."

The look in his eyes reminded her of her hotel room in San Francisco. Right before he rushed her into the room and started kissing her. Anticipation made her breath hitch as their gazes locked and held. His body heat wrapped around her and through the scent of the wine, she could detect his cologne. The spicy sweetness she doubted she'd ever forget.

"I wonder if you still taste as sweet as you did…" Slowly he bent his face toward hers, and all she could do was stare into his eyes. Eyes that smoldered, reminding her of heat and uncontrollable feelings, the strength of muscle beneath hot skin.

A car door slammed somewhere in the garage, and the light in his eyes dimmed. "Let's get you upstairs. That gown must be awfully uncomfortable about now."

"It—it is," she stammered, then cleared her throat. "Yeah, it's getting sticky, and I'm sure my face is a fright of melted makeup. Raccoon eyes, you know."

One half of his lips curled upward in a crooked grin. "Not so bad, but let's go."

Still holding her hand, he led her to the elevator. In the lobby, she waved at the security guard who looked astonished when he got a good look at her. The second elevator was already waiting, so she didn't stop to explain. Thankfully no one else had been in the lobby or in the car racing upward.

Ozzie chuckled at their reflection in the shiny chrome lining the walls. "You definitely got the worst of the splash, but I didn't fare so well myself."

"Most of that came from hugging me, you dork." God, it felt good to laugh a little.

Ozzie threw an arm around her shoulders. "I said I'd match you if you told me what you were wearing tonight. Now we have matching wine stains."

It was just too stupid for words, and she bent forward with a good, deep belly laugh. "I don't think that's what either of us had in mind."

It was worth looking ridiculous to see, and hear, him laugh too. In fact, she couldn't remember ever seeing him let go enough to really guffaw. If she'd thought removing his glasses and watching him smile transformed him from a stiff toad, laughing really changed him. Much like watching a video of David Gandy playing with puppies, Oswald laughing completely melted her heart. He'd never looked better to her.

Their eyes met in the polished chrome, and their laughter quieted just at the car arrived at their stop. Oswald's arm slipped down her back until his hand rested on her hip. "Get your key out, Courtney." His voice, low and growly rough, stimulated something down deep and low in her body. The memory of him humming against her, the vibrations traveling up her body from down *there*, sent a flash burn of heat over her skin once more. This man was going to burn her up.

She kept her face down as he hurried her toward the entrance of the flat. When her hand trembled, he took the key and opened the door. She disabled the alarm as he closed the door. Once she finished, he spun her around and backed her against the wall.

"Courtney." The sound of her name spoken like he was a desperate man was enough to convey the question. Did she want him?

Soggy and sticky, smelling of wine, she wanted him to kiss her. No longer caring if she ruined his tux, she reached for his shoulders, sliding her hands up and into the hair at his nape.

Ozzie groaned, but he gathered her close and their lips collided, like two magnets irresistibly attracted. The kiss was neither gentle nor sweet. They only pulled back a hair when their teeth clashed, but that wasn't enough to make them stop. Instead they repositioned their mouths and went back to devouring each other. The cold, sopping material pressed against her body, heating as his body lent its warmth to the combination. He must have felt it too, because he grunted and reached for the fastening behind her back.

"How do you undo this thing?" he muttered, his fingers fumbling.

"The dress is already ruined, Oz, just rip it."

Chapter 15

As much as he wanted to do as Birdie demanded, the thought of ripping off her dress, here in the foyer of her father's flat, put a damper on his libido. All he had to do was lift his head and remember they weren't in his flat several blocks inland from the river.

Besides, if he ripped the dress, thousands of tiny beads would scatter in the foyer, on the tile, making the floor dangerous to walk on. Impossible to clean up before Court and Randi came home.

Courtney's head thunked against the wall, her face to the ceiling. "Your mind is working far too hard, Ozzie. What could possibly be more important than kissing me senseless?"

"The thought of all those beads on your gown scattering over a tile floor. And getting them swept up before your parents walk through the door and kill themselves on the beads."

Courtney laughed. "Of course. Safety first." She raised her head, her eyes twinkling with laughter, but also shadowed with frustration.

He needed to pull this in. Right now. A dozen curses flashed through his head. Tipping his head down, he rested his forehead against Courtney's. "While I check out your necklace, you need to get in the shower before I offer to scrub your back. And front. And bottom. Wouldn't do to get caught in the shower together."

A rosy blush painted her cheeks. "I feel like such a teenager instead of a full grown woman."

Oswald kissed her nose. "In many ways you're still as innocent as a young girl. Don't rush to be grown up. Fortunately for me, you are grown, so I don't have to feel guilty or pervy about lusting after you." Purely indulgent on his part, he let his hands slip under the oversized jacket she still wore, to re-familiarize themselves with the very womanly shape of her body. "You are definitely a woman. One I should keep my hands off." One more kiss, he told himself. One more and then he'd slap her on the butt and send her to the showers. "And more to the point, your first time shouldn't be up against a wall while wearing a wine soaked dress. Your first time deserves champagne, roses, and silken sheets."

Courtney shivered and he immediately felt guilty for keeping her from cleaning up. "Give me the necklace and go. Now. Before I forget you're the boss's daughter and follow you in."

Her lips opened, to argue he presumed, but he stopped her with a finger over her lips. "Please. I'm trying to preserve both our dignities. What we have left, anyway."

Certainly not happy, she nodded, cheeks stained with more than the wine. "I'll see if I can dig up at least a clean shirt for you. Think one of Drew's will fit you?" She lifted the chain from around her neck and held the locket over his open hand, slowly lowering the chain until it all puddled in his hand.

"I'll go digging in his room. Go take care of yourself." How many times did he have to insist? The sooner she got away from him the better. It wouldn't take much for him to forget where they were, who she was, who he was.

Finally, she nodded and sidled away from him. He watched her walk down the hall toward her room, hips swaying, bedraggled tendrils of hair swinging with her movement. He wanted nothing more than to pull the jeweled pins from her hair and peel that sodden dress from her body, licking every spot where the red liquid stained her skin. If he could suck hard enough, he'd surely not only clean her, but grow drunk on the combination of her sweetness and the alcohol. Hell, who needed alcohol when she was around? All he needed was time to explore the neckline that plunged dangerously deep to the bottom of her cleavage.

Thankfully she disappeared into her room, carefully shutting the door behind her. Oswald heaved a sigh, running a hand through his hair. He looked down at himself and realized just how stained he was. Some of the splash had landed on him. What his shirt bore now mostly came from holding Courtney close. Spinning, he looked into the hallway mirror. Damn if he couldn't see the impression of her body from where he'd held her against him. A damn near perfect hourglass outline was imprinted on his starched white shirt. He might have to keep the shirt and frame it.

He heard voices in the outer hall. Although it was too soon for Court and Randi to have returned, it did remind him they would sooner rather than later. He entered Drew's room, now Drew and Meilin's, and headed for the closet. They were fairly close in size. However, Drew had slightly more bulk when it came to muscle from playing rugby. Since Oswald preferred mixed martial arts, he was leaner, tighter. Still, one of Drew's shirts should fit him well enough to be decent. He set the necklace on the dresser.

And while he was changing out shirts, it wouldn't hurt to find a towel and wipe himself down.

He grabbed what looked like an older, white button-down with one hand while working the studs on his tux shirt. There were times clothes certainly were a pain to deal with, but he'd learned well the lessons of being well-groomed at an early age. It was all about blending in. His wardrobe was mostly suits, casual to formal with business wear the most common. Yes, he owned jeans, even wore them sometimes, but rarely. The only other clothes he owned were of the workout variety. He could have dug in the drawers for something along those lines, but didn't feel like mixing formal trousers with a Cold Play T-shirt.

Damaged shirt off, studs and cufflinks in his trousers pocket, he headed for the en suite bare-chested to find a towel to sponge off the worst of the wine stains.

The door easily pushed open, but before he could find the switch, the row of lights over the double vanity flicked on.

Coming into the bathroom from a door opposite, was Courtney.

Beautifully, gloriously, nude.

"Oh," she said, coming to a stop, one arm coming up in a poor attempt to cover her breasts.

"I—" He didn't quite know what to say. His brain checked out, and his body took over with an instant salute.

Courtney laughed a little, her face flushing pink as she let her arm drop. "I guess you've seen it all...."

"Doesn't mean I don't appreciate viewing it all again." He waved toward the separate room that held the shower and toilet. "You jump in there, and I'll just use the bath in the hall. I was looking for a towel to wipe down." The explanation was weak at best, but he couldn't seem to move with that beautiful tanned skin on full display. Full breasts, slim waist, flaring hips, and the small patch of pale fluff that shyly hid the location to heaven on earth. Yes, he knew what naked females looked like, had admired them in paintings, photographs, sculpture, and in the very decadent flesh, from afar and up close. With eyes, hands, and lips, he'd worshiped the female form in many variations. But none so lovely as the perfect form he admired this very moment. A form he very much wanted to worship over and over again.

"I'll just leave you to…" He backed from the space and pulled the door shut. Then thunked his forehead against the panel. If he wanted to keep their relationship on a non personal plane, he had to get out of there right now.

Behind the door, water ran in the sink. A moment later, the doorknob turned under his hand and was tugged from it. The door only opened a few inches. Enough for a slender, feminine hand to push through the opening with a damp cloth wrapped inside it.

"Here. Maybe this will do," she said softly.

"Ta." Oswald took the offering, then pulled the door shut again. "Lock the door," he advised her.

Courtney merely laughed, and a few seconds later he heard water rushing through the pipes, hitting tile in what he presumed was the shower enclosure.

But he never heard the door lock engage.

Calling firmly on his strictest discipline, Oswald used the cooling cloth to wipe his torso down. Not just the wine, but also the sweat breaking out. The sensation left his heart racing, cock harder than reinforced steel, and his head reeling in confusion. Since he'd taken his first woman to bed, he'd never had such a feeling in his life.

On a deep breath, he forced himself to shrug into Drew's shirt, pick up the necklace, and exit the room. Buttoning as he went, he headed for the kitchen and started the process of making tea. He'd been to the flat often enough he almost felt at home going into the cupboards while the kettle heated. The last tea cup had barely settled on the tray when a key in the front door alerted him to the arrival of Court and Randi. He double checked that the shirt was buttoned, and he had it tucked by the time the couple walked into the kitchen.

Randi rushed over to him and pulled his head down to kiss his cheek. "Thank you for taking care of Birdie. I'm so furious. All I wanted to do was slap that spoiled brat and her friend for putting my daughter through that. Sad to say, but we had to talk to her father like they were in grade school or something. It's also a shame so many people seemed to catch it on their phone cameras, or rather the aftermath."

Green eyes swimming with checked tears and emotions surely only a mother could feel, Randi gazed up at him. How had this tiny woman produced a daughter several inches taller than her? "I only did the right thing," he said.

"Yes, you surely did do the right thing," Court added with a slap to his back. "I'm very proud of how Birdie handled the whole thing and am so grateful to you for ushering her out in the least conspicuous way. However, I'm afraid Randi is right. Pictures are already popping up on social media. I wouldn't be surprised to see it in the tabloids come morning."

Oswald winced. He did his best to stay out of the tabloids, usually showing up only as an accessory to the star of the day. Sort of like a floral arrangement. Part of the scene.

"Where's the locket?" She glanced at the kitchen island. "Oh look, Court, he's already set up the tea." Randi turned her attention to the tray, then reached for two more cups. "Hope you don't mind us barging in, but a cup would settle us as well. Birdie in the shower?"

"Yes. Least I heard the shower turn on while I was knicking a shirt from Drew's closet. Hope you don't mind."

Randi looked over her shoulder enough for him to see her roll her eyes. "Oswald, I keep telling you, you're family. Take what you need. Drew won't miss the shirt, I'm sure. He has more than a few just like it."

So did he, but that wasn't the point. The point was he didn't go around carrying spares in case someone tossed wine on him.

The water came to a boil. "Court, darling, would you look at the locket? I'll take care of this." Randi warmed the teapot with a swish of hot water, added some loose leaves, then filled it with the rest of the boiling water. She added a strainer, then lifted the tray. "How's it look?" She nodded at the now open locket cradled in Court's hand.

Court stood under a bright light looking intently at it. "It looks perfect. Maybe a tiny bit made it in, but not enough to ruin the contents."

Randi let out a huge sigh. "My mom gave it to her right at the end. It's very precious in a sentimental way more than anything else. Birdie has a few other charms, but none mean more than that one."

Court handed the locket to Oswald. "See if your sharper eyes can see something mine can't."

Oswald held a towel and used it to polish the edges of the tiny gold book. The woman in the photo was beautiful, her features more like Randi's than Courtney's. "It looks pretty good to me, but Courtney will be the final judge."

Randi nodded. "Excellent. Let's take this into the living room."

Oswald set the towel-wrapped bit of jewelry on the tray, then took it from her hands and gave her a smile, one she returned with a little smirk.

"Thank you, Oswald. Always such a gentleman." She patted his arm and led the way.

Court went ahead of them into the lounge and switched on the gas fire. Beyond the windows a terrace looked over the city glittering on the other side of the river. Raindrops began to splatter against the wall of glass protecting them from the elements.

Randi snapped her fingers. "Let me see if I can find some cookies to go with this. Be right back."

Oswald set the tea tray down on the coffee table and took a seat in one of the club chairs. No risk of having Courtney sit beside him that way. Across the low table from him, Court leaned back and stretched out his legs, his bowtie undone and dangling from his collar.

"Lord, what a night. I don't think I've ever been involved in such a scene." He ran a hand down his face. "Mind telling me about it? I've only had half explanations."

"I'm convinced it was deliberate."

Randi came back with a plate of biscuits as Oswald went through the event, detailing his suspicions. Court nodded, his face scowling, while Randi's lips drew tight. At the end of the telling, she started pouring.

It was then Courtney came into the room, her long, wet hair combed out, a soft blue robe over hot pink pajamas, and her feet shoved into fuzzy green slippers. The shy smile she gave him reinforced the image of her as being very young. He needed to remember her innocence and treat her as if she were a much younger sister or cousin. No touching.

"Hey," she said softly, and her parents twisted from their seat on the sofa to look around at her.

Randi immediately rose and went to her daughter, wrapping her arms around Courtney's waist. She may have been shorter than her daughter, but there was no mistaking who the mother was as she comforted Courtney.

"I'm fine, Mom. Really. Oswald got me out of there, and now that I've had a shower I feel one hundred percent."

Randi cupped her daughter's cheek with a tiny hand. "I'm proud of you for how you behaved. You came out far and away the better woman in that attempt to draw you into a cat fight. You kept your head up and didn't cry or fight back. It was the perfect response."

Courtney smiled. "Frankly I was in too much shock. Otherwise I would have slapped both of them. Catherine, whoever she is, and Deirdre."

"The tabloids and her father will take care of that for you. No need to drop yourself down to their level." Randi tugged Courtney over to the sofa and plunked her down next to her father before flanking her on the other side. "And both Dad and Oswald looked over the locket. They think it looks undamaged."

The domestic scene was heartrending. Oswald watched as Courtney's parents practically smothered her between them. Randi lifted the necklace from the tray and handed it to her daughter. The three of them bent over the bit of gold and examined it closely.

After a few seconds, Court laughed. "There we go suffocating you. Are you really all right?"

"One ruined dress, a few stains in my hair, pride dented, and locket rescued, but overall, I'm in good shape. It's almost becoming funny. Or it would if it had happened to someone else." Courtney slipped the chain over her head, then took the cup her mother handed her and blew on the hot liquid while first Court and then Oswald accepted their cups.

"Well, you'll have the last laugh. I'm pretty sure the tabloids already have the full story from multiple witnesses. Wouldn't be surprised if they came calling to get your side." Court sipped his tea, then smiled at his wife. "Perfect again, love."

Oswald's heart skipped at little at the pretty blush on Randi's cheeks, and the coy smile she gave her husband. The two of them again made him want the same thing for himself.

Needing distance, he quickly drank his tea and refused the sweet. "It's been a long night, and I'm sure Courtney will want to sleep soon. I'd best be on my way." He stood and set his cup on the tray. "I thank you for the tea. Courtney, I hope we can have a do-over sometime. In fact, I know of several balls coming up. I'll let you choose which ones you want to attend, and I'll make sure no wild wine lands on you."

They all chuckled and rose.

Courtney set her cup down. "Let me get your jacket for you. Or better yet, leave your shirt and jacket, and I'll make sure they're returned to you cleaned."

"No worries. I'll take them along with me now. I have a pile for the dry cleaner already. And the shirt is probably beyond redemption."

Randi spoke up. "We'll see about that. I have a few tricks up my sleeve.

With nothing left to say, Oswald nodded, accepted Court's handshake, and promised to see them in the office on Monday.

Chapter 16

Unfortunately, Birdie thought the next morning, the annoying news about the tabloids was dead-on. Embarrassing pictures of her with wine streaming down her face appeared on more than one website, along with accounts from witnesses. Fortunately, Catherine and Deirdre came off the worst in the comments.

So far so good for Birdie.

Not good for Deirdre's charity.

Birdie knew that much from the two extravagant flower arrangements and hand written apologies that arrived the next day along with dozens of phone calls to Court. He stood firm in that he'd find another organization to take his check for refugee relief. Birdie penned a reply to both Catherine and Deirdre that the apologies were accepted and left it at that.

After spying the street filled with paparazzi, they chose to have a quiet day in. Her mother filled it with pictures of gowns for the two dozen or so events Birdie would have to attend before Christmas. And since her parents would be home for the holidays, her mother promised they'd go shopping for more dresses then.

"Mom, when did we turn into ladies who shop and lunch?" Birdie teased her.

Mom sighed. "I know. It's so different from how we used to live, and I don't do it nearly as much as the other women in the circles we now travel in. I've even worn the same dress to more than one event." With a gasp of mock horror, she held a hand over her heart. "I'm a real disgrace around here." Giggling, she rolled her eyes. "Your father doesn't really care one way or the other, but he does insist I usually wear something recognizable as designer couture. Otherwise, he leaves it up to me."

Shaking her head, Birdie bent back to the computer with the intent of discovering a designer she liked.

"I'll set up an appointment with a stylist," Mom said. "It will save us time."

"Great." Birdie only wished she felt more enthusiasm.

The next morning when she and her father left the building for their usual walk to work, Birdie was relieved to see only a couple cameras pointed their direction.

"Is it crazy like this very often?" she asked.

Dad shook his head. "There's usually someone far more interesting stirring up scandal somewhere else. I've never even made the front page." He smiled down at her. "As horrible as it was, you still looked like a lady in those pictures. I'm pretty proud of you, puddin'."

Birdie wrapped her hand around his arm, just like a lady being escorted by her knight. "I'm glad Ozzie was at my back. He didn't give me time to behave badly. Given another minute, I might have chased her down and slapped her around a few times. Ozzie caught her first, then wrapped me in his jacket. He's the one who called them on their little scheme, then got me out of there. He was in control the entire time when all I wanted to do was slap someone, then sink through the floor."

"Oswald has a good head in a crisis." Dad's eyes twinkled at her. "I tried to keep your mum away longer, but she was worried and wanted to rush right home."

"No reason for you to stay away from your home."

"Our home." The correction was gentle, but firm nonetheless.

"Right. Our home." They walked a few more steps in silence. "I guess, with you two taking off, it would be silly for me to look for my own flat."

"It would, but I'd also understand. There's something about having your own place when you're just starting out. A real declaration of independence. A chance to prove you can stand on your own two feet."

"Exactly. But then again, with you two taking off around the world, and leaving your flat empty, it doesn't make sense for me to spend money on my own place."

"Whatever you want. Of course you know your mum will want to help you get your place set up. Bet she did it when you moved into the dorms the first time. And I know she did it when you and Drew moved into the apartment off campus."

Birdie nodded. "And with departure imminent, she doesn't have time to help me find a place and get moved in."

"Very true. So, although I understand your desire for your own flat, I'd prefer it if you stayed in ours. At least until Christmas."

Birdie nodded. "It will give me time to look around and be choosy." And save up her own money to pay for it. Although the folks were generous with the cash, it felt important to set up her own space with her own wages, which were also generous. Surely more than a normal intern would make.

"Whew." He pretended to wipe sweat from his brow, then grinned at her. "That takes a load off my mind. I'll let her know. She hasn't said anything to you, but I know she's been worrying about it."

Birdie laughed. "Got to love her."

"Yes, yes we do." The dreamy look on his face said it all. Courtland Robinson was as giddy as a school boy in love. For the first time, Birdie considered that was exactly the kind of love she wanted for herself.

Once she made it to the mailroom, the teasing, and the dark looks, started. Several issues of the tabloids, all showing the same scene from many angles, were scattered about. Even Dennis was reading one when she walked in.

"Funny, guys."

That cracked up most of them.

"Look what 'appens when you try to move onto their turf," one girl said. Since she was dressed in all black with several painful looking piercings, Birdie didn't take her too seriously, just kept her head down, doing her sorting.

Later when she checked in with Dennis, he said, "You made them look like spiteful bitches, which I guess they are. Good on you, but watch yer back."

"I plan to," Birdie said. "Anything special to add to the first delivery?"

"Nah. But I notice you didn't bring any of those cinnamon buns today." Dennis cocked a wizened hair brow at her.

"Didn't feel much like cooking yesterday." She shrugged and was about to turn away when he stopped her with a hand on her forearm.

"Stay true to you," he said. "You're more a lady than either of them will ever be, title or no."

It was the kindest thing he'd ever said to her, and she had to blink back a sudden rush of tears. "Thanks, Mr. Redford. My mom never believed in playing the social games. Guess I don't, either."

"It's Dennis to you, young lady. Just stay true and you'll come out smelling of roses rather than wine."

"Thanks." She meant it from the bottom of her heart.

The sensation blew over quickly, Dennis got his treats, and before she knew it her parents were headed out the door with their luggage, bound for Europe. She had their itinerary posted on the bulletin board in the kitchen, and she moved from the mailroom to the accounting department. Now she was much more firmly under the tutelage of Oswald. He'd introduced her to the department head and outlined the steps she'd take, starting with filing shipping documents.

Before he left her there, he took her aside. "Dinner tonight? To celebrate having the flat to yourself? Or were you planning on dancing naked from one end to the other?" The way his eyes twinkled belied the blank expression he held with seemingly no trouble.

"I was planning to cook something decadent. You're welcome to join me." There was a giddiness already inside her at the thought of being alone in a high rise flat overlooking the Thames. She'd been growing accustomed to her father's style of living, something far beyond what she'd grown up with. At times her mother still had a little trouble adjusting to the luxury of a housekeeper and cook, something that came in handy while she long-distance trained and worked with the accounting department she'd left behind in California. Grandpa wasn't ready to let her cut her ties to his business just yet, so Mom didn't always have time to cook. And she was always happy to leave housecleaning to someone else, not that Birdie would argue with her about it.

Oswald nodded. "Red or white wine? Or have you sworn off wine for now?" A hint of laughter lightened his face.

"Oh bring a good red. Something that will go with steak. I asked the housekeeper to find some filet mignons while doing the shopping. I plan to be most decadent for a few days at least. Then I'm sure it will all settle down into a dull, very quiet routine."

"Will do. I love a good piece of beef." With that, he turned and headed for the elevator and his own office. With Dad on the road, Oswald's tasks had more than doubled and she doubted she'd see much of him.

"Seven o'clock," she called after him.

Without turning around, he raised a hand in acknowledgement.

At the clearing of a throat, Birdie turned to smile at Abigail Smith, her new supervisor for the time being. "Ready to get started."

"Excellent, Miss Robinson."

"I'm happy to go by Courtney."

"Very well, let me show you the file room."

* * * *

Oswald straightened his tie before knocking on the door to the Robinson flat. The bottle in his hand was a very pricey bottle of Bordeaux. As a woman raised on California wines, he hoped she appreciated it.

The door opened and Courtney stood there with a shy smile. "Come on in," she said, barely loud enough to be heard over the crazy laugh and the opening strains of "Crazy Train."

Oswald smiled at the taunt, even as he noticed she'd changed from the plain skirt and blouse she'd worn to work that day. Instead she wore a lemon colored sundress currently covered by an apron. Her feet were bare, her hair in a messy knot high on her head, only a small amount of barely there makeup on her face. Every time he saw her she looked more beautiful. What the hell was he doing here? Why had he asked her about her dinner plans? Why hadn't she accepted his invite to go out? He ran a hand through his hair as if he could clear his mind. Coming here was a bad idea.

"The grill is nearly hot enough," she said stepping back to allow him in. "Dad had one installed on the terrace last summer."

Oswald had heard about it multiple times. Had even had some good meals Court had cooked on it. Well, the meat portion. As Randi reminded him, she'd been responsible for the salad, the sides, and the desserts. Hardly a night off from cooking for her. One American tradition that had found its way across the pond.

"It's nice enough I figured we'd eat outside," she said over her shoulder, leading him deeper into the flat. The sliding doors to the terrace stood wide open. He could see the outside table was set.

"What can I do to help?"

"Open the wine and bring it out. Might as well lose the jacket and tie while you're at it," she said with a smile. "Roll up those sleeves, and we'll kick back like we're in California."

Oswald chuckled. "Can do." He set the wine on the island and unknotted his tie.

Birdie made a stop at the audio center and adjusted the volume down a little. "Just a little rock to get us started on relaxing."

"It's good. I like metal. I like all kinds of rock."

Birdie gave him a look of shock, accompanied by the Robinson raised brow. "The man has hidden depths. And here I thought I'd have to introduce you to something beyond baroque."

Oswald tugged off his tie, rolled it up, and stuffed it into a pocket before shrugging off his jacket and hanging it on the back of a bar stool.

"I like many kinds of music. Baroque helps me concentrate on work better is all. On my own time I've been known to do a little head-banging."

"Well then, seems my music mix will be just fine tonight." She sauntered back to the kitchen and picked up a platter with two bacon wrapped filets and a pair of tongs. "The wineglasses are on the table. If you could just grab that bread basket and follow me…"

He also picked up the wine opener on the counter.

Like her nickname, Birdie, she chatted lightly through the cooking of the steaks, then through dinner. He felt himself relaxing in her presence, something that didn't happen often. Maybe the bottle of wine helped. Maybe it was the conversation. She was all on about London, asking questions about the surrounding area, where to live, where to go on a spare afternoon if one wanted to see something more than the usual tourist spots. She never mentioned clothes, or gossip about who was doing what or whom. She asked about the countryside and the various places he'd traveled. Although she kept sending him shy looks, the conversation never faltered.

Neither did his unruly libido.

Oh, he'd answered her questions, learned a little more about her—she loved lemon curd and Scottish shortbread—and what she wanted to do at Lynford. She wanted to save up and be able to travel more, getting a feel for the countryside, maybe find her own little cottage to buy. But she also wanted to get out and about London more. The museums, art galleries, a club or two where she could dance. And friends. She wanted to make friends.

"I know I can't really look for friends at work, but since I didn't grow up here, didn't go to school here, I've missed those opportunities." The little slice of loneliness in her voice just about gutted him. Although he had gone to school, grown up here, he still experienced loneliness on a depth she'd probably never encountered before. But he thrived in loneliness. Courtney was a social creature and needed the whirlwind of many friends to keep her energy up. In fact, he should choose another social event for them to attend. Something other than hitting the club scene.

"Have you considered joining a club of some sort? Ballroom dancing lessons? Hanging out at a bookstore? Painting or music lessons? You'd meet people there."

Birdie wrinkled her nose most adorably. "Something more active. You do martial arts, correct?"

"Yes." Surprised, he tilted his head and regarded her with a raised brow. "Are you interested?"

She sipped the last of the wine in her glass, carefully devoting all her attention to it, her eyes definitely not looking his way. "I've considered it. Any recommendations for a beginner?"

"I know a few senseis who would be good to work with." Put his name at the top of the list.

"I don't want to embarrass myself. Think you could show me a few moves to see if I have any talent for it before committing to do it in front of a room full of strangers?" She gazed out across the river. A breeze blew a strand of long golden hair across her face, and she gently removed it with a graceful hand. He could see through her fragile veil of indifference. The pulse beating at the base of her throat and the slight pinking of the tips of her ears gave her away.

"I could do that." He too feigned a casual attitude when all he could think of was tussling with her on the mats of his workout room. Physical, indeed. "I have a room in my house dedicated to working out. We could do it Friday night after work."

Finally she turned her blue gaze on him. "That would be great. I take it yoga pants and a T-shirt would do as workout gear?"

He nodded. He'd seen her in just such an outfit and looked forward to seeing it again. In fact, he'd already held her in his arms while she wore it. The next time there wouldn't be chaperones around when he wrapped his arms around her. In the name of teaching, of course.

"Right. Friday night works," she said with a firm nod. "Go straight from the office?"

"Bring a bag with a change of clothes and we'll be set. I'll feed you dinner after."

Courtney smiled at him, brilliant and blinding. His breath stilled in his lungs for a long moment.

The sun dipped behind a building, sending the terrace into shade, and he saw Courtney shiver. The warmth had gone the way of the sun as a breeze raced down the river.

"Let me help you get the dishes inside." He stood, then helped her push back her chair.

"Thanks. We can do coffee, or tea, inside."

Between the two of them they gathered the dishes and toted everything into the kitchen. The utter domesticity of sharing such a mundane chore with a woman was far more thrilling than he'd ever imagined.

"If you'd go secure the cover on the grill," Courtney said, "I'll get the dishwasher loaded."

There was no extra food to put away. Everything she'd made had been perfectly proportioned and exquisitely tasty. Steak wrapped in bacon, topped with Stilton crumbles, baked potato, tossed green salad. Basic food, standard American steakhouse menu, but still better than anything he'd ever tasted along those lines before.

The cover went on the grill easily enough, and he'd just entered the kitchen when the in-house phone rang.

"You expecting anyone?" he asked.

Birdie shook her head as she finished drying her hands. "Only you."

"Want me to answer?"

"Sure." She gave him a brilliant smile.

The phone buzzed again, and Oswald lifted the receiver. His greeting was met with silence and then a chuckle he recognized.

"Larry? What are you doing here?"

"I was going to ask you the same, my dear boy," his uncle replied. "I can see neither of us wanted to leave Birdie on her own tonight."

"It's always an adjustment. Want to come up?"

"Not if it's going to cramp your style. I'll take my carton of cookie dough ice cream home with me."

Hell yes it would cramp his style, but Larry as a chaperone was probably a very good thing right now. Oswald was thinking thoughts, imagining things he shouldn't. More than once he'd wanted to drag Courtney's chair over to him and pull her into his lap. He didn't want ice cream; he wanted Courtney's cream for dessert.

Courtney's hand landed on Oswald's shoulder. "Larry?"

"He has ice cream," Oswald said.

A wide smile brightened her face again. "Let him come up."

Of course she couldn't say no to ice cream. "Come up. She's already getting the bowls out."

Sounding particularly pleased with himself, Larry responded, "On my way."

Oswald hung up, cracked open the door a bit, enough he wouldn't have to wait for the knock, then followed Courtney back into the kitchen.

"Coffee or tea?" she asked him.

"With ice cream, coffee."

"Right. Half caf, it is then."

Half caf. The woman needed some schooling, but not tonight. It was like saying half-hard, a state no man wanted to suffer. All or nothing, and he didn't want to be sporting a full-on right now.

"What can I do to help?"

By the time Larry let himself in, the coffee maker was gurgling out the last stream. The bowls and spoons were out, the cream and sugar on the dining room table, and something along the lines of mellow rock played from the speakers.

The intimate setting allowed Larry to tell the stories Oswald preferred to keep private. Like a proud parent, Larry rolled out the stories of Oswald's early days living with his uncle. The stories of scrapes at school. The academic and sporting awards. The first social events and the sometimes disasters as Oswald learned the ways of a different world from what he'd known.

Courtney laughed and cooed in the right places. Sometimes he'd look up from his coffee to see her gaze firmly on him. He also was privileged to see a softer side of her. The one that reminded him of her mother. At the thought of Courtney round with child or rocking an infant in her arms, his heart pinched. Why she wanted to run the company, he didn't know. She was far more suited to being a wife and mother. And wasn't that sexist of him, he who claimed to be a feminist? Let a woman set her own course, and all that. Girl power, rah-rah-rah.

At last Courtney delicately hid a huge yawn. "I'm terribly sorry. It's not the company."

Oswald glanced at his wristwatch. "It's the hour. We're going on midnight here."

"And oh how the hours flew by," she said. "Thank you both for the company this evening. I really wasn't quite sure what to do with myself, to tell you the truth."

Larry reached over and patted her hand. "We're here anytime you need company. I promised Court I'd check up on you from time to time. And if you ever need an escort to an event, consider me among your list of available arm candy. I'll understand if you pick the lad first."

Oswald rolled his eyes. Like he'd give his uncle a chance to be Courtney's escort anywhere. Only, he supposed, if he had to be out of town, Larry would be better than half a dozen men he could think of.

"Which reminds me, there's a horse racing thing this weekend," Oswald found himself saying. He originally hadn't planned to attend, but what the hell. "It's King George weekend, very fancy, two days. Held at Ascot. You'll need an appropriate outfit for each day, complete with hat."

Courtney's eyes crossed adorably. "Mom hired a stylist to help me. I'm sure I'll come up with something fascinating to wear. That's assuming jeans, T-shirt, and cowboy boots aren't appropriate."

Larry managed to get a napkin in front of his face before spewing coffee everywhere. "I'd pay you twenty-thousand just to see that. Can you impersonate a rodeo queen?"

Now Courtney laughed. "No, sorry, only once had cowgirl boots growing up. I was quite little when they took me to a rodeo. It wasn't something we did often."

"Ah well, it's a good fantasy," Larry said. "Maybe next time I visit California we can take one in. Live like the wild west for an afternoon." He stood and stretched. "These late nights are finally getting to me. Growing old isn't for the meek, I tell you."

Oswald shared an eye roll with Courtney. "You aren't old, Larry."

"That's what you think. Well, I'm off. Be good, chooks."

Courtney was smiling as they cleared dishes once more and the front door closed behind Larry.

"Chooks. Chicks, right? As in baby chicks?"

"Or just chickens, but yeah, basically."

"I've heard it often enough, just never really took the time to figure it out."

Courtney finished putting the few dishes in the machine and reached for a towel to dry her hands.

"So, an Ascot weekend? Sounds like fun. What do I need to know?"

"I'd suggest flat sandals."

"Right. Long day, walking on grass, picnic?"

"Yes, but it's fun to people watch. Might see royals and celebrities, if you're interested in such things."

"Who doesn't want to get a look at Harry up close?" She winked at him. "Although gingers aren't quite my thing."

The temptation was too great to resist. He backed her against the bench and trapped her there with a hand on each side of her. "What is your thing?"

The look she gave him was direct. "It seems to be tall, reserved, Englishmen who wear glasses. Very hot."

Oh he was hot all right. "Hmm, and I seem to have developed a thing for innocent young women with blonde hair, blue eyes, and golden tans."

Courtney laughed. "That's at least the third time someone commented on my California tan. Something that is already fading away. Soon I'll be as pale as anyone here."

"No, you'll always be golden."

"Are you...will you..." Courtney cleared her throat and looked down with a pretty pink flush warming her cheeks. "Ah, that is to say..." She blushed deeper.

"What? You can ask me anything."

She reached out a hand and toyed with one of the buttons on his shirt. "I don't know how to ask this question without sounding like an idiot."

Oswald moved closer, his body touching hers. "Ask me."

Once more she cleared her throat. "Are you planning on...oh hell..." She cast her gaze heavenward, drew in a deep breath, then looked down again, both hands now fiddling with the button. "Are you staying tonight?" The words rushed out of her as she stared at his throat.

The air stalled in his chest. Oh how he wanted to stay. His memory immediately began replaying the night of her brother's wedding. Courtney on the bed. Naked. Ready for him. Crooking her finger, calling him to her...

But no, he wouldn't do that. Not tonight. Not any night soon.

"I want to," he said quietly. He touched her chin with a finger and gently lifted until her gaze met his. "I want to very much, but no. I'm not staying tonight. There are so many reasons why I can't. Won't. I don't know how long I can hold out, but right now, I can't. I shouldn't have touched you in San Francisco as it was."

She lowered her eyelids and a tiny moue of disappointment graced her lips. "Okay. I just wasn't sure if that's why you hung back. I mean, after that night, I thought..."

"I know. And right now I want to," he repeated. "I can't tell you how much. But not tonight, Courtney. I owe your family too much to jump on you the second you're left alone. I've sworn to be your protector, your mentor, and that's a pretty big vow. I won't dishonor it, or you, by taking advantage. There are so many other reasons, but I won't list them now." Maybe he needed to list them to remind himself.

When she tried to turn away from him, he stopped her by cupping her cheek. "Oh Courtney, there's so much more for you to learn. You're just starting and you deserve the right to have fun and explore your world. I'm here to help you do that safely. I'll do better than I did at the refugee event, I promise. That has to be enough. For both of us."

"I'm not a little girl, Ozzie. You're my mentor at work, but I'd hoped you'd be my friend outside of it." A trace of hurt lingered in her eyes with a healthy dose of confusion. He hated that look, but knew she had so much to learn, see, do before he could let her choose him. As, he strongly suspected, he'd already chosen her. Most unwisely.

"I know you're not a little girl, but this world is very new to you. I'd be doing you a disservice by not letting you experience it your way."

She pinched his side. "Then let me choose my way without the patronizing words."

She had a point, but it was all the defense he had right now. By keeping her innocence in mind, hopefully he could keep his distance. Remember why he needed to.

"Kiss me good night and I'll be on my way." He lowered his lips to hers and let himself indulge once more, losing a bit more of his self control as she eagerly met him halfway.

Chapter 17

Bemused, and more than a little frustrated, Birdie enjoyed the kiss, then walked Oswald to the door. He backed her into the wall and kissed her again, leaving her wilted and breathless when he told her to secure the door behind him. His footsteps didn't move away until she'd set the locks. She stayed there, ear to the door, listening until she heard the elevator doors close and begin to move downward.

He'd warmed her up, then walked away. Okay, so it had been obvious he did so reluctantly, but still. He'd left. And that hurt a little, along with intriguing her.

Quiet, stern, stiff Oswald wasn't nearly so stuffy as she'd assumed. The man had layers, as evidenced by Larry's stories and their conversation over dinner.

And now she had two dates with him. Friday night to learn a little self defense, and races at Ascot over the weekend. She'd have to look that up on the internet, but not tonight.

She set the alarm, turned out lights, and headed for bed wondering what her parents would say if she adopted a cat. A living, breathing creature to keep her company. Maybe then she wouldn't beg Ozzie to spend the night. She drifted off dreaming of curling around Ozzie like a cat purring in satisfaction.

The next day she woke feeling flustered and frustrated, a feeling she tried to dispel on her brisk walk to the offices and buried under a mountain of filing.

On her lunch hour she called the stylist and made an appointment to meet at Harrod's. Dad had left her with a handful of credit cards and told her to use them to fill out her wardrobe, decorate her room, or eat out as her heart desired. She also had a car, a sporty little SUV, she could easily maneuver around town or drive out to the country house as she wished.

While nibbling at the salad she'd brought from home to eat, she contemplated her current social life. What she didn't have were local friends. The ones she had on Facebook all seemed so distant now.

What she needed was a girlfriend to hang out with. She'd had a few friends in college, more in high school, but she didn't know anyone here as of yet. If Deirdre and her posse were who she was supposed to befriend, then London was going to get lonely. Maybe Ozzie would introduce her around more over the race weekend. Surely there were nice people who attended the social events it seemed she was now expected to show up at. If only Mom and Dad had stayed around another month...

No, another month of them in town wouldn't have helped much. They were now in France, heading for Belgium, and the Netherlands, passing through Germany toward Denmark, before winding their way through Poland, crisscrossing Germany, then back into France and Paris. They had a twisty itinerary they were following, including Austria, Italy, Spain, and Portugal. They'd be home for Thanksgiving and Christmas, as would Meilin and Drew, before heading into Greece and Turkey. From there they'd hit South Africa and a few of the countries on that continent. India, Australia, New Zealand, Indonesia, and the South Pacific were also part of their plans. They'd promised to fly her to China for a mini family reunion there.

Of course, still being the new kid at work, Birdie couldn't afford more than a one week vacation sometime next spring. She had a ladder to climb, things to learn, and part of not being pegged as Daddy's girl meant she had to concentrate on work and not be gadding about the world.

Reminded of work, she glanced at the clock and noted she had ten minutes left to her lunch break. Enough for a trip to the loo and refill of her coffee cup.

A part of her was irritated that her family all got to bounce around the world, but the bigger part of her knew if she was ever to be taken seriously at work, she had to do her best and learn everything she could.

At the end of what felt like an endless day, she stopped at home for a quick dinner and accepted a call from her grandmother.

"I'm in town," Gran announced. "I hear you're headed for King George Weekend at Ascot. I'm going as well. Do you know what you're wearing?"

"Meeting the stylist in an hour."

"Harrod's, of course."

"Of course."

"I'll meet you there. One hour you say?"

"Yes."

"Better yet, I'll pick you up. Be downstairs in forty-five." The phone went dead.

"Love you too, Gran." Birdie grinned and dug into the chicken casserole she'd found in the fridge. Cook had made her several in single portion containers, each one clearly labeled and stored in the freezer. If she didn't want to, she didn't have to cook for the next two weeks.

Being picked up by Gran meant riding in a Bentley with a driver. Martin as it turned out.

"Miss," he said, while holding the door for her.

She gave him a cheeky grin and climbed in the back with the cranky old lady she adored.

"Any idea what you want? Where are your seats?"

"Clueless, Gran. Ozzie merely said he'd pick me up Saturday morning. Wear flats and something I could sit on a blanket in, if we choose to have a picnic."

"Nonsense. My box has room for the two of you," she said. "Tell him you'll be joining me. Still, flat sandals, or something with a square or wedge heel, would be a smart idea if you go down to the paddocks."

"Of course. Shall I text him now?"

"Yes. We'll also tell him the color of your dresses once we have them picked out so he can match his tie." Gran gave her a long look. "The weather is supposed to be sunny, so maybe a sundress so you can get some of your tan back. You should be sitting on the terrace as much as you can. Winter white will come soon enough. Maybe the weekend after we'll go down to the house and get some sun there."

Birdie made a non-committal hum. The idea had possibilities, but that didn't leave room for going out dancing. Oswald didn't seem like the type to go clubbing, so maybe she'd have to touch base with Phillip after all. That was more his scene.

By the time the store began closing, Birdie had three outfits, complete with matching hats, handbags, and shoes. The third was a spare in case of an accident, or could be used for another weekend. Surely someone would get married before summer's end. Oswald also had photos of the dress colors, but not Birdie in the dresses. Gran declared that was a surprise for him.

"Tomorrow night we'll go shopping again. You'll need something for the fall."

"Gran, Mom promised we'd have time to shop when she gets home. I don't think I need to prepare that far in advance."

"Girl, you can never have too many clothes. I understand your work choices, but when out in social situations, you must dress better. I saw those awful photos from the fundraiser."

"I liked that dress, very much." Gran dissing her dress didn't sit well with Birdie.

"I'm sure it was lovely before its bath in wine." The older woman sniffed. "And while I'm not thrilled with today's fashion of using so little cloth, I must admit you carry it well. Still, a little more taste would go a long way."

"Yes, ma'am."

"Don't sass me." The laser blue gaze was directed at her through narrowed eyelids. "Now, do you have everything you need in the flat? Are you set?"

"I'm very well set, Gran. I have food, clean laundry at my fingertips, a housekeeper to do the chores, and more movies than I can count to keep me entertained. I also have a library of both print and ebooks to keep me curled up in a cozy chair for twenty years. What I don't have are friends to hang out with."

"Oh, well, I can help with that."

At Birdie's raised eyebrow, Gran shook her head. "My friends have granddaughters who love to hit the clubs and 'hang out' as you call it. They're much nicer than Miss Portman-Wright and her crowd, while still being fashionable. You'll meet many of them this weekend."

If only. Well, it was worth a shot.

The next night Gran again took her shopping. Birdie found three hats she adored, followed by dinner. Dad was going to notice when the credit card statement arrived. The night was, however, informative and she had a better idea of what to expect from the weekend. At least Gran had no shortage of stories about past races and who had been the best and least well behaved. She thoroughly approved of Wills, Kate, and Harry. Of course the Queen was above reproach. She made no comment on Charles and Camilla.

Before bed that night, because of the race weekend, Oswald called with the suggestion they move their training night to Thursday. The very next night.

"So you'll be well rested for the weekend. Days at Ascot can be long and tiring," he explained.

Since Birdie had no other plans, she agreed. Excitement got her through the long day spent in the filing room. Once five o'clock rolled around, she grabbed her purse and a tote stuffed with new yoga pants and a sports bra she intended to wear as a top. Of course she had a T-shirt and jeans to wear home.

Oswald was on the phone in his office when she knocked and entered. He held up a finger. She got it. He'd be done in a minute. She dropped her tote and purse near the door.

With his sexy accent in the background, she looked around his office. Sure, she'd been in here, but she'd never stayed long enough to really look. Like her dad's office, it had a wall of windows that overlooked the river and the far bank. Unlike her father's office, his furnishings were much more in keeping with the modern theme of the building. Chrome and frosted glass desk. Matching credenza behind him with a sculpture and a speaker designed to hold an iPod or MP3 player. Currently silent. A sleek laptop rested to his left on the desktop, but few papers littered it. Phone to the right. Efficient.

And Ozzie sitting in a large executive, black leather chair, looked exactly right in the room. Today he wore black trousers, white shirt, blue tie, his leather shoes polished to a high shine. Even his shirt still looked crisply starched. She looked forward to the day she could go home without dust or toner ink on her clothes. Or papercuts on her fingers, and mascara smudged beneath her eyes.

Not much of his personality filled the space. No personal photos, no awards or trophies. A black leather and chrome sofa with a matching glass and chrome coffee table sat off to one side. Across from it some low black lacquered bookcases. On top of one sat a tea service with a small coffee maker and a stark modern sculpture in white marble. An obelisk, about twelve inches high. She placed a hand on it, feeling the cold, smooth surface. A few black framed pieces of unidentifiable modern art hung from steel cables mounted to the ceiling, since it was pretty hard to hang pictures on frosted glass walls held in place by crisscrossed steel beams. The floor was gray and white marble with the only soft feature in the room, a large Persian rug in muted tones of gray and white, covering the center.

Overall, the effect was cold and stiff. Much like Ozzie presented himself to the world.

Only she was getting to know him better. He wasn't always Mr. Stiff and Proper. He could be improper when properly motivated. Maybe tonight some of that propriety would slip.

Then again, she wouldn't mind him stiff like the sculpture under her hand. He could laugh and be passionate when he wanted. Did he only loosen up with champagne and a private room? Would he loosen up tonight while teaching her a few basic moves?

A vision of Ozzie teaching her how to pin him to the mats certainly piqued her sense of intrigue.

At the sound of Ozzie clearing his throat she realized he was no longer on the phone. She turned, hand still on the sculpture, to see him watching her.

"Like marble, do you?" he asked. The question was mild enough, but the intensity blazing from behind the lenses of his glasses spoke of his interest in her hand stroking the obelisk.

Abruptly embarrassed, she pulled her hand away as if it had just turned to super heated metal. "Oh. Um, no, not particularly. It…just…" She sighed and moved away from it. No, she wasn't going to think of how it had looked. Her burning cheeks were enough. As was the amused expression on Ozzie's face. "So, uh, you ready to go?"

Ozzie rocked back in his chair and folded his hands over his stomach. "Actually, right now I want you to bring that thing over to my desk and fondle it some more."

Birdie spun away and headed for the door and her bags. There. See? Ozzie could leap over his walls and play the perv just like any other man. The action also hid her super hot face.

"I'm ready to go, are you ready?" She asked the question without turning. It was a good opportunity to bend and retrieve her bags.

Ozzie's quiet chuckle floated across the room. "I might need another minute."

"I'll wait outside." She tugged open the door and stepped into the reception area, tote and purse slung over her shoulder.

"Now that's just a damn shame," Ozzie said behind her.

How had he moved so fast? A second ago he'd been seated at his desk and now here he was, beside her, reaching for his suit jacket and shrugging it on. She glanced back as he locked his door.

"Want me to carry the larger bag?"

"No, I've got it." Although maybe she'd offer to let him carry her purse. Almost as if he'd read her mind he shook his head.

"Come on," he said. "I've got my car in the garage."

Birdie followed him to the elevators. Lifts. Whatever. Although her co-workers gently teased her about her Americanisms, she was determined to hang on to them. It wasn't like her accent would change anytime soon. Maybe slowly, but she'd always stick out as American. No use fighting it.

When a car came, Ozzie stepped back to allow her and a few other people to board first. Since they were headed for the garage level below the building, she braced herself in a back corner. Ozzie stood just in front of her, chatting with a man she recognized from Marketing.

Two floors down when the car stopped, Birdie's supervisor, Mrs. Smith, stepped on.

"Garage please," she said to Ozzie who stood at the panel. "Oh, already selected. Excellent." She then noticed Birdie. "Good evening, Courtney. Thought you'd left already?" The older woman raised a dark brow in inquiry.

"Had to pick up something on my way out."

"Have fun plans for this evening?" The woman's eyes went to the tote bag over Birdie's shoulder.

"Taking in a workout."

"Oh? Aerobics? A spin class?"

"Something along the lines of self-defense. If I'm going to sweat, figure I might as well learn something useful at the same time."

"God forbid you ever need it." Mrs. Smith shifted closer to her as three more people boarded at a lower level.

"I hope not, but just in case, makes sense to be prepared, right?" Birdie looked up at the number flashing downward. Ten floors to go. "You have fun plans?"

Mrs. Smith laughed a little. It was the first time Birdie had seen her smile. "Oh big plans. Nag teens into doing homework, cook dinner, and then if I'm lucky, a little laundry and watching the telly. Might even toss in an argument with the spouse."

"Sounds like a familiar routine." Birdie smiled at her. "Only I was the one getting nagged into doing the chores."

"Not so sure it's better from the other side. Enjoy your single status while you can." Mrs. Smith's expression grew wistful. "Parents enjoying their trip?"

"Mom's relaxing a bit. Only called once today. She's really trying to respect working hours." Birdie had seen the looks when her phone buzzed on vibrate in the middle of the workday. Personal calls were frowned on when there was work to be done. No one had said a word, but the expectation was still clear. Even if her dad was the CEO. She still had to conform to the office etiquette. Her mom really did understand that, but now Birdie was alone in London, rather than safely tucked away on a college campus, Mom worried just a little more. And it was the kids who were supposed to get separation anxiety.

Mrs. Smith sighed. "Well, I see it from both sides. I suppose we can make an allowance for your mum."

Birdie gave her a tiny smile. "This time she wanted to know how much Belgium chocolate to send home. I told her to send enough to share."

Mrs. Smith looked at her with another raised brow and definite amusement in her expression. "Well then. Talk to your mother as much as you like, Miss Robinson."

In front of her Ozzie coughed. Oh yeah, he was listening. As was everyone else in the elevator car.

It was probably her own paranoid imagination, but it seemed a little awkward when those remaining in the elevator, after dumping half the load on the ground floor, filed out into the garage. Mrs. Smith and the Marketing guy particularly noticed when Birdie followed Ozzie to his car parked only a few spaces away from the elevator. He had use of Dad's CEO reserved spot while Dad was gone. The fact Ozzie opened the passenger door for her, further emphasized whatever it was flashing through those other two minds. If only she'd asked him for an address in order to meet him there.

Ozzie climbed in the driver side and reached for his seatbelt as she clicked hers into place. "Where are we going, anyway?"

"We'll use the workout room at my place. Figure it will be easier to get your first lesson out of the way there."

"You mean less embarrassing for me that way?"

Ozzie's smile was small and a little crooked. "Something like that."

Birdie snorted and watched out the window as he navigated the garage and out onto the streets crammed with rush hour traffic.

"Damn, I always forget how busy the streets are just after five," he muttered.

"That's right, you usually leave later. Come in earlier too? How many hours a day do you typically work?"

"Oh anywhere from twelve to fourteen, depending what's going on. Makes it easier to stay in touch with folks around the world."

"Isn't that what e-mail is for? Send a message, have an answer back the next day?"

"Sometimes communication needs to be faster than that."

"I suppose." True, she'd seen her dad up at two in the morning talking with India or Australia. Even touching base with London when he was in California.

"Mobile phones and laptops help with some of that, but sometimes I just need to be in the office at odd hours." Ozzie's fingers tapped on the steering wheel while waiting for the light to change.

"How far away do you live?"

"Not far. I have a terrace house. You might call it a townhouse. Narrow, tall, no garden, but the whole place is mine. I got one that hadn't yet been broken up into two flats. The workout room is in the basement."

"I'm most curious." She truly was. Mainly because she wanted to check out the various areas around the office where she might consider moving after Christmas. Now was as good a time as any to start looking around.

It took twenty minutes for Ozzie to maneuver onto his very narrow street. On the right side the houses were plainer, red brick with brightly painted doors. Both sides had wrought iron fencing keeping people from falling down the stairs to the basement level.

"Not very wide, are they?" She commented more than asked the question.

"Two windows wide, four levels total."

On the left side of the street the individual homes were no wider, but they were white with columns holding up small porticos covering a slightly deeper walkway to the front doors.

"In case I haven't mentioned it, I'm sort of keeping an eye out for a place of my own. I'm dying to see the inside."

Ozzie gave her a long look. "I can either help you look or put you in touch with a good agent." With minimum fuss he parallel parked on the side with fancier white homes.

"I'm looking to rent, not buy."

"Doesn't matter. Someone with neighborhood knowledge is invaluable."

Birdie released her seatbelt. The front of Ozzie's house was unadorned other than the white columns, unlike some of his neighbors who had green thumbs and somehow had managed to turn planters into lush green mini gardens. She climbed from the car onto the sidewalk and slung her bags over her shoulder.

Ozzie shut the car door, then led her to the front door of his home. "I've only been here about a year, so there's not much inside."

"Doesn't matter. I've seen a bachelor pad or two in my time."

Ozzie merely glanced at her as he turned the key and swung the door open. "Enter and look around. There's a loo down the hall a bit if you want to change."

"Thanks."

He wasn't kidding about there not being much in the way of furnishings. This floor had a small sitting room, the half bath tucked under narrow stairs, and she could see a small kitchen at the back. The sitting room had a couple black leather club chairs and a large flat screen TV. A small table sat between the chairs facing the TV. No artwork on the walls.

"I'll be down in a minute. Just need to change out of the suit."

For some reason, Birdie wanted to follow him up the stairs and watch him remove the suit. The whole suit. Instead she ducked into the powder room and changed out of her skirt and blouse into the stretchy blue yoga pants and matching sports bra that covered about what a tank top would, but with more support. She also removed the pins holding her hair in a twist and gathered it into a high ponytail. And guessing working out would melt what remained of her makeup, she found a clean towel and rinsed her face to remove the faded foundation, blush, and mascara smudges.

After packing away her clothes, she swung open the door and looked up and down the hall. She could hear Ozzie moving around upstairs, and she wondered how the upper two floors were arranged. Was his room on the top? An office on the middle floor?

Before she could move, she heard his footsteps coming down. The doorbell rang.

"Should I answer that?" she called up.

"Go ahead. It should be Hammond."

"Hammond?"

"Phillip. He was at the weddings."

There was no time to question the addition to their workout she hadn't expected. Instead she pulled the door open to Drew's friend and onetime groomsman.

"Hello, Phillip."

His friendly smile widened across his face. "Bird. Oswald said he could teach two of us as well as one, so I'm here to get an intro to MMA." He stood on the stoop already in designer black sweats and a T-shirt, with a small gym bag hanging from one hand.

"Interestingly enough, so am I." Her smile was probably more of a grimace, way too toothy, but she stepped back and let him in. Of course his gaze swept her from head to toe and back again, taking in her bare feet and the sports bra. Had she known Phillip would be here too, she would have pulled on a T-shirt.

Oswald hit the bottom of the stairs just then. "Hammond." He extended a hand that Phillip eagerly shook.

"Looking forward to this. I've followed a little of your tournaments and don't know much more than what Drew has said over the years. Glad you remembered I was interested. And to train with Birdie"—here he smiled down at her, rather her chest—"is just all around good luck."

Birdie grimaced again and shut the door behind him. "So,"—she turned to Ozzie—"where do we go now?" The glare she gave him for not mentioning Phillip bounced right off him.

"Back this way." Barely sparing her a glance, he turned toward the kitchen. Stopping at the fridge, he opened it and pulled out three icy bottles of water, passing one each to Birdie and Phillip. "Down here," he said and headed down a flight of stairs.

The glimpse she had of the kitchen looked like it had been updated with impeccably polished cherry cabinets, black granite counters, and stainless appliances. To the right was a tiny eating area. All neat and sparkling clean.

The stairs ended in a room that took up the entire basement. The long wall opposite the stairs was mirrored from floor to ceiling. Only a small section at the back was closed off with louvered bifold doors. The washer, dryer, furnace, and hot water tank, she guessed. In the rest of the room, well, it was a gym. Complete with blue mats from wall to wall, a kickboxing dummy, punching bag, and at the front end, a set of hand weights side by side with a small fridge. A player dock sat on top of the fridge. Mounted high in the four corners of the room were small black speakers. Maybe she'd get a taste of what he considered head banging music.

Phillip tossed his bag at the base of the steps and kicked off his shoes.

"Might as well lose the socks too," Birdie suggested.

"All right, then," Ozzie said. "First things first, we need to warm up and stretch. No point in tearing muscles this early in the game." He touched a few buttons on the music player, and Ozzy Osborne's "Crazy Train" screamed out of the speakers.

Birdie laughed at the sly look he shot her over his shoulder. "You brat," she accused him.

"Never said I didn't like the song," he answered mildly, then indicated he wanted them positioned in front of the mirror. "If you have a warm up routine, fine, but you can watch me and follow along."

Oh Birdie watched, all right. He wore clothes similar to Phillip's. The sweats might have passed for man-tights had they been a hair snugger. His pants were black, his tank top white. His bare white feet were long and, she couldn't believe it, actually looked sexy. After a day in leather shoes they probably stunk, she told herself. *But after a shower they wouldn't.*

Groaning under the cover of the music, Birdie watched Ozzie in the mirror and followed his stretching routine. More than once her gaze was snared by his in the mirror. Usually when she was bent forward and both men had a pretty good chance to look down her bra. She especially liked the way Ozzie's eyes heated up. If Phillip was looking, she pretended not to notice.

After fifteen minutes, Oz stood up and looked at his two students. "Ready? We'll start with the basic moves tonight. Those will tire you out."

Birdie merely gazed at him. *Bring it*, she thought.

"Ready to go," Phillip said.

"First is the bus stop stance." Ozzie demonstrated. Feet shoulder width apart. Shoulders relaxed. "You're both right handed?"

Birdie and Phillip nodded.

"Then put your right foot back and turn forty-five degrees. Rear heel up." Each step they took, he explained why it was important. "Heel up for faster movement. Taking time to lift the heel is time lost." Each movement was like a part in a ballet as Ozzie moved. Natural and part of the routine. He made it look as easy as breathing.

Next came how to make a fist and how to hold them up in front of the cheekbones. "Keep your shoulders relaxed or you'll be too sore to move tomorrow." Ozzie's gaze moved over her body in the mirror, then moved down to take in Phillip's stance. "Good. Easy enough, hey?"

Birdie soaked it all in. Ozzie had them practice getting into position a couple times before going on to the next step.

"If you want to move back, lead with your rear foot." He danced backward, looking as springy as Tigger. "Remember to keep that heel up. Lead with the left foot to move forward. Right foot to move right, left to move left." He demonstrated the small steps, slowly at first, then with a show of speed. It looked like he was dancing as he demonstrated how quickly he could turn and move. "Little crab-like steps. Keep them loose." Birdie made a bet with herself that Ozzie could probably dance a Lindy with style.

Okay, the heel up made sense to Birdie. Even Phillip nodded. It took only a few minutes to gain Ozzie's nod of approval. That small acknowledgment was like the highest praise to Birdie. Or maybe her blood was warming from the exercise. She didn't have time to stop and contemplate it now. Watching herself in the mirror, she put on her mean face and concentrated on the small crab-like movements until Phillip started laughing.

"Now that's a scary look, Bird. Just like that, you'll scare off any potential mugger," he said.

"She's smart enough to not be out on the streets after dark by herself," Ozzie barked.

"Of course she is," Phillip agreed. "But just in case, that's a good move to start with."

Ozzie grunted. "Next is the jab. With that and a cross punch, it will make your stance more believable. This is your range finder, or in other words, it's how you gauge how close your opponent really is. Using your left arm…"

The next sequence took a little longer to perfect for her. Obviously no one had ever taught her how to throw a punch. Aim with the first two knuckles because they're the strongest, Ozzie demanded. After a few punches she understood the mechanics and the importance of a straight arm and wrist. Stomp with the left foot, strike out with the left arm.

"This is where it helps to build up the muscles in your legs," he said. "The power comes first from your legs, then your core"—he slapped his abs—"shoulders next, and then your arm."

Every body part he touched, she wanted to touch too. Seeing this authoritative, teaching side of him was also a turn on. She couldn't ever remember him stringing so many words together at once. Then there was how he moved. Poetry with power in motion. Of course she'd seen hints of his coordination in how he walked and danced. However, now, stripped down to workout clothes, for the first time she could fully enjoy seeing all those sculpted muscles in movement.

As a teacher, Ozzie wasn't one to let her daydream. So she followed his instructions. Stomp, jab, exhale on the jab, then pull the arm back into position, all while keeping the right fist up by her cheek. The movements were not intuitive for her, but she thought she did okay when Ozzie told them to take a short break and shake out their arms and legs. Then there was the gleam of approval in his eyes, although he kept his facial expression neutral. For Phillip's benefit? Trying to deny whatever attraction he felt for her? Is that why Phillip was there? As a chaperone?

"Before you actually start punching things, we'll make sure you have good wraps," he told her. Even that tiny consideration sent a thrill down her spine.

Satisfied with her progress—Phillip got there first—Ozzie demonstrated the cross-punch with the right arm.

Birdie's thighs were starting to burn, as were the muscles in her left arm, as she resumed her stance, but she was damned if she'd complain. Phillip wasn't whining. No way would she be the wussy girly girl now.

"This is your power punch," he told them as they made their first stabs. "Although you can knock out an opponent with a perfectly placed jab, the cross is more likely to be the one to do it."

Birdie watched as Ozzie twisted his rear foot, the one with the heel up, the resulting twist of his shoulders adding power to the punch. After a few throws he nodded in satisfaction, and Birdie was ready to sit down and rest.

Ozzie had other ideas. "Now we're going to put it all together in a sequence."

"Can I get a sip of water first?" she asked.

Ozzie glanced at Phillip first, then her. "Good idea."

He also turned on a fan, and Birdie wanted to sigh in relief. The small hand towel in her bag was also a joy to find as she wiped sweat from her face and neck. She sensed a prickling at the back of her neck and turned to see Ozzie motionless, his eyes on her toweling the sweat from her upper chest.

"Hey," Phillip said, interrupting her moment with Ozzie. "You're doing great. Have you had any martial arts training before?"

Birdie snorted and swiped the towel across the back of her neck. "Some ballet and gymnastics, but martial arts? No."

"Can't tell." He gave her a big grin. "Must be the ballet and gymnastics, muscle memory and all that. You move well."

"Thanks."

"All right," Ozzie said. "Not much left to do, but we're going to go through all the steps at once. Once you have the moves smoothed out, we'll do a five minute session with you throwing a jab every ten seconds."

"Only five minutes?" Phillip dropped his half full water bottle on his gym bag.

Birdie reluctantly did the same. If she downed the entire bottle, she'd probably spit it back up in five minutes.

"Five minutes will be enough for tonight," Ozzie said with a crooked smile. "You can practice that each day until we get together again."

Phillip nodded. "I can't make it this weekend. We're doing the races. King George Day at Ascot and all."

Birdie glanced at Ozzie who was nodding. "We're going as well. With Courtney's grandmother."

"Old Mrs. Robinson?" Phillip looked suitably shocked. "You're brave, mate."

Ozzie shrugged. "When you're offered a ride and box seats, it's best not to disappoint the lady who offers."

Birdie snorted. Offered. Right. More like Gran had demanded, but whatever. Birdie was actually a little excited. Okay, a whole lot excited.

"We'll get you introduced around this weekend, Bird," Phillip said. "Okay, I'm ready. Let's do this."

Ozzie nodded and herded Birdie back to her spot in the middle of the mat. One man on each side. Not a bad place to be, once she thought about it. Both men were fit, ripped, and handsome. Ozzie with his dark blond hair, Phillip with his darker brown, a girl would be crazy to not have fun standing between them. Still, it would have been more fun with only Ozzie there. She'd had fantasies of his getting closer, wrapping his arms around of her as she followed his instructions.

Ozzie's sharp instruction to pay attention cut off that thought.

Lined up in front of the mirror, Ozzie led them through the sequence. Set the stance, fists in the guard position, then stomp, jab, exhale on the throw, pull the fist back into position, throw the cross, exhale, dance around and set the next jab and cross combo. He made them do each step perfectly, complete with exhale, heel twist, and movement.

"Slowly now, increase the pace…"

Working to the music, they flowed from punch to punch.

Birdie glanced at the clock and Ozzie caught her. "I'll tell you when time's up."

Rolling her eyes, she focused on the mirror, making sure she moved correctly.

It was the longest five minutes of her life. And considering the three wedding ceremonies she'd stood through in the last eighteen months, that was saying something.

"Three more sequences," Ozzie called out from behind her. "Keep those fists in place when you're not punching."

Beside her Phillip bounced around, dancing left, right, front and back, spinning every now and again, his form perfect.

"Two more," Ozzie said. "Hands up! One more!"

Birdie put on a burst of energy for the last sequence, then stopped moving the second she finished. Her arms dropped as if she held ten pound weights in each one.

"Walk and shake it out," Ozzie said. "You did well." He patted her on the shoulder before moving over to the music player.

"High five!" Phillip came toward her with his palm in the air. "You looked great!"

"Thanks." She couldn't help the grin as a small surge of adrenalin kicked in. "You did pretty well yourself." Palm connecting with palm sent a small sting through her hand and down her raised arm. The slap sounded loud in the suddenly quiet room.

Birdie glanced at the big clock on the wall. "Wow, we've been going over an hour?"

"Yep." The short affirmative was almost ridiculous in Ozzie's high brow accent. "So, five minute routine each day until we meet again. Take it slow the first few times to make sure you're practicing perfect form. If you're not going to do it right, it's better to not do it all."

Birdie nodded. "Perfect practice prevents piss-poor performance."

Phillip laughed. "Such language from a lady."

She smirked back at him. "Don't make me demonstrate my full range of sailor curses. I learned from the best."

Ozzie merely lifted an aristocratic brow.

"My grandfather can turn the air icy blue given the right circumstances. Especially if he thinks I'm not around."

"Birdie, you need a lift home?" Phillip looked so hopeful she didn't quite know how to answer. Ozzie hadn't said a thing about after working out since the other night. Did he remember his promise?

"I'll take her," Ozzie said. "I promised to feed her."

Phillip smiled, but it was somewhat dimmer than his usual. "All right then. When do we do this again?"

"I can set aside Thursday evenings," Ozzie said. "That way it doesn't get in the way of your usual Friday night plans. It's also usually my most free evening."

"Thursdays are good for me." Phillip stooped to pick up his bag. "I'll show myself out, and will look for you this weekend. My sister wants to meet Birdie."

"I'm looking forward to it," she replied.

Phillip rested a hand on her shoulder and gave it a tiny squeeze. "Don't worry, she doesn't associate with Deirdre unless she has no choice."

Birdie laughed. "I like her already. Thanks, Phillip."

He nodded at Ozzie. "I'm off. Have a great rest of the evening."

Chapter 18

Listening to Hammond bound up the steps and out the door, Oswald stood and stared at Courtney. The look they shared was deeply intimate and if her stomach hadn't chosen that moment to grumble, he might very well have gone with his fantasy of taking her down to the mats and making love to her.

It had been hard to keep an eye on Hammond in the name of teaching because watching Courtney had been like watching a ballerina. The woman moved with such grace and ease, surely it would translate to extraordinary sex.

"Oops!" Courtney clapped one hand over her stomach. "Guess it heard you mention feeding time."

"What would you say to the best fish and chips in town?"

Courtney had bent over to retrieve her bags and the half full bottle of water. She looked up at him as she straightened. "You can make fish and chips?"

This time he laughed. "I could, but I'd rather take you to the pub down the street. Have a shirt to throw over that gear?" Not that he wanted her to cover up, but neither did he want anyone else to see her looking deliciously pink and glowing from the workout.

"Shower first?" She sniffed and wrinkled her nose. "I'm a little stanky."

"You don't stink, but if it would make you more comfortable..." And he couldn't quite stop the vision of Courtney in his shower from forming. Since he'd already seen her naked—twice—it wasn't hard to imagine at all. "Come on, I'll get you some fresh towels. Unless you brought your own potions, you may come out smelling a little manly, but it won't bother me."

"It won't be the first time. I've accidently used Drew's shower gel a time or two."

A sweep of relief went through him like a breeze. Of course, they'd shared a bathroom when sharing an apartment at Stanford.

Oswald swept out a hand, encouraging her to go up the stairs first. She only hesitated a beat, then took the steps two at a time. Except for passing too quickly, he had a fine view of her backside. She waited for him in the kitchen.

"We have to go up one more floor for the guest bath."

"Okay."

It only took half an hour for them both to shower and dress in clean clothes. He was somewhat surprised she had a complete outfit of jeans, T-shirt, and trainers in her oversized red leather tote bag. He hadn't expected her to plan so far in advance. Not that he'd ever had a woman over to workout in his home gym before.

Most of the women who stopped by whatever gym he'd been at for evening workouts had showed up in work clothing, then went straight home still in their workout togs. More comfortable to shower at home whenever possible, one had said to him once. He got that.

Still, Courtney hadn't known they'd be going out for dinner. Then again, Americans seemed to be a little more fastidious when it came to bathing.

Settled in a booth, ale in front of them and order placed, Oswald took a long look at her. "So, what do you really think?"

"About the workout?"

He nodded.

"Feels like a good start to me. I know we've barely begun, but I like the way you explained each step as we went along. I like knowing why a certain position works best. What do you think? Did I do well?" She threw the question back at him.

"You did great. Better than many beginners I've worked with." And that was the honest truth. "Of course these next few weeks will take some tweaking of your form. Until you build some muscle memory, you're going to have to constantly check it." Or rather he would check her form. "If it would make you feel better, we can get in some extra workouts before Thursday."

Ah. That earned him a raised brow. So much like the rest of her family, she had the aristocratic demeanor no one in his family could seem to grasp.

The delivery of their meals interrupted the conversation. Just as well. He offered her the vinegar, and she took it without batting an eye. So she'd had true fish and chips before. Then again, after half a year living with Drew, it was to be expected. He vaguely recalled Drew talking about some fish and chips shop not far from campus.

"So what about Phillip?"

The question came out of the blue, and Oswald wasn't sure how to answer it. "What about him?"

"You didn't tell me he'd be there tonight."

Feigning nonchalance, something he'd practiced for years, he shrugged. "He's been after me for a year or so to do a little private teaching. He wants to come off experienced when he goes into a real training facility. Can't stand to look like a fool."

"More acceptable if one is young and adorable rather than grown?"

Oswald pointed a chip at her. "Got it in one."

Courtney threw back her head and laughed. "Does that make him a git?"

"Determined to learn the lingo?"

"Have to be able to understand when someone is being just a little too vicious with their insults." Although her shrug looked casual, he imagined she was reliving the memory of the refugee fundraiser.

"I won't leave your side this weekend. If someone gets out of line, I'll take care them for you."

Courtney gave him a funny look. "You can't protect me in all areas. I need to be able to stand up for myself."

"Where can't I protect you?"

"The ladies' loo for one. Going about my day to day duties for another. You can't run the company and stick to my side like glue."

"Got me there. Guess we'll just have to skip the rest of your internship and move you right up the exec suite." A solution and a problem in equal measure. "Who's been mean to you at Lynford?"

Since she'd just taken a bite of her fish, she waved the rest of the piece at him to wait a moment. Finally she swallowed, then delayed answering by sipping her ale. Finally, seemingly having her words sorted out, she spoke. "No one's been mean, specifically. I can't give you any one example. I'm probably just being hyper sensitive what with my *privileged* position and all. I mean, I've only been in accounting four days, filing invoices no less, so no one is accustomed to me being there. We're still dancing around the issue, ya know?"

"No, I don't know. Explain it to me."

The huff of exasperation was adorable with her rolling eyes. "I can't explain it. I mean, well, tonight on the elevator? I know you were listening. Everyone was, but that's the first time Mrs. Smith took the time to really talk to me. You dropped me off Monday morning, she sent me straight into the filing room with a junior clerk who was polite enough, but also clearly didn't want to show me how the filing is set up. Like she thought I should already know how it's done just because my last name is Robinson."

"Your father explained this, didn't he?"

"Of course he did. But how long has it been since he started with the company? More than twenty years? He'd be clueless if he stepped into that file room. You too, most likely. How long has it been since you set foot in there?"

"I can't imagine it's changed much in six years, but I do get your point. So nothing specifically evil has been directed at you, and yet neither has anything specifically friendly been offered."

"Right. Is that just the way it is? Or is it because of my family affiliation? I just don't know."

"Bring in a few pounds of Belgian chocolate and neither will matter. You'll suddenly be the rock star of the department."

Birdie gave him her brightest smile. "Good point. Until the chocolates arrive, maybe I can think of something else. Like cinnamon rolls."

Oswald narrowed his gaze. "Better call me to help you carry them in. Tomorrow?"

A spear of chip was pointed at him. "You just want one."

"One dozen. You caught me." He caught the chip she tossed at him and ate it.

Chapter 19

When Birdie told Oswald the news their date had been hijacked by Gran, he hadn't reacted noticeably. Instead he'd gracefully accepted the invite to ride with Gran and met them on the street when Gran's car arrived to pick up Birdie Saturday morning.

Gran was polite, but not overly friendly with Oswald. He was exceedingly polite and proper with Gran. Birdie wanted to poke them both and figure out why they were so stiff with one another.

"Let's get settled in the box; then you two can go wandering about as much as you please. I have some friends who will join us. Oswald, please introduce Courtney to some appropriate young women. She needs girl friends."

"Part of my master plan, Mrs. Robinson," he replied smoothly.

"We want no more incidents like the last time you escorted her." Gran peered at him intently. "Although I can see where that came completely out of the blue. Who'd expect such an attack at a fundraiser?"

"Actually, Gran, Ozzie saved me once before they grew more determined and hit me in the face with the wine. It would have been a far smaller stain, and less humiliating, but he did get me out of the way in time. The one that landed came quickly on the heels of the first one, and you're right, who could have anticipated that?"

Gran's expression grew thoughtful. "Good man, Mr. Attenborough. I'm beginning to approve of you. Keep up the good work."

Oswald blinked, clearly surprised. "Yes, ma'am."

Ascot was fun, Birdie decided as they left the car and entered the grounds. The people, the hats, the air of festivity, all of it was a party for the senses.

And she was grateful for Gran's advice when dressing for the event. Her first day's dress was a silk Oscar de la Renta watercolor floral. Perfect for a summer event, the stylist had said. Large pink flowers on a white background, the dress had a fit bodice and a pleated skirt that flared and swished around her knees just right. With her hair pinned in a low bun at her nape, she wore a brimmed, flat crowned hat in deep pink that matched the flowers perfectly. The day was warm enough, her legs still tanned, so she left off the pantyhose and wore beige pumps. And Gran had insisted she carry a purse of pink as well. The one inch shoulder straps of the dress were wide enough to conform to the dress code and narrow enough to leave her arms and shoulders bare to catch the sun promised for the day. The ensemble felt fresh and flirty. And since they'd sent along the color for Oswald, his tie matched her dress and paired beautifully with his white shirt and gray suit.

Once Gran was settled in her box, Oswald took Birdie, their picks, and a handful of Gran's money to place their bets after looking over the horses. Based on appearances of the beasts and their jockeys, she changed her choices a bit from what Gran had chosen. She carefully kept the tickets separate.

Oswald was the perfect gentleman, never leaving her side. Even when they met up with a group of his friends. A group that included Phillip and his sister, Anne.

"Like the Queen's sister," Anne confided after introductions. "Our elder sister is Elizabeth, of course. I'm the baby," she cheerfully announced as she shook Birdie's hand. "I've heard good things about you, and I see Phillip hasn't over exaggerated your beauty for once. He has a habit of doing that."

Birdie smiled at Anne's run-on mouth while Phillip looked slightly abashed. Birdie had a feeling while she might not always like what Anne had to say, at least she'd say it up front.

"I would have met you at the wedding, the second one, but I had a touch of the flu, and we didn't want anyone else catching it," Anne confided. "Could have sworn I was going to die; it was that bad. Still, I'm very glad for this opportunity."

Anne made sure Birdie had a drink in hand before beginning her interrogation. "So. Oswald Attenborough finally shows his face at Ascot. How did you accomplish that?"

Birdie kept her surprise hidden. "He invited me."

Anne blinked in what Birdie surmised was astonishment. "Really? But didn't you also arrive with your grandmother, the elder Mrs. Robinson?"

A snort of laughter burst from Birdie. "Excuse me. I'm sorry, elder Mrs. Robinson? Is that what people call her? I'm not sure she'd like that very much."

Anne shrugged with a cheeky grin on her face. "It's how it goes. Your mother is now Mrs. Courtland Robinson, the reigning Mrs. Robinson. Your brother's wife is the younger Mrs. Robinson. That puts your grandmother in the background now to keep things straight. So, you also arrived with her. How did that happen?"

"Simple. Once she heard we were coming, she took my wardrobe in hand, then told us we were riding with her and sitting in her box. When we aren't gallivanting around the race track, that is." Birdie sipped from her drink, a light sparkling wine Ozzie had procured for her.

"Well, I'll tell you this, she did an excellent job dressing you. When I saw that outfit in Harrod's, I was sure it was meant for the middle-aged crowd, but you've proven me wrong." Anne's gaze cut sideways to where Ozzie and Phillip talked horses with a couple other men. "And the boys certainly approve. Not only can't Phil and Oswald stop themselves from looking at you, but neither can their friends and every single man walking past us."

Birdie choked on her sip. "I doubt that. I want to know where you got your dress. I'm sure there are other stores besides Harrod's, much as I love it."

"We'll go shopping next weekend if you like. I need to find something for a wedding. One of my classmates caught herself a Viscount in line for an Earldom. Lucky trollop."

By the end of the day Birdie was tired, but happy. She'd made a fast friend in Anne and met half a dozen of Anne's friends. Every single one of them seemed to like her. She'd never felt more certain when one of them called her a baggage. Had they been staying at one of the nearby hotels, Birdie and Oswald would have been included in the plans to party the night away.

As it was, she was more than happy to trundle the hour back to London. But soon, she wanted to join Anne and her friends for a night of clubbing. Phillip had offered to squire them about. Birdie wasn't sure if Phillip had seen the look on Oswald's face or not. If she were to guess, it would be a cold day in Hades before Oswald let that happen, and yet, the closer Phillip had moved toward Birdie, the farther Oswald had stepped back. But true to his word, she'd remained in his sight all day long.

"You look happy, girl," Gran said.

"I am. It was a very fun day." She glanced at Oswald and found his eyes gleaming in her direction. "One of my horses won, so I'm fifty pounds richer, I made some friends, and finally laid eyes on Prince Harry." From a distance that required binoculars, but still. She'd been within a hundred yards of him. "The sun shone all day, my tan is refreshed, I'm drunk on horsey smelling fresh air, and I get to do it all again tomorrow in excellent company. What more could a girl want this weekend?" Well, besides a good night kiss from the enigmatic man sitting across from her.

Gran laughed softly. "Well then, a highly successful day. Your parents will be pleased."

* * * *

Sunday morning Birdie was a little slow getting going. At least she'd been smart enough to load the coffee pot the night before. A check of the weather report showed sunshine was expected all day. She hadn't needed the pashmina she'd tucked into her purse the day before, but she'd take it again. Just in case. Her brain was slow enough she was a little behind from choosing her dress for the day. In the end, she went with a simple, boat-necked sleeveless two tone dress. White linen bodice, lime green knee-length skirt of moiré silk separated by a waistband of embroidered flowers. The large white hat with a mess of fabric flowers circling the crown was just right and only needed a couple pins to hold it in place. The white pashmina from the day before would be perfect. White purse, white strappy sandals. As they hadn't walked nearly as much as she'd expected the day before, she felt it was a safe choice for the day. The two and a half inch heel was also modest enough she wouldn't kill herself.

As she was locking the flat door, her cell phone rang. Gran's tone.

"I'm on my way down," Birdie said first thing.

"Fine. We're waiting. Even Mr. Attenborough is here. I just stopped him from running up to get you."

"Elevator opening now"—she stepped in—"there in two mins max." As she disconnected she noticed the battery was down by fifty percent. Oh well, she hadn't needed the phone yesterday other than for a few photographs for the family. Not like she'd need to use it for an emergency call. Both Gran and Ozzie carried phones. And everyone else at the race track.

Oswald was waiting when the elevator doors opened. The slight irritation in his eyes disappeared as he took in her outfit. He held out an elbow as she drew near him. "Ready to go?"

The minute she wrapped her hand around his arm, the electric buzz she felt every time she touched him showed up with a vengeance. And that was a hand over skin covered by at least two layers of cloth. "Yes, Ozymandias. I'm ready. Sorry I'm late." Instead of staring at him, she forced her eyes forward, the goal being the door, and then the car beyond the side walk parked at the curb.

Ozzie tipped his head closer and spoke quietly. "Ozymandias? Really? Didn't realize you read Shelley. Besides, you're not so late, and looking like that makes up for it." She could feel his minty breath on her cheek.

"You look dapper." She smiled at the doorman, then looked at Ozzie again. Today he wore a charcoal suit, white shirt, and a paisley tie, white and black with spots of lime in it. He also had a top hat. "I don't think I've ever seen you with a hat."

"After the sun yesterday, I figured it might be a good idea today."

Martin smiled from where he stood by the rear door. "You two look like a very fashionable matched set today," he said.

"Thank you, Martin. I'm trying to fit in." Birdie briefly touched his arm before climbing into the back of the car with Gran. Ozzie followed and took one of the rear-facing seats. The one directly across from Birdie, setting his hat on the seat beside him. Like yesterday, she had a whole hour each way to look at him. Not a hardship.

Although, considering his behavior last night, she didn't quite know what to think. After a fun day, once Gran and Martin had dropped them off, he'd reverted to his old stand-offish self. Sure, he'd seen her to the door of the flat, then kissed her hand, pulled the door shut between them, and waited until he heard her engage the locks.

The fun and friendly guy had completely disappeared. She'd been hoping to invite him in for…well, anything, really. Instead she'd taken a long bath, then dropped into bed where she'd tossed and turned for an hour before exhaustion dragged her down into sleep.

"Looking a tad peaked, my dear," Gran noted.

"Just a little tired, but excited for today." Not exactly a lie. Mostly she was feeling confused and more than anything wanted to smack the man sitting across from her. To avoid his gaze, she looked out the window as Martin eased into the traffic.

"If you're not feeling well, we don't have to go," Gran said.

Birdie turned her head to smile at her grandmother. "Of course I'm fine. Just waiting for the caffeine to kick in. I'll be right as rain by the time we get there."

Gran winced. "Don't say the R word. It's not in the forecast, but that means nothing."

"Right. Sorry. We'll talk of sunshine today. So, who are you betting on?"

Ozzie pulled a racing form from his suit pocket and Gran pulled one from her purse. These two were serious about this racing business. Mostly she listened while Gran and Ozzie discussed each race and made notes on their forms. Birdie decided she'd take a look at the horses when they arrived and then make her choices. It had worked the day before. She could afford to buy her own food and drinks today because of it. Not that her parents kept her poor, but she liked the idea of paying for herself whenever she could. She didn't have to be radical about it, and by living at home she was able to put most of her paycheck in the savings account. Only a tiny part of her felt a little guilty about that. So many of the people her age were struggling to start careers and live on their own. Had Dad not shown up in their lives so many months ago, she'd be doing the same, she supposed. Then again, she could have lived at home and commuted to her grandfather's office easily. Not so much different than her situation here. Really, there was no point to make things hard just to feel like she was accomplishing something. Things would get plenty hard with each step of her internship, specialized though it was.

Dad was right about one thing, she faced subtle accusations of nepotism every day. No one came out and said anything directly—they were far too polite for that—but there was an undercurrent. Making cinnamon rolls for Friday morning had taken some of it away. For a day. How would things go tomorrow? She'd be too tired tonight to make a treat to carry in. Maybe she'd make it a Friday only thing. But then she'd be cooking right after working out on Thursday evenings.

If the Thursday training continued. With Ozzie's sudden distance, she didn't feel confident about that. Hot and cold. And here she'd thought women had reputations for sending mixed messages. He was the king of it.

She looked away from the window to see Ozzie gazing at her. A question rested in his eyes, but she wasn't going to play that game. Instead she let her gaze slide right past him and turned her attention on her grandmother.

"What do you think of this horse, Courtney?" the older woman asked. "His stats are quite impressive."

"Whatever you think, really. It's not like I know anything about racing."

"You did all right yesterday," Ozzie reminded her. "I'm inclined to follow your choices."

"Beginner's luck. Nothing special about my betting abilities."

"Far too modest, my love," Gran said. "Why don't you just point at the form, and we'll choose that way. It ought to work as well as any other method."

They all chuckled. "Might at that," Ozzie said.

Shrugging, Birdie reached out and pointed at the paper.

"Who'd she pick?" Ozzie asked Gran.

Presenting their tickets at the entry gate, they received a nod of approval from the Fashion Police. Birdie still privately chuckled at that. The Fashion Police were real and working hard at the Ascot race grounds. Anne had explained the previous day how they carried around pashmina shawls for the women who showed up not wearing dress code approved clothing. Shawls to cover strapless dresses, or dresses with too little strap. Fascinators for women without hats for the Royal Enclosure. Ties for men who'd forgotten theirs.

Today there were just as many cameras out as there'd been the day before. Birdie smiled, but she really wanted to cringe away from them. At least she wasn't being asked to don a shawl and her hat was modest by the standards set by other race-goers. In fact, Anne was waving them down with something huge and floppy on her head. The flowers on her hot pink hat looked like real peonies.

Anne wrapped her arm around Birdie's arm while greeting Gran. "You look lovely today, Mrs. Robinson."

"As do you, Miss Hammond. Looking forward to another day of racing?"

"I'm hoping Courtney will share her betting suggestions with me. Oi, Phillip, bring champagne for my friends here."

From a stand nearby Birdie saw Phillip, standing next to Calvin Whetmore, wave a hand and turn back to the barman.

Ozzie turned to Gran. "Shall we escort you to your box?"

Gran shook her head. "I see my friends right over there. I'll go up with them. Come up for lunch."

"Yes, ma'am," he promised her. "We'll place the bets and drop your tickets off."

"No need. Just collect my winnings for me." With a smile, something that nearly shocked Birdie's hat right off, Gran headed toward a couple Birdie remember seeing at the second wedding just a few weeks ago. Mr. and Mrs. Longley? She'd had so many names thrown at her that day she'd forgotten most of them. She'd been too upset with Ozzie that day as well. Seemed to be a theme going on.

Ozzie headed off to place the bets, and she didn't have time to think about anything other than remembering names as the crowd of Anne and Phillip's friends she'd met the day before descended on them, everyone holding a glass of something alcoholic. Phillip handed her one—after a sip she noted it was the same sparkling wine as she'd had the day before—while Calvin handed out a few more to Anne and her friends, then went back for more.

Birdie was laughing over a joke from Christina, the one who'd called her a baggage the day before, when a strong arm went around her waist. Fortunately she recognized Ozzie's scent and grip before she flinched.

"Bets all placed." He held the tickets out for her to place in her purse as she had the day before.

"Why don't you hang on to them?"

"No. The formula worked well yesterday. Why tempt Fate?"

She glanced up from under the brim of her hat to see him smiling down at her. Oh damn. The hot smile.

Anne came to the rescue. "Why tempt Fate indeed? Did Courtney win yesterday?"

"Fifty pounds." Ozzie turned his smile on Anne who blinked before recovering.

So Birdie wasn't the only one who reacted to that smile. She knew that, but it was nice having the reminder. A deeper sip of her drink was meant to buy her time to slow the racing beat of her heart even as she moved a tad closer to Ozzie's warm body. The fit felt so right she wondered how she'd lived this long without him so close.

"Well, fifty quid is nothing to sneeze at. I've not placed my bets yet, so tell me who you bet on today, and I'll see if your luck is holding. Lord knows I never win at the races!" Anne said.

The circle of friends laughed and added their own tales of bets lost in the past. It seemed a few of them had lost hundreds, and on occasion, a few thousand pounds on what was supposed to be a sure bet.

Phillip pulled out his racing form. "Come on, tell us."

Birdie glanced up at Ozzie who shrugged. He consulted the tickets he still held, then told them what bets they'd placed.

"You've got to be kidding me," Phillip finally said after gaping at Birdie for nearly a full minute. "A couple of those are longest shots in their fields. Seriously?"

Heat touched on Birdie's cheeks. "I think I had beginner's luck yesterday. I really, really don't know what I'm doing here. I've never bet on a thing in my life." With a shrug, she drank some more.

"But you won," Anne stressed. "How did you pick the winning horse yesterday?"

"She picked two winners, but because the odds were so bad, she only bet a fiver on each one. And came out with fifty pounds total winnings." Ozzie looked down at her, and she experienced a warm flush of pleasure at the approval glinting behind his glasses. "Beginner's luck? Maybe. I'd be willing to splash down a coupl'a quid on that."

"So how did you choose today's bets?" Phillip pressed.

"Well, I just… This is going to sound completely stupid, but I just closed my eyes and…pointed."

At least eight faces gaped at her.

Christina was the first one to burst out laughing. "Bloody brill! Sure beats my system." She held up her cup in a toast. Birdie touched her cup to Christina's before both women sipped. At this rate she'd finish her drink in minutes. Already a warm buzz teased the blood rushing around her body.

"What's your system?" Ozzie asked before Birdie could get the words out.

"Alphabetically," Christina answered without a touch of shame. "Depends on who is in the race, but the first one is any horse with a name starting with A, or B, or whatever letter comes up first. Second race is the next letter in the alphabet."

Her friends all laughed, but they started confessing their own systems for choosing. Phillip was the only one who studied the stats in agonizing detail. Granted, his win rate was a bit higher than most of them, but not by much. Patricia looked at the jockey arses. She bet by who had the tightest one. As they went around the circle, Calvin rejoined them.

"What're you all hooting about?" he asked. He held up a cup. "Anyone need a top off?"

Birdie shook her head, and Phillip was the one to fill him in, although Calvin's gaze was on her. He'd certainly made note of Ozzie's strangely possessive hold.

"You all are delusional," Calvin announced. "The best way to bet is to flip a coin between the top two contenders."

Phillip scoffed. "Your way is no more reliable than anyone else's."

"And yet, my thousand pound win yesterday puts you all to shame." Calvin bowed at the laughter and applause that greeted his announcement.

Anne had the last laugh. "Well, I'm not seeing any improvements here. However, I need to go place my bets. Meet up at the Panoramic in an hour?"

"We're meeting my Gran in her box. I don't know how many people she's invited," Birdie said.

"Oh, ain't she posh!" Anne adopted a pose, one hand on a hip, another behind her head, nose in the air. "See how y'are?" She dropped the pose and giggled. "What the hell? It's the best way to see the races, you know. Have to see what I can do about scratching up a box invite next year. For now, we're slumming it with the general population and regular grand stand seating."

"How about we meet up after lunch?" Birdie suggested.

"Aye." Anne whipped out her phone. "Give me the digits, trollop."

They exchanged numbers, and Birdie tucked her phone away.

Calvin leaned over and looked into her cup. "Looking a little low there, darling girl." Without asking, he tipped several ounces into her half full cup.

"Oh. Thank you." She returned his salute, then sipped. More of the sparkling wine, but something about the way Calvin watched her was off-putting. Some warning about accepting drinks flitted across her mind. Phillip she trusted. Calvin she didn't. Standing beside a flowering bush, she wondered if she could surreptitiously dump most of her drink without anyone being the wiser. A large pink bloom caught her eye, and she leaned a little to sniff it. Apparently she'd startled a bee because one shot right out of the center of the flower.

Birdie flinched backward, but not before the thing landed on her neck and stung her.

"Ow!"

Oswald immediately spun her around to face him, her wine cup dropped into the bush, and several drops splashed on her foot and ankle. "What happened?" he demanded.

"I...I think... I was just stung." She blinked back tears as the site of the injury grew hot. "I've never been stung before."

He pulled her hand away from where she was instinctively trying to cover the wound. "You don't know if you're allergic?" One hand cupped her chin and gently twisted her so he could see.

"No. I don't know. I've never known anyone who was."

"Looks like it's bloody painful," Anne said, leaning in close to look. "Phillip, flag down someone to get a medic."

Birdie sensed the small crowd around her mobilizing, but she could only see Ozzie and the deep concern in his eyes. "Is it...?" She didn't even know what to ask. Just the pain from it was making her dizzy.

"Let's find a seat and some shade." Ozzie looked up at Anne. "Can you find some water?"

"On it," one of the men said, and departed.

Arm tight around her, Ozzie half carried her to a bench under a spreading tree. It felt wonderful to lean on him as she blinked back tears of pain.

"This is silly," she protested, not sure what she was protesting.

"Just relax, Courtney," his calm voice soothed her. "I don't think you're allergic, but we'll have a medic check you out, anyway. If nothing else, he'll get the stinger out and put something soothing on the welt."

"Something soothing sounds good."

"Let's get rid of this. Where are the pins?" A moment later her hat was off, and he used it to fan her face.

Shamelessly she leaned her head on his shoulder and allowed that the breeze on her neck felt pretty good.

Phillip sat on the side of her injury. "I've got a credit card here. According to the web, it can scrape the stinger out if it's there."

Ozzie held up a hand. "Can you see a stinger? Unless we know what kind of bee it was, it's better to wait for a medic, don't you think?"

Phillip held up his phone. "This site says if it was a regular honey bee, it takes a few minutes for the venom sack to empty. Better to get it out as quickly as possible."

"But if the stinger isn't there, you're just hurting her," Ozzie pointed out. "Look, here comes a medic now. Move out of his way, Hammond."

By then they had a small, very polite, crowd around them.

"Hammond, shoo everyone along," Ozzie ordered.

The medic bent over her and examined the site. "No trouble breathing?"

"Just a little dizzy," she answered. "Oh, and it hurts. A lot."

"Stings do at that," he said cheerfully. "Looks like a honey bee stinger in there. We'll get that out, some cream on it, and see if we can't get an antihistamine in you."

With Ozzie's strong arm still around her, she rested her head where his neck and shoulder met. The medic talked, but she concentrated on Ozzie. The warm, spicy sweet smell of his skin. Like cinnamon and lemon, or lime. A note of bay leaf. Whatever it was, he smelled good.

"She's looking a mite woozy there, mate," the man treating her said. "But her blood pressure is good, and she's breathing well; I don't think she's allergic. Have you got seats in the shade?"

"We're headed for a box."

"Best idea. Get her someplace shady and somewhat quiet. Not that there's a quiet seat to be had around here."

Birdie opened her eyes and caught the young man's grin.

"You'll be all right, luv," he said and patted her arm. "I've put a loose plaster over it. It will hurt for a couple days, but the swelling should go down and any hydrocortisone cream will ease the itch."

"Thanks," she whispered. For some reason she was feeling sleepy and didn't want to move.

"Up, Courtney," Ozzie said. "Let's get up to the box and park you in a comfortable seat."

"Sounds like a great idea." The medic snapped his case shut. "What box will you be in? If you notice any signs of wheezing, just give us a call and we'll be right up."

Ozzie told him, shook the man's hand, then stood and pulled Birdie up, keeping his arm solidly around her waist.

Someone pushed an opened bottle of water into her hand. "There you go, Birdie. Drink up, you'll feel better soon."

She sipped at the cool water, accepted an antihistamine tablet from the medic, and swallowed it down with more water.

"Oh, and take this." The medic smacked a plastic pack against the bench, then shook it before handing it over. "Cold pack. Helps reduce the swelling about as well as an antihistamine."

Birdie straightened up enough to notice he had dark hair and a cute beard and mustache. Maybe a few years older than her. But definitely cute over all. "Thank you," she said. She handed the water bottle to Ozzie so she could hang on to him and hold the icepack.

As Ozzie steered her toward the grand stand and a bank of elevators, she wobbled a little on her heels. They weren't so high, or the heels so narrow that she should feel so unstable on them. Anne showed up on her other side and took her by the elbow.

"Nasty little sting there. You all right, strumpet?"

"I'll be fine. Don't understand why I'm so shaky, though."

"The shock," Anne said. "And probably that horrid wine Calvin used to top off your cup. Smart of you to dump it in the bush like that. When I stooped to grab your cup, I used the opportunity to dump mine as well. Don't ever trust that bugger. I never drink anything he gives me."

Birdie sensed rather than saw Ozzie's head turn Anne's way. "He's been known to slip a mickey?"

"Only suspected a time or two. Haven't ever actually caught him in the act." Anne shrugged. "Meant to tell you before you got that sip in. Then the bee attacked. Think it's a good idea to park you in the grandmother's box for the day. I'll look you up in the next day or two and see how you're doing. Friday night we usually go dancing and I think you'll like our usual spot, okay?"

"Sounds fun," Birdie said. "I'd like that. Haven't been out clubbing since I got here."

"Well, now that's a true crime! Just for that we won't invite Oswald," Anne said. "Here we are now, at the lifts. Oswald will get you settled, or he'll answer to me!"

"Thank you, Anne. I've got her from here," Ozzie casually dismissed Birdie's new friend.

Birdie gave her a small wave as the doors closed. The sting site on her neck felt about five inches wide, hot, and it throbbed.

"Put the cold pack over it," Ozzie ordered.

"What happened, luv?" one of their fellow passengers asked, a short, round woman with two other women. The three of them were dressed in matching hot pink dresses and hats.

"Bee sting," Ozzie answered for her. "Mind the flowering bushes when you're about."

"Oh dear," another woman said. "That's an awful thing to happen, especially so early in the day."

The lift stopped and the trio filtered out, each one passing on their regards.

The door slid shut and the two of them were alone. Ozzie turned her to face him, using one hand to cup her cheek and lift her face. Serious icy blue eyes stared deeply into hers.

"You look a little off, love, and I don't mean the site on your neck. Your eyes are a little glazed."

"Pain."

"Maybe. Hold on, we're almost there. Just another couple levels."

"I'm sorry."

"Nothing to be sorry for. I'm worried about you. Not like you asked the bee to sting you. And now I'm concerned you got a sip of something pharmaceutical slipped in your drink. Add that to the tablet the medic gave you and I think it best if you stick to water or tea the rest of the day."

"Yeah, I feel a little drunk, now that you mention it." Which made her frown because she hadn't had more than a teaspoon of wine once her cup had been refilled. The half cup beforehand wasn't enough to make her tipsy. "You think Calvin...?" The lift stopped and doors opened, interrupting her thought.

Ozzie secured her against his side once more. "I wouldn't trust Whetmore any further than I could throw him." He glanced at the half empty water bottle in his hand with a frown.

"Hmm. Funny Drew having a friend like that."

"There's one in every crowd, love. The trick is figuring out who it is and then keeping a respectable distance from them. Never accept a drink from him again."

"I won't."

* * * *

The instant they entered the box suite, Oswald knew Courtney's grandmother was no fool. Mrs. Robinson pushed her friends aside and met them not five feet into the room.

"What's wrong with her?" The tone was sharp, but the eyes said the older woman was worried. Intent blue eyes zeroed in on the cold pack Courtney was barely able to hold to her neck. The fact was, he was very worried.

"Bee shting, Gran."

Oswald looked down at her. Her speech was slurred far beyond what he'd expected. How concentrated was the dose of roofies she'd been fed? Had she had more than a teaspoon? Had it been in the drink before Whetmore had poured more in? If indeed that had been in her drink. His fingers tightened around the water bottle Whetmore had fetched for Courtney. Had he opened the bottle just before handing it over, or had he opened it much earlier? Oswald couldn't remember.

"Indeed. Are you allergic? Your mother never said a word." Mrs. Robinson took Courtney's other arm. "Let's get her into one of the outside seats." Then she stopped walking and looked up at him. "Unless we should be heading for hospital?"

Oswald frowned. The same thought had just been rushing through his head. "I'm not sure. The medic who treated the sting said if she had trouble breathing to call down right away, but she's not wheezing."

"Then what else is wrong?"

"It's possible she's been exposed to a tiny dose of a date rape drug," he reluctantly admitted. "She didn't have more than a sip of a refill when the bee stung her. The rest got dropped into the bushes. But she'd had a few ounces of wine before that." He tried to remember the sequence of events. Hammond had given her the initial cup of wine. Whetmore had added at least a few ounces after she'd already had some. There was no way to know if both men had tampered with her drink, or only one. Then there was the water bottle in his hand. No point in over-alarming Mrs. Robinson, he decided not to mention it now. He would hand it over at the hospital for testing.

"So no proof from the container." The older woman pursed her lips. "Well, I'm not willing to take the risk. Call those medics, Oswald. Have them get an ambulance on standby."

"Let's get her comfortable first." A glance at the gathered guests showed them all focused on the trio.

"Right." Mrs. Robinson considered her guests. "Marlow, call the medics. Everyone else clear the way. We're setting her down by the rail. Oswald. You're in charge of making sure she doesn't fall over and hurt herself."

Oswald nodded at the man heading for a phone. "Tell them it's the girl with the bee sting. They have the box number and promised to be here quickly if called."

"On it," the man said.

Although Mrs. Robinson hovered, Oswald managed to get Courtney into a seat next to him, her head on his shoulder as her eyes drooped.

"So tired," she sighed against him, her voice barely a whisper.

"I know, darling. I've got you. Just rest. Everyone will think you're a little drunk, but that's not unusual here on big weekends."

"I don't, not really, get drunk. A little tipsy from time to time, but never shhh-tinking drunk. And, and, I dinna drink shenough even for slightly buzzed."

"I know, love. Just rest. We're marshalling the forces and will have you out of here soon. Your grandmother is right; I think a stop in hospital would be a good idea."

"Don't tell..." She sighed and seemed to fall asleep.

Don't tell who? Her parents? Her brother? Too bad, he was going to spill the beans just as soon as he knew she'd be okay.

"All right?" One of Mrs. Robinsons friends sat down on Courtney's other side. She put out a motherly hand and brushed Courtney's forehead. "Not feverish. The medics treated the sting?" She took the cold pack from Courtney's limp hand and gently held it over the plaster.

"Got the stinger out. Said it came from a common honey bee."

"Poor dear. First that awful bath at the refugee event, and now this. I'm sure the bee isn't part of a conspiracy, but if someone tried to slip her roofies..." Her voice trailed off as she shook her head, lips pressed in a hard line. "What is it with young people these days? Not that a few girls in my class hadn't been slipped mickeys back in the day, but this seems just so much...more. More malicious."

Yes, the incident had a very dark overtone to it. And he didn't like it one bit. Like Hammond, Whetmore had been after Oswald for a matchup. Unlike Hammond, Whetmore had some experience in the fighting cage. Had this been a gauntlet thrown down? Or was the arsewipe really after Drew's sister?

Chapter 20

Birdie woke with a headache, a throbbing, itching neck, and a male arm draped over her waist, complete with a large hand cupped around one breast. Light beyond the curtains made her think it was morning.

She was on her side with a wall of warmth at her back. Warm puffs of air caressed her neck. At least she recognized the scent. Ozzie. What she didn't recognize, didn't remember, was how they came to be in her bed. Because it was her room. That much she did recognize. And it was nearly ten in the morning according to her alarm clock.

Still, other than a great need for the bathroom, she was quite comfortable, and wearing something other than a sheet and a man's arm. She looked down at herself and recognized her nightshirt. The oversized green one she sometimes used as a pool cover-up. Experimentally she shifted her legs and discovered they were bare and entwined with a harder, hairier male leg. And she seemed to be wearing panties, but not a bra. Had she undressed herself, or had someone done it for her?

Ozzie started to stir behind her. His hand flexed, lightly pinching her nipple, and she felt something very male begin to stir against her rear. Suddenly the hairy legs molded behind hers seemed to bring out goose bumps all down her legs. This was almost sexier than his lips touching her bare skin that night in San Francisco. And much more wicked, since it was in her bed, in her parents' flat.

The hand on her breast started to move, and she slapped hers over it to keep it right where it was. Behind her the sleepy body stiffened.

"Courtney?" His sleep rough voice vibrated right through her. "Are you all right?"

"Ozzie, what happened? I remember getting stung, I remember walking toward the elevators, but I seem to be missing a whole bunch of hours."

His big exhale tickled the fine hairs on the side of her neck. "In case you're wondering, we didn't have sex."

"I never said we did." Although she had wondered and it was too damn bad they didn't, although she would have liked to remember it. "But I'm wondering about a few other things."

"We made a stop by hospital on the way home from Ascot, which was before lunch could be served. Blood tests proved you'd been roofied, but mildly so. The combination of the drug with the antihistamine for the bee sting mixed with however much wine you'd had, really knocked you out. However, after a couple hours of observation they set you free with the promise we wouldn't leave you alone over night."

"Was I asleep this whole time?"

"With help, you walked out of the clinic and managed to get into your night clothes and crawl into bed mostly under your own power. Sort of like a drunken sailor."

"Oh there's a lovely picture."

"Actually, it was. You make the world's prettiest drunken sailor, and had it been only play acting, I might have taken you up on your very blatant offers." Teasing touched Ozzie's tone, something she hadn't ever heard before from him.

A hot flush rushed to every nerve ending she had. "I propositioned you?"

Ozzie's chuckle vibrated against her back. "It was very flattering, but I wouldn't take advantage of a woman so obviously under the influence." She tried to wiggle away, but his arm held her secure. "Don't be embarrassed."

"Of course I'm embarrassed." She wrapped a hand around his wrist and tried to pull his arm away.

"Steady on, darling. I'm not awake enough to wrestle."

Birdie groaned. Yes, she'd wondered about waking up in Ozzie's arms, but this wasn't how she'd imagined it all.

"I need to…um…get up."

"Of course. Forgive me. I'll meet you in the kitchen. What you need now is plenty of water, and probably a cup or two of tea."

"I want coffee," she said just to be contrary.

Ozzie slowly removed his hand from her breast, sliding it down her stomach, around to her waist, and landing on her hip.

"Got to admit, I don't want to move from here," Ozzie whispered against her ear. "You're soft and smell very sweet. And you're oh so warm."

"And if it weren't for calls of nature, I wouldn't dream of leaving this bed," she assured him. His lips tugging on her earlobe melted whatever remaining resistance she had. If she'd ever had any to begin with. For the life of her she couldn't remember why she'd ever disliked this man.

"Go on, then. I'll make breakfast."

Reluctantly, Birdie rolled from the bed and bee-lined for the bathroom.

"And don't change out of your nighty," Ozzie called after her. "It's back to bed after sustenance for you. Grandmother's orders."

The door slammed on her groan. She was twenty-four. Would she ever escape orders from well-meaning family members? Maybe she should go ahead with finding her own flat. As much as she enjoyed the luxury of this one, especially all to herself, it was still too accessible to family members. Hell, if Drew and Meilin flew into London tomorrow, they'd be staying in the flat right alongside her. For now, she freshened up, brushed both teeth and hair. A long look in the mirror confirmed wrinkles from the pillowcase pressed into her cheek and shadows under her eyes. If she calculated right, she'd slept the better part of eighteen hours. Damnit. She was horribly late for work.

Reaching for the shower knob, she jumped when the door from Drew's side of the bathroom opened and Ozzie came through with a mug in his hand.

"Unless you really want a shower, there's no hurry. You've been excused from work for the day." His gaze traveled over her body, from bare feet to bare thighs, then up the baggy shirt she wore for sleeping, to her face. "You need more sleep after you eat and get some liquids in you. Still need to flush the last of the chemicals from your system." He set the mug on the vanity, gave her one last, long head to toe visual scan, then turned on his bare heel and left the bathroom. It was only then she realized he'd only been wearing a pair of what were probably Drew's basketball shorts.

She leaned against the counter, hand over her wildly beating heart. The man hit her like a hurricane, then disappeared like a wisp of smoke. Then his words hit her. Excused from work for the day. Well, she wouldn't miss the filing room. Did that mean he was spending the day with her? Maybe she could talk to him about some of her budding ideas…or seduce him.

Twenty minutes later she sauntered out to the kitchen, freshly showered and wearing a summer set of pajamas. The set was made up of shorts and a camisole, blue with little anchors printed on the fabric. Perfect for lounging around the flat on a warm sunny day. Rare for London after a sunny weekend, but according to the news, Londoners were taking advantage and thronging the streets instead of tending to their jobs.

Ozzie took in her look, then turned to open the oven and pull out a steaming dish. "Frittata," he answered her unspoken question. He set the pan on the stove as he shut the oven door. With a smooth movement he pushed down the handle on the large toaster Mom bought last year, the one that toasted four slices of bread at once.

"Get the butter and jam, would you? Everything else is on the table."

"Smells wonderful." She wandered right up to his side and leaned over the bubbling egg casserole. "Mmm."

Ozzie looked at her as she straightened. "You seem to be feeling chipper."

"Actually, all things considered, I do feel pretty good. Other than the hideous welt on my throat."

Using a gentle hand, he brushed her damp hair back and took a good long look at the site of her sting. "It's already shrinking, the welt fading, but it wouldn't hurt to use the cream and cover it again. After we eat I'll help you with that." The light brush of his fingers against her neck made her want to forget food, but the delicious scents reminded her she hadn't eaten lunch or dinner yesterday. Or had she?

"Did we eat last night?"

"You had a few sips of soup and tea, but mostly you were too out of it for more than that. I spent several hours trying to rouse you to get water into you."

She frowned. "I don't remember. I have vague dream-like impressions of sitting on very exposed toilets, like being on a market street with several stalls, but only with half-height walls. No privacy at all."

Her embarrassment flared when he chuckled and reached beyond her head to get two plates from the cabinet. "Grab the butter and jam. I set the table on the terrace. A little sun and fresh air will do us both good."

Birdie carried out her job and sat at the table. Oswald had set their places side by side so they could both appreciate the view. It was a rare day with no clouds and a soft breeze. Not too hot, not cool. Sunlight sparkled on the surface of the Thames, and boats moved up and down the river. Working barges, sightseeing cruisers, even a couple speedboats pulling skiers. Walkers filled the footpaths that traveled along the riverbanks and crossed the many bridges, stopping to pose or take photos, or merely to admire the flow of the river.

A plate appeared in her line of sight, then was set in front of her. "Smells wonderful."

"Eat while it's hot." Oswald settled into the chair beside her. "I hope you feel special, brunch on the terrace on a perfect day. This happens rarely more than once in a lifetime in London."

"I'm appreciating it."

They ate with little conversation. Birdie was too busy shoveling in the food to talk. And far too aware of a nearly naked Ozzie beside her. Without a shirt on, all his impressive muscles were on display. Each one flexing under smooth skin as he quietly ate his food, as proper as always. The man had more inborn grace than anyone she'd ever met, including her very proper father and brother. The only thing he lacked was the golden tan the other two had acquired in California. But give him a summer over there and he'd be a bronzed god.

At last she put the last forkful of eggs, cheese, and fresh vegetables into her mouth and moaned. Drew had proven he could cook a time or two while they'd shared their apartment, but Ozzie did more than cook. He created manna from heaven. Setting down her fork, she leaned back and savored the last bite before swallowing. "That was delicious."

"Thank you. Nothing more than a fancy omelet."

"Still fabulous." She patted her stomach. "Do we really have the day off?" She slapped a hand over the yawn that surprised her.

"Yes. Your grandmother made me swear I wouldn't leave your side all day. Not until you could string two coherent sentences together." He shifted in his chair and sat back with his hands wrapped around a large coffee mug resting on his flat stomach.

"Well, I'm feeling coherent, but I don't feel much like moving from this spot."

"I'm not much in favor of moving myself. Haven't taken a day to sit on a sunny terrace in longer than I can remember." She caught him turning his head to look at her. "You should lie down again. I'd say you're maybe seventy-five percent recovered. You should be good to go by morning."

"Just fifteen minutes in the sun. After, I'll find shade, but I'm short on natural vitamin D. Wouldn't hurt you, either."

Ozzie laughed. "Me lying about in the sun. I'll burn to a crisp."

"Fifteen minutes won't burn you. It will give you a light touch of color. And if you're really worried about it, I'm sure I can dig up a tube of sunscreen and rub it into your back."

Ozzie's eyes heated behind the lenses of his glasses. Hair normally neatly combed was a little disheveled, partly from the breeze, and partly from sleep. Only he didn't look sleepy.

"I'll pass. Help me get the dishes cleared; then you can nap outside under the umbrella if you wish." His gaze slid down her body again, surely taking in the way her nipples tightened under the soft cotton of her camisole. She hadn't put on a bra or panties, and the short bottoms were almost as revealing as short boy-cut panties. Rubbing her thighs together didn't relieve the ache building there. The fact he noticed the movement and swallowed deeply, his Adam's apple moving beneath his unshaved skin, only made her restlessness worse.

"Sure. Let's clean up." She either had to do something mundane or jump into his lap.

Swinging her hips, she carried her load into the kitchen, set it in the sink, then opened the dishwasher. When she heard Ozzie behind her, she bent over to get the detergent from beneath the sink and took her time filling the cup. Ozzie's hip bumped her bottom as he set his load beside hers in the sink. Shifting her weight, she rubbed against him, sure her invitation was unmistakable. When Ozzie's big hand cupped her bottom, she was positive.

"You're sending out signals you can't possibly understand, Courtney," he said gruffly.

"I understand." She straightened and leaned back against his chest. It was probably an automatic move on his part, but his hand slide around to her front, fingers splayed over her lower abdomen, and pulled her tighter against his body. This time she was sober enough to fully recognize his body's reaction to hers. "Please," she whispered.

"No, Courtney. Not like this."

"Exactly like this. I don't need silk sheets and rose petals."

"It's what you deserve."

"I don't. We have a day and a night to ourselves. If we take it."

Ozzie groaned and dropped his lips to her neck, a tender spot behind her ear she never knew existed. It was like an instant touch point that made her weak and her blood boil in an instant. "Please," she begged. "I want to know. I want it to be you."

The groan against her neck was one of surrender.

"Ever since you first touched me..." She gasped as his teeth lightly bit her earlobe, then nibbled down the side of her neck. His right hand claimed its hold on her mons, his fingers slipping between her legs. His left hand cupped her chin, tilting her head and turning it so his lips could tease the edge of hers.

"Ever since I touched you, what?"

Birdie twisted her hips, wanting more from his hand. "Ever since you made me come, with your hands, your mouth, I wanted to do the same for you."

Ozzie's intake of air was sudden and harsh. "There are so many reasons this isn't a good idea."

"I don't care. I get to choose my first, and I want it to be you."

"Bloody hell. It should be someone else, Courtney."

She also noticed that didn't stop his hand from delving deeper between her thighs, or his lips from traveling down her neck.

"Ozichu, I choose you." She reached behind her and grasped his hips, pulling him closer yet.

"Ozichu? Is that like Pikachu?" He chuckled at his new nickname.

"Because your touch is electrifying. I don't want anyone else. Just you."

And how could a man argue with that? He couldn't; she smugly answered her own question.

"And what princess wants, princess gets." Although the words could be considered sarcastic, the groan in his throat, the rasping of his breath over her skin, turned the meaning around.

"Don't forget it." The tender nip of his teeth against her neck brought out a gasp.

"I never do." A second later she was off the ground, cradled in his arms. "But we're going to do this right. I won't take you bent over the kitchen bench."

Chapter 21

Exquisite excitement coursed through Oswald's veins like a flash flood. Although this was a monumentally bad idea, he could no longer deny himself. Her. Them. The need to touch her had been clawing at him for weeks now. Ever since he'd given in the night of the wedding. He'd tried to be honorable, but screw that. He merely pretended to be a gentleman. That time was over when it came to being near her.

Especially since she'd made it clear. She knew exactly what she asked of him. His only fear was living up to her romanticized expectations. This girl-woman was so very different from the usual ingénues he paired off with. All of them knew the score going in. He was there for their pleasure, and only if they were satisfactorily pleased was he requested again. Beyond inviting Courtney to Ascot, he couldn't remember the last time he'd initiated a date. That time was over. No more playing stud to any socialite who wanted to dabble on the dark side.

Walking down the hall, he made a detour into Drew's room, earning him a look of confusion.

"I'm hoping he has condoms," Oswald explained. "I'm not in the habit of carrying one on a daily basis."

Courtney's reddened lips rounded in a silent O as her cheeks colored.

Sitting on the edge of the bed, Oswald was able to dig into a bedside drawer without letting go of Courtney. Luck was on their side. He found a strip of three almost immediately.

"I had no idea," Courtney murmured.

"Don't think about it," he ordered, then kissed her to get her mind back where it needed to be. On making love with him.

Once she fought for breath, Oswald stood and carried her through the shared en suite into her room. The still rumpled sheets of her bed suited him just fine. While she truly deserved silk sheets strewn with fresh rose petals, he'd take rumpled fine cotton any time. The fresh scent mingled with her lemon fragrance was earthier, cleaner. Much like her sunny California disposition.

Once more sitting on the side of a bed, he settled her on his lap, took off his glasses, set them on the night stand, and took her mouth again. He dropped the condoms beside his glasses, then slid his hand up under the scrap of fabric she probably called a camisole pajama top. Under his palm the muscles of her abdomen fluttered.

"So soft. Warm. Beautiful," he murmured between kisses.

Her hand drifted from around his neck, down over his shoulder, to his chest, and lower to his abs that hardened at the light touch as she studied his muscles like a blind woman memorizing a sculpture. Each place her tiny fingers touched burned as if scorched.

Slowing down, gently approaching her breast, was one of the harder things he'd ever done. Known for his slow hands, he wanted to throw that reputation out the window. He wanted to touch all of her, kiss everywhere, taste everything all at once. Her mouth tasted of coffee and innocence. Her skin as soft as silk. Her body strong and supple, firm and soft, slender yet perfectly proportioned. The bumps of her vertebrae smooth and silky like pearls as his other hand traveled upward under her top, pushing it up as he went. The hand on her stomach also traveled upward, his fingers stroking the underside of her full breasts, his gaze on her face.

Courtney's eyes closed, her face tilted heavenward, she gasped from slightly parted lips. Her profile was a work of art, and given the first opportunity, he'd get a photograph of her just like that.

From her back, he flipped the tiny top over her head. She pulled her arm from around his neck, the fabric sliding off quickly so she could return her arm to his shoulder, holding on. The warm flesh of her torso touched his. Under her thighs he hardened, pushing up against her, seeking the space heating against his thigh. Impatiently she pulled her hand from his stomach long enough for her top to fall away completely with a flick of his wrist.

Slowly, determined to not startle her out of her moment of growing ecstasy, he gently cradled one weighty breast, cupping her, savoring the joy at holding her. Without opening her eyes, Courtney inhaled deeply, her breath catching as his thumb glided over her tightened, berry-pink nipple.

"More."

Oswald watched her face, once more skipping a finger over her very tender nipple.

Courtney's face tilted downward again, her eyes opening only enough to see him through her lashes. Full pink lips parted to form the order, "More."

He curled his forefinger up to join his thumb, capturing her nipple between them. Slowly, drawing out her agony, he applied pressure until he had her tightly clamped and her breath hitched. Just as slowly he rolled her flesh between his digits. A flattering pink warmed her skin and she squirmed on his lap. When he moved to pulling, equally as controlled and slow, she moaned, thrusting her breast into his hand. Against his chest he felt her neglected nipple grazing his skin, exquisitely torturing him, reminding him he wanted to touch all of her.

As her body arched more, he cupped the back of her skull, holding her as she once more gasped toward the ceiling. Wanting her breath, he gently kissed the corner of her mouth, extending his tongue to taste her lips.

With a slight turn of her head, he took those sweet lips as they opened for him, her tongue tentatively touching his lower lip. God, he groaned, she tasted better than the finest whisky, rich and sweet.

Amazed he could focus on more than one sensation, he continued to roll and tug her nipple, feeling her moist heat grow against his thigh.

One small twist of her torso and Courtney pressed both breasts against his chest, the hard points shocking him into momentary stillness. The slow torture was more than he could handle, despite his desire to go slow for her.

Abandoning the plan, for a few minutes anyway, he grasped her waist and lifted her. "Stand up a second, love."

She mewled in protest, but did as he demanded. It barely took a heartbeat for her bottoms to slide over her hips to land on the floor around her feet. Without pause, she reached for the waistband of the shorts he'd borrowed from Drew's closet. Determined to control the pace, he stood. She beat him to the punch by pushing the garment down a second before he lifted her in his arms again.

"Naughty girl. You have to trust me here. I'm the teacher, remember?"

"I think you can speed up the lesson a little." It was her only complaint as she once more clung to his shoulders.

"Patience, wench. Good things to come to girls who wait for them." He turned and lowered her to the rumpled bed and disengaged her arms from around his neck. "Now lie back so I can see you."

"I want to see you too. Last time I didn't get the chance."

Her small pout was adorable. She truly was annoyed he'd kept his trousers on in her hotel room. Well, now she could look, and her eyes glazed over as she drank in the sight of him at full salute. Her blue eyes darkened, and her little pink tongue swept her swollen bottom lip, leaving it glistening. Instantly giving him a vision of those sweet lips wrapped around him. A fantasy for later.

For now, he had a girl to convert to a woman, and she needed special care.

He knelt on the bed, then fell forward to rest on his hands. Gaze firmly captured on her eyes, he crawled over her, using his knees to nudge hers aside enough to settle between creamy golden thighs. The brazen wench crooked a finger, calling him to come to her. Braced over her body, he shook his head. "I'm calling the shots, darling. Lie back and enjoy."

"Ozzie," she huffed out in frustration. "You're killing me."

"Then you'll die with a smile on your face," he promised, then bent to take her neglected nipple between his lips.

The gasp and arching of her body filled him satisfaction. Her nails skimming his scalp as she tunneled into his hair induced a flame of pleasure that traveled from point of contact down his spine to his bollocks. Nothing shy and sweet about this innocent miss. She knew exactly what she wanted even if she couldn't put a name to it.

Resisting her attempt to hold him there, he nuzzled her other breast and treated the nipple to a long suckle, enjoying the writhing of her body rising to his. Following a path previously scouted, he trailed kisses and dots of moisture from his tongue down her sternum, around her belly button, and continued to the trimmed patch of blonde hair at the junction of her thighs.

The soft hair tickled his face, and the scent of her heat filled his nostrils, making his mouth water to taste her again.

He slipped his arms under her thighs and used his hands to hold her hips down. He'd almost forgotten her ability to move against his mouth. Movement reined in for the moment, he took advantage, using his shoulders to press her thighs open wider, opening her to his view.

She shuddered at the small stream of air he blew over her quivering flesh. So wet already. She smelled even sweeter here, and he bent his head to taste her. At the first glancing sweep of his tongue down her outer lips, she moaned and tried to thrust upward, only to be held back by his grip. It was possible he'd leave fingerprint-sized bruises. A small mark to remind her she was his now. A thought he'd never entertained before. Had he ever taken a virgin to bed? He didn't think so. A reminder to slow down and make this memory one they'd both treasure for a lifetime. Draw out every moment until it was engraved upon their memory neurons. Settled in their cells for eternity.

She wasn't the only one changing today. Tonight. From the moment he'd laid eyes on her at Court and Randi's Sussex wedding, he'd been doing his best to steer away from this very occasion. He'd fought to maintain distance, but every event seemed to toss them into the same sphere time and time again. He wouldn't walk away from this without some mark on his soul. What kind of mark was still up for debate.

Under his tongue she quivered and moaned, straining against his hold, whimpering for the release he held just out of her reach. The longer he held it back, the wetter she grew. Very necessary to the impending joining.

Two sides of his soul fought for and against the coming claiming. One side cringed at the pain he'd inflict, the other pushed for the pleasure to follow. At last she sobbed, begging him for mercy. With a carefully aimed flick of his tongue, precisely timed suckle, she broke against his mouth, her body stiffly arching with a wordless cry from her elegant throat, before bucking and calling out his name.

While she quivered with aftershocks, he rose up on his hands and knees, crawling over her body to reach for a condom he swiftly rolled into place. She was still gasping as he pressed his cock into her oh so wet cunny.

"It's time, love," he said through gritted teeth.

Courtney didn't say a word, just nodded and gripped his arms now braced beside her breasts. Lord, she was a beauty, her skin flushed a deep pink, eyes glazed, nipples hard as little red berries. And she was his for the taking.

He slid into her, pausing at the constriction he met. He took a few short strokes, almost fighting her tight muscles for admittance. Each thrust growing easier as she relaxed, and her natural moisture rushed in, allowing him to advance fractions of an inch at a time. When her gaze met his, when she smiled at him, he grit his teeth, pulled back, then thrust forward with a greatly restrained grunt when he wanted to roar.

Beneath him Courtney stiffened with a surprised yelp.

"That's it, love. Just hold still and you'll adjust." The gruff, raspy voice coming from him was foreign.

"That hurt." She lightly slapped his shoulder. "But then again, I knew to expect it," she whispered.

"We'll talk about it later." God knew he didn't want to talk now. He wanted to move inside her. Desperately. "Is it easing?"

Small frown lines formed between her eyes, but he could see the pain fading along with the panic. The panic and pain just about killed him. "Is it better?" He moved a fraction of an inch and her face began to clear.

"Yeah. It's fading. And I feel…"

Slowly he withdrew half an inch and just as slowly thrust forward, going a bit deeper.

"Oooohhhhhh," she drew out the word on a long exhale. "Yeah, Ozzie, *there. That.*"

Thank God, he silently prayed, and began to move. Still slow, far slower than instinct demanded, but slow enough to bring her back, build her passion. In her eyes, he watched the transformation from pain to blazing desire. It didn't take long for her to join him, matching her movements to his.

"That's right, love. Let the passion build again."

Her hands roamed his chest, grazing his nipples, sliding down his sides, around to his back.

His arms shaking from the strain, he lowered himself until his elbows held his body over hers. Close enough her nipples rubbed against his chest, high enough he didn't crush her and he could keep eye contact with her.

The glaze began to spread over her beautiful blue eyes as he felt her body arch and strain against him. "Faster, oh please, faster…"

This is what the stairway to heaven felt like. The writhing of two bodies covered with a light sheen of sweat, her tight channel clasping around his cock, drawing him in deeper, seeking the very heart of a woman. This woman. The woman whose innocent hands stroked his back as if stoking a fire. Soft thighs braced his hips, then circled his waist as she brought her legs up to hug him tighter.

Pinning her arms to her sides, he curled his hands around her shoulders, feeling the fragility of her even as he increased the pace, angling his pelvis to press against her sensitive bundle of nerves. Her gasp was his reward while a streak of lightning traveled down to the base of his spine. He wouldn't last much longer and knew it was iffy for her to climax with him. More than anything he didn't want to leave her behind.

Shifting his weight to his left arm, he wedged the right between them and stroked her.

Holding back waiting for that first shudder of her release just about killed him, but by God he'd take her with him even if it gave him a heart attack.

And just when he thought his heart would burst, she arched up, a thin wail on her lips, before her climax broke with a force that rolled her head back and forth on the pillow.

She called out his name, her nickname for him, over and over again, clutching him tighter as fire brought his body to a boil and he found his own bliss rolling on and on before at last the waves began to calm and his body slumped onto hers.

With the last of his strength he pulled his hand away from where their bodies melded into one and reestablished his semi braced position over her. Both of them were breathing hard enough he feared collapsing and crushing her.

An eternity of her body pulsing around him, massaging the last drops of his energy, passed before she heaved a great sigh of happiness. His face was buried in the fine blonde strands spread over the pillow, inhaling the scents of her, them, the best perfume in the world. Lazily his lips touched her throat and she shivered.

"Oh. Wow." She sighed again.

"The sweet mystery of life," he murmured.

"Oh, how very sweet it is." She kissed his ear and rubbed her hands up and down his back. "I could stay here forever."

It was a weak effort, but somehow he managed a chuckle.

"Oh, do that again. I felt it everywhere."

The baggage was incorrigible. Finding one more spurt of energy, he rolled, taking her with him until he lay on his back with her draped over him, still connected. He needed to deal with the condom, but he didn't want to let go. Instead he nuzzled her temple.

"Disadvantage of condoms, I need to dispose of it before it leaks." Even to his own ears he sounded mournful.

Courtney lightly pressed her lips to his. "Okay. Go. Be responsible, then come right back."

"As you wish." He kissed her, then gently rolled her off his chest, disengaging them.

In the bathroom he took care of business, then rounded up a cloth he wet with warm water. Courtney was sprawled on the bed, more than half asleep.

He sat at her hip and gently used the cloth to clean her. At the look of perfect fulfillment on her face, a glow of something primal filled his chest.

She was his.

And damn his soul, he didn't want another living being ever seeing her like this.

Chapter 22

At Ozzie's touch, Birdie stirred, a little embarrassed to have him tend to her in such an intimate manner. Not so embarrassed that she protested. She was far too tired for that. Far too satiated to care.

Ozzie finished and tossed the damp cloth back toward the bathroom. She opened her eyes as the bed dipped from him once more crawling up the bed, kissing her bits as he came back. First a kiss and a lick on her mound that made her squirm at the tenderness he found there. Then one hip bone, followed by the other. He kissed her navel, each rib, and finally each nipple. She moaned and reached for him, not resisting an inch when he curled his arms under her shoulders, and pressed his lips to hers as he rolled them until once more she was draped over him like a cheap blanket.

Ear pressed to his chest, she listened to the soothing rhythm of his heart, the sound of his lungs exchanging air like the gently shushing of waves on a beach. A natural lullaby that pulled her under.

The sun was considerably lower in the sky when she woke to the gentle stroking of his hands moving up and down her back.

A little moan escaped her. "Am I too heavy?"

"No. You're perfect."

His voice was a rumble beneath her. With his accent, unbelievably sexy. His breath a warm puff against the top of her head.

"You're the perfect one," she mumbled before yawning. To her mortification, her stomach growled right along.

Amusement laced his voice. "Sounds like time for a shower, then dinner."

"Mmm. Sounds wonderful. I can get something from the freezer and drop it in the oven."

"Shower first; then we'll see what we can scrounge up."

Ozzie rolled until she was under him once more. She could get used to this, she realized. "Can we do that again?"

He kissed her deeply, then pulled back and brushed a strand of hair off her face. "Not for a day at least, love. You're probably a little sore about now." The look in his eyes was extremely tender. "I hurt you. Couldn't be helped, but it's over and done now. I'm only sorry we'll have to restrain ourselves until the soreness is gone."

"You've been reading old wives' tales." Birdie let herself pout playfully. "I'm not sore."

Ozzie's smile was crooked. "Wait until you try to walk. You'll probably feel like you've been on a horse for a full day. Bet you look cute walking bowlegged."

Laughter burst from her. "I bet not."

"Still, a warm shower will help."

His palm cupped her cheek and she turned into it. "Sounds good."

Indeed, his sponge bath notwithstanding, she felt a little sticky from the sweat they'd worked up.

Leveraging himself up onto his hands, Ozzie reached for hers and pulled her to a sitting position as he sat back on his heels. "Come, my lady, let me tend to your needs."

Hand in hand they wandered into the bathroom. He started the shower while she dug out a packaged toothbrush from a drawer and reached for hers.

Teeth brushed and shower steaming, he held the door for her and ushered her into the double wide enclosure, just right for two.

Birdie reached for her shower gel, but Ozzie beat her to it. He nudged her under the spray and poured the citrus scented gel into his hand.

Having never showered with a man before, Birdie let him rub her down with the foam, sharing the bubbles with him. The decadence of him massaging shampoo into her hair, then carefully rinsing it out, almost made her swoon. Lord, she was falling hard for him with each caring touch he treated her body to. He was especially gentle between her legs although his erection pressed against her backside. An advantage she pressed when she rolled her hips against him.

"Easy, love. None of that here. First of all, you're sore, I can tell by how you move. Second of all, no condom here."

She turned in his arms and rubbed her lower half against him. "But there's something I can do for you." With a shy smile, she slid to her knees and took him in hand.

"Courtney, there's no nee—"

Wrapping her lips around his crown effectively shut off his protest.

"Lord." His breath shuddered out of his body with each stroke of her tongue.

No, she had no experience here, other than what she'd read or seen during the one porno she'd watched years ago. But she was already determined to do her best. She owed him at least one after their night in San Francisco.

"Courtney, love." His fingers slipped through her wet hair, his hands gentle as he gripped her head. "Really, I don't expect—"

With both hands wrapped around him, she lowered her head, sucking him into her mouth.

"Oh, bloody hell, that feels good, love."

She looked up at him, only the tip still in her mouth, and found him staring down, his eyes burning with what she now recognized as lust. No doubt, he wanted her, even as awkward as she was. Gaze glued to his, she moved forward, taking him deep, deep, her lips stretched as wide as she could go, doing her best to keep from scraping him with her teeth, until he touched the back of her throat and her gag reflex kicked in.

She pulled back abruptly, eyes watering as he reached for her arms.

"Love, come here."

She shook her head and leaned forward again.

Ozzie groaned. "Easy, love, don't go so far you choke. We can work on that later. Seriously, you don't have to—"

With one hand on his shaft, she wrapped the other around his balls, cutting him off once again. She marveled at how close they'd drawn up to his body. She hadn't expected that.

"Unless you want a mouthful," he said sounding as if he'd just run a marathon, "back off, love. I can't stop it—"

She bent forward again and sucked as if he were a popsicle. A hot, hard popsicle covered by the silkiest skin she'd ever felt. The hand gripping him moved with her head as she bobbed up and down his length. In her other hand his balls tightened more as she gently massaged them until he threw back his head with a roar. In her mouth he grew a little more and then hot streams of thick liquid hit the back of her throat.

Acting on instinct, she pulled off while trying to cover her gagging. She kept her hand pumping and he kept coming, his seed landing on her lips, chin, and finally her chest. His hand covered hers, showing her how to stroke, how to squeeze, until the last drop beaded on the tip.

Ozzie leaned over her, bracing himself with one hand on the tile wall behind her.

Birdie gently kissed the tip of his cock, and it twitched in her hand. He opened his eyes and gazed down at her kneeling at his feet, looking up at him, while little spits of water dripped from his shoulders onto her face.

"Now there's a sight to inspire a man," he said softly. One hand still braced on the wall, he reached down with the other. She placed her hand in his and he helped her to her feet where he hauled her into his arms, hugging her close. Arms wrapped around his waist, she clung to him, the spray now full on her head and back.

Once his heartbeat returned to normal, Ozzie lifted her face. She could feel the remains of his ejaculate on her skin. He rubbed a thumb over one spot on her chin, his eyes warm and affectionate. "You need another washing."

After dinner and cuddling on the sofa through a movie, Ozzie dressed in his Ascot duds and reluctantly left. She had to concede he had a point, he needed a business suit and she needed to heal. Didn't make it any easier to kiss him good night.

But at least they had plans for the following night. She smiled to herself and packed her tote with workout clothes and an outfit for work. In case she went home with him and stayed the night. And while she was at it, she'd stop by the chemist and stock up on condoms.

Chapter 23

Birdie bounced into the office the next day prepared to have the best work day of her life. The rain was light with hints of the sun breaking through on her walk over. Her feet felt light as air, and she nearly floated over the puddles and around the people filling the sidewalk. She even managed to arrive ten minutes early.

In the filing room, she leaned her umbrella against the desk and tossed her purse and tote into the drawer before looking at her desktop. There was a note in a little envelope centered on the blotter. She opened the sealed note and read the words in her mother's handwriting. She'd listed the boxes of chocolates she'd sent and who they were for. A two pound box to share with Birdie's current department, a one pound box for Dennis, and one for Mrs. Cuthbert. Last, one filled with only soft milk chocolates for Birdie.

So she had the note, but where were the chocolates?

Puzzled, she wandered toward Mrs. Smith's office to ask. First of all, why would anyone open a box addressed to her, and then what would they do with the chocolate? Passing the coffee corner, she saw a sight that made her stop. Two boxes sat on the counter. Chocolates. She lifted a lid of one and saw what looked like the combined remains jumbled together. The other box looked about the same. So where were the other two?

"Courtney. There you are. I must say the treat from your mum was quite well received."

She turned to see Mrs. Smith approach with a coffee mug in hand.

"Are you feeling better? Mrs. Cuthbert called down yesterday morning saying you were under the weather." The supervisor's eyes zeroed in on the fading welt on Birdie's neck. "Oh dear. That doesn't look like a love bite?"

Birdie swallowed. "Bee sting. Sunday at Ascot."

Mrs. Smith's smirk turned to shock. "Oh dear. Tell me you aren't allergic? That looks like it still hurts."

"It's not so bad now. No, I'm not allergic. I also had a reaction to something else." She smiled wryly. "Sunday wasn't my day, and between the doctor and my grandmother I got grounded yesterday."

"With good reason." Mrs. Smith nodded. "Well, the package from your mother arrived yesterday and before I could stop her, one of the clerks opened your mail. Since you'd said your parents were sending chocolate to share..." Suddenly she didn't look so sure and glanced at the note Birdie still clutched. "Oh, dear, did we err?"

Looking at the ground, Birdie took a moment to think. Yeah, she was bummed her surprise had been stolen, or rather over anticipated. But the damage was done now. Maybe Mom could send another package. Only this time directing it to the flat or Dad's office with clear instructions to be opened only by Birdie.

"I'm guessing it was addressed to the department," Birdie said.

"It was, but it did have your name on it." Mrs. Smith frowned. "It seems we took advantage?"

What a dilemma. Complain about it and come off looking like Daddy's privileged spoiled princess, or let it ride in the name of peace? She shrugged. "I'd hoped to spread it out a little, but what's done is done." She crumpled the note and tossed it into the nearby trash can. Forcing a cheerful smile, she did her best to sound nonchalant. "I'm glad it was enjoyed." Turning to the counter, she noted the empty coffee carafe. "Looks like we get to make the first pot of the day."

It was silly, really, considering how wonderfully yesterday had turned out, but the chocolate debacle cast a shadow over her day. It took everything inside to hide her disappointment behind a bright smile, especially when Sally, the senior clerk who'd taken it upon herself to plunder Birdie's treasure, made a half-hearted apology. Clearly forced into it by Mrs. Smith, Sally barely made a show of pretending to be repentant, and Birdie took it a face value. From Birdie's first day in the department, Sally had made it clear she wasn't impressed with Birdie's family connection or education.

When Mrs. Smith told her later in the day she was being moved across the department to learn data input of the invoices and manifests, it gave her a slight lift. She'd be away from the filing clerks and working with people who might have more respect for her abilities.

At least she had tonight with Ozzie to look forward to. A training session, hopefully followed by more love making. Yeah, that new activity had certainly caught her attention. Just thinking of Ozzie's muscles, lips, hands, and the way he used all his intriguing body parts definitely lifted Birdie's mood as she finished her stack of filing. Since she had five minutes left and had cleared her desk, she texted her mom.

Chocolates received and enjoyed.

Mom's reply was nearly immediate: *Lovely to hear. But Mrs. C. didn't say a word when Dad called in this afternoon. Did she not get her box?*

Damn. The simple message hadn't done the job. *No, sorry. Box was intercepted while I was out and Accounting reaped the benefit of your generosity. They're still moaning over the deliciousness.*

Mom pinged back: *Next time I'll ship to the flat or Dad's office. How are you feeling? Better?*

This she could answer truthfully. *Yes. Much better. Ozzie makes a good babysitter. He's promised to investigate the suspected culprit.*

Mom apparently was glued to her phone: *I can't believe you got roofied. It took some fast talking from your Gran and Dad to keep me from flying back immediately. I wanted to be home with you yesterday.*

Sending silent thanks to her father and grandmother, she typed out a reply: *I wasn't hit so bad. Recovery was fast. The bee did more damage. Enjoy your trip and stop worrying about me. I have an army of support here.* And to forestall more texts: *Time to run. Learning a little self-defense tonight.*

Mom: *Excellent. Lovies from Dad and me.*

Birdie sent back a heart and stuffed her phone into her purse.

Cheerful mood back in place, she arrived outside Ozzie's office with a smile on her face for Mrs. Cuthbert. At a pang of disappointment for not having Mrs. C's treat, she smiled brighter to cover.

"There's the lovely girl." Mrs. Cuthbert smiled at Birdie. "Looks like you're recovering from your unfortunate experience at Ascot. Did you enjoy Saturday? I hope Sunday didn't put you off the races."

"Oh I had a great time. Very fun. I even won fifty pounds on Saturday." Ozzie's door opened, and she flashed him a smile too. "Come to think of it, wonder if I won anything on Sunday?"

"You did," he said, apparently back to his aloof demeanor. Not even a twinkle in his eye indicated how he felt about seeing her. "I asked Hammond to collect your winnings. We still need to figure out how much belongs to Mrs. Robinson, but you did well from what Hammond said."

"Awesome!" She restrained her glee to a smile instead of bouncing and clapping like she wanted to.

From behind her the sound of a woman's heels clicked on the marble flooring. She glanced over her shoulder to see Mrs. Smith approaching with a piece of paper in her hand and a worried look in her eye. When she noticed Birdie, Mrs. Smith slowed to a halt in front of Mrs. Cuthbert's desk and shot a glance at Ozzie.

"I thought you'd gone home, Miss Robinson," Mrs. Smith said.

"I'm heading out in a few."

Mrs. C jumped in, fortunately. "Is there something I may help you with, Mrs. Smith?"

"I was wondering if I could take a moment of Mr. Attenborough's time." She looked at him directly.

Ozzie nodded. "If you don't mind waiting a moment, Mrs. Smith, I need to have a word with Miss Robinson."

"Oh, no. I'm in no hurry." Her smile looked a little forced, but Birdie wasn't going to worry about it.

"Courtney?"

She turned to see him holding out a hand indicating he wanted to speak to her in his office. Okay. She gave him a brilliant smile and sauntered through his door, which he closed after following her. In anticipation, she turned only to watch him walk right past her, headed for his desk. Not what she expected.

"What's up, Ozzie?"

"In the office, please call me Mr. Attenborough," he said curtly, surprising her.

That was annoying, but technically he was correct. "All right, Mr. Attenborough."

He held a hand to his chest, holding his tie back as he shot her a sharp glance while settling into his chair. "Have a seat." A wave of his hand indicated he meant one of the chairs across the desk from him.

Heart sinking, Birdie sat as he ordered. What the hell was going on?

Once she was sitting, he cleared his throat, but he gazed at her steadily, his eyes blank of any emotion.

"I'm afraid I have to cancel our plans for tonight. Something's come up."

"All right. Anything I can help with?" From his manner, she didn't like what she was feeling, but maybe it had nothing to do with her.

"No. I'm sorry, but I can't discuss it." Gaze still steady on hers, he didn't elaborate.

"Well then. Okay. I'll figure out something…" She bit her lip. This was not how she expected to end her day. The night suddenly stretched before her long and empty. A hurt like she'd never experienced pierced her chest. She needed to get out of there. Needed air. She pushed to her feet. "Guess I'll see you later, then."

Desperate to get home and try to figure out what had just happened, she spun on her heel and headed for the door. She wasn't going to beg. If he didn't want to talk to her, then fine. If he was having regrets about the day before, then he could come find her to tell her. Obviously he wasn't prepared to do that in the office.

"Wait a minute, Courtney. I'm not done."

She froze, but didn't turn around.

"Your father sent out a company-wide memo today, regarding the handling of mail. Do you know anything about it?"

Oh great. Mom had told Dad, and he'd jumped right in with a memo. "What did it say?"

"It was along the lines of personal mail not being opened by anyone other than the addressee. It went to all the managers."

Birdie nodded, her head bent forward. "Yeah. There was a mistake made yesterday. No big deal. However, he shouldn't have done that." Because now what had merely been uncomfortable with one senior clerk was now going to be a near war. Probably what Mrs. Smith was there to discuss with Ozzie. Mr. Attenborough.

"Explain it to me, please." His tone was crisp and commanding, and it rubbed her exactly the wrong way. Be cool, she reminded herself.

Refusing to face him, she lifted her head and stared at his closed door. In the briefest of terms she gave him the facts.

"I see. Well, then the memo makes sense, however ill-advised. I'm sorry it happened. I've never heard of anything like that taking place here before. Nevertheless, you should have told me."

Birdie turned then to look at him. His gaze was still stern, but there was a flicker of something softer, more human in his eyes.

"When was I supposed to run up here and tattle?" Hoping to calm her pounding heart, she took in a lungful of air and slowly blew it out. "Look, I didn't want to make a big deal out of it. Mom is sending more chocolate for Dennis and Mrs. C. They'll get the treats I wanted them to have. This time she'll either address it to this office or she'll send it to the flat. No more personal mail for me, no more issue. It's a done deal, and I'm of the opinion you should let it drop." She held up her hands, spread open in a plea for peace. "To make a big deal out of it now will only make my life more difficult. I already have one senior clerk directing attitude toward me, based mostly on what she believes my situation is. I haven't discussed it with her, or anyone, in keeping with the game plan of hoping I'll just slide into the corporate structure."

Ozzie continued to stare at her. "So you've encountered some hostility."

"Not unexpected, and not anything I can't handle. Besides, tomorrow I move to another section of the department, and I won't be near the filing clerks anymore. No big deal. It's done and over. Let it lie."

The cold stare continued, but now it was beginning to unnerve her. She blew out a big breath. "Just leave it. Mr. Attenborough. I'll fight my own battles, thank you very much." For good measure she gave him a hard glare then spun on her heel once more. "Catch you later. Mr. Attenborough."

"Courtney."

Finally he spoke with a little emotion, but what it meant she had no idea. Right now the blood was pounding in her ears, and she just wanted to get out of there before she did something stupid like burst into tears.

She reached for the doorknob, but his hand slapped against the door, holding it closed. His arm was close to her ear, and she felt his body heat all along her back. More than anything she wanted to lean against him and draw in his heat and the comfort she knew he could provide.

And by the sudden burning behind her eyes, she wanted to turn around and cry into his suit. Why was he being so cold? Why had this day turned to crap?

"Courtney, please."

And why did his voice have to soften now?

"What?" She couldn't do bitchy, but she could snap.

"Talk to me. Please."

"I just did. You have the facts, and I'm guessing Mrs. Smith is here to discuss the issue. Please tell her I didn't come running to you. I'm doing my best to listen, learn, and not make waves. Make up something. Say the memo came about because of something from another department. I don't want anyone getting reprimanded because my chocolates went astray."

Ozzie took her by the shoulders and turned her around, pulling her close into a hug. God help her, but a few rebellious tears leaked from her eyes.

"You've had a shit day, haven't you, love?" His softened voice still rumbled against her cheek, but she refused to put her arms around him.

"I've had worse." She shrugged and tried to pull back. It was true she hadn't had many worse, but this one rated in the top five. Maybe top three.

One of Ozzie's hands slid up into her hair, holding her head against him. "I'm sorry I have to cancel tonight. Tomorrow is impossible, and we'll have to see about Thursday. Maybe I can set you and Hammond up with an instructor at my gym."

"I don't want anyone else. If you can't do it, then no big deal. Maybe I'll take up photography or watercolor painting." Against her wishes, her hands found his waist. His shirt smelled of clean starch and cologne warmed by his skin. Similar to her father, well, both of them, the combination was the ultimate in masculine comfort. Only on Ozzie there was the added layer of sexual attraction. He soothed her on the one hand, but excited her on the other. And completely confused her with his hot and cold treatment.

Ozzie pressed his lips to the top of her head. "I have to attend a meeting tonight. The rest of the week will probably be shot, but this weekend we'll do something. Drive in the country, or maybe try your betting skills at the track again."

That made her laugh a little. Enough she could pull away from him. "Go do what you need to do. My supervisor is waiting outside your door, probably wondering what's happening in here."

Ozzie gave her a tiny, crooked smile. "No doubt." His hand cupped her face, and he used his thumbs to dry the wetness beneath her eyes. "You all right?"

"Yeah. I guess. Just warn me when you're going to shift back into stick up the arse mode."

That earned her a bark of a laugh. "Expect it at the office. Can't have anyone thinking I've got an especially soft spot for you. No preferential treatment, right? If I recall, that was your edict."

Now she could smile up at him. Humor glinted in his eyes, and he seemed more like he'd been the day before. "Right. Okay, fine. You can be a stiff-neck at the office, but outside of it I like how you were yesterday. Come to think of it, this whole past weekend you were pretty nice."

Ozzie groaned, and with hands still cupped around her face, he bent and placed a very fast kiss on her lips. "Go on with you now, baggage. I have work and you're distracting me. Mrs. Cuthbert won't leave until Mrs. Smith does, so I need to address her concerns and get on to my own meeting."

"Aye-aye, boss." She stepped back and gave him a snappy salute. "Oh no…" She raised a hand to a small patch of mascara that had washed off her face and onto his pristine white shirt.

"No worries, I'll put on my coat. Now get out of here and send your supervisor in."

* * * *

Ozzie was straightening his jacket as Mrs. Smith entered and shut the door. "What may I do for you, Mrs. Smith?" He moved toward his desk and indicated she should take a seat. He noticed that she glanced back the way Courtney had just exited, with signs of her rapid distress still ghosting her face.

"Everything all right with Courtney? She looked a little upset walking out of here." Mrs. Smith peered at him uncertainly.

Oswald took his seat and considered just how much he should say. "She learned of the memo regarding mail and was distressed to think it had something to do with some hijacked chocolates."

Mrs. Smith closed her eyes and lowered her head. "That's what I was afraid of."

"Please tell me what happened." At the unhappy look on the woman's face, his fist clenched beneath his desktop.

"I'm afraid one of the clerks has taken a dislike to Miss Robinson. The box came in yesterday, and she took it upon herself to open it and then set out the chocolates for the whole department. Because Courtney said she'd asked her mother to send some to share, I didn't think too much about it. Then I saw her this morning and from the expression on her face, it was clear something was wrong." The older woman swallowed and pulled a wrinkled bit of parchment from her pocket. "After we spoke, Courtney crumpled this up and tossed it into the dustbin. I grabbed it, and well, it's obvious a crime has been committed." She handed the note card over the desk and Oswald took it.

A quick glanced confirmed Mrs. Smith's story. "All right. Yes, the clerk was wrong. If you haven't already delivered a verbal reprimand, I'd like you to add something." He stood and began pacing behind his desk. What he was about to say went directly against Courtney's wish to make her own way. Lord help him if word got back to her, but this was for her own good. "Courtney does not wish us to make a big deal of her association with Courtland." He stopped and faced Mrs. Smith. "However, what these lower level people need to understand is that Courtney is Courtland Robinson's very beloved daughter. She's been educated at one of the top universities in the world, she's smart, kind, and has a cheerful disposition that is easy to take advantage of. But first and foremost, as much as Courtland values those qualities in every employee, she is his daughter."

Leaning on his fists, he braced himself on his desktop. "Like any parent, he gets upset when she gets upset—if he finds out about it. I can assure you, she doesn't go running to him with every imagined slight, like some might believe." He leveled a significant look at the woman before him.

"He's especially sensitive to her upsets because he's only just found her and can't stand the thought of her being hurt by anyone." Taking a deep breath he stood straight. "If there are whispers that she's taking advantage of him, squash them. She was there when Martha made such a hash of things that she wants to be his exec assistant so no one will take advantage of his kind nature ever again. Like father, like daughter. They're looking out for each other. Are you understanding their relationship better now?"

Mrs. Smith stared back at him with eyes like wide blue saucers. "Yes, I see things in an entirely new light. And you're right. She is very much like her father. And her brother."

"Yes, she is. Only far prettier." Oswald allowed himself a small smile, a hint of a joke.

Mrs. Smith grasped on to that and chuckled. "Yes, yes. That makes the wrong done to her far worse than first glance showed. And it illustrates her kindness and grace all the more because she chose not to make a complaint. I'll remind my department that someday Courtney will be in a position to affect their careers, and it would behoove them to demonstrate the same respect they'd give anyone in upper management. The same respect she accords them."

"The same respect they'd extend to any coworker, I'd hope. After all, we want all our employees to not only treat others with respect, but to feel respected themselves. Exactly as they should treat any new hire, regardless of their family associations," Oswald added dryly.

"Of course." Mrs. Smith nodded, then looked up with worried eyes. "Poor girl. Did she have to suffer hazing in the mailroom?"

"Nothing more than pushing a reluctant trolley. And, by the by, Dennis adores her."

Mrs. Smith nodded vigorously. "A good indication of her true character. Dennis can sure sort them out quickly. He doesn't adore just anyone."

"Exactly. Your senior clerk might need to know that."

Mrs. Smith slapped her hands on her knees and pushed herself up to a standing position. "Thank you for taking the time to talk with me. There'll be no more trouble from my department on that score," she said briskly.

"Thank you. We have enough real troubles crop up often enough without these personnel issues."

"Have a good evening, Mr. Attenborough."

"You as well, Mrs. Smith."

She stopped at the door and looked back at him. "If something comes to my attention, do you wish me to bring it right to you?"

Oswald sighed. "If she's in over her head, yes. Since she's just assured me she can fight her own battles, I'll let her do that to a certain point. However, because of the family connection, I fear she won't speak up soon enough."

"Very good, sir. Good night."

This one Abigail Smith would handle, and Ozzie felt good about the rest of Courtney's time in that department. However, with Finance up next on the agenda, a department with few women and a whole lot of old school boys, well, he could only hope Abigail gave Courtney a good injection of confidence. She was going to need it.

But that wasn't his worry right now. A glance at his wristwatch showed he just had time to make it to the meeting at his gym.

Chapter 24

Other than a one pound box of Godiva chocolate being hand delivered to her desk, by Freddie no less, and no note indicating the giver, the rest of Birdie's week was downright boring. Although she noticed people were excruciatingly polite to her, she put it down to being in a different part of the department. And since she was doing a lot of data entry, she plugged in her headphones, put her head down, and did her work without fuss or interaction. Ozzie was boring too. She didn't see or hear from him at all, and she'd had no excuse to go up to the exec offices, so she'd stayed away.

So when Anne called Thursday night to invite her out dancing on Friday, Birdie decided she'd had enough of being huddled up in the flat, even if she had beat Drew's ass at Rocket League the one night Meilin had something going on he couldn't attend. It had been a good time catching up.

Friday after work, Birdie hurried home, nuked a quick dinner, and dressed in one of her more conservative dancing dresses, a royal blue dress that stretched to hold her curves from mid-thigh to shoulder. She piled on the makeup and sparkly costume jewelry, including piles of thin silver bangles and wild chandelier earrings. Posing in front of the mirror, she decided she looked pretty good. She hadn't had a chance to tart up since moving to London. Excitement bubbled in her veins. Hell yeah, she was ready to party and was anxious to see what London had to offer on the club scene.

Birdie had just reached the ground floor lobby when she received a text that Anne was outside. Not bothering to reply, Birdie pushed through the door to the sidewalk and saw her new friend waving from a Mini.

Patricia, another new friend, pushed open the rear passenger door, then slid over to make room for Birdie. Christina sat in front with Anne.

"Looking good, strumpet!" Anne greeted her. Like Birdie, the three women in the car had dressed in short, tight dresses, hadn't spared the makeup, and all wore platform heels. "We're going to kick ass and take some names tonight, right, ladies?" Without waiting for an answer, she pulled into traffic. "We're stopping for some food first, and a few rounds to warm us up. Then we're headed for a killer dance club. You have the important Cs?"

"Cs?"

"Cash, Credit, and Condoms!" the other three yelled.

Birdie laughed. "Yes, and I have a key and ID as well as lipstick." She patted the small purse strapped crosswise across her body. And yes, she had tossed in a condom. Just in case. Maybe she'd stumble across Ozzie. Or stumble into his house later. Although with his silence this week, he might not appreciate a surprise visit.

"The trollop knows how to party, for sure," Christina said.

With an expertise Birdie was sure she couldn't emulate, Anne steered the car over a bridge and through winding streets, managing to find parking near a pub. Across the street the pumping of bass could be heard. The neon sign over a plain black door only said Karma Temple. There were no velvet ropes and no lines.

"That's our spot," Anne said, pointing at the club. "Not a huge tourist trap, so you won't find it on a list of London's Ten Best, but it's popular with our friends, and you might find one of the younger royals there from time to time. Best kept secret in town."

Birdie piled out of the car with the others and followed them into another unassuming storefront of a pub. Much like the one near Ozzie's house. She didn't have time to nurse the pang of loneliness as she recalled the night they'd had dinner a week ago. A lifetime ago.

The bartender called out to them, and the women hollered back. The man, tall, barrel-chested, with a gray grizzled beard, nodded toward a booth on the far wall. To Birdie's mind he looked a little like a biker.

They settled in the booth and a waitress headed their way with a tray loaded with drinks. Some kind of beer and shot glasses full of clear liquid. Tequila or vodka, she wondered, and made a mental note to not try to keep up with these women. She wasn't that much of a drinker.

"Just assumed your new friend there might want what you all usually 'ave," the woman said as she set her tray on the table and started passing around beers and shots.

Birdie nodded at the woman's piercing look. "Sounds good to me."

"Yank, eh? That'll make you a novelty around 'ere."

Anne threw her arm around Birdie's shoulder. "Drew's sister, so she's only half Yank. Just sounds like one." She faced Birdie. "This here is Wanda, and behind the bar is her man, Matt. They've been serving us since we got old enough to come in. Rumor has it they served our parents when they were at Uni."

Wanda laughed. "I 'ave stories that'd curl your eyebrows about what yer parents got up to. They pay me well to keep silent." The woman looked at Birdie again. "And wot might yer name be, luv?"

"I'm Courtney Robinson."

"Robinson like Drew? Like Courtland?"

"Yes."

Wanda nodded. "One day you'll have to come in between rushes and tell me your story. Want to make sure I got me facts right. All sorts of rumors floatin' 'round."

Birdie blushed. "Didn't realize I was a topic of conversation."

"Oi, luv, yer 'alf famous 'round these parts." Wanda cast her eyes on the other women. "Wot're you tarts 'aving tonight, eh?"

Birdie listened to the orders, then added her own for a basket of chips. She wasn't particularly hungry, but the fried potatoes would help absorb the alcohol.

The beer was warm, the shots tequila, the chips hot and crispy, and the pub lively as a mix of all ages wandered in. In the corner a woman dressed in black leather plucked out Celtic love songs on a battered guitar. Birdie mostly sat and soaked up the conversations and the atmosphere. At last Anne reached for her purse. It was the signal to the other women, and Birdie zipped her bag open as well. Ten pound notes started hitting the center of the table until Anne nodded. "That should cover us and make Wanda a happy woman tonight."

Thirty pounds per person certainly ought to cover that bill. Not that Birdie had seen one. Wanda appeared at the booth and considered the pile of money. She picked it up, separated out two tens, and held the money out to Birdie.

Birdie blinked and lifted a brow in question.

"Drinks on the 'ouse for you tonight. Now you 'ave to come back and talk t'me." Wanda winked at her. "Get out of 'ere, wenches. I need some paying customers in the booth."

Laughing, Anne and Christina led the charge toward the exit. Birdie stayed back long enough to give Wanda a long questioning look. "Then consider this part of your tip." She stuck the money into the pocket of Wanda's apron.

"Go on. Come back Sunday afternoon if yer not spoken for. And give Drew our love." Wanda patted her on the butt and gave her a little shove.

Shaking her head, Birdie smiled and followed her friends across the street where they were quickly absorbed into the dark shot through with laser and neon. The music was predictably loud, the establishment comfortably crowded, but not so crowded they didn't find a pair of tables to pull together.

Anne shouted in her ear, "The boys will come by later. They had a thing tonight, but they'll want to dance off some steam when they're done."

Birdie nodded, ordered a seltzer and a Caipirinha to start. She downed the water fast, and sipped the lime infused drink slowly. Her head was already spinning from the drinks at the pub. When the girls got up to dance, Birdie waved them off.

"I need to sit a minute," she shouted back at Anne. Lord, did she really think sitting in a loud bar was fun? It had never occurred to her before that maybe the loud music could be painful.

Three songs later Christina came back to the table, fanning her sweaty face. "Go dance," she told Birdie. "I'll watch the drinks."

Birdie blinked at her. "I'm just letting the water catch up with the booze."

"Sure you are," Christina said while blotting her face with a napkin. "I'll keep an eye on the drinks so no one gets roofied tonight. We'll all take turns, although I can guarantee you, it's never happened here before. Besides, been on my bloody feet all day, and I'm ready to sit for a bit. Go on with you." She nodded toward the dance floor where Anne and Patricia waved at her.

With a reluctance she'd never felt before, she guzzled down her drink, then made her way onto the dance floor. Before she'd even made it to the floor, Christina's gaze was tight on her mobile.

It took a couple songs, but finally Birdie began to relax and enjoy herself. A variety of men worked in and out of their dance circle, Anne traded out with Christina, and then Patricia had her turn at the table. Birdie let the alcohol in her system do its work, and she twisted, jumped, wiggled, and spun, enjoying the suppleness of her body. One song had her remembering making love with Ozzie, and she closed her eyes, losing herself in the lyrics and the beat until large hands caught her around the waist.

Her eyes flew open and she saw Phillip grinning at her. Indicating he'd scared her, she patted her chest, then mimed fanning her face. With sparkling eyes, Phillip pulled her pelvis to his and preformed a dirty dance move. No big deal, Birdie went with it. Phillip would only get covered with her sweat if he pulled her too close. When she stumbled after not following his lead, she laughed and tried to get into the dance again. No, Phillip wasn't Ozzie when it came to dancing. There was a man whose lead she could easily follow. A handful of other men she'd met as Drew's friends joined the ladies on the dance floor, and for several songs they gyrated around, no one dancing with anyone in particular. She danced by herself, and she danced with all of them, men and women alike. Other than making love to Ozzie, it was the freest she'd felt since arriving in England. No stuffy rules. No grandmother clucking over her manners, or dress. Just pulsing music, writhing bodies, and fun.

And loneliness. She didn't really know these people. They were nice to her, well, nice enough to insult her as they insulted each other, but there was still a reserved air about them. Was that because they still weren't sure of her or was it merely a byproduct of their upbringing; she didn't know. Only time would tell. Intellectually she knew that. But her heart longed for the deeper friendships she'd known growing up.

No, that wasn't quite right, either.

She longed for how Ozzie had made her feel on Monday afternoon. The connection she'd felt in her soul looking into his eyes as his body entered hers. Suddenly the club held no appeal for her. Smiling and waving, she made her way back to the table where she found Anne sitting and watching something on a phone. Birdie sat beside her and Anne let out a cheer.

"Way to go, Attenborough!"

"What? Did Ozzie do something?" Birdie leaned forward to look over Anne's shoulder.

"Ozzie, eh?" Anne's smile was mischievous as she glanced over her shoulder. "Now that it's done, I suppose you can watch this. It's where the guys were earlier." She fiddled with the phone, then handed it to Birdie.

At first she couldn't quite make out what was happening. Some sort of sporting event judging by the crowd. In the middle was a…cage. An octagonal cage. Her heart stuttered.

Fortunately the video taker zoomed in then, and Birdie could make out two men bouncing on opposite sides of the cage. The camera zoomed in on the profiles. Calvin Whetmore in loose red shorts. The video panned to the left and she gasped. That was Ozzie! Wearing black shorts with a tighter fit than Calvin's. No mistaking those lean muscles and ripped abs. Definitely an Ozimander moment. Seriously hot.

"What is this?" she shouted at Anne, her gaze glued to the screen.

"Cage fight between Oswald and Calvin. Oswald challenged him for putting the roofies in your wine on Sunday. Serves the arsewipe right." There was no mistaking the glee in Anne's attitude.

While Anne talked, the two men met in the middle of the cage. Birdie's heart beat so fast she wasn't sure she'd avoid fainting. Was this why he'd put her off all week? Anger drove her heartbeat up another notch.

"Hey," Anne said and put a hand on Birdie's arm. "You all right?"

Still fixed on the screen, Birdie shook her head, scowling at the tiny screen. "Why?" she demanded.

Anne wrestled the phone from Birdie's grip as the first series of strikes flew. "Now I know why Ozzie didn't want you to know." She punched the screen and the video disappeared. "Bugger. Now I'm in for it," she muttered.

"Anne. Explain." Birdie clamped a hand around her friend's wrist. "What happened tonight?"

Anne sighed and shot a desperate look at her brother still on the dance floor. "There was a cage fight tonight. Oswald set it up Sunday while you were sleeping off the roofies. Of course Calvin never confessed, but he has a history and he accepted Oz's challenge. That right there was as close to an admission of guilt as we'll ever get."

Large hands settled on Birdie's shoulders, and she flinched before she realized it was Phillip.

"What's going on, Anne?" he demanded.

"I screwed up, okay?" she responded. "I couldn't wait to watch the vid, and then Courtney shows up and sees it over my shoulder. Since she'd seen that much, I figured what the hell, and started it for her. Only apparently she doesn't like fighting and nearly passed out."

Phillip's hand flexed on Birdie's shoulders while her head swam. "I didn't almost pass out. I'm pissed off. Now show me," she managed to spit out the words. "Show me the video."

Phillip took the phone from his sister. "No. Oz didn't want you to know about it at all, much less see it. It's my arse he's going to kick from here to Beijing."

Birdie held out her hand in demand. "I want to see it."

"No," Phillip said. "All you need to know is Oswald wiped the floor with Cal. You don't have to worry about him ever again. Word is out that he's a rapist and he'll be shunned. Oswald, of course, is your knight in shining armor, and you won't find any of our crowd willing to cross him by asking you out." The crooked smile on his face said he was one who'd keep his distance. "Well, unless you need an escort and he can't make it."

Birdie narrowed her eyes, something Phillip should have seen as a danger signal. "Are you saying he's claimed me?"

Oblivious, Phillip grinned. "Exactly. God, it's so great when women get it."

With a snarl, Birdie lifted her glass, nearly full of the rum and lime drink, and tipped it back, swallowing it down, before slamming the empty glass back on the table. "Like hell he's claimed me." She grabbed the nearest full shot glass and drank that down in one swallow and slammed that glass on the table. Ugh, tequila. There was one more on the table and she grabbed it too. "I have something to say to him about that."

Now Phillip and Anne looked a little nervous. "Um, Courtney, Birdie, what's wrong?" Phillip asked.

"Never you mind, mister." Birdie stood tall, threw her hair over her shoulders, and shoved past the Neanderthal blocking her way. The stupid man actually reached out and grabbed her arm. It was most satisfying to see him step back at her glare.

"Where I'm going is none of your business, Phillip." She yanked her arm from his hold and started pushing through the crowd blocking her way to the front door. So what if her steps were a little wobbly? All that dancing, on those stupid shoes, it was enough to wear out anyone's legs.

"Birdie," Phillip pleaded, using the nickname he'd heard Drew using.

"My name is Courtney," she shouted over her shoulder, then stopped and glared at him. "Remember that or I'll start calling you something like dipshit."

Hands up, he didn't step back this time. "Sorry. Courtney. You came with Anne. There's a law that says you leave with who brought you."

Imagine that, he managed to deliver that line dry as dust, totally deadpan. "I'm taking a cab." Mid-spin she grabbed the side of a booth to steady herself.

"Where are you going?" he pressed.

"I'm going to Ozibutt's. I'm going to give that man a piece of my mind; then I'm going to kick his ass into next week." After that, she'd probably pin him to a bed and do him silly, until neither of them could walk.

"Um, that might not be a good idea…" Phillip's voice sounded pained.

"Not your problem." She continued her march toward the door, Phillip hard on her heels.

"How are you getting there? Do you even remember where it is?" The man was like a damn leech.

"A cab driver can figure it out."

"It's clear on the other side of the city. A cab will cost a fortune, and I know you girls never bring enough cash. Let me drive you."

"How much?" she asked, mentally calculating how much cash she had left. No, she'd have to give some of it up for her share of the drinks. What would cover that? Thirty? Forty pounds? Damn, that would mostly kill the hundred she'd tucked into her purse. Pushing her hair back she took a moment to steady herself. Damn these stupid shoes. She was throwing them out the minute she got home. After digging in her purse, she counted out the money, then handed the bills to Phillip. "Give that to Anne. For my drinks."

Phillip turned and handed the money to his sister. "Take this."

"It's too much," Anne protested.

"Put it toward next time," Phillip told her. He took Birdie's arm. "I'll drive you over there, but don't yell at me if he won't let you in, right?"

Oh Ozzie would let her in. Even if it meant taking an axe to his door.

Chapter 25

Oswald rolled his neck and adjusted the ice pack on the knuckles of his right hand. Why was it always the right hand? Just once he'd like to place a left jab just right and knock his opponent out. Just one clean hit, over and done. Of course Whetmore's head was a little too hard for something so simple.

Not that the fight had taken very long. It was almost a shame all those spectators only getting a five minute show. Which was why Jameson had lined up six other fights before his against Whetmore.

Still, as short as it had been, it had been incredibly satisfying to take the bastard down. Hard. First he'd played the guy. Let him get in a jab or two. A block. And just as he'd gotten cocky, Oswald knocked him clean out. TKO.

Whetmore was probably still trying to figure out what his own name was, much less which decade they were in.

The best part was the investigator Oswald had put on Whetmore had turned up photographic evidence of the arsewipe putting drugs in a girl's drink. The young woman was extremely grateful when the PI had told her not to drink it. Her boyfriend had required restraining by the club's bouncers when he'd been told what had happened.

As a result, Whetmore's name was ruined. A couple of the tabloids had been given the story complete with photos. So much for his ancient and proud family line. He'd have to take himself into exile before the crown got wind of it. Which meant he'd have to be on a plane to anywhere sometime tonight. The sooner the better to Oswald's mind.

The investigation had also turned up dozens of accusations that his father's money and influence had managed to get swept under the rug.

Public knowledge of that little fact was going to be more than a bit embarrassing for the family.

The victory would be even sweeter if he could somehow tie Deirdre into Whetmore's sick schemes.

Oswald lifted the cut crystal glass filled with whisky to his lips, contemplating his next move. Turn on the telly or haul his slightly battered self up to the whirlpool? It meant climbing two flights, which he'd have to do eventually to get to bed, anyway. While contemplating, he savored the smooth burn as the whisky flowed down his throat and into his stomach. The smoky flavor lingered pleasantly in his mouth. Water of the gods indeed.

As his last taut muscle relaxed, his doorbell began pealing. Like someone was holding the button down. What the bloody hell?

He pushed onto his feet only slightly, babying his sore ribs where the bastard had gotten one good kick in. That was going to hurt for a few weeks. His own fault for toying with Whetmore when he should have gone straight to the beating.

Not in the mood for whoever had the misfortune to choose his door to pound on, he had to remind himself to not throw a punch first and ask questions later. Probably a pissed friend of one of his neighbors. Just one issue he had with the nearly identical terrace houses. Sometimes the numbers were hard to see in the dark, and he wasn't known for leaving the front light on.

Just for the hell of it, he flipped the light on before throwing the locks and jerking the door open.

To his surprise Courtney fell into his arms. A nearly naked and drunk Courtney. He could smell the alcohol wafting off her as she pushed against him trying to find her balance on a precarious perch of platform stiletto heels. At the end of the covered portion of the walk, Hammond stood looking wary.

"She insisted," Hammond said. "I tried driving past her building, and she practically caused an accident by grabbing the wheel."

"Ozzie, you stinking rotten misogynistic rat fink!" Clutching his arm for balance, she used her spare hand to poke him in the chest. After a few pokes, the hand flattened over his heart, then began petting him. "Oh, damn, you look hot," she muttered. "Why do you always look so hot?" She stared up at him blearily, mascara and smoky shadow smudged around her eyes, her lipstick half chewed off. Around her shoulders, hanging down to the middle of her back, her golden hair looked as wild as if she'd been in a windstorm. Probably created by her own mouth, he'd wager.

"Where the hell was she?" he snapped at Hammond.

"Out with Anne. Karma Temple. Dancing. Stopped at the pub across the street beforehand and met Wanda and Matt."

Oswald rolled his eyes and pulled Courtney up against his chest. He told himself it was to give her more stability on those ridiculously sexy shoes. Not that it felt good to hold her. Not at all.

"What is she going on about, anyway?" He couldn't make out a word she said buried face first against his shoulder.

Whatever Courtney was muttering didn't sound exactly complimentary to him.

"She saw part of the video. Anne was watching it." Hammond shrugged. "Didn't tell her until she nearly passed out after only watching the first round of punches."

Oswald looked down to see her glaring up at him with bloodshot eyes while one arm gripped his waist, fortunately not on the side of his sore ribs, and the hand on the other patted his chest. In a demented way, it was actually kind of cute.

"I'm mad at you, Ozimantis," she said. "No, don't you dare smile at me, dammit. You're not going to get around me with your wicked sexy smile. You aren't. You went and scheduled a big ass deal fight without telling me, you rotten fink, fighter-insect." At least that's what he thought she said. It was a little hard to tell through the slightly slurred words with her American accent and some off the wall mix-up of his name with a video game character.

"What happened to Ozichu? That's my favorite."

"Anyhow," Hammond said, shifting on his feet, "I got her here. She's your problem now."

"That's right, Mr. Knight in Shining Armor," Courtney added while patting his chest.

On the one hand she was giving him hell, but her actions were more telling. Especially since the hand on his waist slipped downward to grope his arse. All while she snuggled up closer to his chest. At least she wasn't gripping his sore side. Yet.

"I'm your problem and you're my problem." She emphasized each statement with a pat over his heart. "And you, I have a big problem with you going around defending my honor behind my back."

"And you're making absolutely no sense at all." He pulled her tight and dragged her deep enough into the hallway he could close the door, but first, he had more to say to the other man witnessing this scene. "You're a first class idiotic git, Hammond. I'll talk to you later about what it means to keep things just between the men and to not involve the women."

Hammond gave him a cheeky salute and turned away.

Sighing, Oswald shut and locked the door, then stood there looking at the top of her head. Good God. He was going to have to carry her up the stairs. Like that would help his ribs.

"Now I've told you what I think," she said, "it's time for me to kick your ass."

He couldn't help it. He laughed.

"Don't you smile at me, or laugh at me, neither." She probably meant to shout, but her voice lacked the power.

"I was just headed up to the whirlpool. Why don't we discuss this there, hmmm?"

Courtney cocked her head to the side. "Like a Jacuzzi?"

"Big enough for two." He nodded when she smiled. "Think you can walk up the stairs?"

"Of course. But first, the shoes come off."

"Allow me." He lifted her thigh even with his waist, then trailed his hand down her smooth calf until he reached her shoe. He gripped it and tugged it off her foot. A flip of his wrist sent it flying into the parlor. All done without taking his gaze off hers. Courtney's mouth dropped open in a sweet little O, her blue eyes wide as saucers.

It was the sexiest thing he'd ever experienced, and despite his aches, he hardened against the notch of her body fitted exactly right against his.

He let her leg down slowly before shifting her to his other arm and reaching for her other leg. The height difference without the one shoe was dramatic enough he lifted her onto the first step of the stairs. In tune with him, she lifted her thigh into his hand. Moving even slower, he repeated his moves until he tugged the second shoe off and tossed it after the first one. Not once did they break eye contact. Both of them were breathing as hard as if they'd run a race by the time he pulled her body even tighter against his.

Damn, he had to kiss her now.

Courtney met him halfway, their mouths meeting, already open and hungry to devour one another. The hand holding her thigh moved to her perfectly rounded ass, slipping under the tight, stretchy material of the thing she probably called a dress. More like a rubber band the way it molded to her body. Despite the booze, he was still able to breathe in her lemony fragrance as his tongue plundered her mouth. She tasted of rum and lime, and surprisingly it mixed well with the whisky still coating his mouth.

Courtney moaned and slid her arms up his body and around his neck. He wanted more, but dammed if he'd take her on the stairs. It took little effort to urge both her legs up and around his waist. The eroticism was so drugging, he barely noticed the discomfort to his ribs as he firmly held both cheeks of her bottom and hefted her closer. From there it was a matter of counting steps to reach the first floor. There was a guest bedroom there, along with his home office, but he wanted her in his bed. That meant one more flight. Dammit, there were advantages to flats. For one, they were usually flat, as in one floor.

To buy himself a little more strength, he pressed her back to the wall without once breaking the kiss longer than it took to take her mouth from another angle.

Courtney broke the deep kiss to pepper his cheeks with tiny pecks. "I can walk, Ozichu. Sounds like I'm too heavy for you, what with all that grunting."

"I've got you, love. Just one more floor. Easy peasy lemon squeezy."

To the sound of Courtney's laughter, they made it, but he didn't know how. Maybe it was her brilliant smile at his use of her kitschy line that carried them on wings. All he was really capable of understanding was his cock wanted inside her in the worst way. Beside the bed, he let her legs down to the floor. Once more she took him by surprise. With only two fingers in the middle of his chest, she pushed him down onto his mattress.

Dumfounded, he watched while she began divesting herself of first her jewelry, which she wore almost like armor. A dozen or more thin enameled bracelets slid off her arms and clattered when she set them on his bedside table, reminding him of that night in her hotel room. Next came large dangly earrings, followed by the string crossing her body holding a tiny bag. Probably didn't have room for more than a lipstick in there, he guessed. Only once did she sway a little, reminding him she was still drunk and liable to pass out at nearly any moment. He'd catch her then, and hold her all night long, just as he had the previous Sunday night. Heaven and torture at the same time, but he'd survived that night; he could do it again.

Only this time it would be worse because he intimately knew exactly what was under her incredibly tight dress. So tight he could clearly see her nipples and a hint of the texture of her areola. At once his mouth started watering remembering having those luscious nipples in between his lips.

Courtney reached for the hem of her dress and started tugging it up over her creamy, bare thighs. No stockings, which was partly a shame, but not really because he'd surely ruin them at some point in the night.

The way she wiggled, it looked as if the poor girl needed assistance. He sat up and, gripping her hips, pulled her between his legs.

"You look like you could use a hand or two."

"Mmm, Ozimantis the helpful," she all but purred.

But she didn't push his hands away. Oh no, he slipped his hand down over her flared hips to the hem of her stretchy dress. From there it was easy to slip up underneath, the fabric gathering and pushing upward like a wave before a boat leaving a tiny blue lace thong behind.

The dress was easier to push upward than he'd originally calculated. He'd figure it out another time, but for now his tired muscles were glad so little effort was required. At her waist his fingers nearly met at the small of her back. Sure he had large hands, but she was tiny in the waist. It was damn sexy.

The fabric gathered at her waist was easier for her to grab, arms crossed over her stomach, pressing her breasts closer, deepening the already gorgeous cleavage. Now his head was spinning, and he hadn't had more than a sip of his drink.

In the act of tugging her dress upward, Courtney swayed again. Right. Pissed. Drunk. God, he really shouldn't be planning his moves for making love to her.

With the dress now half off and covering her face, she wiggled, then all motion stopped and he watched as she drew in a deep breath, then huffed it out with a quiet, "Damn."

He couldn't help the grin spreading across his face. "Um, need a little help there?"

Her body slumped and she said miserably, "I'm stuck," in a tiny voice.

"Well, it seems you have a knight on hand. The armor isn't shiny at all, but he's quite handy."

"Please," she whispered. "I can't breathe all that well."

Oswald stood, took the upside down hem in hand, and pulled straight up. A second later the dress nearly popped as it came off. He tossed it in the direction of a chair in the corner of his room.

"One damsel de-distressed." And what a damsel. Her stretchy lace bra matched the thong, the items clearly making the most of her hourglass figure.

The look she gave him was disgruntled to say the least.

"What's wrong, love?" He crooked a finger under her chin and noted the wobbly lower lip.

"So much for my grand seduction. I had it all planned to do it in such a way you'd tackle me to the bed and ravage me." The lip wobbled again. "And I messed it up. Had to ask for help like a toddler."

Oswald wrapped his arms around her waist, pulling her closer. "Aw, love, now there's where you're wrong. First of all you're nothing like a child, thank God. And second, there's not a man alive who wouldn't be thrilled to rush to your side to help you undress." With her hands on his chest, creeping up toward his shoulders, it took but a heartbeat to release the catch of her bra. "See? There I go, helping without complaining a bit."

Courtney laughed, her natural cheer reasserting itself. "You are so, so helpful." The way she cooed at him was beyond sexy.

Too bad her next move was to fall asleep in his arms. Standing up. Just his luck.

Chapter 26

Birdie knew it was an awful cliché to say she woke with a drum corps in her head and desert in her mouth, but that was exactly how she woke when a sunbeam tried to burn a hole into her forehead.

She rolled over in hopes of putting the evil light out of her sight and immediately realized she wasn't in her own bed. The pillow didn't feel right, and the sheets smelled of...Ozzie.

Memory crashed into her the same time queasiness hit her stomach.

Upon cracking one eye open she discovered what she'd already figured out. The bed was empty, but Ozzie had slept there last night. That much she remembered from stirring a few hours earlier. She had a vague recollection of him helping her find the bathroom and forcing her to drink a full glass of water.

At the edge of the bed, beside a pile of her bracelets, sat a glass of what looked like tomato juice and a bottle of aspirin. Universal hangover cure.

Moving slowly, she pulled herself up and leaned against a firm headboard of tufted leather. It felt cold against her bare back. A struggle to pile some pillows behind her followed; then she pulled the white sheet up over her breasts, tucking it beneath her arms. That much effort required a few minutes of resting, eyes closed, and forcing her lungs to exchange some air. A fresh breeze scented with rain came from a window opened a few inches. Air was good, she decided.

While she rested, she listened to the house, hoping for some sound indicating Ozzie was nearby. Or not, in this case. She could only imagine what she'd looked like last night and how much worse she looked this morning. If she had a mirror nearby, she might see a green cast to her skin. She certainly felt green.

Well, sitting there thinking about it wasn't going to make her feel better any time soon. Cracking one eye, she glared at the juice and aspirin on the far side of the bed from her. Wincing, she shifted her pillows and crawled to his side of the bed. Settled once more, she reached for the glass and sipped the thick red juice. Tomato. No fancy seasonings added. Or vodka. Just the straight stuff. Hard core.

Fifteen minutes later the aspirin started kicking in and the juice had settled her stomach. The house remained silent. As the clock read well after eleven, she wasn't entirely surprised. He'd had plenty of time to shower, dress, eat a four course meal, get in a full workout and probably do business with half a dozen offices around the globe.

Certainly he didn't have the time or desire to deal with her pathetic ass.

Somewhere she found the strength to make her way into his bathroom, large enough to nearly take up half of the top floor. Sure enough, he had a Jacuzzi tub big enough for four and a shower filled with nozzles and bench seating for three, deep enough one could lie down.

She turned on the simplest of the nozzles and dug into his vanity looking for a toothbrush while the hot water came up from the basement. She found one in the bottom drawer, along with a bottle of her favorite shower gel. Well. That was a surprise.

Deciding not to look a gift horse in the mouth, she appropriated both. With a minty fresh mouth, already a huge improvement, and another full glass of water in her, she grabbed the gel and stepped into the shower. She wanted to linger, wanted to play with all the settings, but also didn't want to get caught in his house when he came home.

Ten minutes later, wet hair combed out, towel wrapped around her, she frowned at the clothes she'd worn the previous night. Really, she had little choice, and remembering her shoes, she grimaced. Steal sweats and a T-shirt, then walk home in platforms? No. She'd have to do the walk of shame in her own clothes. Or take more time digging through his closet for a raincoat.

Decision made, she dressed, grimacing at the dirty clothes on a clean body, gathered her jewelry, tucked it into her purse, and inventoried her remaining cash for a cab. Surely she had enough. Ozzie's house wasn't that far from the flat. Cab or walk it in her silly shoes? Cab. Surely she'd pick one up on the next street over. It'd be faster than calling. And she'd feel like a streetwalker the entire way. At least her face was now clean of the makeup mess and her washed hair combed.

Deciding to forego the streetwalker parody, while she walked down the stairs, she pulled out her phone and checked it for the number of the cab her dad had insisted she keep there. She also noted half a dozen texts from Anne and Phillip. Anne's included an offer to pick her up and take her home at any time. If Oswald didn't take her home, that was.

No, Birdie remembered her behavior the night before. There'd be no calling a friend, or shouting out to an audience member for that matter. Nope, she was on her own today.

She called the cab, then started searching the floor for her shoes. It took a little doing, because remembering how he'd held her while removing them created a heat flow to rival a lava eruption.

Oh, yeah, he'd tossed them into the room with the TV. Once she had them on, she stood and faced the door.

On it was a sheet of printer paper with one word written boldly across it.

Stay.

Birdie snorted over the fact her heart stuttered just a little at his command. Why use five or ten words to explain where he was when he could use one to demand obedience. Like a damn dog.

She didn't think so.

Outside she heard the beep of the cab horn. Relieved the cab had arrived so quickly, she swung open the door, stepped out, and slammed it shut behind her.

Oh, she survived the trip home, and the stares from other residents in the building's lobby and elevator, but other than thanking the cabbie, she didn't say a word to anyone. Just kept her head up and eyes forward.

The relief at being home was intense. And stifling. If she stayed there, Ozzie might come looking for her. Well, it was a good day to get out and see a few sights.

Changed into jeans and a light sweater, she pulled on her raincoat and hit the sidewalks under drizzly skies. To drown out the city noise, she pushed earbuds into her ears, set her playlist to rock loud enough to filter all but the loudest car noise, and headed for Vauxhall bridge. She could have jumped on the Tube and head north, but she wanted to walk and breathe in the atmosphere. Besides, how did one explore the gardens and shops on the north side of the river from an underground train?

Halfway across the bridge, she slowed, her attention caught by the river itself. So wide and placid looking. With the sun beginning to burn through the mist, her raincoat became too warm. Setting down her overlarge shoulder bag, she shrugged off the jacket and shoved it into the bag. With her back to the railing, she looked downstream. Like a wide road, the water lay flat. The view showed a few tall buildings, more than a few cranes building newer, taller ones, and in the far distance she could see the London Eye. Just out of sight by a bend in the river were Big Ben and Parliament. Not on her agenda for today, but maybe tomorrow she'd play tourist over there.

She shouldered her bag again and turned to look upstream. To her left, the very modern St. George Wharf, across the road from the building housing MI6, the British Secret Intelligence Service. Definitely one of the most impressive building complexes in London, she had yet to take full advantage of living there. Time to do more exploring, although she found the cafés convenient. Beyond the Wharf, an even taller building stood. And beyond it, more cranes, on both sides of the river.

But it was the water she was drawn to. Leaning her elbows on the railing, she stared straight down at the gentle ripples of the vast quantity of greenish water slipping below the bridge.

So different from the cold beaches of Northern California with the Pacific pounding on their shores. Not much like the waters of the Bay, which could be still or whipped into a frenzy of white caps and the white sails from weekend warriors racing across the water.

Here, the Thames flowed just as it had for thousands of years. So old. So massive, at the moment so calm and non-threatening. She knew it was only one face of the river that could become wild with floods, wind, tide, and careless boaters. It had a history all its own.

The water was calming to the thoughts in her head. She could feel the burn of her shame from the last fifteen hours cooling, slipping away like the mindless water below. She let it go, washing away to eventually find the sea.

God, what had she been thinking storming Ozzie's house last night? Throwing herself at him only to… She didn't remember anything clearly after he carried her up the stairs. Or did she? She did remember him grunting as he carried her up the last flight, and laughing at his use of her silly phrase. Far too silly for someone as dignified as him to use. Guess she'd better slow down on the chips and booze if she ever wanted him to carry her again. There, there was the burn of embarrassment.

Once more she focused on the water and let it and the music carry away her shame.

When had life grown so difficult? Oh, she understood her problems were small in the overall scheme of things. But she'd never had these troubles before. Friends had never been an issue before. She'd been known for the ability to fit in with many groups. Here she was so clearly the outsider. She'd always made friends at school or work, and if not close friends, at least her co-workers had been cooperative. Was it the change from school to career? The move from California to England? So many changes in the last eighteen months. Twenty months.

She bent her head to rub her temples. She'd never felt so unprepared for anything in her life as she had the big changes she'd been so eager to embrace, and, as long as she was admitting things to herself, she might as well put Ozzie at the top of the list.

Why had she ever thought she could get him to take her seriously? Especially here, in his world. Maybe her problems settling into London life stemmed from not knowing her place in this arena. By being related to the Robinsons, she had history here. Deep roots. But they didn't feel like her roots. On her mother's side she had deep roots in California. She'd been born and raised there, each year growing with the state. There she had friends. Family she'd known all her life. Here she was the newcomer. Sort of like being new money. Crass and unpolished, unlike the old money folks who were as polished as the marble that lined their homes. Here she was raw and uncut. Her father might say a diamond in the rough, ready for shaping into something indescribably beautiful.

She smiled thinking of her father. Fathers. Wyatt had been the daddy of her childhood. Court was the daddy of her adult life. She'd have much longer with him, God willing, but they'd missed so much. For all the time she tried to spend with him, they'd never have the years of him teaching her to ride a bike, how to swim, or even how to drive a car. They'd had some time of him teaching her to drive in right hand drive cars on left hand driven roads. But it wasn't the same. Not really. And he was supposed to be here teaching her the family business. Instead, he and her mother were off touring Europe.

Which she had to admit was fair. As much as she wanted him here, and her mother too, of course, she was the one who had demanded no preferential treatment at work while she learned her way through the different levels. Yes, she was impatient to be working side by side with him every day, but she did have to learn and this was the best way, as much as she found herself resenting it. Had every assistant worked their way into their position from the mailroom up? She didn't think so.

The main reason she didn't like her current situation was because she was in limbo. Not really one of the workers, separated by her family relationship, and not truly free to make friends with those workers her own age. There was a wall there she couldn't, wouldn't breach. They didn't want to make friends with her because one day she'd be in charge of them. She couldn't bring the entire company up with her. They had their roles, and hers was outside of their spheres. Did that make her the poor little rich girl, forever outside, beyond, never belonging? Well, she did belong somewhere, but her place was populated with middle-aged managers and people like Drew's friends who were all raised within a privileged system she couldn't truly understand. Again, she was the outsider. The only person she knew who also felt like an outsider was Oswald. She just didn't know why he felt that way.

Even then, he wasn't as far outside the inner circles as she was. This past week had only drawn a big black line around that fact. He was keeping his distance from her, but other than vague references to some sort of class difference, he wasn't exactly convincing. He said he wasn't worthy of her, when in fact, she wasn't worthy of him. He called her princess, but in reality he was far closer to royalty than she'd ever be.

Lord, she was depressing herself. She dropped her forehead to her hands folded on the wide rail of the bridge, feeling more pathetic than she'd ever felt in her life. It didn't help that Celine Dion was wailing in her ear about not wanting to be all by herself anymore. A cover of the Eric Carmen song her mother had on her playlist. Well, she could take care of that. She straightened, pulled her phone from her pocket, and pushed the fast forward button on her player app.

She also noticed a few missed calls. All Ozzie. Guess he'd discovered her vanishing act. The texts from Anne and Phillip still sat unanswered. And they'd stay that way for now. She slipped her phone into her pocket and went back to watching the river, staring down into the water, letting her mind wander.

Something up river caught her eye and she leaned forward, stepping up on the lowest rung of the railing, trying to make it out. As it drifted nearer, she could see it was a branch. Probably knocked off a tree far up river, she watched it and let her mind wander. Her imagination could almost make out a miniature Huck Finn and Tom Sawyer sitting on top, holding on to smaller branches sticking up. Wanting to watch it as long as possible, she hitched up onto her elbows. It was almost out of sight when someone grabbed her arm and pulled her backward with so much force she landed on her butt and one earbud popped out.

"Don't do it!" a man in a police uniform yelled at her. "It's not worth it!"

Shaking her head as she tried to figure out what the hell he was talking about, she heard cars pulling up with wailing sirens. They screeched to a halt behind her, lights flashing. From below the bridge came another siren.

Birdie threw up her hands as more cops gathered around her. "I didn't do anything," she yelled. "Everyone just calm the fuck down!"

Chapter 27

Oswald stared at the door to the Robinson flat and wondered how much hell he'd catch if he kicked it in.

He'd gone out to get breakfast, not even away thirty minutes, and returned home to find Courtney missing. She'd had the juice and he assumed some pain reliever. She'd showered and even gathered all her belongings, including the jumble of bracelets she'd worn the night before. When he was parking, he'd seen a cab turning the corner at the end of his street, and from her absence, he guessed that had been her bugging out.

Obviously she hadn't liked the note he'd left for her. Women and their need for pretty words.

Okay, he could have been a little clearer that he'd be back soon. Frankly he'd expected her to still be sleeping.

His phone rang and he pulled it from his pocket. Number unknown. "Attenborough."

"Mr. Attenborough, this is Constable Gavin Barnaby, sir. Do you know one Miss Courtney Robin Ferguson-Robinson?"

Oswald's blood chilled. "I do. Where is she?" He started moving for the lift.

"We have her at the Vauxhall station, sir."

But was she alive? Of course she was, otherwise it would be the coroner's office or a hospital calling. "Is she all right? Did something happen to her?" Because for the life of him he couldn't imagine her doing something that would get her arrested.

And where was the damn lift when he needed it now?

"She says she's fine, but it is my belief she was about to jump off the Vauxhall Bridge. She swears she's not suicidal, however she was observed for more than thirty minutes leaning on the bridge rail, and then she hoisted herself up…'tis the truth I managed to pull her off before she got a leg up."

Courtney? "Suicidal you say?" Of course disbelief poured right out of him. She might have been upset, but if anyone had a brighter attitude toward life, he didn't know them. He'd seen her bounce from disappointment to cheery optimism at the snap of two dainty fingers.

"She was up on her elbows, head down, leaning toward the water. Several people on the bridge observed the same thing." The defensive tone of the constable puzzled him greatly.

"What does she say about all this?" The lift finally arrived and he boarded, stabbing the ground level button twice to be sure it got the message.

Fortunately he didn't lose cell service while the car traveled downward.

"She says she was watching a stick in the water," the man admitted grudgingly. "She's been, well, a bit mouthy since I pulled her to safety."

A snort of laughter left Oswald before he could stifle it. "I bet."

"Please, sir, you were the last one to call her mobile. Would you please come get her? We can't let her go on her own, and she refuses to talk to our psychiatrist. We must insist she have someone with her for the next twenty-four or we'll have to commit her for observation."

In the background he heard Courtney spluttering in protest. "YOU are the one who needs psychiatric observation!"

That did it. Oswald burst out laughing. After confirming the address, he said, "I'm on my way, Constable. I'm not far."

"Thank you, sir. She's quite a…handful."

Oswald rang off with a tiny bit of pity for the poor man.

If last night was any indication of the temper she could get up to, Courtney was more than a handful; she was a force to be reckoned with. Oddly enough, his blood heated with anticipation of the battle to come, for if her exit this morning was any indication, she would not welcome his appearance at the station.

It took less than twenty minutes to get to the station and find parking. Inside he was directed to the desk of a young man who gazed at Courtney as if she were not only the most beautiful woman he'd ever seen, but also the most demented one as well. Couldn't fault the constable for that. Despite the glare and snapping energy in her eyes, the heightened color on her cheeks reminded Oswald of the night before when she'd been giving him hell and petting him at the same time. Minus the smeared makeup of course.

The second she caught sight of him she stood and grabbed her shoulder bag. Unfortunately, she was also handcuffed to the chair she'd been sitting in, bouncing her right back onto her arse, making her wince. Which didn't do anything to improve her mood or attitude. Once more she stood, this time slowly, without pulling on the handcuffs.

From the corner of his eye, he noted the officers around them all watching her. The men and the women. Some with curiosity, a few with lust, and many with wariness. Just what had happened on the bridge?

"Miss," the constable said as he rose with her. "You can't just walk out. We need to go over a few things with your, um, I mean with Mr. Attenborough here."

Contemptuous blue eyes raked up and down Oswald, then turned on the constable practically burning with a blush on his pale cheeks. "*Mister* Attenborough is not my anything."

"He's on your phone, miss, and if what you tell me is true, then isn't he your employer?"

Courtney's nose went up in the air. "My father is my employer. *Mister* Attenborough is not."

"Ah, but in this case, Courtney," Oswald said, "I am your father's representative. Therefore, I am your superior in the office, as well as a trusted family friend who has been given the task of watching out for you." He returned her glare with a single raised eyebrow, the one aristocratic gesture he'd had from birth, apparently. It was enough to make young sods like Hammond and the like beg to do his bidding. Had even worked on Lynford's Board of Directors a time or two. Didn't work on Courtney.

"Constable," Oswald spoke to the nervous younger man. "Is there someplace a little more private we can discuss this?" He waved at the cuffs still holding Courtney to the chair. "I don't think those are necessary. Unless you're charging her?"

The eyebrow worked on the poor man who hurried to release Courtney. "Come this way, please. We have a room open…." He turned away and led them to what looked like an interrogation room, complete with one-way viewing window.

Not what Oswald considered optimal, but it was better than sitting in the open room.

He held a chair for Courtney who sat as if she were the queen, stiff and regal, arms and legs tightly crossed.

Oswald took the chair next to hers, the two of them facing the blushing constable. A moment later an older man entered the room. He certainly had the look of authority about him, wearing a three piece suit, his salt and pepper hair cropped.

"All right, now, let's see if we can sort this out and let you two be on your way," the older man said after introducing himself as the lieutenant in charge. He settled back in his chair, hands folded over his slightly soft stomach. "Miss Robinson, I haven't heard the story from you. Please tell me what you were doing on the Vauxhall Bridge."

Courtney drew in a breath, then spoke with her most polite tone, dropping her hands to her lap. "I was intending to walk across the bridge. I've only been in London a short time, and with the rain letting up, I thought to do some exploring. Maybe have lunch. I haven't eaten since last night, and I planned to treat myself today. However, as I reached mid-point of the bridge, I was struck by the magnificent view. I'm also not terribly familiar with large rivers, being more used to the Pacific ocean and the San Francisco Bay, and wanted to study the differences. It's really the first time I've been out in the city by myself. Up until now there's always been someone playing nanny, and honestly, it's starting to drive me a little crazy. I just wanted the peace."

"I understand you had music playing through your headphones. How is that peaceful?" The lieutenant cocked his head, looking puzzled. "Apparently loud enough you didn't hear the constable calling out to you."

"I enjoy music. With all the bands that have come out of England I'm fairly certain rock and roll is no crime. In fact, a cousin of mine was once rather famous in the music world."

Barnaby's eyes lit up with questions, but his superior merely nodded. "You are correct; there is no law against listening to music."

"Music is an old friend. And today I realized I'm missing old friends. I've had little contact with people from my former home."

"You're from America, obviously. Where was home?"

"California. The Bay Area."

Again the lieutenant nodded. "A beautiful area I believe."

Courtney nodded back. "It is. However, if you've checked, you know I have a dual citizenship. My father is British. That would be Courtland Robinson."

"Yes, CEO of Lynford International. Your mother is American."

"Yes."

"So you stopped in the middle of the bridge to admire the view," he prompted.

"I did. I've had a difficult time lately, and with my parents wandering around Europe and my brother in China, I suddenly felt very much alone, and wanted to figure out why."

Oswald held his blank face, but inside his gut clenched. Courtney was a social creature, and she'd had plenty of difficulties fitting into her father's world. His world. He'd hoped the previous evening she'd have made progress in cementing one or two true friendships. He'd have to ask about that.

"And what prompted you to hoist yourself up on the railing of the bridge?"

"I was watching a branch float down the river."

"A branch."

"Yes. It seemed out of place and it was interesting. I leaned forward to watch it as long as possible. That was when your constable leaped to the conclusion I meant to jump." Contempt filled her expression as she flicked a glance over the younger officer. "Without warning, he grabbed my arm and practically threw me to the ground. I'll wear the bruises on my butt for weeks to come. And I'm pretty sure my lower back was jammed. I'll need to see a chiropractor for an adjustment, which will mean time off work. Time off I can't afford."

To his credit the lieutenant barely blinked. The constable blushed furiously. Probably imaging those bruises on Birdie's perfectly curved ass. Something Oswald planned to do his best to kiss away.

"I thought your father was the boss?"

"He is, but I requested he not give me preferential treatment. I'm a worker just like the managers and workers who keep the company running day to day. In order to earn their respect I have to show up and do the tasks assigned to me like everyone else."

"Do you intend to claim injury against the department?"

It was a reasonable question, Oswald thought.

Courtney drew back in her chair with an extreme look of distaste on her face. "Of course not! I'm appalled you'd even think so. I was on that bridge minding my own business, enjoying the flow of the river, admiring its power, when I was rudely accosted, but I also understand where the constable was coming from. I understand he—incorrectly—feared for my life. However I'm reasonable enough to know it's better he do what he did than hold back and wait for someone to actually jump before concluding they needed psychiatric help. I'm embarrassed he thought me so desperate. I'm angry I'm being held here against my will. But I'm not litigious and won't seek damages."

Relief of varying degrees crossed the faces of the men across the table from them. "I'm happy to hear that, Miss Robinson. However, you have to understand several people rushed to the scene, including the Royal National Lifeboat Institution, our river rescue volunteers."

Oswald held up a hand to stop the man. "Would it help soothe inconvenienced souls if a donation was made to their cause? As a volunteer service, I'm sure some of their funding has been diverted to the refugee situation."

The lieutenant's eyes narrowed and he murmured the word, "Refugees..." Recognition hit his eyes a half second later. "You were accosted at a refugee fundraiser, weren't you, Miss Robinson."

Oswald watched her nose rise another quarter inch.

"Yes," she answered shortly.

"And," Oswald continued, "she was stung by a bee at Ascot on Sunday, and the target of a roofie in her drink that same afternoon."

"Ozzie," she snarled under her breath. "That's not germane to this situation."

The lieutenant shook his head. "Oh, but I think it is. It further illustrates the difficult time you've recently experienced and surely contributed to the extremely sad expression my constable here noted on your face, another indication of distress that might have sent you over the rail and into the water."

Courtney rolled her eyes and uncrossed her legs as if preparing to stand. "May I go now? I'm not suicidal. I didn't mean to upset your troops. I had no idea anyone was watching me. I was merely trying to sort out some thoughts and enjoy one of the major attractions of this city. End of story."

Oswald glanced at her, then turned his attention to the officers with a shrug. "I believe her. She's a fighter. Can't see her giving up like that."

With a sigh, the lieutenant shrugged. "Very well. Unless you wish to press charges regarding the roofie incident?"

Oswald shook his head in unison with Courtney.

"No? All right. However, I request that she remain in your charge for twenty-four hours at least, Mr. Attenborough."

"Are you serious?" Courtney huffed out her exasperation. "I don't require babysitting."

"It's merely a precaution, Miss Robinson. Otherwise I'll be obligated to commit you for psychiatric observation." The lieutenant's expression was kind, but it also said he would do his duty if required.

Mouth open, Courtney leaned over the table, but Oswald put a hand on her arm, forestalling whatever she'd been about to say.

"I'll keep her in sight, I promise. No harm will come to her. I give you my personal guarantee." He shot Courtney a look that had her pressing her lips into a hard line.

"Good enough for me." The senior officer stood. "Get the release papers ready, Barnaby."

Chapter 28

Hunger was gnawing a hole in her spine by the time Oswald escorted her into a pub somewhere north of the river. When she caught sight of the silent Karma Temple sign across the street, she almost refused to get out of the car, but the constant rumbling of her stomach put down that particular rebellion.

The touch of his hand on her lower back sent involuntary shivers of excitement shooting out to all the extremities of her body as they passed through the door into a familiar pub. The very same where she'd been the night before. Matt nodded at them from behind the bar and shouted for Wanda.

Oswald waited for her to slide into a booth with high sides, then slithered in beside her.

She gave him her best stare-down-the-nose glare. "I don't think they meant you have to keep this close of an eye on me. Across the table is close enough."

Of course he ignored her. "How hungry are you?"

"Absolutely starved. In fact, unless you move, I might take a bite out of you."

The damn man laughed at her. Actually laughed. Complete with twinkling eyes. It would have been less shocking if he'd gotten up and danced a can-can.

"Beef sound good?"

"Either a half pound burger, or a side of beef. Either will do."

"How about the steak pie? It's very good here."

"All right. Throw in a salad and a pile of fries and you've got a winner."
She reached for the napkin-wrapped flatware. If she had to, she could
easily stab him. Fork or knife, she didn't have a preference.

"Welcome, luvs. Didn't expect to see you so soon." Wanda set two
glasses of water down for them, her gaze locked on Birdie. "What
can I get you?"

Oswald glanced at Birdie. "Ale?"

"Oh, God, no. Lots of water, please, Wanda."

"Rough night?" the older woman asked. "Ye look a bit dehydrated, luv.
We'll get ye settled; then you can tell me all about it."

"Coffee American style, with a cream pitcher, and a large tomato
juice for the lady." From there Oswald continued the order for them,
the steak pie for her, a half pound burger for himself. And a starter of
bread and butter.

"Comin' right up, 'andsome." Wanda winked at Ozzie and he grinned
back at her before she turned toward the kitchen.

"Come here last night?" Ozzie asked, pushing both water
glasses toward Birdie.

"Yes. Wanda promised to tell me stories about my dad when he was in
college." She picked up the first water glass and started sipping.

The moment the bread hit the table, Birdie was on it, slathering butter
on a thick warm slice.

"Guess she's not ready for talkin'," Wanda observed with
great amusement.

Birdie merely shook her head and bit into the best bread she remembered
ever eating. Probably the hunger talking, but that didn't stop her from
moaning over the taste.

Oswald was slower about helping himself, but at least he didn't try to
talk to her. If he knew anything about starving women, he'd wait until
she'd made it halfway through her main dish before badgering her.

No, he didn't have talking in mind at all. After taking a bite of his
bread, he slipped his free arm around her shoulders and pulled her close
to kiss her temple.

Mouth too full to speak, she gave him the hairy eyeball instead.

The man had the nerve to smile down at her. The lady-killer, panty-
melter smile. Damn him. She shifted on her bruised butt, beginning to
feel her lower back tighten up as predicted.

He must have read the discomfort on her face because he gently
cupped her head and pulled it to his shoulder. "We can get the food to go
if you prefer."

Mouth full once again, she shook her head. She didn't think Wanda would like it much. For now Wanda puttered around the pub, serving other customers, taking time to chat and charm while keeping an eye on their table.

"All right. As soon as we eat we'll head back. Your place or mine?"

She started to say her place, but then she remembered his magical shower and the huge tub. Yeah, her parents' flat had a good sized Jacuzzi, but they didn't have the exotic shower. Using her bread, she pointed at him and kept on chewing. A bit of her stress melted at the laugh he let out. It was a wonderful sound.

Lunch was consumed quietly, and Birdie finally relaxed, eventually leaning against the arm he'd had to withdraw in order to eat. Didn't stop him from pressing his leg against hers and dropping kisses on her head every chance he had.

This new Oswald was confusing the hell out of her, but today, she wouldn't complain.

"All better?" Wanda asked as she cleared their dishes. Birdie's was nearly licked clean.

Resting her head on Ozzie's shoulder, Birdie patted her stomach. "Much better. I was starving."

Wanda laughed. "Ye look too sleepy to 'ang out here this afternoon. Have a wild time last night?"

While Ozzie chuckled, Birdie's face flamed. "You might say that. I'm trying to forget most of it."

Wanda laughed more and slapped a ticket down on the table at Ozzie's elbow. "Ye take good care of 'er, Oswald. Ye don't get 'round 'ere often enough yourself."

Ozzie pulled out his wallet, thumbed through a wad of bills, stacked them on the ticket, and handed the lot to Wanda. "We'll try to catch you when there's time to sit and chat. I've heard there are tales to be told."

"Right ye are, mate. Now don't be strangers." She waved them off and turned toward the kitchen, carrying her tray loaded with dirty dishes.

From there it wasn't but a ten minute drive to Ozzie's house.

By the time Birdie settled into his tub, with him at her back, she'd lost the will to fight with him.

"Have I thanked you for breaking me out of jail?" She moaned as his fingers began rubbing her shoulders.

"No, you've grumped at me. But I'm sure you'll think of a way to help me understand your gratitude. There's a time honored way a lady usually rewards her knights.

Birdie snorted. "I don't think a scarf tied around your lance will be suitable."

"I don't know. It sounds like an intriguing start."

His voice was just lecherous enough a shiver of delicious heat ran through her. One that had little to do with the hot water surrounding them and more to do with the hot man holding her.

"What hurts the most?" he asked. The fact his lips were nibbling near her ear didn't hurt.

"My butt is bruised, and my lower back is stiffening up. I really need a massage." She rubbed her head against his neck. "Aren't you sore, too? Don't you need a massage as well?"

"Not so much. I think I can figure out a way to help us both. Let's start with the water jets." He pressed a button and the water began madly bubbling.

"Is there anything you can't do?" She tilted her head and he took advantage, nibbling his way down her neck.

"Plenty. But whatever you need me to do, I'll do my best to figure it out."

She let him have his way, enjoying every touch, every caress, every kiss until even her back relaxed and she hovered on the edge of sleep.

"Why the change, Ozzie?" she asked.

"What change?" His fingers plucked at her nipples, and she nearly forgot the question she'd asked.

"Monday you were so wonderful, and then Tuesday you were back to being cold. You avoided me all week."

"No I didn't. I very clearly remember kissing you in my office. Something we should never, ever do. At least not until you're head of the company."

"Something that is likely to never happen, as I have demonstrated my lack of leadership." She was more the power behind the throne than the figurehead to sit on the big chair type, anyway. "But before that kiss you were back to being a hard ass. And then you hid from me the rest of the week. I can't keep up with your moodiness."

Against her back, Ozzie's laughed rumbled pleasantly. "I'll give you that one, only in regards to Tuesday. Just before you came in I'd finished setting up the meeting about last night's event. I'd been on the phone most of the day with a private investigator I hired Sunday afternoon. What he told me made me extremely angry, and I was having trouble not punching something."

"And then something so petty as unintentionally shared chocolate led to a memo from Dad. So silly, and yet, so disrupting." She shifted, pressing her breasts upward, wanting his hands on her more fully.

"Maybe it seemed silly, but it was a blatant show of disrespect for you. I haven't heard of anything else, so I'm assuming they've either left you alone or have made a show of respecting you."

"Left me alone. I've had my head buried in data entry for the last three days. I now know when a huge shipment of Belgium chocolates will arrive for the Christmas season."

"Insider information. What will you do with it?"

"Get my boxes out before the rest goes to our customers. By the way, thank you for the Godiva."

"Godiva?" He feigned ignorance well, but she didn't buy it.

"I took them home. Not sharing that box. You did good. All soft milk chocolate."

"I'm afraid I'm being thanked for something I didn't do. But you can thank me for this later." His hand slipped between her thighs.

"We're not done talking about your high-handed ways."

"For now we are."

His kiss silenced the subject.

* * * *

Later, much later, as Courtney lay in his arms, Oswald took the time to reconsider his future. Their future.

In the final throes of her amazing climax, one he felt very proud of, she'd let slip the best three-word sentence he'd ever heard in his life.

"I love you," she'd gasped, sending his own release off the charts, before she'd collapsed into a blissful sleep. In fact, she still lay on top of him, using his body for her personal mattress. Something he liked very much.

Not just liked. Loved.

There went that funny little feeling of warmth exploding from the region of his heart, sending waves of contentment throughout his entire being.

He loved her too. More than he could ever say in words.

But he could show her.

He loved her cheeriness that lightened his darkness. He loved the way she teased him, making silly nicknames depending on her mood. It was hard not to smile back at her when she smiled at him. All her smiles, from coy to outright joy. He loved her wide-eyed innocence and wanted to shield her from the ugly truths of the world so she never lost it.

Which led to the next logical leap.

Forever.

Hell, he was going to have to marry her sooner or later. Damned if he couldn't stop from smiling over it.

He stroked a hand down the smooth skin of her slender back, stopping to lightly massage the sore spot from where her spine had been jammed into her pelvic cradle. She was also right about her very beautiful arse being bruised on the right side where she'd landed the hardest. He'd rubbed some arnica gel into her skin, and promised to do it often until the bruising faded. She'd done the same for the bruises over his left ribs with a light touch.

She was tender, his woman. And it was up to him to see she stayed that way.

He'd already made a good start by removing Whetmore from the picture. Rumor had it he was on his way to Italy. Wouldn't take much to put a word into the ear of the local authorities to keep an eye out. Eventually Whetmore would either get thrown in prison or run out of the country until he had no place to go but the far Outback of Australia or deep into someplace like Libya. Time would tell, but there were people watching his movements enough Oswald didn't have to worry about him.

Word had started filtering through the management levels at work. Eventually she'd find out, but he'd deny his words to the end. Only a few more months before she was working in the executive office, anyway. Hopefully her internship through the rest of the departments would be much smoother. She'd learn the ins and outs, and at least put names to the faces of the management structure. That was exactly what her internship was about, Courtney having daily contact with the people who reported to the top so she knew how to best work with them.

So, with that much laid out, all he had to do was figure out the timing.

Rushing her didn't seem wise. They were far too new in this relationship to immediately make a lifetime commitment. He was committed, but he didn't know her idea of how fast she wanted to move toward a wedding. Maybe they'd date for a few months with occasional overnights, but still living in separate quarters. She'd talked of having her own place, but was it really necessary? After a few months of dating he could see her moving in with him. Another logical step as they grew closer. It would certainly increase the odds of sex on a nightly basis and no one would quibble with the desirability of that plan. From there, a Valentine's Day engagement? How fast would her parents push for a wedding? He didn't see the need for a long engagement, or a huge society wedding, but he was certain Randi wouldn't hear of anything smaller. Neither would Court, knowing his need to spoil his daughter as much as she'd allow him.

Right. Date until November. Move in, enjoy the holidays, maybe take a skiing trip in January, or combine it with a proposal in February, then sit back and let her and her mother plan a June wedding.

There. He had a timeline set. Right after the wedding he'd step away from Lynford and put his business plans into motion. Perfect.

Simple, logical, practical. Courtney would love it.

He'd discuss the plan with her later.

Right now, he needed to tell her something important. She'd confessed her love for him. It was time to return the sentiment.

Chapter 29

Like living a dream, Birdie floated through the rest of the summer buoyed by a pink cloud of love—yes, he loved her!—spending most of her free time with Oswald. Walks in green parks, drives in the country, and even one day punting on the Thames, far upstream from London.

On the few days they didn't spend together outside of work, Birdie shopped and dined with her grandmother or her new friends. It was if the day on the bridge had been her turning point. From that night onward, life became golden. Oswald's turn toward tender lover had much to do with it. Most nights they had dinner together. Sometimes out, sometimes at her place, other times at his. At his house they also made use of the training room for actual training, but just as often for playing. Some of those memories had the power to make her blush at inappropriate times.

By unspoken agreement, they kept their affair under the radar at work, where things had improved as well. She suspected Ozzie had stepped in at one point, or Mrs. Smith had. Or her father as he touched base with his executive team. Word had somehow filtered down, and Birdie was treated with careful politeness. It was frustrating because she knew people didn't exactly feel comfortable around her. But there were no more hazing incidents, and for that she was grateful.

Their life was also blissfully free of Deirdre and her cohorts. They still saw her at the social events Ozzie figured they were obligated to attend, but by mutual distaste, they stayed on opposite sides of the room. The tabloids had certainly noted Ozzie's constant companion, her, and the fact Deirdre had a new man on her arm at each event. She changed them out like she did her dresses.

One afternoon in mid-October, Birdie finished her work and headed toward Ozzie's office. They had plans to work out at his gym where the owner had asked him to teach a beginner's class for a couple weeks. She had her tote with clothes over her shoulder and was excited to see how a real class worked. Ozzie had told her she could easily hold her own, and she wanted to see if it was true.

Mrs. Cuthbert told her she was free to go in. Ozzie was on the phone with her father.

She knocked and entered when he called, "Come!" that created a pleasant burn in her.

Opening the door, she heard Ozzie say, "Your favorite rising star just walked in, Court."

"Birdie!"

She smiled at the joy in his voice. "Hope I'm not interrupting plans for world domination."

"As if we'd leave you out of those plans," her father said with a chuckle. "Actually, I'm glad you're there. Your mother wants to talk to you. Not that I'm trying to get rid of you, but why don't you use the phone in my office? Oswald and I still have a bit of business to discuss."

"Oh, I see. You really do want to get rid of me," she teased. "Fine, I'll happily talk to Mom on not only company time, but on their dime."

"Nice rhyme there." Oswald winked at her.

"Your mum will catch me up on the details after you two talk. But I'm very much looking forward to spending time with you when we get home in just a few weeks."

Birdie's heart melted a little. "I miss both of you too. It will be fun to see everyone over turkey again."

"Our own Thanksgiving, as in we're thankful for bringing our family together."

Birdie grinned at Oswald who smiled back, and answered for her, "You're about to send her into tears. Enough of the mushy stuff."

Dad laughed. "Well, you're expected at the family dinner too, Oswald. In fact, we're inviting Mrs. C as well. Feels like a good year for a big celebration."

"Oh boy," Birdie responded. "I'll go call Mom now. Sounds like I need to get a handle on these plans early."

"Excellent idea, puddin'. Ah, there Mum is. She has her phone charged up and ready to settle in for a long chat. I'll let you two get to it."

"Love you," she called out as she sailed out the door.

* * * *

Without thinking, Oswald called back at the same time Court did. Then there was silence on the other end of the line. A pause, during which Oswald felt his cheeks burn. Shite.

"That's the way it is, eh?" Court's voice was mild, but Oswald wasn't fooled by the man's apparent disinterest.

With a heavy sigh, he pulled off his glasses and tossed them on his desk. The better to scrub his face with both hands. "Yeah. I love her."

"Congratulations. Now what are your intentions?"

"Sure we don't have more business to discuss?"

"Nothing as important as this topic."

Oswald sighed again. "Yeah. You're right. This is pretty big news. Especially to me."

Thankfully Court laughed. "I bet. For the man who said he'd never marry, I have to wonder if love will lead to matrimony."

"And you're the one I need to talk to, although this is way premature. I was holding off until Christmas to speak to you, face to face. Ask for her hand properly and all that."

"And when did you plan to propose?"

"Valentine's? While on a ski holiday? Possibly in Switzerland?"

Court was already tsking by the time Oswald finished speaking.

"You know the tradition of asking over a big family gathering. It's not just the Robinson men. Albert asked Liza the same way," Court patiently explained. "The whole family would be disappointed to be excluded."

"Yeah, well, I'm not big on public displays."

"Why not propose at the Thanksgiving dinner? We'll help you plan it if you like."

"Oh that takes the pressure off," Oswald said in his driest tone.

Court merely chuckled. "She's worth a little sweat."

"Absolutely," he replied immediately. "Of course she is."

"Good answer, my boy. So, are you going to ask me?"

Sensing there was no room for squirming, he didn't even pause before saying, "Courtland, I request the honor of your daughter's hand in marriage."

"You have my blessing, Oswald. Welcome to the family."

A few minutes later Court rang off, and Oswald flopped against the back of his chair, a layer of sweat soaking his shirt, he was sure. Felt like buckets were pouring off him. Now that it was over, he reflected it hadn't been so bad. At least he didn't have to spend the next few months working up to it, trying to be clever. Instead, he had about four weeks to plan a proposal that put Court and Drew's to shame.

As Courtney would say, easy peasy lemon squeezy. Whatever the bloody hell that meant.

Over the next three days he began to learn just how determined the Robinson clan could be. Mostly it was kind of cool, but also a little annoying. Like he couldn't come up with an idea on his own?

First was a call from Drew.

Then Albert, Court's brother-in-law, of all people.

Then Court and Randi together.

"We'll do the family dinner on Thursday, just as we would back in the States," Randi said. She said it sweetly, but Oswald caught the hint of steamroller behind the velvet curtain. "If you want to ask her then, that's perfect. We'll help however you want."

"Okay," he said slowly.

"We don't want to step on your toes," she assured him with a mild purr in her voice, but to him it sounded like the growl of a lioness. "And we're adding a ball the next night to celebrate and announce the engagement."

Now that alarmed him. "What if she says no?"

"Easy, Oswald," Court said. "She won't. We have our own spies, not to mention the pictures that have been showing up in the tabloids. Everyone confirms she has the look of love in her eyes."

Good. God. He hadn't been following the tabloids. Never had. "What pictures?"

"Usually back on page three or four, so you've haven't been front page news, but someone has the paps keeping an eye on you," Randi confirmed. "The pictures are very nice, and all the commentary is complimentary. They're all speculating on whether you've finally been lassoed or not."

Oswald groaned. "I appreciate the help, I really do, and I've had many offers. About the only people who haven't called yet are my uncle and Courtney's grandmother."

"Oh dear." Randi sighed. "We're pressuring you. We're just so excited it's hard to hold back."

"I promise you can go to town on the wedding," Oswald said. "But I think this part is up to me to figure out. I just have no idea how to put on a show Robinson style."

Both his future in-laws laughed. "You're a smart man," Court said. "I'm sure you'll figure it out. Just a hint, she prefers gold to silver."

"And something personal makes it more special, like the tea bag Court gave me," Randi added. "Just think back on your defining moments and something will come to you."

They rang off, leaving Oswald to figure out which defining moment stood out the most. There were so many. When they met at Court and Randi's wedding, followed by the trip to California. Birdie's graduation from Stanford. Dancing at Drew's wedding. A troublesome trolley. Wine. Ascot with the winning bets and the bee sting. Her first fancy hats… There were so many moments in his head he couldn't sort them out. How could he pick just one? And if he managed, how would he work it into a proposal?

Larry was the next to call.

"Uncle, if you're calling to give me advice on how to stage a proposal, I have to tell you many have already voiced their opinions."

Larry laughed. There was nothing he loved better than being in the middle of a big secret. "What are you thinking?"

"Randi suggested selecting a defining moment as a theme."

"Ah, which Court managed with a jewel-filled tea bag."

Yeah, it only cost him about fifteen thousand pounds, on top of a ring that matched the family necklace and earring set Court had given Randi.

"I'm not quite *that* loaded," Oswald grumbled.

"Of course not, but I do believe Birdie likes jewelry. A bracelet might work. Or you could get Paul Robinson to sing for you while you go down on bended knee. Or have him play backup while you sing her a sappy love song."

"Sing?" Appalled, he held the phone from his ear and stared at it. "I like the idea about Paul doing the singing. I can't sing a note."

"Bollocks. You were in the school choir. You can sing."

Of course his uncle would remember that. The man was a vault of Oswald's childhood memories. As bad as any over-proud father.

"I'll think of something." Once more Oswald's glasses came off and he rubbed his eyes. "I have three and a half weeks. I can do this."

"I'm here if you need me. Just say the word, and I'll help in any way you need."

"Thanks. Just what I need, more helpers."

"Sometimes it takes a village, Oz. It's a sign of great love that they all want to help you. It's also a sign of great approval. Can't expect anything like this with another girl. Most of the families we know would be demanding to see your financials before giving approval. Court didn't flinch, did he?"

"No, he certainly didn't. In fact, he outright demanded I ask him. Wasn't planning on asking until Christmas, if the truth be told."

"Always tell the truth," Larry said cheerfully and rung off.

The most surprising call of all came from Court's mother. The elder Mrs. Robinson. Who invited both he and Courtney to dinner.

Over coffee and cake she got to the point, her blue eyes focused solely on him. "Oswald, I've just heard you two are in a relationship, and before you two go further, I want to clear the air about something that has bothered me for some time."

While his head spun in confusion, she continued. "I always figured you were too proud of that family title to deign to speak with us commoners. Nevertheless, this summer I began to think maybe I was mistaken."

Oswald nearly choked on his tongue. "Pardon me, Mrs. Robinson? I'm not following you."

"Oh you." He'd never seen her roll her eyes, but she came close then. "Ever since you were a boy, you always stood off to the side watching. I've never had a child make me feel so pedestrian in my life. Haven't changed much in that regard, young man." She sniffed before taking a sip of her coffee.

"I beg your pardon?" Oswald repeated himself because he really couldn't think of anything else to say. If she was saying what he thought she was saying, she had it all wrong, and he wasn't sure how to go about correcting her.

"Just because you come from a titled line doesn't make you better than anyone else. Didn't your Uncle Larry ever teach you that? Oh sure"—she waved a hand as if to sweep away the importance of his possible, long-shot at a title—"you're in line for a Barony, but you're pretty far down the line, aren't you?"

Oswald coughed to cover his choke. "Sorry, ma'am, but you've got it all wrong. It wasn't me looking down on you and your family, it was me doing my level best to not impose my unfortunate circumstances on you. I'm not good enough to be in your circle to begin with, so I always figured if I was quiet no one would notice me. Fewer chances of getting kicked out to sleep in the stables that way."

"Not good enough?" Across the table from him, Courtney choked out the question with indignity. "Who says you're not good enough to hang out with the Robinsons?"

"That would be the whole of upper crust society," he said with no small sense of irony. "I'm not quite a bastard, but probably the next worst thing. The dependent fringe relative. The poor relation who had to be taken in and raised with those more privileged."

The sound of Courtney scoffing echoed in the dining room of her grandmother's town flat.

Mrs. Robinson plowed onward. "What utter rubbish. Not good enough for the likes of us? I'd say you're a sight better connected than we are. Damn your relatives for making you feel any other way. I'll have to have words with Lawrence myself," she added darkly.

"I'd say so," Courtney added. "Not good enough? That's bull—I mean that's garbage." A glance showed her shooting a fast look at her grandmother.

"Mind your language, young lady, or you'll prove my point we're not good enough to be seen with him."

Courtney took her grandmother's admonishment with a heavy sigh. "See?" she said to Oswald. "You're better mannered than I am."

"Almost everybody in England has better manners than you," Mrs. Robinson snapped.

"Easy, Mrs. Robinson," Oswald interrupted. "That's my girlfriend you're casting aspersions on. She has very nice manners."

"She could have better manners."

"Maybe, but she's damn near perfect as she is. I don't mind a little imperfection to spice things up."

Mrs. Robinson answered with a sniff. "In any case, Oswald, you need to get that chip off your shoulder. You're better than a great many people who claim to be upper crust. You don't make scenes, you are unfailingly polite and courteous. You open doors for ladies, make sure everyone is taken care of. You are also thrifty and resourceful, don't waste time or money, and know how to dance. Your table manners are impeccable, and you never make a boor of yourself. Many a snooty young woman has missed the opportunity to catch your interest, instead they used you for arm candy, then dropped you the moment someone richer or more entitled came along." The older woman reached over and poked Courtney in the shoulder. "In fact, you should marry him. You'll not find anyone better."

Oswald and Courtney choked together.

"Thank you. Grandmother," Courtney said. "I'm not ready to marry at this time. I figure it will be a few years before I am." A pretty blush covered her cheeks as she shot him a shy, uncertain smile. "And then I'm sure Oswald already has someone in mind. Someone more appropriate to his social standing."

Not bloody likely. Marriage was something he'd never imagined for himself because most of London knew his circumstances. He didn't bother setting anyone straight on that score, and Courtney would know soon enough, but he wasn't prepared to take that step tonight.

Instead he apologized to Mrs. Robinson for the misunderstanding, ignoring the reference to matrimony altogether. "Was never my intention to make you think I set myself above you, or anyone in your family. I was just grateful you let me in the door, let alone at the dinner table. Drew's mother always made it clear I was accepted only because my uncle was a great chum of her husband."

"Beatrice." The older woman sighed. "The best thing she ever did was have Andrew. The rest, well, I'm ashamed of her."

The whole conversation was making Oswald extremely uncomfortable. Probably why he seldom interacted with the elder Mrs. Robinson. Although he'd had no idea she'd thought he thought he was above her family. Truth was, she'd always intimidated him.

So, what message was she sending him now?

At the door, Mrs. Robinson put her cheek up for him to kiss, then patted his arm. "You'll do, Oswald. You'll do very well, indeed."

The tight knot around his lungs loosened. She'd just given him her blessing.

In the car, Birdie nervously twisted her fingers together. "Please don't let my grandmother twist your arm. I assure you I'm not pushing for marriage, or any kind of long-term commitment. I'm very happy with how things are right now." Even in the darkness of the car, he could see her cheeks burned bright red. "I'm so embarrassed over her behavior tonight. I mean, it's good she's decided to like you; that part was great. But the rest?" She buried her face in her hands. "I'm not sure I can face you now."

Oswald reached over and pulled the closest hand away from her face. "It's okay, Courtney. The moment was painful, yes, but now we have a clear understanding. And I'm relieved. I didn't realize how much I wanted her approval all these years. The fact I have it makes me feel ten feet tall. The fact you love me makes me feel twenty feet tall. Practically invincible." He shot her a quick grin before turning onto a busy thoroughfare. He raised her hand to his lips and kissed each knuckle without taking his eyes from the road. Eventually her embarrassment would fade, and he wanted to give her what time he could. Hopefully by the time they parked outside his house, she'd be over it.

Chapter 30

It was a familiar scene. Ozzie pulled his car up in front of Lynford Hall, the country seat of the Robinson family for too many generations to count. He glanced over at Courtney who vibrated with excitement. Although the Thanksgiving holiday was a mystery to him, he couldn't help but absorb her joy. After all, hadn't the pilgrims who'd left England celebrated their survival in the New World with this feast? What were good queen-loving Brits doing celebrating it?

In this case he knew the family was celebrating the day two years ago when Court and Randi met again for the first time in more than twenty years. Court called it feast of giving thanks for finding not only his true love, but another piece of his heart. His daughter.

That alone was reason to celebrate in Oswald's book.

Courtney smiled at him, the big one that lit up his life. The one she used to announce she was happy in the best way. Hopefully in a few hours she'd be even happier.

Wanting a kiss, and so much more, he reached out and cupped the back of her head to gently tug her to meet him over the console for a kiss. A kiss for now. Tonight... Well, he hoped he'd get the so much more he'd planned for.

As they were the last to arrive, the front door opened, and people began spilling out into the chilly autumn air.

"Damn," Courtney softly swore. "Not a moment's peace to be found down here."

"Tonight," he promised her and took his kiss before the doors on both sides of the car were thrown open.

"Kiss her later," Drew demanded. "I flew halfway around the world to see you; he's had you to himself for months. Come on now, out of the car, you two."

Oswald reluctantly let her go, and hit the boot button so Martin could unload their luggage.

Court met Oswald first with a firm handshake that turned into a manly back-slapping hug. Which was a first.

Randi was next with a hug and a kiss on the cheek, her green eyes sparkling. It seemed he was due to receive a hero's welcome today. Fortunately Courtney didn't notice as she faced her own enthusiastic greetings from Drew and Meilin.

"What did you come up with?" Randi asked quietly.

This one he had. "You'll have to wait and be surprised."

Randi gasped, so much like her daughter, and then she slapped at his arm. "You're as bad as Court," she declared much to her husband's amusement. "He won't tell me a thing."

"That's because he also has no clue." Oswald gloated just a little.

Both he and Court laughed at her disgruntled look. "Fine. Be that way." She turned away, leading them into the house as she spoke over her shoulder. "It's a good thing you arrived dressed, no time to change, dinner will be on the table in fifteen minutes. You have time to quickly freshen up and say hello to the rest of the family."

On her way into the house she took time to hug Courtney, then drag her along.

"So," Court strung out the word as Drew hurried over to them. "No hints?"

Oswald shook Drew's hand and endured another manly hug. "Yeah, let's see the goodies," Drew said.

"Not on your lives," Oswald told them. "You two, and the rest of your family, harassed me enough this past month, so now you have to wait until Courtney sees it. It's her gift after all."

Court slapped a hand on his shoulder and guided him toward the house. "I just never dreamed of putting on a wedding for a little girl. Now it's all I can think of and my wife is no better. We just want to see you both happy."

"Thoughts appreciated. Although this family thing will take getting used to."

Drew barked out a laugh. "At least you're not arguing with five thousand years of Chinese tradition. We're now negotiating where the first child will be born."

"Oh?" Oswald stared down his friend. Soon to be brother. Somehow the acknowledgement felt as right as marrying Courtney.

"Shhhh." Drew placed a finger on his lips. "That news is for later this weekend. Today is your day. Well, Birdie's day too."

A glance at Court showed his smug smile. "A new son and a grandson at the same time. Can't imagine a better life."

Inside, greetings were quickly exchanged with the members of the Robinson family who could make it for the mid-day feast. Most surprising of all was Oswald's own Uncle Wilton and Aunt Penelope. There was little time to contemplate that oddity before they were called into the dining hall.

Apparently there was a rule Thanksgiving dinner had to be served no later than two o'clock on the fourth Thursday of November. The elder aunts and uncles were missing, but Court's sister, Liza, and her family were there. As was the elder Mrs. Robinson who made it clear she expected Oswald to kiss her cheek. The old lady was actually growing on him. Getting their misunderstanding out of the way had helped a lot. Smirking beside Mrs. Robinson was Courtney's grandfather, also a guest at the dinner two years ago. No, he wouldn't miss this, Oswald acknowledged as he shook the man's hand.

Uncle Larry of course was there, right beside Uncle Wilton. Oswald's cousins were missing, but he didn't mind. This was mind boggling enough. Even Meilin's parents, Mr. and Mrs. Wu, were there. A fine film of sweat began to gather above Oswald's lip. He hadn't expected such an audience.

Paul Robinson also waved from across the room, his guitar discreetly tucked away. Courtney didn't seem to notice it, which was a good thing. At the end of dessert, the plan was for champagne to be served. Paul would then pick up his guitar and start playing in the background while Oswald made his way toward Courtney. He even had a speech memorized, and at the end, he'd go down on one knee and beg her to marry him. He'd gone over the speech a hundred times, mentally rehearsed the entire proposal, every step and action. She'd be dazzled and unable to say no.

All too quickly, or not soon enough, depending on one's view, Martin appeared at the doorway of the drawing room dressed in traditional butler togs. "Dinner is served."

Court held out his elbow to Courtney while Randi grabbed Oswald's arm. "We're separating you two during dinner," she announced cheerfully.

Courtney tried to protest the seating arrangement. "Dad, shouldn't this be Gran's seat?"

"Not today, darling girl. I haven't seen my daughter in far too long. You can flirt with your boyfriend later. This afternoon you're mine."

From his end of the table Oswald could see her blush while he pushed in Randi's seat. Probably just as well he was at the far end from Courtney. She'd pick up on his nervousness too easily.

Court stood to give the blessing. The vicar would have been far more brief. It seemed Court had a lot to be thankful for.

At last the prayer ended and the parade of food began. Oswald let Randi dish out everything that passed their way. Turkey, dressing, mashed potatoes, corn, salad, rolls… The bounty rolled on and on.

"We don't serve this as individual courses," Randi explained to the company in general. "Most Americans don't have servers, and it's sort of a tradition to just pile it all on. Take a little of everything, and you can go back for more of what you like best. Pass the gravy, Drew, if you please."

Of course Oswald had tasted some of these dishes before, but not all. The sweet potatoes with melted marshmallows on top didn't appeal to him one bit. Most of it was quite excellent, and it wasn't long before he began to feel very full. Call him a civilized man, but he preferred the courses served separately and in proper order. When he and Courtney hosted the feast, they'd adjust the tradition slightly and slow down the food service.

Then again, like his courtship, nothing had worked out properly. Normally deviations from a civilized plan annoyed him, but not today. Today he saw the value in relaxing and going with the flow.

He glanced down the table toward Courtney in time to see her throw her head back in unrestrained laughter. The intoxicating sound soared to the heavy Tudor beams overhead. Everyone stopped talking and turned their heads to watch, and listen. From the corner of his eye, Oswald could see his Uncle Wilton smile at the vision before them. Uncle Wilton who had an even bigger stick up his arse than Courtney accused Oswald of having. Oswald met his uncle's gaze and was completely gobsmacked when the man actually smiled and nodded his way. Uncle Wilton approved of Courtney.

Shocked to his very soul, Oswald blinked, then nodded back. For once in his life, Uncle Wilton approved of Oswald's decision. It was mind blowing. So much so, he didn't want to wait for dessert to be served.

Scraping the floor with his chair as he stood, Oswald had everyone's attention. Only he didn't see them. He only saw Courtney as the room fell silent but for the crackling of the logs burning in the large fireplaces on either end of the great hall.

Gaze firmly locked on her questioning stare, he started walking toward the head of the table. Somewhere in the back of his mind some vague words floated around. He had a speech prepared, but for the life of him he couldn't remember any part of it except the last two words.

The world narrowed down to just the two of them as he passed behind Court's chair and came to a stop beside Courtney. The soft strains of an acoustic guitar came from somewhere, and he remembered the request he'd made of Paul. "Unchained Melody." Letting the tune carry him back to their first dance, he silently held out his hand to her, and she took it. He drew her up and into his arms, eager to kiss her. She met him with a hint of hesitation, and then the fire between them flared and she kissed him back, with her whole heart. All he ever wanted.

Eventually, the clearing of a throat broke through, and he reluctantly ended the kiss.

"Say yes, Courtney. Please."

"Yes. But what's the question?" A little smile playing around her lips teased him for forgetting his words.

"Marry me." Those were the only two words of his speech he remembered. "Please."

"Oh good lord," Drew cried from the end of the table. "He forgot the speech!"

"Shut up, Drew," Courtney said. "Yes. Yes, I choose you, Ozichu."

Drew laughed the loudest, but everyone else broke into applause.

"I forgot my speech," Oswald told her.

"No you didn't. It's all there, in your eyes and in your kiss. You didn't forget a word," his beautiful Courtney said. And in her eyes he saw the same.

"The ring, Oswald." Court's reminder kicked Oswald in the gut.

"I have something for you, but first, the ring." He let go long enough to hold out his hand to Court who slapped a ring box into it. Holding the box with one hand, Courtney with the other, he told her, "Open it."

She used her free hand to open the box, still looking into his eyes.

"Take a look. If you don't like it, we can choose another."

"Doesn't matter what it looks like. You picked it out; I love it."

Joy so large it filled not only his heart and soul, but the entire room, he kissed her hard, then let go to release the ring from its velvet bed. With shaking hands he slipped the three carat princess cut diamond set in eighteen karat gold onto her finger. Her hands shook as well until she finally looked down and gasped.

"Oh, Ozzie, it's perfect."

"Like you."

Courtney's laugh sounded a little soggy, but she grinned enough to chase away the snow clouds gathering outside. "I'm not perfect." She threw her arms around him and hugged him tight before pulling back to rub his chest. "What's that?"

For a moment his mind blanked out again. "Oh, right. Your engagement gift."

"The ring is more than gift enough."

"No it's not. This one is even more special." Reaching into his breast pocket, he pulled out another jeweler's box, this one long and flat, and handed it to her.

By now everyone in the room was straining to see, especially Randi at the far end of the table. Not a breath was heard as Courtney snapped open the lid.

"Oh my…" Wide eyed, she ran her finger over the solid gold bracelet carefully secured on a bed of velvet. "Charms. It's beautiful…Wait, is that Vauxhall Bridge? And…" Her mouth fell open as her finger touched a tiny pair of handcuffs.

Oswald met her shocked eyes with laughter. He took the box from her and started pointing out the tiny charms, each one found or made to his exacting specifications. "Tower Bridge and the Golden Gate, those are obvious. A horse for Ascot, a hundred pound note for your winnings."

"A bee, also Ascot." She grinned up at him, then looked back down. "Platform shoe, fancy dress, Ascot hat, Godiva chocolate box, mail trolley, earrings?"

"Fancy dangling earrings," he confirmed.

"Punching bag, lipstick, champagne, a bird! Oh, Ozzie, it's perfect!"

"All right," Randi said from behind Oswald. "We all want to see!"

Courtney clutched the box to the front of her. "It's mine."

Randi laughed. "Of course it's yours, but I get to be nosy. What do the charms mean?" She gently tugged the box from her daughter's hand.

"Defining moments," Oswald answered. "Each one represents a moment we shared that added to my love for Courtney."

How he loved the blush on her cheeks as Meilin and Mrs. Robinson joined the circle.

"Handcuffs?" Randi asked. "When did handcuffs come into play, or do I want to know?"

"The police, Mom. When they thought I was about to leap off Vauxhall Bridge, they handcuffed me for a short time," Courtney answered and swiped the box back. "Ozzie, help me put this on."

"Handcuffs? Police? Vauxhall Bridge?" Court demanded as he pushed his chair back to join the fray.

Courtney rolled her eyes and held out her wrist. Oswald concentrated on securing the clasp to hold the decorated chain on her wrist.

"It's a long story, Dad. Maybe I'll tell it over dessert."

"Dessert!" Randi cried. "Who wants dessert when we have this for excitement?"

"I want dessert," Drew said, his words echoed by his younger cousins.

Albert raised his hand. "I want to try the pumpkin pie."

Shaking his head, Oswald finally secured the clasp and turned the chain around to show her two charms secured together. One a heart, the other...

"A Chinese symbol?" Courtney asked "Do I need Meilin to tell me what it means?"

Oswald cupped her cheeks, loving the sound of the charms tinkling as they moved on her wrist when she grasped his arms.

"The character means forever. Which is how long you'll have my heart."

The End

See where the story began, with a special excerpt from

Her Foreign Affair

Twenty-two years ago, she ran out on the love of her life—and took a secret with her.

When Randi Jean Ferguson fell for Courtland Robinson while studying abroad in London, she was ready for a life of tea and crumpets. But when she discovered Court was being forced into a shotgun wedding, there was no way she could stay—or tell him she was also pregnant with his child. Now widowed, Randi is just starting to consider finding Court—when he shows up at her door. With his son. Randi's not ready to reveal everything to Court, but if she doesn't, will both their children end up scarred?

The best thing to come out of Court's unhappy marriage was his son. But he's spent the last twenty-two years thinking about Randi, his California girl, his first—and only—love. Now a widower, he takes a chance he's only fantasized about and seeks her out. At last he'll solve his heart's greatest mystery—but that won't be the only surprise in store for him.

A Lyrical e-book on sale now.

Learn more about Shea at
http://www.kensingtonbooks.com/author.aspx/29498

Prologue

London, England
Mid-late 1980s

A soft spring breeze tugged a long curl from Randi Jean Dailey's carefully styled up-do. She paid the cabbie his quid, stepped from the car with the help of the hotel doorman, and gave him a smile. The cabbie let out a satisfactory wolf-whistle before zipping back into London traffic.

Jean's heart pounded with excitement. Instead of climbing on the plane to go home after her semester abroad, she'd primped and polished and put on her perfect little black dress accented with proper pearls and sexy stilettos. The ones Court had bought for her two weeks prior. The ones that made her short legs look a mile long, he said. The black shoes she'd worn to seduce him last night. The ones that had driven him so mad with lust he'd made love to her all night long.

With a long bittersweet kiss, they'd parted at noon. His promise to follow her to California as soon as he possibly could were the last words spoken between them.

She adjusted the lace shawl around her shoulders and headed into the hotel where the Lynford International Importers new hire reception was being held. As an only-just-hired summer intern, she'd received her job acceptance and invitation to the reception shortly after Court had left her studio flat. The afternoon had been spent madly running around making arrangements to stay in England another three months. To start.

But that wasn't all the good news she had for Court. Instead of only the summer, she'd be extending her stay indefinitely. Forever. The thought made her dizzy with delight.

Upon reaching the doors to the reception hall, Jean stopped and rested a hand over her abdomen. She had one more surprise for Court. One she prayed would thrill him to his bones. One that would give him the leverage to work around his father's manipulations. Like the song from a few years before, their future was so bright, they'd both have to wear shades. A silly grin crossed her face as she started through the wide open doors.

Soft string ensemble music drifted across the room. The event was exactly as Court had predicted. Proper Englishmen and their ladies talking quietly, mingling, as much to see as to be seen. For a week, he'd bemoaned the fact that instead of seeing her off at the airport, he had to attend this stuffy reception put on by his father's company. Not interested in the décor, she searched the sea of bodies in semi-formal wear, looking for one particular blond head. The men wore sharp suits of worsted wool with silk ties, the women cocktail gowns in various levels of fashion and expense. The student interns and freshly graduated new hires were easy to pick out, by not only their youth, but by the less expensive clothing and the nervous smiles on their faces. Because Court's family owned the company, she looked beyond the students and concentrated on the older attendees. The people Court had known since the day he'd been born.

One bright head stood out. Danielle Richards, the hiring contact. If not for Danielle's call hours before, Jean would have been boarding a plane just then. Jean headed for Danielle, who certainly knew Court and could help Jean find him. She merely had to work her way through to the other side of the large ballroom.

Descending the steps into the crowd, she plowed ahead, exchanging nervous smiles with the three or four people she recognized from classes.

Among the glittering bodies, various scents perfumed the air and queasiness assaulted Jean for a moment. Something that had never bothered her before the past week. She and Court figured she had a mild touch of flu, or possibly food poisoning like she'd had right after arriving in January. The call from the student clinic this afternoon had negated that theory.

A glint of Danielle's bright copper hair through the crowd assured Jean she was still on the right path. A few more steps and her gaze briefly met Danielle's. Someone stepped in and cut off the line of sight before Jean could take a second look at what appeared to be mild alarm on the other woman's face. Jean glanced behind her to see what might be happening that would cause the hiring director's reaction. No, nothing unusual there. Jean pressed forward once again.

Like the sun prying back a thick layer of dark clouds, she saw his golden blond hair through a parting of bodies. His back to her, he stood near Danielle, part of a circle of immaculately groomed men and women, a mix of older and younger.

Finally, she eased past a knot of distinguished men and stood directly behind Court. On a deep breath, she assessed the situation. The group he stood with contained two older couples, important looking men and their society wives, all perfectly dressed and bejeweled. A younger woman with a sleek blond bob stood at Court's left. Too close, but he came from people who knew people and had friends he'd been raised with. This could be one such. Across the small circle, Danielle was the only other person Jean recognized. A person who'd been friendly. Although the expression on Danielle's face wasn't exactly comforting.

Court began to speak, and Jean was able to hear him clearly, see clearly as his left arm came up to encircle the waist of the blond woman at his side, the action surprising her. If his shoulders looked a bit stiff, the movement a tad forced, she seemed to be the only one who noticed.

"Danielle, I'd like you to be among the first to know, Bea and I will be married next weekend. There isn't time for formal invitations,"—his chuckle was forced—"we're expecting, however, we'd love you to attend."

The timbre was Court's, but the tone and the words couldn't be his. Dizziness surged in Jean's head. She took a step back and clamped both hands over her now roiling stomach. The air had evaporated from the room and darkness framed the edges of her vision.

"Court..." Danielle said, doing her best to keep her face clear of emotion. Jean could see it, could hear the strain, as the other woman's electric blue gaze locked on her.

Jean swallowed against rising nausea and took another step back, bumping into someone's chilled glass of something. The shock of cold liquid dribbling down her back froze her in place.

In an almost dreamlike parody of slow motion, Court's arm dropped from the woman, and he slowly turned. Jean's gaze flew to his face as it came into view. His skin took on an ashen cast, as his eyes widened above his slackening jaw. For a long moment, it was all she could see.

"Courtland?" The sharply spoken word from the blond woman broke the spell. "What is it, darling?"

Jean's breath rushed back into her starved lungs, and her heart jolted into triple time, rushing adrenalin into her system. It was the spark she needed to turn on her heel and push through the crowd.

"Jean!"

She heard him call after her. Heard Danielle call after her, but didn't stop. Escape was the one thought in her head. Later she'd think about Court's announcement. But now there was room for only one instinct pounding through her veins. Run.

Snippets of his history came to her as she forced her way past people now expressing their shock at her rudeness. The girl he'd practically been engaged to since they'd been in nappies. The horrible break up days before Jean had tripped him in the library. The stories of his family and how he was expected to take over the business one day, like generations of Lynfords and Robinsons before.

Above all, the vision she couldn't reconcile with the words he'd just said, Court's face smiling down at her. His voice saying, "I love you. I'll come for you. We'll have a wonderful life."

As she broke through the edge of the crowd and rushed into the lobby, she thought she heard Court call out her name one more time, but from a distance. She didn't look back. Couldn't look back. Adrenalin pounding through her veins powered her forward. A doorman opened the heavy outer door.

"Miss?"

His enquiry went unacknowledged as she rushed by, headed for the cab parked at the curb.

"Taxi!" she called out.

Surprised, the doorman who'd recently helped her from a cab, leaped to open the door for her.

"Miss? Everything all right?"

She shook her head and climbed into the cab.

"Where to, miss?"

"Home." It was all she could think of. She could be at Heathrow in a few hours where she'd wait until a seat opened on a plane headed for New York. From New York she'd get a plane to San Francisco. There, she'd figure it all out.

"Where's home, miss?"

"Away from here." Tears blurring her vision, she met the cabbie's gaze in the rearview mirror. "Just drive." No one had followed her out the door. Especially not Court. His words echoing in her head tore her heart to shreds. The cabbie turned around and slowly eased into traffic.

Unable to stand it, she gave into temptation and looked back through the tears welling in her eyes and spilling down her cheeks. The sidewalk remained empty of anyone she recognized. Only the doorman looked after her.

The image of Court's face rose in her mind. Merry blue eyes, laughing at her driven need to experience everything Anglo, jokes about her attempts to learn the Brit accent, the little presents of Earl Grey tea, crumpets and flowers he brought her. The rose petals he'd scattered on her bed last night where they made love pretending to be in an English garden. The flower pressed between the pages of her favorite novel, a sweetly scented bookmark and reminder of his promise they'd be together.

From the dark and dreary February day when she'd accidentally tripped him in the library, her world had been filled with sunshine and laughter. He took her places, both physical and emotional, she'd never have discovered without him. Small shops, hidden parks, intimate pubs, classic tea houses, historical sites, and the places known only to locals. To heaven, where he wrapped her in soft clouds of love, like the weekend in the country where they hiked green fields and pretended to be Robin Hood and Maid Marian. A better friend, guide, and lover she couldn't have asked for.

"I need an address, miss. Or an intersection at the very least."

Of course the man needed a direction. Jean wiped tears from her cheeks and wrapped her arms around her middle. "Houghton Street," she said. She needed a direction, too, knew where she was headed in the next twenty-four hours, but had to take baby steps to get there. "Houghton Street and then Heathrow." One step at a time.

Chapter 1

Twenty-two years later
East Bay Area, Northern California

Bent over the open oven, Randi figured only serendipity could have timed her daughter's arrival for Thanksgiving dinner quite so well.

Already up for six hours, most of that time spent in the kitchen, Randi was ready for her first glass of wine. A real glass, not a sip from the bottle she'd poured over the bird. So much for her resolve to become a new woman in her fabulous forties. A couple years in and she still harbored doubts about how fabulous the forties were. However, a person should always seek to improve herself, right? All well and good, nevertheless, this new woman clung to a few old habits she didn't want to give up, such as nipping from the bottle of wine intended for basting the turkey.

"Mom!" Birdie's voice rang through the house like a bell.

"In the kitchen," she called back. Steam from the oven frizzed her hair and bathed her face as she basted the bird. There went the efforts of an hour spent plucking eyebrows and applying her makeup just so. Well, instead of a fashion plate, the picture of a sophisticated California hostess, she'd be Wyatt's picture of the perfect woman—glowing from the heat of the kitchen and probably smelling of turkey as well. Too bad he wasn't here to celebrate. Death had a way of ruining family gatherings.

Instead, Randi expected her father and Birdie, both bringing visitors from out of town with no place else to go. Strays had always been Randi's specialty, especially for holiday dinners.

"Smells great, we're starving!" Birdie moved into Randi's peripheral vision. As bright as a sunny day with her long, honey blond hair, Birdie lit up any room, especially with her smile, cheerful disposition, and her clothing. Occasionally, Randi considered her child's bubbly nature positively nauseating. But not today. The semester had dragged on and contact with her daughter remained too infrequent. Stanford may have been a mere hour across the Bay, but it might as well have been across the country for all the time Birdie had to spare.

Randi shoved the heavy bird back into the lower of the stacked double ovens and straightened with a hand on the small of her back as she lifted the door shut. Yeah, cool sophisticate she so was not. Had she wanted to present such an image, she would have ordered the complete meal, cooked and ready to serve, delivered from the upscale grocery store down the hill. "Bird should be done on schedule this year. This time I bought a fresh one, not frozen."

"Your dinners are always perfect, and thirty minutes late doesn't count. Mom, come meet our guests."

Ah yes. The mysterious Drew, a grad student from overseas Birdie had met the previous week after tripping over his big feet in a coffee shop. Not only Drew, but his father, as well, visiting the states on business, timed for Drew's first big American holiday. The widowed father. A match to her widowed mother status.

Great. It was bad enough her father also asked to bring a guest, a single man of a certain age. In other words, old enough for Randi. But now her daughter had joined the game? Lately, it seemed as if an invisible milestone had passed, one declaring her mourning period complete, and, apparently, someone had declared open season on finding dates for her. Funny, her heart hadn't reached the same conclusion yet.

Well, let these possible future dates get a good look at the new woman. The one thinking about thinking of dating again.

Since Birdie generally preferred jeans, Randi raised an eyebrow at the dress her daughter wore. Navy flats were more in keeping with her personality, though Birdie showed off a pair of still nicely tanned legs. Randi was about to comment, but Birdie beat her to it.

"Wow." Birdie stopped and stared for moment. "Great look," she whispered, then took Randi's arm and dragged her into the foyer where two tall men stood. So the extra hour of shaving, shining, plucking, and painting had been worth it? Despite the steamy glow she certainly sported at the moment, and no time to powder it away.

Not wanting to acknowledge the matchmaking attempt of her daughter—the man was a foreigner for crying out loud and wouldn't be around long enough to get to know—she wiped her hands on her apron, then extended one to the younger of the two. Dark blond, he had deep blue eyes and a smile every bit as cheery as Birdie's. As Randi gripped his hand, hers warmed with dreaded perspiration. She made her shake firm and brief, dropping his hand almost immediately.

"Mom, this is Drew. Drew, my mother Rand—"

"Jean?"

"—ee Ferguson," Birdie stumbled to a stop.

Drew hadn't interrupted. No, it was the man behind him. The boy's father. The one Randi didn't want to look at. The resonance of his voice, the rich British accent that made the plain name she'd used for one semester sound exotic, it was an illusion, an echo from the past, a hallucination induced from too little sleep.

Reluctantly, Randi let her gaze slide past Drew's startled eyes and collide with those of the older man one step back, looking more stunned than startled. More amazed than surprised.

"Not Jean Dailey?" he asked, head tilted a fraction as his gaze bore into her.

There was only one thought in her mind as her heart thudded to a momentary stop, and her blood froze into crystals. *It can't be.*

This must be a delusion leftover from last night's dreams. The ones brought on by the romance novel she'd found in a box last week. The one sitting on her bedside table still exuding the soft scent of the rose pressed between the pages of the love scene. He'd been invading her thoughts too much lately. He couldn't really be here, in her foyer. This scene was purely a figment of a mind set to wandering by plain old loneliness.

Randi grasped Birdie's arm, holding her as much to stay standing as to keep Birdie from moving to the side of the younger man. There was no way God would play this cruel a joke on her after so many years. Yet, as she stared into those blue, blue eyes, the years peeled away.

"Jean is my mother's middle name," Birdie supplied helpfully, despite her apparent confusion, breaking the silence that had held for nearly a full minute. Words abandoned Randi, leaving her throat too tight, too dry for speech. "Her full name is Randi Jean Dailey Ferguson."

Hell, no point in trying to hide her true identity now, as if that had ever been a remote possibility. Not only did Birdie give it all away, she babbled to fill in the extremely awkward silence.

The gaze of the apparition who resembled, well, *him*, sharpened, and his lips quirked in satisfaction. The heat of his regard wouldn't allow Randi to deny the exceedingly male presence in her house. All the air evaporated from the foyer, and her heart kick started so hard it threatened to leap from her chest. Her mind might be screaming denials, but her body knew. And despite the first sluicing of ice through her veins, heat rushed in behind.

Those damn blue eyes stared into hers, and a spark of something ancient and irrepressible settled in her heart, causing it to beat triple time.

Yup. God was that cruel.

From her past, the one man she never once imagined she'd ever see again stood in her foyer. Impossible that he should have found her. Dad would have never given her away had anyone knocked on his door looking for her. Google searches on the various combinations of her name turned up little other than notices in school newsletters. All those years ago she'd married, changed her name, given birth, and moved from the parental home to start a new life as a new woman. The girl he'd known as Jean Dailey became Randi Ferguson. All the heartache of betrayal had been left far behind in Merry Old England more than twenty-two years ago. The only reminder? The nearly twenty-two-year-old beauty standing at her side. The child who towered over her, so like her father, if the truth be known.

All those years ago, God had held her feet to the fire to face her future, but this time she faced the past. And why did that past still have to be so damn handsome?

No, not a hallucination. He was real. So very, very real.

It was him, looking barely five years older than he had so long ago. His thick hair still gleamed gold under the soft glow from the skylight, though there were hints of silver at his temples, and his forehead seemed a tad higher. Great, gray looked good on him. He was still lean, his eyes remained as piercingly blue. Light blue that looked right into her soul. His face had filled out a little, developed a few lines at the eyes, and the cheekbones were no longer quite so prominent, the jaw a slightly smoothed granite instead of freshly chiseled stone, but essentially the same.

Yes, he still looked the same while she'd grown rounder and squatter. Thank heavens for the impulse that sent her to the salon a week ago. At least she wasn't gray. At the moment. And of course, makeup, underwires, and Lycra hid a multitude of other imperfections.

Whereas he… Well, he looked damn fine in his light blue tailored shirt, gold cufflinks, perfect navy slacks, and expensive leather shoes.

Just like his son.

She wanted to push them out of her house right then, send them both back to England, far, far away from Birdie.

Oh, no, no, no. This did not fit with Randi's plans. She needed to regain control of the situation. Time. She needed time. Yes, she'd planned to tell Birdie all about this part of her past, but after Christmas. Before the New Year. After getting some more information from an investigative resource. Not like this, not now. Lord, not now! When Birdie was already looking at her as if she'd lost her mind.

Control. Right. Shut the rest away and pretend there was nothing going on. Randi eased up on her daughter's arm when she murmured a protest.

Oh God. Birdie's attracted to... She couldn't complete the thought too horrible to think.

A first date she'd said, right? Did that mean they hadn't progressed beyond coffee? No hand holding? No kissing? God forbid... How would she break this up without Birdie knowing she'd brought home not only her brother—half brother—but father, for dinner? Her very gorgeous, missing from her entire life, father.

As she watched his face, drinking in every detail, his eyes warmed, then hardened. He didn't seem nearly as surprised as she felt. Had he been looking for her? Had he used his son to find her through her daughter?

Birdie pinched her arm, bringing Randi back to the moment with a small jolt. Oh Lord, she was standing there like an idiot, everyone looking at her with expressions of curiosity and puzzlement. Hoping to find her cool hostess voice and not a strangled, choked voice, she gulped.

"Hello, Court."

Meet the Author

Shea McMaster lives for traditional romance. Born in New Orleans, raised in California, Shea got moved to Alaska in 1977, where she attended high school before running back to California to get her English degree from Mills College. Alas, once back home she met and fell in love with her own forever true hero, a born and raised Alaska man. Since then she's had a love-hate relationship with America's largest state.

With her one and only son half way through college, and mostly out of the house, Shea is fortunate to spend her days engaged in daydreaming and turning those dreams into romantic novels and novellas featuring damsels in distress rescued by their own brains and hunky heroes. She also writes under the steamy romances under the name Morgan O'Reilly.

Discover more about Shea at sheamcmaster.com, and on Facebook: http://www.facebook.com/pages/Shea-McMaster/240251469328338